WITNESS
———————

AN ASH PARK NOVEL

MEGHAN O'FLYNN

WITNESS

Copyright 2019

This is a work of fiction. Names, characters, businesses, places, events and incidents are either the products of the author's imagination or used fictitiously. Any resemblance to actual persons, living or dead, or actual events is purely coincidental. Opinions expressed are those of the characters and do not necessarily reflect those of the author. No part of this book may be reproduced, stored in a retrieval system, scanned, or transmitted or distributed in any form or by any means electronic, mechanical, photocopied, recorded or otherwise without written consent of the author. Assume she's watching you—or that someone even more scary is.

All rights reserved.

Distributed by Pygmalion Publishing, LLC

For those who've seen more than they ever wanted to.

WANT MORE FROM MEGHAN?
There are many more books to choose from!

Learn more about Meghan's novels on
https://meghanoflynn.com

PROLOGUE

The corners of the bedroom held more than just shadows—or so he imagined. Piotr rubbed his eyes. The smoke from the candles made his eyeballs ache, like how it felt if he looked into the sun. He didn't do that anymore. Father had said not to.

But there was no sun now, just the steady flicker of candlelight that made the walls wavery, and that didn't hurt at all. The woman on the bed sure looked like she was in pain, though, her face all squinched up, eyes closed, lips peeled back showing all her teeth the way the dog did when he was mad. She was panting like the dog, too, but Piotr didn't think she was hot. Maybe she needed water—should he get some? But there was another woman next to her who could get it, maybe, and no one had told him to go. He wasn't to move unless Father said so.

And Father was watching. Father was at the foot of the bed now, his gaze on the wall above the headboard, wearing that weird robe thing Piotr liked; all white with little gold trim. It reminded Piotr of the robe his mother had worn in pictures. Before she died. That thought made his eyes burn, too, even hotter than the sun did, but Father said not to think about that either. It was better not to think about things that hurt—things that made you want to cry.

As if on cue, the woman screamed, one hand on the round bulge at her middle, the other twisted in the white blankets. The woman beside her rubbed her back, her curly black hair falling down like a curtain around the crying woman's face as she murmured something into her ear.

He sighed. This part was always so boring. You had to sit and wait while the air hummed and listen to them talk about how the baby was coming—there was always another baby coming. Father liked to be there when new ones came, to welcome them into the world, he said. Into the family. But the babies never stayed here—none but Piotr got to stay with Father, not even his older brother, Roman. Piotr was special. Father had chosen him. He hoped this baby wasn't any different; he hoped that it wasn't special too.

If it was...

Piotr frowned and drew his gaze up to the wall above the bed where Father had been looking. A giant golden tiger's head glowered from its spot on the plaster, its huge teeth like fangs ready to lunge down and snatch the baby from its mother when the thing finally came out. He shuddered, the skin between his shoulders tight and itchy.

Piotr looked away and sighed, and this time, Father turned his gaze on him—his steely eyes were usually the color of the lake, but they were black in the dim light and as dull as coal. Gooseflesh rose on Piotr's arms, and his belly soured. But he forced himself to smile.

If there was one thing you didn't want to do, it was upset Father.

1

THE NIGHT WHISPERED with the thick anxiety known to criminals and cops alike; an unspoken world navigated using the hairs along your spine—where the twitching of your belly feels inexplicably linked to your trigger finger. But instead of a nasty prickling between his shoulder blades, Detective Edward Petrosky felt only the heavy weight of responsibility, its sharp edge muted by booze. Relapse had come more easily than he'd anticipated, without fanfare or preamble. One day he was sober, the next he wasn't, and he hadn't decided if he'd stop again. Maybe he didn't have to. Maybe it'd be fine. Logically, he knew that was stupid, but he wasn't sure he cared.

He narrowed his eyes at the wall where twin smears of blood eked their way down toward the floor. Shattered glass adorned the hall table like glittering flakes of snow, though Petrosky could practically feel the heat coming off the wet edges of the wood—the blood was still fresh. It speckled the floor, smeared the baseboards in ruby, stained the wall between the hall and the kitchen.

"Front lock's been jimmied," Regina Jackson said, and Petrosky turned to see his partner kneeling by the front door, her eyes on the knob. The March wind had been mild today, but now it hissed out of the dark like a frozen blade, biting into his flesh through his sweatshirt. Jackson did not appear to notice. Her shorn black hair did not move in the breeze; even the lapels of her cream peacoat remained stiffly in place, brilliant against her dark throat. How the hell did she always manage to look like she'd just walked off the cover of *GQ Detectives Monthly*? It was four o'clock in the fucking morning; his socks didn't even match.

Footsteps to his right made him turn. Michaelson—shit, he hated that guy—strode in from the kitchen, his jacket barely missing a watch sitting on the edge of the Formica counter. A Rolex? Petrosky stepped closer, squinting. Yes, and a real one, the glass on the front magnifying the date. It didn't belong here, not in this house, not in this neighborhood. Michaelson stepped into the living room, blocking Petrosky's view of the counter, and gestured to the glass on the hallway floor. "Weird thing for a burglar to do, smashing picture frames. What'd he think, that there was money hidden behind them?"

"Maybe the intruder didn't want the family looking at him," Petrosky said. But no family, no children, smiled from the portraits behind the shards of glass; a single man appeared in all of them, sometimes with other dark-haired, broad-chested fellows, though one featured a fortysomething woman with a bouffant hairdo, her leathery skin sallow and sagging. The man was familiar, but Petrosky could not place him. *Maybe you shouldn't have had that Jack before bed, old man.* But, no, he was good, he'd just had a drink or two last night— okay, this morning—at the bar near his place. So far, he'd avoided drinking at home.

Michaelson frowned. "What's that smell?"

"Probably the garbage," Jackson said, but she wrinkled her nose. Michaelson stepped back to the sink and swung open the cabinet underneath—a trash bin. "Yup, hasn't been taken out in a while. The perp would probably have found more to steal in here than behind the picture frames, right?"

Was that asshole smiling? Petrosky turned back to the living room instead of looking at Michaelson any longer, but the view there was only marginally better. The couch was trashed like the pictures, the gray pillows strewn on the floor. The coffee table had been knocked over, too, its wooden legs sticking up like the stiff limbs of a roadkill corpse. "This isn't a burglary, Michaelson."

"But they jimmied the front door, and the caller said—"

"Callers lie." And so did supposed victims. The homeowner hadn't even been the one who called—a neighbor had phoned in the disturbance. Throwing picture frames was a noisy matter, as was tossing other humans into walls and over coffee tables. Burglars tended to move with a little more stealth.

"It sounded like the caller was plenty serious to me," Michaelson said, a note of whiny defensiveness in his voice. "What else would it be but a burglary? The owner wasn't even here when the break-in occurred."

"And yet there's blood all over his jacket," Petrosky snapped. Petrosky had walked past the ambulance on his way in, the homeowner inside still wearing his bloody coat—getting his hand stitched up. "Does that sound like a man who just stumbled in on his house being robbed?"

"No I mean, yes, but his hands were bleeding. He ran in because he saw the front door open, and he cut himself on the glass. But he doesn't want to press charges."

Petrosky frowned at the hall table; all those broken frames. The only reason to ignore a home invasion, to give a "burglar" a pass, was if you didn't want the police involved. But why? Was the homeowner protecting a friend? Family? Unless he was protecting himself—a bookie, maybe. Hiding the intruder to hide his own sins, Petrosky had seen that enough times. But whatever it was, it had ended in a scuffle, and the owner of the house rubbed him the wrong way—even looking at his picture made Petrosky's shoulders tense. "Get out, Michaelson. We've got work to do."

"But I—"

"Now." Petrosky could feel the daggers in his back, the kid glaring at him, but the rookie shuffled toward the door and out onto the porch, probably with a commiserative pat on the back from Jackson. He scanned the wall again, the twin trails of blood that marred the paint—fingers and a palm, probably someone trying to grab the wall. There was way too much spatter on the floor to support this guy's claim of slicing his hand on a broken picture frame. Petrosky's eyes lit on the photo nearest him: the homeowner in a button-down dress shirt, beer in hand, dark chest hair peeking from beneath his open collar.

Who'd you fight with, dickhead? "Did Michaelson check the bedrooms?" he asked. "The bathroom? The basement?"

"Yep. No other signs of struggle, nothing disturbed—neat."

Petrosky grunted. He'd seen a lot of home invasions, and there was a pattern to them, even when it was punk kids; thieves knew that valuables were usually kept in the bedroom so they wouldn't have started in the living room, and they sure as hell wouldn't have left that damn Rolex. So why jimmy the lock? Why break in?

Petrosky turned to see Jackson closing the front door, pulling her phone away from her ear, though he hadn't heard her talking to anyone. Maybe he did have a little too much whiskey in his system—what time had he stopped drinking again?

"Outside isn't quite as neat, though. Looks like someone ran out the back," Jackson said. "Michaelson followed the blood to see if there was any trace of another person, but the trail petered out in the grass near the back gate."

"What's the homeowner's explanation for that?" If there

hadn't been a struggle, blood in the grass was pretty weird unless their burly homeowner had sacrificed a goat to the gods of rich, luscious chest hair—that would explain a lot, actually.

"Homeowner says he ran out there in a panic after he cut himself. Wanted to see if anyone was still here." She shrugged, but her face said: *bullshit.* And whether or not it was true, a burglary, even a domestic call, wasn't their usual case—no rape, no dead people...well, probably not. There were plenty of flatfoots to take a statement on a B&E, even with a possible assault.

"Why are we on this?" He glanced once more at the living room, at the upended coffee table—one wooden leg was stained dark with blood.

She cocked her head. "The chief didn't tell you?"

Nope. He hadn't spoken to Chief Carroll in a month.

Jackson seemed to sense his confusion because she said: "This guy, the homeowner...you know him."

"I don't think so." But when his gaze dropped to the photos once more, he felt it again, that prickle of familiarity. *Why don't I remember him?*

"Piotr...something. I can't pronounce it. He's got a few priors, but nothing significant until about five years ago. His girlfriend, Louisa, said he slapped her around, raped her, and threatened to kill her if she called the police. Ring any bells? She was one of yours."

Now he knew why this guy looked familiar. Piotr Wójcik —that was his name. His victim, Louisa Parson, had stopped cooperating soon after he'd taken her statement, suddenly claimed the three-inch-long weeping gash along her eyebrow was "just a misunderstanding." Without her testimony, the prosecutor kicked it back and said there was nothing they could do, but Petrosky had felt certain Piotr had done it before—he had seen that much in the dull, unremorseful glitter in Piotr's eyes. And these assholes had a pattern; at the very least, Piotr had surely earned a few enemies besides Louisa. Had one of them come after him? That would explain why he was reluctant to tell them what had happened here. He could suddenly see Louisa's face, the dark, deep wound on her head, and was struck by an intense urge to find her—to make sure she was okay. "Need to call her," he muttered.

Jackson raised an eyebrow. "For what? It's not like she did this."

"Just...worried about her, I guess. Piotr messed her up bad." Petrosky shifted his focus to the upended coffee table, the bloody wood, and...something was peeking from beneath it. He edged closer, grabbed the opposite leg—the clean leg—and pulled. *Uh-oh.* Beneath the table, the carpet was shiny, wet. A puddle of blood the size of his fist glared at him like an angry eye.

Someone had been hurt here. Severely. And their homeowner was still standing—no way that was his blood.

He glared at the stain, his chest tightening with unease.

What'd you do, asshole? What the fuck did you do?

2

HE SIPPED AT HIS COFFEE, letting the steam melt the frost in his nostrils. The icy air had picked up as dawn broke, a hazy gray morning heavy with precipitation. Soon, the clouds would dump slush onto the streets—happy fucking spring. "Piotr left the scene; can't we jam him up for that?"

"Michaelson took him to the coffee shop while we were poking around his place; it isn't like he walked off. You should just be happy Michaelson brought your cantankerous ass a coffee." Jackson braced herself against the wind on Piotr Wójcik's front porch and frowned as her cell binged. Instead of asking what that was about—he hated it when his phone rang, too—he grabbed one of the granola bars the neighbor had stuffed in his sweatshirt pouch this morning when he'd dropped the dog off. Dry with a nasty cardboard aftertaste. *Gross, Billie.* Was she trying to kill him? At least there was an ambulance nearby.

"You can relax." Jackson shoved her cell back into her jacket pocket and started across the lawn. "Louisa Parson is fine, visiting friends in Tampa according to her social media. She'll be back in a few days."

Friends—five years ago, she hadn't had a single one. Like most abusers, Piotr had done a good job of isolating her from any potential support system so he could have his way with her. He finished the granola bar in one more bite, swallowed it down with another slug from the coffee cup, and shoved the wrapper back into his sweatshirt pouch, feeling the sour burn in the cave of his belly. The cold bit at his toes through his sneakers, the patchy ice of the sidewalk slipping beneath his soles.

"Detective!" He turned to see a man hustling up the walk. Rory something, a gingersnap EMT with eyes so blue it was like staring into a pair of glittering crayons. "Update for ya, like you asked. Lots of lacerations, but no glass in his wounds when I was cleaning him up. And no injuries deep enough to explain the amount of blood in the house."

Petrosky nodded. "Did you hurt him a little?"

"I disinfect slowly, what can I say." Rory winked and headed back to his ambulance.

Jackson sipped at her coffee, steam leaking around her face and vanishing as it edged toward the pregnant clouds. "What was that about? He was kissing your ass like it belonged to Beyoncé, and you didn't even seem to mind."

Petrosky shrugged. "I let his brother slide on marijuana possession a few months back." So he'd had a little too much non-prescription weed at the nursing home; marijuana was cheaper on the street than the legal way, and when you were on a fixed income, every little bit helped. Petrosky would have looked the other way no matter what, but it was nice to have an EMT owe you one.

And now for the main event. Michaelson's car was at the curb across the street, flashers off, engine running. Michaelson stood against the front passenger door, arms crossed like a bouncer, light hair glaring in the gray morning. In the back, Piotr sat facing straight ahead, his dark hair still seemingly neat despite having been up all night, the angles of his face sharp enough to cut.

Michaelson opened the back door like a goddamn chauffeur as they closed the distance between them, exposing Piotr and his half-unbuttoned shirt to the morning wind. A silver cross caught in Piotr's chest hair glittered. Damn—guy worked out almost as much as Michaelson's dumb ass. He could take Petrosky in a heartbeat, provided Petrosky didn't have his sidearm.

"Piotr, long time, no see."

The man's nostrils flared. "Had to be you, huh?"

Better me than another woman you raped. Petrosky forced a smile. "Me? I'm a delight."

"Has to get boring going after innocent men." He crossed his arms, his hands clean and bandaged—no coat now. Michaelson must have taken it into evidence.

"You see anyone innocent around here, Jackson?" Petrosky sipped his coffee though his belly felt oily, sick, as often happened when he had to deal with abusive dickheads. The wind hissed. Piotr glared. "Listen, this isn't about the past." He plastered on the most understanding facial expression he could muster. "Why don't you just tell us what happened here."

Piotr shrugged one thick shoulder. "I already told the other guy."

"I know this is a pain," Jackson said. "I know you're tired. But it would help if you could tell us again." If there were discrepancies between what he told them versus what he'd told Michaelson a few hours ago, that might help them flesh out the truth. For now, Petrosky wanted to read him. "It looks like there was a fight inside," Jackson said.

Petrosky watched the man's bloodshot eyes, the telltale twitch in one shoulder as his muscles tightened. "There was no fight, I already told you people that."

Liar. Petrosky kept his voice low and as kind as he could manage. "You aren't in trouble here, Piotr, not this time. If you caught someone trying to break in—"

"There was no one here when I got home! Jesus Christ."

Jackson said, "Now that one's hard for us to believe, Mr. Wójcik. There's definitely evidence of a struggle—lots of blood." She leaned closer, near enough to Petrosky that he could smell her hair—coconut. "Do you know the person who broke in? Maybe you don't want them to get into trouble."

Piotr sniffed and blinked—his eyes were spiderwebbed with fine red lines. "That's ridiculous. If I knew who broke in, I'd tell you." He sighed, face sagging—he suddenly looked ten years older. "Let's just drop it, okay? I want to go to bed."

Not gonna happen, assface.

"You're certain it was someone unknown to you?" Jackson said.

The man's shoulders pulled back, rigid, straight. Proper, but not in the way of a gentleman—more like a drug dealer posturing for status on the street corner. "Of course I'm sure."

"The blood in there..." Petrosky began, "we'll trace it, see what comes back. Maybe we'll get your burglar that way." *Or your victim—did you bring a woman home from the bar? Did you hurt her like you did Louisa?* But the lock... If he'd brought this person home with him, they wouldn't have had to jimmy the door.

"A trace is not necessary. I don't want to press charges." His nostrils were working overtime, expanding, contracting, expanding like a bull's.

"It's a little late for that, Mr. Wójcik," Jackson said. "With the mess, the blood, we have to look into it. Make sure no one got seriously hurt." *Or killed.* "The more you help us, the easier this will be." Jackson flipped open her little notepad. She tended to remember everything, but the process of writing seemed to make suspects—and victims—relax. Maybe because they didn't have to look her in the eye. "You said it was a home invasion, a burglary? So what'd they take?" she asked.

Piotr blinked as if trying to decide whether to tell them anything, then relaxed back against the seat—a decision had been made. But had he decided to cooperate or had he just figured out what line to feed them? "The only thing I saw missing for sure was my laptop; it was in the kitchen. Got all my work stuff on there, but it has a bunch of security features for that reason. No way they'll be able to get into it." He smirked. "The boss is going to be pissed. Sucks to be him."

Petrosky leaned closer, resting his shoulder against the doorframe. Piotr had said...*him*. About the intruder. A slip of the tongue or deception? *"Him" makes sense; you have no reason to assume he hurt another girl like Louisa—stop.* Petrosky cleared his throat. "Just the laptop? Good thing he didn't take that watch on the kitchen counter. I guess not everyone recognizes a Rolex when they see one." What did this guy do for a living again?

Piotr's gaze hardened. "The watch is fake."

Petrosky would have bet his right foot that watch wasn't fake. But instead of pressing the point, he said, "It's a damn a good fake. Not something any run-of-the-mill burglar would leave sitting in plain sight. Even a fake will pawn."

For this, Piotr had no answer. He stared. *Keep at it, asshole, I have all the time in the world.* Petrosky downed the rest of his coffee and eyeballed Piotr's front door. If this had been a burglary, the intruder would have abandoned that computer in their struggle to get away. And if someone had broken in to settle a vendetta, maybe break Piotr's kneecaps, they wouldn't snatch up his laptop. He was probably lying about the computer, too; Piotr just needed an excuse, something to explain the intruder's presence, something to suggest the intruder was still alive. But with all that blood...

Petrosky turned back to Michaelson's car—to the dickhead in the back seat. "It's odd that someone would break into your house, smash your pictures, bleed all over your living room, and take nothing but your computer," Petrosky said slowly. "Was there something important on it? I'd sure hate to see them come back if they can't find what they're after."

Piotr shook his head. "There's nothing on there of use to anyone else. It's just bookkeeping for Joe's Hardware."

Something about that pinged Petrosky's memory, but he brushed it away. Jackson's pen scritch-scratched against her notepad. "Those are some nasty gashes on your hands," Petrosky went on. "You want to tell me how you did that?"

"I already told you everything I know!" His voice got louder with each word, echoing against the metal grates inside the police car. "I was at the bar until three. I got home, found that someone had broken in, and cut myself on the glass."

Petrosky rested his forearms on the top of the car and hung his head inside the opening, and the musk of Piotr's cologne assaulted his nostrils—woodsy but sharp. And booze...definitely booze. His mouth watered, though he forced his lips into a line of placidity. "It looks like someone died in your living room, Piotr. I'm shocked they walked out of there on their own." But maybe they hadn't made it far. Would their intruder be found later today, dead in a ditch?

Piotr shook his head. "Whatever happened in there, I had nothing to do with it. I came home, the place was trashed, I cut my hand, that's all."

Enough, asshole. "You know it's illegal to hide a body, right?"

His eyebrows hit his hairline. "What? A body? I—"

"Thank you for your time, Mr. Wójcik." Petrosky slammed the door before the man could say anything else—before the undeniable urge to slap the bastard took over.

Even yelling at him might appear extreme. Regardless of this man's past, regardless of Petrosky's gut feeling on the matter, they had no proof that Piotr Wójcik had done anything wrong.

But he had. Oh, he had.

3

THEY MADE their way toward the neighbor's place—the woman who had called in the disturbance lived a few houses down from Piotr—the icy street feeling more oppressive now than it had in the dark. When everything had been buried in shadow, he could imagine sparkling windows, fine shoots of grass greening between the porch and the street, and early pops of color peeking through the mulched flower beds. But the cookie-cutter brick houses, most with dark wooden shutters of blue or brown, made the overall effect more akin to walking through a western ghost town. Petrosky glanced at his cell.

```
Are you okay? If you died on me, I'll be
            super pissed.
```

Shannon. His ex-partner's wife, the closest thing he had to a daughter, lived in Atlanta now. It had been at least a week since the last time she'd tried to call, and he hadn't answered then either, a thought which made guilt burn hot in his guts like the first shot of booze. *That's why you're not calling her back, she'll know you're drinking again.* Shannon had always had a sixth sense about that; slapped him once for it, right in the face. She and the kids should probably just forget about him. And yet...

If you died on me, I'll be super pissed. He slipped the phone back into his pocket, but he could hear Shannon's voice like she was there on the frigid sidewalk with him, one corner of her lips turned up, the other side deadly serious. He suppressed a grin and finished Billie's second granola bar, the icy wind biting at his fingertips harder than when he'd arrived at the scene. Ah, sobriety. He'd be lying if he said he didn't hate it.

"What's so funny?" Jackson asked.

"Your mother. As the kids would say."

"What the hell is wrong with you?"

"Lots of shit. You're going to have to be more specific." Frost crunched beneath his sneakers; he blew warm breath into his cupped hands.

Jackson stopped in front of a well-kept but older home, the salted walk damp with melted ice, the navy paint chipped along one corner of the garage. Not a carport like Piotr's. A single hyacinth poked from an otherwise empty flower bed beside the front porch; one tiny overachiever that would surely die in the next freeze—sometimes optimism destroyed you.

A woman flung the door wide before they had a chance to knock, bags beneath her eyes that matched the navy on the garage right down to the odd, mottled-bruise effect of the chipped paint. Her wiry, ash-blonde hair boasted a single streak of gray, a shimmering river running through a field of dry wheat. Sixty, maybe seventy. She introduced herself with a much-too-animated grin—hadn't she called them at three in the freaking morning?—and showed Petrosky and Jackson into a living room set up almost exactly as Piotr's had been. A single couch, a table on the far wall near the hallway, pictures hanging neatly in their frames: three smiling families, all with small children.

"We have a lot to talk about." Marylyn's eyes gleamed as Petrosky and Jackson settled themselves on the flowered sofa. A lot to talk about indeed, and damn if she didn't look pleased about it. Like this was an amusement park ride instead of a police investigation.

"Can you tell us exactly what you heard this morning?" Jackson asked her. If this woman had heard shouting, arguing, they'd have more ammunition when they talked to Piotr again—that prick was lying through his slimy teeth.

"Well, there was some crashing—breaking glass. I didn't think much of it, to be honest, not at first."

Jackson raised an eyebrow. "Is shattering glass at three o'clock in the morning a normal occurrence?"

"Well, it was just the one crash, no yelling or anything. Like someone dropped a vase. I wouldn't have even heard it if I'd been in the house, but I'd gone out on the front porch for a smoke."

"At three in the morning?" Petrosky said.

"I'm an insomniac, dear. Gets worse as I get older. Sometimes, I go back to bed, but..." Her smile fell. "If I'd been inside, I wouldn't have seen her."

Her? "Saw who?" Jackson prodded.

"The woman. She came running through the side gate from the backyard and out to the road. Turned right at the corner." Marylyn nodded sagely. "She was holding her arm against her body real tight, lots of blood. Missing her right hand."

Missing her— "Why didn't you tell the dispatcher that?" If they had known a bleeding one-handed woman had been running from Piotr's house, they'd have had a much more interesting conversation with the man, and they'd have put out an APB instead of just having Michaelson call the hospitals. Who was she? And how had she managed to escape with that kind of injury?

Marylyn sniffed. Her shoulders had straightened—defensive. "You have to understand, detectives, she's had it really hard. I didn't want to make trouble for her, but I'm not willing to lie to you."

Wait, what? Had it hard? "Sounds like you know a lot about this woman," Jackson said.

"Yes. She used to live four blocks from here."

Jackson and Petrosky exchanged a glance. All they had to do was go ask this mystery woman what had happened. Hopefully, she'd still be alive when they got there.

"Do you have any idea why she'd be at Piotr's?" Jackson kept her voice low, but the edges of her words were sharp; she sounded as frustrated as he felt.

The woman frowned. "No, I don't know that."

"Was she carrying anything?" he asked. *Like her own severed hand?* That sure hadn't been in the living room.

Her brow furrowed. "You know…she was. A silver rectangle, a laptop, maybe."

So, Piotr had told the truth about that, but why tell them about the laptop at all? As a cover for a more serious crime? Maybe he thought they'd recover it before they realized he was the real criminal, but if he'd hurt this woman, ripped off her hand…he'd be praying they didn't find her. What the hell was going on?

"Her name, ma'am?" Jackson asked.

"Oh, dear, I can't remember her name. Memory's not as good as it used to be, I guess."

Very helpful. His cell buzzed again, and this time, he turned it off. "But you just said—"

"I didn't know her personally, but I'd know her face anywhere. And she was always missing a hand—can't mistake that. That's how I knew it was her today. That missing hand."

So Piotr hadn't done that? At least that explained why there wasn't a severed hand on the countertop. Petrosky and Jackson waited for the woman to continue, but she just nodded again and blinked. *Jesus tap-dancing Christ, spit it out!* This woman was needling the soft spot between his shoulders; this wasn't a goddamn movie, here for her entertainment. There was a woman out there, bleeding, maybe dying.

"This woman you saw—where can we find her?" Jackson asked, her words pressured, harsh.

"Well, she doesn't live here anymore, but you should be able to look her up pretty easily; she was on the news all the time back in the day. Missing, you know. *Kidnapped*." She met Petrosky's gaze, and her face clouded. "I know what you must think, detectives, I can see it in how you're looking at me. That I shouldn't know so much about her life, not without knowing her personally. But I don't have a husband, and my children all live out of state; they don't call too much." She shook her head. "Turns out, these news stories... they're the only things that keep the days interesting."

THE RIDE back to the precinct was filled with stony silence, Jackson's fingers tapping maniacally on the steering wheel, her mouth set in a grim line. They'd knocked on the doors of all the surrounding homes, including those on the street Marylyn saw the woman run onto, but no one else had seen anything useful. He glowered at the hazy gray sky. Piotr had definitely done something he wasn't supposed to, but what? Had this one-handed woman managed to get one over on him and run off? Why had she taken the laptop? Was the neighbor right about her identity? Witnesses sometimes made associations that didn't exist based on familiarity, and if this mystery woman had gotten a lot of media coverage... Well, hopefully, the DNA would give them something to work with—ammunition for when they went back to confront that shithead.

When they arrived at the precinct, Jackson headed for the far side of the L-shaped bullpen where detectives Decantor and Sloan were already at their desks. Sloan had been nice enough to pull the file Petrosky had called about in exchange for the espressos Jackson was now delivering. Sloan grinned at her and nodded to Petrosky; Decantor, too, turned to glance his way, waved, then turned back to his own work, or, more likely, back to whatever Kardashian fan club website he was scouring. Petrosky collapsed into his seat with a cup of coffee-house coffee clasped in his fist just as the slush began to spit against the windowpane.

His old PC gasped to life with the electric rattle familiar to every cop who worked at an underfunded precinct. Jackson was already on the mystery woman, so Petrosky flipped open the folder on his desk while he waited for the thing to boot up—different case, but it felt relevant deep down in his guts.

Louisa Parson, twenty-three, graphic designer, had shown up to Oaklawn Hospital with a deep gash over her eye, bruising on both arms and legs, and signs of sexual assault according to the ER doc. She'd told Petrosky that the assailant, Piotr Wójcik, was her boyfriend and that he'd attacked her after a night of heavy drinking at a local dance club. The next day, she'd called the station and told dispatch she was leaving town to decompress; she'd vanished for two weeks. Petrosky had visited Piotr at his work—the hardware store—questioned him in front of his boss, hoping the hardware store owner would fire Piotr's rapist ass. No luck. And no Louisa. Petrosky had been ready to send out the bloodhounds, but she'd resurfaced just in time to recant, ten pounds lighter, and the bags beneath her eyes…the hope had been drained out of her like someone had stuck a silly straw into her soul. Without her cooperation, the district attorney had refused to charge Piotr, and Petrosky had been dragged away on a homicide before he could even smear egg on the bastard's windshield. People healed in different ways, but letting a rapist walk wasn't ever something that sat right with him even when he had no legal recourse.

The PC beeped, and he glanced up. Maybe this was his fault for not convincing Louisa to testify. Maybe Piotr had hurt this woman who'd once lived around the block, and she'd come back to get even; maybe jimmied his door and stolen his laptop because she thought there was something damning on it. Or the intruder was some new woman that Piotr had also abused. One thing he was sure of: Piotr wasn't a victim.

He pulled the keyboard closer and let the heavy tapping of his fingers soothe his tattered nerves. His eyes felt gritty, like they were full of sand.

Piotr Wójcik... The coffee churned in his belly as he read. No marriages, no kids, no probation or parole, no liens on his property—it looked like he owned that little house outright. Nothing at all to nail him on. A guy like Wójcik should have a rap sheet, but the only things listed here were unverified claims from Petrosky's report on Louisa Parson.

And if Wójcik owned the house outright, with no wife, no kids, hell, maybe he really could afford a Rolex. It was odd that he'd been able to pay the place off on a bookkeeper's salary, but it wasn't impossible. Petrosky shouldn't be able to afford two houses on a detective's salary, but he didn't have kids or a wife or a fancy wardrobe to worry about—the sneakers on his feet had been with him for a good four years, the sweatshirt for fifteen, and he expected to make them both last another ten. All he really needed was his dog, Duke, and his whiskey. A nightly shot or two at the bar, that's all. And coffee. Lots of coffee.

"Piotr's story checks out," Jackson said, and he turned to see her striding toward him from her desk. "Witnesses put him at a bar on the east side until nearly three a.m., and he left alone—got a few security cameras that picked him up driving back all by his lonesome. Looks like he got home exactly when he said he did." She sighed, exasperated, and tossed the files on his desk, narrowly missing his nearly empty coffee cup.

"If he surprised a burglar, he wouldn't be hiding it," Petrosky muttered. "Unless he did something far worse to her."

"Right, but even if he raced home, he had less than ten minutes before Marylyn's call came in." And Michaelson had responded twelve minutes later to find Piotr in his driveway, his hands slashed to pieces, with blood on his jacket. And Petrosky had read Michaelson's notes on the way back to the station; Piotr had told Michaelson the same thing he'd told them.

"You can do a lot in twenty minutes," he said.

"Yeah, but whatever he did, we know this woman was there waiting for him; she jimmied that lock. And Piotr definitely didn't hide a body—Marylyn saw her run out of her own accord with the laptop. But there's a bigger problem with Marylyn's story." Jackson slid into her chair at the corner of his desk, her mouth tight, her eyes narrowed at the window, jaw working…and yet, she didn't look angry. Perplexed?

"What's wrong?"

Her eyes stayed locked on the bullpen window, the slushy mess of a sky. "You know the woman Marylyn was so positive she saw running from Piotr Wójcik's house? The one that went missing years ago?" She tapped the folder on his desktop with one clipped fingernail. "She's dead."

4

Twenty-two-year-old Rebecca Kowalski stared at Petrosky from her driver's license photo, the image thirteen years old. Vibrant blue eyes, nose like a razor, thin pink lips, freckles, dirty-blonde hair highlighted to perfection and layered cleanly around her heart-shaped face.

"This whole thing is just so bizarre," Jackson said. "The witness at Wójcik's clearly got the woman's identity wrong, but what are the odds of two women with missing hands showing up in that neighborhood?" And where was she now? They'd already contacted local motels and hotels to see if they had a one-handed woman renting a room, and they'd come up empty. But that didn't necessarily mean she wasn't there. It was cold—easy to hide an injury inside a jacket or under a scarf, and if she was up to no good, she wouldn't be stupid enough to flaunt her most discernible feature.

But Jackson was right: two women with missing hands within a four-block radius seemed unlikely unless they had some sicko running around lopping off limbs. It was possible Marylyn was mistaken about the missing hand—it was dark, after all—but...she'd seemed so certain. And he couldn't imagine her making that up, not even to make her life *inter-*

esting. So where did that leave them? "Walk me through the chain of events that led to…" He gestured to the file, then raised his fingers to massage his aching temples.

"Like I said…bizarre." Jackson leaned in like she was going to tell him a secret. "So, seven years ago, Rebecca's kidnapping was reported by the media—vanished early one morning, and no leads or at least none leaked to the press." Which didn't necessarily mean they didn't exist. "Just under a month later, she was involved in the car wreck that claimed her hand, but by the time of the accident, the media buzz had died off. There were only a few local articles on her return, but from what I can tell, the car wreck happened right about the same time she resurfaced from the abduction."

Jackson shuffled the papers and pulled a photo from near the bottom of the stack: an old Wrangler, wheels up—looked like a rollover after she careened off the road and into a ditch. For anyone to walk away from that would have been a miracle, and yet, a severed hand seemed a little clean for a car wreck. Who hung their hand out the car window in the middle of winter? Sub-zero wind on exposed fingertips was a recipe for frostbite. "Did they catch the kidnappers?"

"No, but there's a problem with that too," Jackson said. "The file on the kidnapping? It's gone."

"Gone? What do you mean—"

"It isn't listed as checked out, and because it was so long ago, it could have been pulled at any point within the last seven years."

He frowned. Even if you wanted to hide something specific about a case, you didn't need to steal the entire file—more suspicious if the whole thing was gone anyway. "And you said she's dead? Complications from the car wreck?" He turned the page.

"Fire, actually; a warehouse explosion three months after she rolled her Jeep."

Damn—what a shit year. Petrosky flipped to the death

certificate. Method of disposition was listed as cremation, and she'd been transferred to a mortuary in West Bloomfield for that. No report from a medical examiner and no photos of her crispy remains in this file, but the mortuary had signed off; they'd cremated her charred corpse. Highly doubtful she'd put herself back together to go visit Piotr this morning.

His cell buzzed. He shut it off without checking the caller ID, his brain churning. First, a kidnapping, then a car wreck where she'd lost her hand, and finally, burned to death in a fire, all within a few months? This woman had wicked-bad luck, and he didn't believe in luck any more than he did coincidence. But how did all this relate to their case? Sure, it deserved attention, justice, but if Marylyn was wrong about the woman she saw, it had nothing to do with Piotr Wójcik. But with the missing paperwork and the bizarre links to kidnapping and amputated hands and suspicious death… they had to at least ask a few questions.

A headache throbbed behind his right eyeball. *Goddammit, who the hell would take a kidnapping file?* It could have been misplaced, but that felt too convenient, and for someone to steal it…there had to be something of interest inside, right?

He straightened. "Did they do a press conference on the kidnapping?" With all the media hype, maybe someone had mentioned the original detectives by name. He grabbed the keyboard and scrolled through the old *Ash Park Today* articles —*there*. They both leaned closer to the screen. Rebecca Kowalski stared back from the monitor, standing on what was probably her front porch, her good arm linked with that of a dark-haired man who looked remarkably like Piotr; one of her hands was missing, the stump wrapped in gauze just above her wrist bone. From after the accident, after the kidnapping, so no detectives were listed—*perfect*. Once the cops got people home safe, their names vanished into oblivion. He clicked a few more times, seeking articles from before she returned, news pieces on the abduction, a missing persons alert... *Bingo.* Detective Jamaika Apmada was listed on the kidnapping press release as the one to contact with information.

"You really think she remembers?" Jackson asked as he pushed himself to standing.

"I don't know." They didn't have definitive evidence that the cases were connected, but they did have a missing kidnapping case file and a witness claiming to have seen this same kidnapped woman—a woman who was supposed to be dead. And Piotr was a very bad man, Petrosky knew that from the dropped rape charges. This guy got off on brutalizing women. And bastards like him didn't just stop.

Whoever had broken into his house had done it for a reason.

JAMAIKA APMADA still worked as a detective, but she'd moved to a neighboring precinct up the road in Hazel. Apmada was waiting at Rita's Diner when they arrived, her shiny black hair pulled into a tight bun, her brown eyes surrounded by fine lines, her wide smile brighter than the brazen fluorescents. Why wasn't she scowling at him? He'd basically told her she had an hour to pick a meeting place, though he had no authority over her whatsoever.

She waved them into the faux leather booth across from her and picked up her glass, the thick liquid pink and icy—milkshake? "I would have ordered you one, but I wasn't sure which flavor you liked."

"What are you having?" he asked, the seat squealing as he edged in after Jackson.

"Strawberry." She smiled again. "Got fries coming. If you don't like those, I don't think I can be seen with you." A bead of condensation slid down the side of the cup to the tabletop as Apmada drew the straw back to her lips. "So how can I help? You said you wanted info on a kidnapping case?"

"Yeah," Jackson said. "Rebecca Kowalski."

Apmada nodded and set the milkshake aside. "One of my first abductions. I was terrified of the press, the conferences... I would much rather work my magic behind the scenes."

"Tell us what that magic looked like in this case," Jackson said.

She shrugged. "Unfortunately, there was no magic on Kowalski—all I had were suspicions. I remember thinking her creepy husband probably had her body hidden in the walls, but he let us search their place from top to bottom. No Rebecca."

"How'd they find her?" Petrosky asked. "I'm not clear on exactly how she was taken or how she came to be back home. We're starting at ground zero." *Because someone stole the damn file.*

Apmada leaned forward conspiratorially. "It went down like this: we got a call from someone claiming to be Rebecca around two thirty a.m.—just her name, and a plea to help her."

Petrosky put up a hand. "You said, 'claiming to be Rebecca.' Do you think it wasn't really her?"

"I think it was, but after she returned, Rebecca denied making the call, and we could never prove it either way. It came from a pay phone three blocks from her house, but there was no sign of a struggle when the patrol drove by it, and the only witness didn't see a person, just a dark-colored sedan peeling away at around the same time the call came in."

They all paused as a tall redheaded waitress arrived with a tray—three plates laden with fries, one topped with orange cheese, one with chili, and one with both. His kind of order. Apmada pushed a plate his way, and Petrosky snatched up a fork to attack the chili fries—*screw that granola shit*. The meat slid down his gullet on a river of grease. Spicy. Salty. Amazing.

The waitress tucked the tray under her arm, revealing a bulge beneath her apron. Pregnant. "Anything else, folks?"

"Two more milkshakes," Petrosky said. "Strawberry."

Jackson nodded agreement and brushed imaginary lint from her fancy cream-colored jacket—*is that camel hair?*—then pulled the chili cheese fries closer to her. "And an extra bowl of chili."

"Coming right up."

Apmada watched the waitress walk away, then said, "Anyway, I was coming on duty as the patrol was coming off his shift—he thought it was a crank call, didn't even bother to drive by Rebecca's house, which pissed me all the way off. I guess he just figured he'd pass the buck—to me." She rolled her eyes. "I raced over around six thirty that morning."

Petrosky nodded. He'd have done the same. Well, after he grabbed that idiot by the shirt collar and slammed him into a locker for being incompetent. But this woman was probably a better detective than he was—probably a better person, too—just like Jackson. He glanced his partner's way, but she was watching Apmada and shoveling fries into her face.

Apmada forked up another fry, too, and said around a mouthful of potato: "The husband was skittish—almost tweaky, you know? But without the druggie eyes." Petrosky knew exactly what she meant. It was a mannerism he'd learned to watch for—liars were almost always a little twitchy. "He was all smiles at first, said his wife wasn't home, but when I told him we'd gotten a call from her, his story suddenly changed. *Then* he says it's a ransom thing."

Petrosky frowned. Sometimes folks hesitated to involve police if the kidnappers told them not to; they thought they could pay the money as demanded and get their loved one back, those hopeful bastards. But Apmada's eyes…

"You didn't believe him."

"You can read me like a book, Detective." She shoved another fry into her mouth and... Did she just wink at him? *Probably has something in her eye.* "I didn't believe anything her husband said, especially once I found out that she'd filed a police report on *him* less than a week before she vanished—domestic violence. I thought maybe he'd killed her for it, that we'd be dealing with a homicide, but there was no evidence of that—she'd clearly been alive when she called from that pay phone. So we ran with it as a kidnapping, put her photo out, slapped her smiling face on television...well, for as long as they would run it. Turns out, there's not a ton of interest in a missing housewife after three weeks."

Three weeks. Getting closer to the car wreck. They paused as the waitress returned, bearing two more shakes and the chili. She smiled. One of her front teeth was chipped, the sharp edge stained with red lipstick as if someone had recently hit her, the blood still fresh on her mouth. Petrosky's back tightened, though he knew the chip was neither new nor purposeful—probably. *You've been on the job too long, old man.* He sipped at his milkshake, sickeningly sweet, the cold freezing his molars and making his brain throb.

Jackson dabbed at her lips and said, "You obviously weren't ready to let it go."

Apmada shook her head and picked up the shake. "No, especially with that weird vibe from her husband...Lucius was his name. I think." She took a long swallow of her milkshake before continuing. "We put a line on the husband's cell, tapped the home phone—Lucius gave us permission, if you can believe that. And we stationed an officer out front in case he tried to run or sneak out to pay a ransom. But he didn't. No kidnappers ever called or showed. And Lucius's bank accounts stayed exactly the same—Rebecca's husband never took any money out for a ransom payment."

"Yet she still came home," Jackson said. Which was weird

—he'd have expected to find a body. Then again, she had turned up dead three months after she returned. They'd have to look more closely at that fire...in all their spare time.

"Was there any evidence to suggest that Lucius was involved in her disappearance?" Petrosky asked. He'd seen that more times than he wanted to admit. Homicides, kidnappings—you always looked at the family first.

"Nothing. No calls in or out to unknown numbers—not even the ransom call Lucius claimed came to the house." Apmada shook her head. "Lucius's story about that changed, too. First, he said he got a ransom call, then later, he said he got a letter but that he burned it in the sink as instructed by the note."

Which sounded like absolute bullshit, but... *Burned*. That was some creepy foreshadowing. Burn the note, burn the girl. He reached for the fries, though his guts had gone sour.

"So, how did Rebecca end up coming home?" Jackson asked.

Apmada shrugged. "We found her in a ditch under her Wrangler."

Petrosky lowered his fry. Jackson leaned over the table so far Petrosky thought she might stain her fancy camel-fur jacket with chili. "The auto wreck?"

Apmada nodded. "Yup. Never found her hand, though." She pointed to a spot on her arm just above the wrist. "They tried to say an animal ran off with it, but we were on the scene so quickly that seemed unlikely. And she was alone in the car—no trace of any kidnappers. It was like they just gave her the keys and waved." Apmada glanced at the shake as if trying to decide whether to take another swallow, then met Petrosky's eyes. "She woke up after surgery and said the domestic violence thing with her husband was a misunderstanding, that she hadn't been abducted, and hadn't made any calls from that pay phone—that she'd just needed some time away to decompress."

Bile rose in his throat. Shit. Now *that* sounded familiar—that was almost word-for-word what Louisa had told him after she dropped the charges on Piotr. And she'd also vanished for weeks before coming back and recanting. What were they dealing with? Some kidnapping ring who taught your domestic partners a lesson if they stepped out of line and called the cops on you? It made no sense.

Jackson was shaking her head, the food forgotten. "So the only evidence you had that it was a kidnapping—"

"I know how it sounds," Apmada said. "We pressed her, threatened her with filing a false report, tried to get her to admit that something happened, told her we could protect her. In the end, it came to nothing. She was stoic, or numb, maybe, but she denied being hurt or kidnapped, denied any wrongdoing, claimed to be nothing more than a woman who needed a break. And she was driving herself home—weird after an abduction. Case closed, right? Everyone thought I should drop it, and I had to eventually, but there was so much...wrong. That family..." She stared at the plate, the fries, and wrinkled her nose as if she'd smelled something bad.

Petrosky's appetite was shot, too. Yeah, there was a lot wrong, but hearing those words from Apmada's lips and not just inside his own head gave the statement more weight.

"Sounds like you're talking about more than the kidnapping." Jackson leaned back in her seat, the vinyl squealing. *At least my ass isn't the only one that makes the bench cry.*

Apmada sniffed. "The husband's family...I can't for the life of me remember their names, but they were shady as hell. Lucius's friend was a suspect in a double homicide, but there was never any evidence to hold him—the bodies were found in Lake Huron two weeks after they disappeared, all the evidence conveniently washed away or eaten by the fish. His father did time, too." She narrowed her eyes at the plate and snatched up another chili-soaked fry, but stopped short of putting it in her mouth—it drooped. "I know the criminal activity of associates isn't definitive, but I didn't trust a single one of them. Or Lucius. They were all liars, criminals, even if I couldn't prove it."

Petrosky nodded. "I trust you on that."

"I bet that's rare coming from you." She winked at him again—definitely winking. Maybe she was winking at Jackson. But his partner was raising an eyebrow…at him.

He cleared his throat and said, "Sounds like you had a lot of reasons to suspect that Rebecca's later statements weren't true; that someone had actually kidnapped her."

Apmada's eyes clouded—the look of a seasoned detective, tired of the whole damn world. "Yeah. I investigated for a few more months, looking at Lucius, mostly; I wanted to nail her husband on something, give her a chance to get away from him. But after she died in that fire… I mean, it was over." Apmada grabbed her napkin and wiped her hands. "If you have more questions, I'm happy to help. I was actually pretty surprised that you wanted to talk about this case. I figured you already knew about it."

Petrosky cocked his head. "Why is that?"

"Well, the guy posted at Lucius's house, keeping tabs on him during the kidnapping investigation? He was your partner."

5

THE BULLPEN FELT DIFFERENT, tighter, the walls closer than they'd been just this morning. Even the air felt heavier in his lungs as if each breath were coated in lead. Morrison. His partner, a man he'd come to see as his son. How was that possible? But of course it was; they hadn't known one another at the time Morrison would have been posted on Lucius Kowalski's door, but that California boy had started on the beat just like everyone else had, even if he did have some fancy English degree to go with his handcuffs. Cali— damn, he missed the kid. He still had Shannon, Morrison's wife, but he was screwing that up too. Like he fucked up everything. He pushed the thoughts aside, ignoring the tight heat in his chest, and ran a hand over his face—prickly. Twelve hours on the job already, and at least four too few cups of coffee, but thankfully, Jackson was on her way to remedying that; she set a Styrofoam cup on his desk and slipped into her seat with her laptop.

His cell buzzed in his jeans pocket. *Shit. Didn't I turn that off?* Probably Shannon again, but he couldn't talk to her right now, didn't want to have to tell her about Morrison, that her late husband was somehow involved in this case, even as a bystander. At least hitting *Ignore* wouldn't hurt her—he could blame it on a faulty signal, or working too much, or just being, as Jackson said, "a cranky, introverted, non-phone-answering bastard." Actually, it'd probably tip Shannon off that something was wrong if he did pick up.

Jackson raised an eyebrow. "Popular guy."

"Yeah." The phone buzzed again.

"Might be important," she said, opening the laptop and tapping the space bar. "Maybe you should at least see who it is."

"It's fine, Jackson. Let it go." She'd already grilled him about Morrison, as if he'd know what the kid had done before they'd met. He had no idea why Apmada thought he'd know about the case either; Rebecca's kidnapping and return were a bit more sensational than the norm, but Ash Park was a crime-a-minute place, and it wasn't like he and Cali had been in the habit of talking about old bullshit. The phone buzzed again, and Jackson looked at him pointedly. He ripped the cell from his pocket, hit the button to silence the call, and tossed the phone into the desk drawer without looking at the caller ID. "And stop looking at me like I'm ignoring a call from the fucking pope."

"I *know* you wouldn't answer for him." She rolled her eyes, but her lips stayed tight as her own phone buzzed. Unlike him, she turned it over in her hand and squinted at the screen. "Scott." She hit the button for speakerphone and put it on the desk between them.

"What's up, kid?" Petrosky said.

"Oh, hey." Scott's voice was low, momentarily confused, but surely that was Petrosky's imagination. Scott was a genius, a twentysomething forensics expert with more knowledge packed into his brain than Petrosky could ever hope to know. "I just tried to call you."

Oops. "Battery's dead," Petrosky said, earning daggers from Jackson. "So, what've you got?"

"This robbery thing…there's more to it."

Duh. "The fingerprints pop in the system?" That'd make their job a hell of a lot easier, and with the bloody handprint on the wall, they should have gotten something usable.

"Nope, no prints besides the homeowner's. Which is very weird. Most people have a ton of fingerprints around their house—it's like he's never had a visitor."

"Fine, so our guy is a loner." Or a criminal who wiped his place down on the regular. Either way, it sounded like whoever had been in that house with Piotr was smart enough to wear gloves. "So, what's the issue?"

"Well, it's with the DNA. Specifically, your homeowner's."

Uh-oh, dickhead. Maybe they had a cold case they'd never had a DNA match for; with Louisa dropping all charges, they'd never gotten a DNA sample from Piotr. But now they had his blood. Would they be able to nail him on an unsolved rape? Not that it'd necessarily solve their current case, but… "How'd you get it back so fast?"

Scott's laugh rumbled through the phone—the kid was getting old, but damn if he didn't still seem like a teenager. "I got the chief to buy that 'test on a chip' system—four hours or so, and I can see if they're in the database. And more importantly, for this case, I can check for specific identifying markers."

"So, the blood from the scene is in the system?"

"Well, not exactly. So I've got two blood types. No matches on the first blood sample, but it's definitely female, and far more blood from her than your homeowner." Which they already knew—he had to believe Marylyn had been right about seeing a bloody woman, even if she might be wrong about the specific woman. "I'm surprised she walked out of there," Scott finished.

His belly tightened—*me too, kid.* But they'd canvassed the whole damn neighborhood after they'd talked to Marylyn, called hospitals, too, and no one had seen her. And they sure hadn't found a body.

Scott continued: "The homeowner, Piotr Wójcik, isn't in the system either, but a few familial matches popped." They listened to the rustling of papers, then the tapping of Scott's keyboard. "Is your homeowner involved in organized crime?"

Organized crime? "You mean like the mafia?"

"Well, maybe. Lots of criminal activity in this family, but these names don't sound Italian or Irish—not what most people expect when they hear the word 'mafia.'"

"Right. Wójcik is Polish."

"And so are the rest: six others in total. But there's also some strangeness paperwork-wise—like, Piotr Wójcik is *legally* the son of Joseph Rericha, but Rericha is in the system, and the DNA says Piotr is not his biological son; Wójcik is Rericha's *grand*son."

"His grandson?" Petrosky echoed. And that name, Rericha… *Damn.* During the Louisa Parson case, Petrosky had interviewed Wójcik at work, Joe's Hardware—owned by Joseph Rericha. That explained why Rericha hadn't batted an eye; he wasn't going to fire his own blood, rapist or no.

"Yeah, I thought it was weird, so I looked into him a little," Scott went on. "Rericha's pushing eighty, has a history of arrests for burglary, and a charge for drug trafficking almost fifteen years back—served five years on that one. Mostly small-time stuff. Wife died fourteen years ago, and he had one daughter, Miranda, died eight years ago. He still lives nearby."

This was the "shady family" Apmada had mentioned, the people who made her uneasy. Jackson frowned, her eyes narrowed at the cell as if deep in thought, but her hand was working overtime—scribbling notes. He hadn't even noticed her grabbing a pen.

"And we've got an even closer DNA match," Scott continued. "Roman Wójcik. Sixteen of twenty DNA markers—I'd say a brother. Accused of sexual assault a few times, but either the accusations were recanted, or the charges got dismissed. He never saw a day in jail."

Like Piotr—*exactly* like Piotr. Maybe the two of them were into some similar fucked-up shit. Hell, maybe Piotr had called his brother to drive by and find that woman after she ran off this morning. Crazy, surely, but... "Where can we find Roman?"

"No can do. Guy's dead, as are three of the others that popped with partial matches. Most look like half brothers to one another—Rericha is everyone's father except for Piotr and Roman Wójcik, and those two are Rericha's grandkids, like I said. But Roman Wójcik and Lucius Kowalski, one of Rericha's sons, died in a warehouse explosion not ten miles from here about seven years back."

A warehouse explosion... Lucius Kowalski... Rebecca Kowalski, the one-handed woman who'd died seven years ago in a warehouse fire, apparently, with her husband—Rericha's son. She and Piotr were in-laws? And Marylyn had seen her *today*. Petrosky sat straighter in his chair and leaned over the desk as if staring at Jackson's cell phone screen would give him the answers he needed. Sure, it was possible that the witness was wrong, but it was more likely that these very odd circumstances were connected. "Was Lucius cremated?" Petrosky asked. He wasn't certain why that seemed so critical, but the question tingled as it left his tongue.

Tap-tap-tap, then: "Nope. Lucius Kowalski is buried at White River Cemetery."

Huh. Why bury him but not his wife? While Petrosky didn't subscribe to the notion of an afterlife, most couples tended to share ideology—it was odd for one to be laid to rest without their partner.

But that missing hand...the kidnapping-that-wasn't. The

domestic violence charges against various members of the family, all dropped. Their witness, Marylyn, so goddamn sure about who she'd seen. And Rebecca's husband, Lucius, sure kept lousy company. Maybe Rebecca had just wanted to get away from him.

Maybe she'd succeeded.

6

"WHAT ARE WE DEALING WITH HERE?" Jackson put her head in her hands, her elbows on his desk.

After talking to Scott, they had returned to Marylyn's with a photo array that included Rebecca—positive ID, though Marylyn said Rebecca's hair was darker now and she was thinner than the woman in the picture. Different enough for them to be skeptical, especially in the dark, but with that missing hand, it was far too much coincidence, and Marylyn remained certain the woman she'd seen had only one wrist, only five digits.

Petrosky had ridden back to the precinct with this weighing heavily on his mind, watching the afternoon sun leak out of the sky like a slowly melting watercolor, his brain throbbing with an electricity that made his teeth ache. Was it possible that Rebecca was still alive? And if she was, what about the others who had supposedly died with her?

Jackson seemed to be thinking the same; she leaned back in her chair and sighed. "I just… If she's alive, how did she do it? To pull something like this off, she has skills on par with witness protection, and we know it isn't that." They'd put in a call, but Rebecca would have to be in danger to qualify for the Witness Protection Program—pending trials and the like. There was nothing like that in the system, and with the abusive histories of the men in the family, it was most likely she was trying to escape domestic violence.

"I'm more worried about her current motivation," he said. "If she lit that fire, faked her death, managed to get away, I can't imagine she'd risk exposing herself by breaking into Piotr's place." What could be that important? Revenge, maybe, but there had to be a damn good reason to wait seven years. His gaze dropped to the driver's license photo of Rebecca Kowalski—deep brown eyes, freckles like ashes across the bridge of her nose. *What are you doing, lady? Was it really you?* And if it was…

He set her picture aside and slipped a file from the bottom of the stack—the reports he'd pulled on the warehouse explosion, the blaze that had supposedly killed Rebecca along with her husband, Lucius, and Piotr's brother, Roman. The fire had started just after midnight at an abandoned warehouse on Ash Park's east side—three bodies inside, charred beyond recognition, later identified via dental records as Lucius and Rebecca Kowalski and Roman Wójcik.

But the Origin and Cause report rubbed him the wrong way. Gas leak? The warehouse was abandoned, defunct—no gas going to the building, and even if there had been a gas leak, the warehouse was huge with plenty of broken windows for the fumes to escape. And what would three working-class people be doing at an abandoned warehouse in the middle of the night? Plus, whether it was a natural gas leak, propane, whatever, to have enough to blow the building, anyone inside would have smelled it—they'd have been ill. They'd have left.

These were points that should have been explored. But they hadn't been. Had someone in arson investigation been paid to lie?

"Is that your phone again?" Jackson asked.

He looked up—his drawer vibrated with a hollow *zzz-zzz-zzz*. "Not mine." He flipped to the next page in the file, squinting; the charred remains of what should have been Rebecca Kowalski glared back—blackened flesh, gray teeth bared in a permanent skeletal grin. And suddenly he could smell it, the stench of blistering meat, the salty bite of melting fat, the acrid stink of singed hair, and then it was Julie, only fourteen, her body cold, her lips blue, the scent of her burned flesh harsh and dry his nostrils—

His guts heaved. *I need a drink.* He glanced at the bullpen window, where the sky was desperately hanging on to the last vestiges of afternoon. Four thirty or so—soon, he could escape to the bar. But not soon enough. It was never soon enough lately.

"So, Piotr…" Jackson said, bringing him back. "According to this, his brother, Roman, and his uncle Lucius died in that warehouse fire. But let's say Marylyn is right—that Rebecca is somehow alive. How would that be connected to a missing laptop and a bloody living room? Why would Rebecca come back to Piotr's home?"

"With the missing laptop, she's clearly looking for something. Maybe it's monetary—it can't be easy trying to make a living without a Social Security number, and I'd venture a guess that the hardware store is more lucrative than either Piotr or his grandpa Rericha is letting on." Piotr hadn't pulled that Rolex out of his ass.

She frowned. "You think she's here to…blackmail them? Steal from them?"

"I didn't say that; it could be anything, really. With her missing hand, her kidnapping, maybe she's after evidence of those crimes. I trust Apmada's instincts that Rebecca's abduction was just that."

"You just like that she's sweet on you."

"That's ridiculous."

Jackson chuckled.

"Focus, Jackson, Jesus." He shook his head, but the tips of his ears were hot—burning. He cleared his throat before continuing, "Louisa, Piotr's victim, and Rebecca had a lot in common. They both called police after being assaulted by their partners—members of the same family—then vanished for weeks, and returned claiming those reports were just misunderstandings. They both got their partners off the hook." And if Rebecca had been kidnapped, had Louisa been kidnapped by the same person? She'd called claiming she needed time to "decompress," but maybe whoever took Louisa had learned their lesson after the manhunt for Rebecca, knew enough to make Louisa call and head off any investigation. And if they kidnapped you for filing a police report, what might they do if they thought you killed two of their own? He couldn't see a reason for Lucius and Roman to fake their deaths—to hide out for seven years. He straightened. "If Rebecca is alive, I can't imagine her coming back here. But what if she was here all along? What if Piotr's been holding her captive all this time, and she finally escaped?"

Jackson raised an eyebrow. "Held her captive where exactly? There was no evidence of that in Piotr's house; the guy doesn't even have a garage."

"But—"

"If that were the case, she'd have gone to the police after she escaped—even if she killed her husband, jail has to be better than being locked up by a rapist. And the front door was jimmied; she didn't escape, damage the doorknob, and then run back inside, and she wouldn't have taken the time to steal a computer on her way out." Jackson shook her head. "The fact is, there is no evidence that Piotr has done anything wrong outside of Louisa Parson's recanted statement. Nothing to connect him to Rebecca's car accident, nothing to connect him to her kidnapping, nothing to connect him to Rebecca's death or that of her husband and his brother."

"Except all that shared DNA."

"But none of us are responsible for what our family members do. Nothing we have will hold up in court, and even if this is a big conspiracy where someone is kidnapping women who get out of line, I can't imagine Piotr is the kingpin."

He glowered at Jackson, but she was right. Piotr was a wannabe goon, a rapist, maybe even a sociopath, but someone who took orders; he'd said that his boss—*his grandfather*—was going to be angry about the missing laptop. "Yeah, okay, fine," he muttered. He squinted at the arson file again, at Rebecca's charred bones. One hand in a permanent claw. The other hand hacked clean off. They'd need to pull up missing persons, look for other women who'd vanished around that time—if it wasn't Rebecca in the photo he was looking at, then who was it? And how had they matched the dental records?

He crossed his arms and glared at his coffee cup as if it should be ashamed of being empty. "Let's call Piotr back in. I want to talk to that dickbag."

Jackson pushed herself to standing, stretching her arms above her head. "We'll go visit him. We should grab some dinner anyhow."

He didn't need dinner; he'd eat the peanuts they kept at the bar. But he couldn't tell Jackson that. He stood and followed, but paused halfway to the exit and turned back to the bullpen. "Hang on a sec."

Jackson stopped with her hand on the stairwell door. "What are you doing, you old codger?"

"I think there's one stop we need to make first. Hopefully, we'll still want to eat afterward."

7

Were Lucius and Roman actually dead? Was Rebecca? They couldn't be sure, but the dentist who'd provided the dental records on all three after the warehouse blaze had an office in Birmingham—if someone had sent the wrong scans to the ME for comparison, they could have said the bodies were anyone. Hopefully, the doc would have other X-rays so they could verify that the dead folks were who they were supposed to be.

Petrosky and Jackson ducked out of the gathering dusk and into Dr. Pureman's waiting room, shaking sleet from their jackets, at 4:59 on the nose. The bell overhead announced their arrival—not the cheap kind you see at gas stations, but some fancy brass antique that made a hollow clunking sound that had to get annoying halfway through a busy day of cavity filling.

Dr. Ivan Pureman was an expensive antique, too, a silver-haired fox if ever there was one. Smarmy-looking, with a Botoxed forehead and the lines of his beard so sharp they might have been stenciled on. He met them at the door to his inner office, already buttoning his gray wool topcoat, eyes as shiny as the patterned wallpaper. "Sorry, folks, no walk-ins, but you can call the receptionist in the morning for an appointment."

"We're not here for an appointment, Doctor." Petrosky flashed his badge, and the man's eyebrows rose. The folder beneath Petrosky's arm suddenly felt heavier.

Pureman unbuttoned the top two on his jacket—still wearing his doctor's coat beneath. "How can I help?"

"We have a few questions about a case you consulted on—specifically, dental records you provided to identify remains. We'd like to verify that the records you provided were indeed those of the victims."

Pureman frowned and crossed his arms as if hugging himself—more self-soothing than confrontational—but his tone was as sharp as his beard. "If I sent them, then they're correct." Petrosky watched Pureman's eyes, the only part of his face that was still capable of expressing a full range of emotion. Sad—glassy. Was he going to cry? But Pureman just sighed. "Can you tell me what this is all about?"

I just fucking told you. Was he stalling?

Jackson cleared her throat, her tone low and soothing—faking patience she surely didn't feel. "We just need to verify that the records you provided were indeed the ones for the right patients."

Petrosky's eyes drifted to the large square of sliding glass in the wall behind the dentist's back—the receptionist's area. Computer. File cabinets. An ergonomic chair with a headrest that looked squishy enough to fall asleep on.

Pureman dropped his arms and sniffed. "I still don't understand."

"Someone saw a dead woman, Dr. Pureman," Petrosky said, dragging his gaze back to the dentist. "Today. So either we have a zombie running around, your records got mixed up, or someone switched Rebecca Kowalski's files on purpose." Or Marylyn was wrong about seeing Rebecca; that was still a possibility, though he no longer believed it.

But Pureman didn't appear to be a scan-swapping mastermind; his jaw dropped to expose the straightest set of chompers Petrosky had ever seen—the man's shock appeared genuine. "Switched the files? Why would anyone do that?"

Because they wanted to disappear. Or they'd wanted to help someone else disappear.

"We don't know yet," Jackson said, leaning her shoulder against the wall, the paper all the more shimmery against her camel coat. "Maybe you could show us your records, save us all some time." Her voice had taken on a hard edge—her consonants had teeth. No one else would notice, but Petrosky felt the sting of it in his bones.

"Patient confidentiality, detectives." Pureman's nostrils flared, but his voice was steady. Jackson stiffened. The doc should try harder, or he was going to feel Jackson's wrath, and while she was hungry at that. The man was brave.

Petrosky gestured over Pureman's shoulder at the glass window—at the file cabinets beyond. "All you'd have to do is swap an X-ray or two to make it look like someone else died, right?" They'd also have to know who the dead folks were— the ME could only confirm a match if they had the correct set of teeth for comparison—but he'd cross that bridge next. Right now, he just wanted to know whether Rebecca was dead, whether Lucius and Roman were dead. In his guts, it felt as if the entire case hinged on this confirmation.

The man's forehead remained as smooth as a waxed floor, but his mouth tightened further still, and his shoulders were set in steel. This wasn't about confidentiality. *What are you hiding?*

Petrosky slipped the folder from beneath his arm—copies of the dental records that had been used to confirm the victims' identities. "I can get a court order, but I'm not sure we have that kind of time."

Jackson straightened beside him, her coat making a whooshing sound against the papered wall. They had no evidence that there was anything pressing, no evidence that someone else might get hurt, but three people had died in that fire—if these three weren't among the dead who had burned in their place?

"Maybe we should start over," Jackson said. "It's after five; you're off the clock. Let's talk human to human before anyone else gets hurt." Pureman did not look convinced, but she continued: "What do you remember about Rebecca Kowalski's smile?"

Pureman swallowed hard, his eye twitching—*he definitely remembers her*—and when he spoke again, his voice had gone quiet. "She took good care of her teeth, had a nice smile; that's the first thing I always notice about a person. You have a nice smile too, Detective." He nodded toward Jackson.

"Aw, now what about me, Doc?" Petrosky flashed him a grin.

"You should smoke less. A lot less." Deadpan. Probably serious, but he could at least have the decency to pretend like he was kidding.

"Got me there." Petrosky opened the folder, squinting at the X-rays. He'd examined Rebecca's picture on the way over—her straight, white teeth. But the teeth in Rebecca's X-rays here looked crooked, crowded, front teeth overlapping the ones on either side, almost rabbit-like. And there were several white spots on the film: root canals. Petrosky knew what those looked like from his own dental work.

"Do girls with nice smiles usually have crooked teeth and lots of root canals?"

Pureman shook his head, frowning at the folder—at the scan. "You really think..." Petrosky extended the film toward Pureman, and the dentist held it up to the light. His eyes widened. His nostrils flared. "Shit."

"Well, that's a little harsh for such a polished fellow."

"I didn't..." He lowered his arm, the sheet making a rattling sound in his trembling hand; his face had paled.

"You look surprised, Doctor." And Petrosky believed that he was, which meant someone else had switched the files. Petrosky stared at the man until Pureman met his eyes. "You ready to go to jail over this, or is there someone else who might have switched up your records?"

Pureman was chewing on his cheek—no good dentist would recommend that. "I had my receptionist send them; I couldn't even look at them. I was hoping…hell, I was *wishing* it wasn't Rebecca."

Interesting, especially since it actually wasn't her. "Sounds like you knew her well." Petrosky raised an eyebrow.

Pureman's hand steadied. "It wasn't sexual if that's what that accusatory look is supposed to mean."

"Sexual? You said it, not me, sir. I don't give a shit who Rebecca was banging so long as you didn't help her fake her death."

"Fake her…" Pureman's eyes dropped to the scans once more, shaking his head as if trying to piece together a puzzle no one else could see. The silence stretched.

"Doctor?" Jackson finally said.

Pureman raised his head. "I…listen, this seems far-fetched, but these look like Miranda's teeth."

Miranda's teeth? How did he recognize a girl just from an X-ray? Did he have a photographic memory, or were her teeth just that remarkable?

Jackson was frowning, her eyes on the semi-transparent sheet in Pureman's hand. "You can tell they're Miranda's from an X-ray?"

Pureman angled the sheet toward them and pointed. "See that dark spot on the back tooth?"

Petrosky didn't, but Jackson's eyes were apparently better because she nodded.

"She had a deep cavity on an impacted molar," Pureman said. "Needed an extraction. Lots of pain, lots of painkillers, but she kept putting it off; Miranda always had a fear of dentists, which was a bad thing for a girl who needed so much work."

"And you didn't know her beyond this?" Despite just learning that the woman's dental records had been used to identify a body, that this woman was dead, Pureman sure hadn't gotten emotional over it—he'd had a much stronger reaction to questions about Rebecca. "You don't seem too upset, Doctor. Or shocked."

"Well, this is all quite distressing, but Miranda just came in occasionally for dental work, and…" Pureman paused, his eyes on Jackson's face. "Oh, you don't know."

Petrosky and Jackson exchanged a glance. "Know what?" she said.

"Miranda Rericha was gone before the fire; died…maybe four months earlier. Her father found her in the bathtub." He drew one slender fingernail across his wrist. "I don't think you ever get over something like that."

Pureman opened his mouth as if to say something else, but his words had faded; Petrosky could no longer hear the doctor over the roar in his brain. Rericha…Miranda Rericha. And Joseph Rericha, father to so many, had a dead wife and a dead daughter, that's what Scott had said. Rebecca had used Joe's daughter to fake her death. This shit was more convoluted than the plot of *Game of Thrones* and far less entertaining—they needed dragons. He glanced at the front window as if expecting flames to come screaming out of the black sky.

But something else was nagging at him, too: Miranda was the only one of Rericha's children to have his last name— Miranda had been different for him. Daughters were different. *And Shannon probably hates you by now, you're choosing the booze over her, you asshole.* As if on cue, a spot of pain brightened just behind his breastbone, and he rubbed at his chest, wincing, then pulled the other dental X-rays out of the folder and passed them to Pureman.

"Roman and Lucius…are these their teeth?"

Pureman frowned but repeated the same procedure he'd used with Miranda's X-rays, squinting at them in the light. But this time, he nodded. "I'll have to double-check the files, but these are theirs, I think. I remember Lucius had a crown on his front tooth"—he tapped his own, then tapped the second X-ray—"and Roman never had cavities." He passed the images back, and Petrosky tucked them away, a pit swelling in his guts. They'd get copies of everything the doc had, but if he was right, they had two accurate sets of dental records—Roman and Lucius had indeed died in that fire. But Rebecca's X-rays had been switched with those of Miranda Rericha…and Miranda's body had been moved to the warehouse to burn.

"So we're back to our original question: who could have done this, Doctor? Who had access to your files?"

Pureman didn't move—he stared. Petrosky leveled his gaze at the man and stared back. Pureman blinked first.

"Come on, Doc. What about the receptionist who sent the scans to the ME?"

"No, no way. She had just started—she wouldn't even know what she was looking at."

Jackson crossed her arms. "There had to be someone who had access."

"I do have a hygienist, but he just started last week."

Definitely stalling. But why? "You already told us the groundbreaking news that Rebecca's dental records were incorrect—that it was Miranda's teeth, her body in that fire. So why don't you level with us about your staff before we have to go through your W-2s? We just need to know who was working here around the time of the giant fire we're here to investigate."

Pureman's jaw clenched. "Back then…it's hard to say. I'd have to pull the employee files." But his voice was tight now, too—strangled.

Bullshit. He remembered dental records, but not his goddamn staff? "Good, let's do that. Let's pull the files. I'll order us up some dinner if it's going to take a few." He slipped his cell from his pocket.

But the man made no move toward the door at his back, a passage which led to his office, to the files they needed—and he didn't have to, Petrosky was sure of it. *He knows exactly who did this.* And Pureman would only protect someone he cared about...someone worth being emotional over.

Petrosky lowered his cell. "You said the receptionist who sent those records to the ME had just started; was she replacing someone?" *Maybe someone who had a reason to switch out those files?* Petrosky stepped closer to Pureman, near enough to smell his cologne: sandalwood. "Let me guess, Doctor. Rebecca Kowalski?"

Pureman's shoulders slumped, defeated. The silence stretched. Finally, he sighed. "She worked here for four months or so. Before she died."

That explained his reaction, being more upset about her death than the others.

"How close were you and Rebecca?" Jackson asked. "You're being pretty evasive, almost like you're trying to help her get away with this."

Did you know what she was doing? But the man's eyes had gone wide. "I'm not trying to help her get away with anything. I'm still in shock, if I'm being honest—it never would have occurred to me that she'd do something like this."

"Why do you think she did?" Jackson asked. "Did she ever talk about her home life?" *Her abusive shit of a husband?*

Pureman shook his head. "I really have no idea. She never talked about herself at all. I do know she was an anxious woman, a little high-strung, but very conscientious."

Anxious. Conscientious. *And calculating.*

Their witness had been right—Rebecca Kowalski hadn't died in that fire. And Roman and Lucius had been buried; all they had to do was exhume them, and they'd be able to prove those men were dead.

But not Rebecca. No, not Rebecca.

Rebecca Kowalski had worked here. Rebecca had swapped her file with Miranda's—had gotten this job just in time to do so.

Rebecca had stolen Miranda Rericha from wherever she'd been buried. Hacked off Miranda's dead hand. Then she'd put Miranda's body in that warehouse to burn alongside two living people, one of whom was her husband.

Rebecca had burned them both to death along with Miranda Rericha's corpse.

8

BLOOD. How was it possible for there to still be so much blood?

The bathtub was cold against the backs of her thighs, the porcelain already stained with drips of red. Rebecca grabbed the towel—rough, harsh, and reeking of industrial detergent—and wrapped it over the wound on her stump. Deep. She'd already removed the glass, the huge pointed shard he'd stabbed into her forearm, but the wound just kept seeping.

It's time. You have to do this now, Becca. You can't wait anymore.

She peeked beneath the towel, her eyes and nose stinging with the fumes from the rubbing alcohol, flesh burning with it too. How had this happened? How had she let him get to her again? She should have known better, should have made sure there was no way he'd show up, but Piotr had always been a man to stay out late, and he often didn't come home at all—it used to be that if he stayed out until one, he wasn't coming back until the morning. *Shit.* Ten minutes, and it hadn't been nearly enough time. She'd screwed up royally.

And it had all been pointless anyway. Piotr's computer didn't have the information she needed. She'd been so sure it would—records were his job, after all. That had always been his job. Well, that and…

She shuddered. Her eyes dropped to her arm, to the stained towel. She let it fall away, exposing the wound.

Blood dripped into the tub.

Rebecca picked up her belt and clenched it between her teeth, the taste of leather and iron filling her mouth—she had to resist the urge to spit. But she wouldn't scream. No, she wouldn't scream. She ground her teeth harder, the belt squeaking between her molars.

Just a few minutes, and it'd be over. It would all be okay.

It's time, Becca. Now.

She gingerly reached for the sewing kit at the edge of the bathtub, its contents wet already, slippery with alcohol. She brought the needle to her arm.

The first stitch went in quickly, but hot, and the burning did not abate. She forced herself to hiss a trembling breath through clenched teeth, jaw tight, molars digging into the belt. *Hang on, Becca. Hang on.*

The second stitch was more difficult, her hand shaking so much she could barely get the sharp tip into position. She pressed harder, the skin resisting the needle, but then it broke through with an almost audible pop, the thread harsh like she was rubbing sandpaper over her arm. Her armpits were slick with sweat. Her teeth ached. The suture was a little off, but it did the job—she tugged the stitch tight and watched the flesh close.

Sweat dripped off her forehead and into her eyes, burning nearly as much as the alcohol but not as much as the needle —the wound throbbed, throbbed, throbbed. She blinked hard, trying to clear her vision. Bile rose in her throat, acidic. *I'm going to puke.*

She sat back, holding her arm steady, careful not to tug too hard on the string lest she break the stitches—she couldn't do this again, she couldn't.

Yes, I can. She breathed, breathed, breathed, trying to calm the roiling in her guts. She'd been through worse. She'd done far worse to herself. Her eyes grazed her stump, the scarred flesh where her wrist used to be. A few stitches in a motel bathroom were nothing compared to that night—even now, she could almost feel the razor-sharp blade biting into her arm, the heavy bulk of the ax handle in her other hand. And now, like then, she could smell the iron and the salty musk of fear.

It was the hardest decision she'd ever made. But it had been effective. It had made people feel sorry for her—made them treat her like an invalid. Made them let their guard down.

Made them believe her.

She had lost her hand, but she had gained a life until Piotr had found her. And now…

Rebecca swallowed back bile and breathed, watching her blood drip toward the drain.

9

Petrosky shoved the cell back into his pocket and stared at the road through the windshield, the sky a watery blue that appeared more like the cloud front before a storm than a world easing slowly into spring. Too early for thinking, for research, but at least he had something worth reporting. "Two days before the fire, someone vandalized the cemetery where Miranda Rericha was buried," he said. "Four graves disturbed, a dozen headstones knocked over, flowers torn up—no one dug deep enough to disturb the bodies themselves, just a little loose soil. The police wrote it off as punk kids."

Jackson shook her head, her hands on the wheel at ten and two like she was trying to pass her first driver's test. "That was smart, creating a diversion so they wouldn't suspect anything serious—knock it down the priority list. But how the hell did she take Miranda's body? You'd need a backhoe to get a casket out of the ground."

"That's the genius part: Miranda was buried in Joseph Rericha's mausoleum at the edge of the property." Vandalism of the mausoleum hadn't been listed on the report, but if Rebecca had taken a sledgehammer to Miranda's final resting place, maybe the cemetery would just fix the busted concrete.

A bag of cement was far less expensive than a lawsuit, and unlike a shattered headstone, no one would notice that a solid concrete tomb was missing its occupant. And who'd want to bury their loved one there once it came out that the place had a tendency to lose bodies?

Jackson sniffed, maybe absorbing that information, maybe just enjoying the silence, and Petrosky drew his eyes to the passenger window. The slush on the roadways had hardened to a frosty skin that was already beginning to melt—like the flesh burning off a corpse. Usually, those thoughts made that old pain brighten in his chest, but the liquor in his guts seemed to have numbed the ache. *Drinking in the morning already, are ya, you fucking lush?* Yeah. In the morning, and last night after the dentist—he'd slept like a baby, his arm thrown over his Great Dane's flank.

"She's a killer, you know that."

He turned. "What?"

"You're giving Rebecca the benefit of the doubt; I can see it in your cantankerous face—those little lines around your mouth are less angry now that the killer is a woman."

He wasn't sure that was true, but he didn't care—either way, they needed to figure out what she was doing here. Most traumatized women didn't form some convoluted plan to fake their deaths and kill their husbands, and one who had done both wouldn't just wander back into the lion's den. Even if Piotr knew what she'd done, she wouldn't wait seven years to go after him. "Did we get approval on the exhumation order for Roman and Lucius?"

"Not yet; we will. But Pureman doesn't have a reason to lie." She shook her head. "Killing Lucius makes sense, honestly—her husband had a domestic violence history, and abusers don't just let their victims walk away. And Roman could have been in the wrong place at the wrong time." Though Scott had said Roman had been accused of sexual assault on multiple occasions as well—the asshole wasn't innocent.

Petrosky shrugged and raised his half-full coffee mug to his lips—stainless steel. Still hot. "Yeah. There's obviously more to this story."

"More to the story? Well, that's the understatement of the century." Jackson glared at his mug as he set it back in the cupholder. "Where'd you get that thing?"

"Billie." He'd stopped by the neighbors' house to drop Duke off this morning—a dog park was in his future—and the mug was a parting gift after pancakes. Jane and Candace had stepped up their breakfast game, and if he were being honest, he couldn't handle one more granola bar.

"Is your harem buying you gifts now?"

"It's not a hare—"

"I know, I know, they're just street girls you let live with you."

"They don't live with me, they live next door. And they aren't *street girls*."

"Not anymore."

"Are you done?"

"There's that angry little forehead line." She raised an eyebrow at him, then turned back to the windshield, squinting at the sun like she wanted to slap the hell out of it.

He tried to relax the muscles in his face, but his jaw stayed clenched. Okay, so they were both a little irritable. They'd stopped by Piotr's place the night before, and again this morning—no one home. Petrosky wanted to confront that asshole about his relationship to Rebecca, wanted to dangle his cuffs when he told Piotr about the witness who had seen a bleeding Rebecca running from his house, but Petrosky sure didn't want to waste time chasing the shithead. Hopefully, Oaklawn would prove more productive.

The hospital crawled from the dawn like a hibernating bear: brown and hazy, though that might have been his eyes.

Jackson parked in the structure, and they hurried through the lot, icy wind biting at his exposed fingertips.

"Is this guy going to be awake?" he muttered.

"I hope so. I'm not sure any one time is better than another."

But better today than tomorrow—bone cancer was unforgiving. They needed to chat with the arson investigator before death snatched him from this earth and took the answers to their questions with him. Because whatever Rebecca had done, it was unlikely she'd been able to pull it off alone, and he couldn't imagine any arson investigator looking at that warehouse and deeming it accidental. Not without a reason to lie.

The doors hissed, the florescent lights glared, the elevator hummed, his hand ached from grasping the file they needed the guy to look at, but all Petrosky could focus on was the harsh bite of alcohol in the air, a scent far too much like the liquor he'd snuck from Billie's cabinet when she was in the bathroom this morning. He was slipping, he knew he was slipping...but how fast? He could call Carroll—the chief had been his sponsor until a month ago—but their relationship, or more specifically, the fact that her husband didn't know she was also in recovery, had almost destroyed what was left of her marriage. He was a lot of things, but he wasn't about to be *that* guy.

He pushed those thoughts aside and followed Jackson into a private room; the walls yellow like the skin of a patient in liver failure, and the meager light that eked through the single window did nothing to brighten the pallor of the man lying in the hospital bed.

Franklin Gargano looked exactly as Petrosky would expect a man on his deathbed to look—barely kissing fifty, but disease had aged him another fifteen years. Sallow skin, pale lips, blue eyes bright with pain despite the morphine drip snaking into his arm. Sparse, dark hair that might have been thinning before the cancer took whatever was left.

"Thank you for seeing us, Mr. Gargano." Jackson sat in the chair nearest the mattress—wooden arms with itchy cushions that had probably absorbed their weight in anguished tears. Petrosky stayed standing at the foot of the bed.

"Of course." Gargano's voice was harsh and raspy, maybe from the dry hospital air. Maybe from the pain. Petrosky wasn't sure what he'd expected—maybe excitement to have visitors like Marylyn—but Gargano just seemed exhausted.

Jackson crossed her legs and leveled her gaze at Gargano. "We have a few questions about a case you worked when you were with the department—a warehouse fire."

Gargano raised his head off his pile of pillows and offered them a wan smile. "You're going to have to be more specific. I've consulted on a lot of warehouse fires over the years."

That was true. The man had worked as a firefighter for ten years, then an arson investigator for another twenty, and his record had all the marks of a conscientious employee. Accolades out the wazoo. His solve rate was far higher than average, and he found arson in more cases than his counterparts, which made this particular fire all the more strange if it hadn't been an accident. "I know. Too many cases to remember," Petrosky said. The man nodded, but the movement appeared to hurt him—he winced. "I read that your expertise in unusual accelerants got you a few calls from the FBI. Consulting on federal cases probably made you quite the celebrity."

A tight smile, but Gargano's eyes brightened. "I'm not at liberty to discuss that."

Petrosky forced a laugh. "Good man." But all working with the Feds proved was that Gargano could pass a detailed background check, and that he was adept at kissing ass. But...*huh*. A metallic glint on the end table caught his peripheral vision, and Petrosky stepped around the bed. Beside a glass of water and the untouched remnants of a bland rice and applesauce breakfast, a series of gold and silver medals glittered, the type one might wear on their jacket at a fancy firefighter's ball. He leaned closer. Was that a Firefighter of the Year medal? Shit, maybe Gargano really was the best. Why he had the medals here was another question, but Petrosky wasn't about to judge how the man derived whatever slivers of comfort he might manage from his past achievements. Maybe this close to the end, that was all he had. Gargano appraised him, but turned back to Jackson as she asked, "Do you remember Rebecca Kowalski?"

The man's eye twitched, but Petrosky couldn't tell if it was recognition or pain—his whole face was a little on the twitchy side, now that Petrosky really looked, a cornucopia of winces and grimaces and forced politeness. *Unless it's the booze dulling my instincts.* He pushed that thought aside, though it might have been true.

"I'm not sure," Gargano said finally. "The name sounds familiar, but my memory these days..." He pressed his head back against the bed pillows, making them pucker around his ears, shifting his weight as if his legs hurt, too—not as thin as most cancer patients' legs, thick enough for Petrosky to discern their shape beneath the blanket. Firefighters didn't mess around on the workouts.

"Kowalski's body along with her husband and another man were found in an abandoned warehouse on the east side about seven years ago," Jackson said, her eyes locked on the man's face, probably hoping that the trio of bodies would make it a bit more memorable. "Your report said a gas leak started that fire."

"Ah. Well...how many deaths again? It's hard to remember details, and I don't want to guess."

"Understandable, which is why we brought pictures to help jog your memory." Jackson nodded to Petrosky, and he slid a photo from the folder and turned it so Gargano could see. Miranda's blackened body lay near the lower right corner, the other two corpses near the top of the shot. "In your report, it says that all three of these victims were on the ground floor?"

Gargano's brow furrowed. "That appears to be accurate. Hard to tell what level they're on from this."

Petrosky pulled another set of pictures from the folder: closer shots, miles of charred flesh, two bodies with meat still visible, the yellow and red striations of fat and ligament flanked by curtains of blistered skin. But one body had only gray bones beneath the blackened outer layer of flesh. That body was missing a hand, the bone severed between the elbow and wrist, and…the amputation did seem a bit higher up the arm than what Rebecca's media photos had indicated. An inch, maybe, not enough to ping any bells unless you were really looking, but he should have seen it. *It's the booze, old man.* He cleared his throat. "Here's my issue, Mr. Gargano: this body appears to have burned at a different rate than the others. Almost as if her bones were more brittle, her flesh drier—more flammable." Which would be true if she'd been dead for months before the fire.

Gargano shrugged one shoulder. "That can happen sometimes."

Petrosky frowned. "I've been in law enforcement a long time, but I've never seen anything like that."

"Law enforcement isn't the same as fire and rescue. No disrespect, Detective, but there are a number of factors that might make a body burn differently, position being one." He raised his hand and pointed to the lower corner of the first shot; his fingers trembled. "Even a few feet can make a lot of difference depending on the point of origin."

Exactly the way he'd explained the discrepancy between the bodies in his report. "Fair enough." Petrosky touched his fingertip to Rebecca's—Miranda's—body, waiting for the bile to rise in his throat, waiting for the tightening of his rib cage that often came when dealing with burn victims—waiting for the stabbing above his breastbone where every parent seemed to feel the loss of a child. Nothing. Had he really only had one drink at Billie's?

Jackson shifted in her chair, her coat hissing against the seat. "To me, it looks like someone poured accelerant over her body, but there's no mention of that in your findings."

Gargano blinked, shifting his gaze back to Jackson. "Whatever it says in the report, that's what I found. Every case is different, and there are a hundred reasons for differing burn patterns." He sniffed. "If the question is specific to the bodies, maybe the medical examiner can help. Who did the autopsy?"

Gargano had spoken quietly, but Petrosky didn't like his tone—almost smug. It raised the hairs on Petrosky's neck. "I'm sure you know, being fire and rescue, that they don't routinely do an autopsy unless someone suspects criminal activity, and your report says gas leak—accidental. And the ME's dead now." Both of which were more than a little convenient, but the assigned ME had been seventy-two at the time of the warehouse fire; whatever else Rebecca had done, they probably couldn't blame her for Dr. Crup's death. "But the gas explosion *is* fully in your purview, and it isn't sitting right. I know I'm just a detective, nowhere near your level of expertise, but this report...it's lacking."

Gargano frowned. "I'm sorry I can't be more helpful to you, but I don't know what else to say."

Petrosky pulled the photos back and slipped them into the folder once more, then edged his way back to the foot of the bed; he suddenly didn't want to be any closer to Gargano than he had to be. "Maybe just tell us how Rebecca Kowalski walked away unharmed."

Gargano's teeth parted—cracked, dry lips. "Unharmed? I'm not sure what you mean."

Petrosky watched his eyes, but Gargano's gaze remained steady. The silence stretched.

"This woman isn't dead," Jackson said finally.

Gargano raised one eyebrow. "Were you looking at the same photos I was?"

That's not her, and you know it. Petrosky couldn't pin down why he was so sure, but something was off with this guy—the hairs along his spine vibrated furiously. "Let's forget the bodies for a minute. Let's talk about the fire." He shifted his weight, the footboard pressing into his thigh. "You have the cause listed as a gas leak, but there was no gas going to the building at the time, which strikes me as more than a little odd."

But Gargano was shaking his head. "The gas being off doesn't necessarily mean it's safe. I've worked at least ten other cases where a supposedly void gas line started a fire. The pipes aren't what they should be, especially in the older buildings down around that area, but the money to fix the infrastructure isn't there. Look at the faulty natural gas pipelines in California. It's the same idea. All it takes is the tiniest of sparks and…game over."

"But they should have smelled it, right?" Jackson cut in. "If there was enough gas to explode, I imagine they'd have taken one deep breath and walked right back out of that warehouse."

The corner of Gargano's lip turned up. "Not necessarily. Gas doesn't have to accumulate within the building, there just needs to be enough gas for a flame to lead back to an affected pipe, and then the pipe itself can explode. From what I recall…I think that's what we're dealing with here. I'm sure it's in my notes."

Petrosky pressed on. "But even if the pipe exploded, is that likely to knock them out cold long enough to burn to death? The way they were positioned makes it look like they didn't even try to crawl away—like they were already unconscious when the fire started. And knocking out two grown men would be hard for one woman to accomplish on her own." Petrosky slipped past Jackson and eased into the chair beside hers. "But what do we know? We're just cops, not fire and rescue, right?"

Gargano's eyes flicked from Petrosky to Jackson and back again. "I'm really not sure what you're getting at."

"I'll make it easier," Jackson said, her voice low but deadly serious. "Did you help Rebecca Kowalski kill her husband?"

Gargano balked. "Wait...what?"

"Did you help her fake her death? File a false report for her?" Jackson leaned toward Gargano, her hands on her knees.

His jaw dropped, face contorting in a way that might have been anger or pain or both. "No. Absolutely not."

"Did you know that one of the bodies at that warehouse was dead well before the fire?" Jackson said. "That it burned faster because it had embalming fluid in its veins?"

"Stop, okay? Just stop." His rasp had turned gravelly, like he had stones in his lungs. "Why would I do this? Why would I risk my career? Have you read my file? I spent my whole life trying to do everything...right." A breath vibrated from his lips. "And look where it got me."

Jackson eased back in her chair, usually a sign that she believed the suspect—if that's what Gargano was.

"I don't know what you're after here, detectives," he said, his voice controlled once more. "I haven't done anything wrong. If I made a mistake on some report I filed seven years ago, all I can do is apologize, but that doesn't mean I know more than that. Honestly, that time period was hard for me—maybe I wasn't as focused as I should have been."

"Why was that?" Petrosky asked.

He blinked. "What?"

"Why were things hard?"

Gargano's eyes drifted away from them and over to the

window, perhaps reminiscing about whatever awful thing had made him screw up his cases. "I was going through a divorce. It was…pretty rough. For me anyway." Gargano stared at the sky for another moment, but the muscles in his jaw had gone hard. He finally drew his gaze from the window. "Whatever happens, leave her out of this, will you? She's a good person, my daughter too. I don't want some stupid mistake to be my legacy."

"It sounds like you really care about her," Jackson said.

Gargano met her eyes. He sighed. "I wish I could help you more here, I really do, but I don't have the answers you need. I do get it, though. It's like that in fire and rescue too—always hoping you'll ask the right question, get the right answer, trip someone up, but…" He reached for the nurse call button. "I'm really tired. If there's something else I can do, let me know. And you can always talk to my boss, too, if you don't believe me—get him to review my notes, have him consult. But I can't tell you what I don't know."

Jackson pushed herself to her feet, and Petrosky followed suit, the chair creaking as if angry at the abuse it had suffered under his fat ass. "We'll be back, Mr. Gargano."

Gargano nodded, then closed his eyes, his thumb caressing the call button. It blinked red.

Gargano wasn't worried they'd catch him in a lie, and he sure wasn't worried about getting caught. Even if he'd killed them all himself, the man had nothing left to lose.

10

Jackson's tires hummed against the asphalt, the damaged street boasting enough potholes and loose stone to turn the sound into a low, angry hiccupping. The slush had melted while they were speaking to Gargano, leaving a dark stain over every surface below calf height—curbs, brick buildings, telephone poles. His spirit felt stained, too, and much too heavy. This case was insanity, all the pieces like tiny slivers on the wrong side of a wood chipper, a mess that had no hope of forming a cohesive whole.

"So Rebecca gets the job with Pureman and swaps out the dental records in advance of the fire," he said to the dashboard. "Then she steals Miranda's corpse—"

"And lures her husband, Lucius, and his nephew Roman to the warehouse so she can kill them." Jackson looked at him pointedly as if expecting him to disagree, but he wasn't about to argue. Yeah, she'd done it, but she was the real victim, wasn't she? Abused by her husband, kidnapped by…someone, maybe even Roman or another family member. Those men she killed were the criminals.

"Then she just had to trigger that explosion with them inside." Jackson frowned at the street and hit the turn signal.

"You think she used drugs to knock them out? We've seen that before."

"Yeah, but did she drug them after they were already inside? She didn't carry them into the warehouse on her own. She's a buck twenty soaking wet, and she only had one hand."

"That's some ableist shit," Jackson said.

Petrosky balked. "That's not... Are you kidding me right now? To drag them, she'd need to...well, grab them, and they were big men like Piotr is. She'd have had a hard time with a wheelbarrow, too, with only one hand." Maybe she could have rigged a rope and dragged them, but up the steps, over uneven ground...it was a stretch. When Jackson's jaw dropped, he raised a hand and went on: "I can use an off-the-rack wheelbarrow, but I can't run a goddamn marathon, Jackson; she probably can. We all have our strengths." He lowered his arm. "It would make sense to drug them once they were inside anyway; she was married to one of them, so they'd probably trust her if she asked them to follow her in. It's that, or she had help, someone to move them once they were unconscious. Like Gargano." The guy seemed decent enough, but there was something off about him that Petrosky couldn't put his finger on. He'd thought it was the report, but...that didn't feel right, or at least, that didn't feel like all of it. So what was bothering him? Gargano's twitchy face?

"There's nothing in Gargano's history to suggest instability, and if he was involved with the fire, they'd have done a better job staging it. Rebecca would've known the bodies would burn at different rates, and she would've put Miranda's body farther away from the others to make it more believable."

Jackson had a point there. An arson investigator as an accomplice shouldn't have left a single indicator of foul play. Fire was one of the more effective ways to obliterate evidence.

Then there was the inconvenient matter that they hadn't been able to connect Gargano to Rebecca prior to the blaze—they'd looked at that before they headed to the hospital. No phone records on Rebecca's end to indicate they'd ever spoken, no credit card receipts from places Gargano would have frequented, not a single coffee shop charge on Rebecca's Visa; the woman was a shut-in, common in abuse cases. And Gargano hadn't followed Rebecca to wherever she'd been living for the last seven years, which he'd expect if the man loved her enough to kill for her. Instead, their hero had filed his arson investigation report as usual and gone back to his boring life.

"So how do we explain the break-in at Piotr's?" Petrosky said now. "After seven years, it's not like she suddenly got worried he might tell on her—if he even knew what she'd done. So how the hell is Wójcik involved?" Because he assaulted his girlfriend the way Lucius had assaulted Rebecca? Because Piotr was related to Rebecca's husband and to Roman, the two men killed in the warehouse fire? And what the hell had she been after when she'd broken into Piotr's house? That particular splinter wasn't even in the pile of wood-chipper mulch—that bastard was wedged in his foot.

Jackson shrugged and eased them off the main drag and into the neighborhood. "Whatever she's after, coming back here is a huge risk for someone who played dead to get away with a double homicide. As soon as anyone realized she was alive, they'd put it together." And lock her up. Or worse. And that blood, all that fucking blood…

"You think she's dead now?" he asked. She'd managed to get away from Piotr's house, but she'd been severely injured—would they find her rotting in a ditch? Putrefying in an as-yet-unburned abandoned warehouse?

"We should know soon; we just released her picture to the press an hour ago, and Acharya's got it out to his sources too.

But if she is alive, she's obviously better than most at keeping her head down."

He bristled at the mention of the journalist. Reyansh Acharya also happened to be Jackson's boy toy, though she hated it when he called Acharya that. Which only made him do it more.

Jackson pulled into the driveway and killed the engine. Piotr's place was a little cheerier today, the sunlight glowing against the front door, but the air felt too still, too lonely. No car in the carport—again.

"Third time's a charm," he muttered anyway as he climbed from Jackson's ride. His sneakers squelched against the muddy lawn, chilling his toes; despite the sun, it was still cold enough to make his ears go numb.

Jackson rapped on the door with a hollow *thunk*, *thunk*, *thunk*. Somewhere in the distance, a bird shrieked once, then again, its sharp cry echoing against the eaves.

The house remained silent. "Do you hear that?"

"The bird?"

"Not the bird. Screaming."

"Don't even try that shit, Petrosky. We have no cause, you can't just say you hear screaming every time you want to bust through someone's door."

"Yeah, yeah." He stepped off the side of the porch into a postage-stamp-sized flower bed, now filled with last season's leaves, and picked his way carefully toward the window—blinds open to the living room. The coffee table was still on its back. Broken glass lay scattered across the floor near the far wall, and a square of carpet was missing near the middle of the room—the techs had taken the puddle of blood. Fine gray powder covered everything else. "The guy hasn't cleaned up yet." And if he was still around, he should have at least swept up the glass. He stepped out of the flower bed and headed for the far side of the house, toward the gate to the backyard. "I definitely hear screaming."

"I swear to god, I will call Carroll if you try to enter this house, Petrosky."

"I'm not entering anything. Just looking." He'd come back later with his Swiss Army knife when he was alone. The gate squealed as he raised the latch.

There was only one window on the side of the house, a tiny high rectangle they weren't going to peek into unless Jackson gave him a boost, but she deserved better than a hernia. And he wasn't picking anyone up. They all had their strengths, and heavy lifting wasn't one of his.

Instead of a walkway and a flower bed, the backyard had a large concrete patio that stretched from one corner of the house to the other, the slab adorned with an outdoor bistro table. An ashtray overflowing with butts—Marlboro Reds— and half a dozen beer bottles stood in silent vigil on the wrought iron. Looked like Piotr spent a lot of time out here, even in the winter.

His wet sneakers slapped against the concrete. He passed the kitchen window—no Rolex on the counter. The back door was locked. On the other side of the back door, one more window beckoned. No curtains.

He stood on his tiptoes and squinted.

A bed with a metal headboard sat dead center, the kind of frame that comes in handy if you're going to handcuff someone to it. Closet doors open. The duvet lay crumped at the foot of the bed, and on top of the sheets…

Jackson stepped up beside him. "Well, fuck," she breathed.

Empty metal hangers had been tossed haphazardly on top of the bed, two on the asshole's pillow. Hangers and an array of rumpled clothing had been thrown near the floor of the closet, too, as if he'd ripped shirts and pants from the fray. The empty spaces in the closet gaped like missing teeth.

Piotr had left in a hurry. Whatever Rebecca had been trying to find, Piotr knew exactly what it was, and he wasn't going to stick around and wait for the cops to figure it out.

But one thing Petrosky was sure of: Piotr wouldn't have run off if this was about something Rebecca had done—this wasn't about the fire, at least not exclusively. Was it related to Rebecca's kidnapping case, or maybe the auto wreck that supposedly claimed her hand? Was it about the family full of men with dropped assault charges?

Missing kidnapping files.

Faked deaths and miraculous reappearances.

"Dammit, Rebecca, what are you doing?" he whispered to the window.

"She's here for something, we know that," Jackson said. "We're just missing the connection—the why."

The connection...the connection. There were lots of webs here—marriages, police reports, deaths—but one man was intimately, or at least biologically, connected to it all: Joseph Rericha, ex-con, Piotr's boss and grandfather, Miranda's father, Rebecca's father-in-law, and father and grandfather to the men who died in that fire. And now that Piotr had run off like a little bitch, Rericha might be the only living person linked to every piece of this puzzle.

And they knew next to nothing about him.

11

Tyler Hudson, the man who'd arrested Joseph Rericha fifteen years prior, was pushing sixty-five, but didn't look a day over…well, sixty-five. Wrinkles softened a once razor-sharp jawline. Wiry white hairs sprouted from each black eyebrow. But his shoulders were wide and square, his belly concave beneath his green T-shirt—the guy might even have abs.

Hudson led him into a sparsely furnished family room, which apparently doubled as an office. Beside one arm of his green love seat sat a stack of three cardboard file boxes, a computer—not a laptop, but an older-model PC—balancing precariously on top of them. Mismatched barstools stood across from the couch. Petrosky took the chair with the cracked vinyl seat.

"Rericha has a history alright, goes back fifty years. By the time he came across my desk, he already had a few arrests for burglary and was suspected of a series of other crimes from sexual assault to firearms trafficking." Hudson leaned back on the sofa and crossed his arms. "But there was no evidence. No one willing to testify against him. The only reason I managed the drug trafficking charge was because I didn't need testimony; I had pictures, and it took me near ten years to get that lucky." He shook his head. "I tried like hell, but I never could get him on anything else."

"What else were you trying to get him on?" Jackson asked. "What did you think he was doing?" That was the reason they were there; even with a criminal record, Rericha's paper trail was sparse at best, and a phone call to Hudson had ended with the man grumbling, "you better come on down—this'll take a while."

"I suspected money laundering," Hudson said now. "With the drug trafficking, there should have been a lot more cash going in and out."

Laundering. That would explain the hardware store front, and why his bookkeeper grandson could afford a Rolex. But was it somehow connected to Rebecca?

Hudson chuckled. "I even tried to jam him up a few years back on the Glock he always kept under the hardware store counter; no guns for ex-cons. But the weapon was legally registered to his only employee, a guy whose name is listed on the hardware store lease. And that asshole is squeaky clean on paper."

Piotr Wójcik—his only employee. "How'd you even know it was there?"

"Rericha killed someone."

Jackson raised an eyebrow. "Say what?"

"Some crackhead tried to hold them up one evening, took two center mass. Justified, according to the DA, and I never could prove it was Rericha—Piotr took the blame. But I'd gone in there lots of times, and I never once saw Piotr up at that counter. Rericha was the only one who ever sat there."

Petrosky nodded, but Hudson's jaw had gone hard; his nostrils flared. Dust motes skittered through the beam of yellow light from the half-open curtains, and Petrosky watched them swirl and settle.

"What are you not telling us?" Jackson said. "You look a little upset, even now."

Hudson shrugged. "It's not that I'm hiding anything, I just don't know everything, and I sure wish I did. My biggest concern was always their church."

Petrosky cocked his head. "The church?" From the files, Rericha didn't seem like the kind of man to be devout—didn't seem like the kind of man who believed in anything. Piotr had been wearing that cross, but a piece of jewelry didn't mean shit, and some of the most crooked people Petrosky had ever met were men of the cloth.

"Well…I called it a church, but it wasn't, not really. Rericha had a place in the warehouse district back in the day—no stained glass, no crosses, no altar, no sign out front, but it definitely *felt* church-y on the inside." He cleared his throat, a low, rumbly growl. "Had a stage set up with a podium, enough seats for at least forty, and that bastard had a bunch of kids by different women like some kinda damn cult. They refused to call themselves a congregation, but I know one when I see one. Hell, one little boy called him Father when I was standing right there and got dragged away by his ear."

Father, not Dad? That was weird on its own.

"And the things they believed…" Hudson ran a hand down his face, and Petrosky could practically feel his own palm prickling with beard stubble. "I only caught the tail end walking in, but it was some damn nonsense. The women weren't allowed to work unless they took a job with someone in the congregation, and the men…it seemed like they had every profession covered. Lawyers, janitors—"

Petrosky straightened. "Dentists."

Hudson's eyes locked on Petrosky's. "You've met Pureman, eh?" He snorted, and Petrosky nodded, but his neck felt stiff—Pureman was another link to Rericha. Another link to Rebecca's case. And he still had no clue what it all meant. What the hell had they stumbled into here? "I tried to nail that smarmy bastard, too, before I put Rericha away," Hudson went on. "The guy was right out of school twenty years back, and suddenly, he had no more student loan debts and a brand-spanking-new office. He claimed it was a gift, that Rericha had taken up a collection, and the congregation backed his story. But it was all low-key—sneaky. A nonprofit status which would have saved Rericha a bundle if things had been aboveboard."

"Sounds like his members all had something to gain by being there," Jackson said. Rericha probably had big plans before prison cramped his style. What exactly had the congregation been following, anyway? The money?

"Yeah, Rericha took care of his people." Hudson sniffed and recrossed his legs. "Wasn't all bad either. Like Piotr's mom…Kazia Grogan, her name was. That woman came up from Florida with a rap sheet a mile long—drugs, prostitution, you name it. She went from homeless junkie to moving into Rericha's warehouse the year after her oldest, Roman, was born; they said she was a caretaker or some shit. But she stayed there, sober so far as I could see, until she had Piotr near fifteen years later. I don't think Rericha was ever into the life, into drugs or anything in particular, he just did whatever he could to make as much cash as he could, and didn't give a shit beyond that."

"Sounds like you followed the members as well as Rericha himself," Jackson said. "Piotr, Roman, Lucius…" Name dropping. But Hudson's eyes brightened.

"I didn't watch all the members, but I know those assholes. Those three were there from the beginning, and they were the only ones who stayed involved after Rericha went away."

Because they were more than members—they were blood. Petrosky cleared his throat. "What does the congregation look like now?" Neither Piotr nor Rericha had any other properties besides their respective houses and Rericha's hardware store, but if there were some hidden holdings, lots of cash, that might be worth coming back for…even if he couldn't see Rebecca risking her life and her freedom for it. Maybe Piotr had already retrieved his hidden fortune and flown off to the Bahamas.

Hudson was shaking his head. "It's gone now. The church, or whatever it was, fell apart after Rericha went inside. Piotr tried to keep it up, but it wasn't the same—he wasn't near as charismatic as Rericha, but I think it was more…entitlement. Piotr didn't want to work, didn't want to share, thought he should just keep whatever he wanted. But in the world of the congregation that meant no more help for the members, and definitely no more women having those babies—not a single child born into the family once Rericha went to jail. Everything Rericha built just dried up, and so far as I can tell, it hasn't reemerged. A congregation without a leader is just an expensive potluck."

Ain't that the truth. And that also meant Rebecca hadn't been involved in Rericha's original cult—Rericha was already in jail when she'd met her husband. All she knew of the "congregation" was her husband's version of it. Piotr's version. A family of misogynistic cult members turned domestic abusers. But Hudson didn't know anything about Rebecca—they'd already asked.

"If you're looking into the family, I assume you know about the rape accusations?" When Petrosky and Jackson nodded, he went on, "I figured as much. Some of the claims are more recent, but none of the cases were mine. Roman, in particular, had a habit of getting himself into trouble before Rericha went away—like he knew he had a way out. Just three weeks before I arrested Rericha, Roman raped a girl in Bloomfield; she was on the horn with the police before he got down the driveway. But the next day, she said it was consensual."

Petrosky frowned. "Do you think someone threatened

her?" Every time they pulled one thread, a whole new blanket unraveled, but at least this piece felt more relevant to Rebecca.

"Nah. I think Rericha paid her to drop her rape accusation. She paid off her student loans a week later, bought a car, too—cash. No legitimate influx of money that I could find. I let it go, it was her choice to make the best of it, get something out of a shitty situation, but that wasn't a coincidence."

Lucius and Rebecca—the assault charges. Piotr and Louisa—her rape. Roman and this girl in Bloomfield—another sexual assault, and according to Scott, Roman had more allegations in his file. The whole damn family had a history of abusing women and getting away with it. But Louisa Parson's rape case, Rebecca's domestic violence claim…they'd ended those ordeals just as broke as they'd gone in. So what was different?

But Hudson was already answering that question. "I think Joseph Rericha, for all his faults, kept things in check with his money. Still wrong as hell, bribing that girl to drop the rape allegation, but the boys…" He shook his head. "They had violence in their blood. I always suspected Piotr was involved in a double homicide I worked…oh, must be a dozen years back. A couple of guys who washed up on the shore of Lake Huron. But there was nothing to link Piotr to them outside of them being involved in Rericha's group back in the day."

"What made you think it was Piotr?" Jackson asked.

"Well, it was between him and Rericha ordering it, and Piotr just seemed more likely. He was in charge of the group with Rericha gone…while it lasted." He shrugged. "Mostly, it was just a gut feeling since neither victim had enemies; no motive for anyone else to hurt them. But those men were leaving the congregation and moving out of state—no other member had ever done that, and it didn't seem like the kind of group you could just walk away from."

So...nothing. He had nothing. No wonder it hadn't led anywhere.

"Names?" Jackson asked. "Of the victims?"

"Clark Jervis and..." He squinted. "Ivan Feeney."

"Did they have other family? Wives, kids?" Maybe one of them could shed a little light on Rericha's "congregation."

He shrugged. "I don't think they were ever married, though I can't be positive on that. The group...they were tight-lipped. Secretive. I got the impression Rericha had something on everyone; hand-picked his members so he could manipulate them. But Rericha's wife? Damn, she was sweet, deserved better than that cancer—she smiled right to the day she died. Maybe if Rericha had let her raise Piotr instead of keeping that kid at the hardware store with him, the boy would have had a chance at being normal." His eyes narrowed. "I might not have anything on Piotr or your missing woman, but I do know one person you could talk to: Robert Lewis. Only other member I've ever been able to pin anything on. Has to be ten years back, but the bastard's still locked up if memory serves."

"I guess they didn't like him enough to pay for his freedom," Jackson said.

"Piotr never did that—he kept all that cash to himself. And Piotr had more to hide than Rericha did." Hudson's nostrils flared. "Some cults need a fall guy too."

12

"What do you know about Joseph Rericha?"

"Who?" But the twinkle in Robert Lewis's beady eyes told Petrosky all he needed to know—this guy knew Rericha, and he was a liar. A terrible one. Every piece of him, from the messy cut of his salt-and-pepper hair to his fidgety little fingers to his uneven shaving job, screamed "second-rate, sure-to-get-busted narc."

Jackson had elected to sit outside and make phone calls, leaving Petrosky inside with this prick. Barred walls cast harsh shadows across the laminate floor and painted lines on one of Lewis's slippered feet. "If you want to be a criminal, you have to at least work at it, Lewis. No one ever taught you how to lie without your eye twitching?"

Lewis managed to keep his eyelids under control, but his nostrils flared instead.

"I'm not here about Joe," Petrosky said. "Someone is harassing Piotr, even broke into his house. I'm trying to figure out why." That wasn't entirely true—the burglary just happened to bring them into a case that had evolved to include rape, kidnapping, arson, homicide, faked deaths, and a cult of megalomaniac misogynists—but Petrosky was betting he was a better liar than Lewis.

Lewis planted his elbows on the table and leaned in, appraising Petrosky, his eyes twitching once more. He squinted, perhaps to still his eyelids before someone mistook him for a manic Chihuahua. "Yeah, well, if someone's messing with him, he has it coming. He's the reason I'm here. They tell you that?"

Petrosky raised an eyebrow. "I thought you were in here for smashing your car into a pair of motorcyclists while drunk off your ass. What'd Piotr do to you?"

Lewis glared, his wide, thin mouth a gash across the bottom half of his face—he kept his elbows on the metal table. His jaw stayed locked. Even if Piotr had something to do with his conviction, he wasn't going to say shit. *That bastard keeping your commissary card full or what?*

"Fine, fine," Petrosky said. He laced his fingers on the table and leaned toward Lewis, the table pressing hard into his gut, and he was suddenly hyperaware of the cottony stretch of the sweatshirt over his belly. The chemical stink of the man's soap bit at his nostrils. "How about telling me who else might have it out for Piotr? Is there a woman out there who wants to kick him square in the taint with a barbed stiletto?" This guy had been locked up before Rebecca had come on the scene, but he might be able to speak to a more general pattern of the group's behavior.

Lewis's eyes narrowed as if trying to decide whether to trust Petrosky's motivations. But maybe Petrosky wasn't the issue. *Are you scared, asshole?* But of what? Not like Rericha or Piotr could get to him in here.

Finally, Lewis's shoulders straightened, his elbows squeaking as he drew them off the steel. He swallowed hard. "A woman, you say?"

Petrosky smiled and hoped it looked genuine—his face suddenly felt heavy, his muscles drained. *I need a drink.* How many hours until quitting time? *Stop it.* He cleared his throat. "Were there any women in particular who had it in for Piotr?"

He sniffed. "Lots of them, I'm sure." But the moment the words were out of his mouth, his lips clamped shut once again.

For god's sake. "Listen, I'm not trying to jam you up—you're already in jail, not like I can do anything else to you." That wasn't true, but maybe Lewis wouldn't think too hard about it.

"You're right there," Lewis said. "I already lost my family."

Petrosky nodded, trying to keep his features soft—understanding. "You have a daughter, don't you?"

Lewis's nostrils flared again. He looked at his hands, now clasped on the steel tabletop, then at Petrosky's laced fingers as if comparing their fist size. Maybe that was a thing you had to do on the inside. "My daughter won't see me."

"Her mother won't either?" But Petrosky knew that answer. He'd looked at the visitor logs—she hadn't been to see him once. "Why does your family hate you so much?"

Lewis kept his gaze on his hands, on his white knuckles. No more twitchy eyes or nervous fingers—just old, long-suffering grief. "For staying around that group as long as I did. For letting them tell my wife how to live."

Here we go. "Meaning?"

"She wanted to give birth in the hospital, but Joe sent a midwife. Stuff like that." He shrugged. "She was a good woman, and I messed it up; I didn't really know there was another way. Joe, Roman, Lucius, they'd been my family since I was a kid, when my mother joined up with them, and honestly…I needed the money. Joe always helped me out. I've never been book smart, and it's not easy raising a kid on a mechanic's salary. Hell, I couldn't even bury my mother without him."

Hudson had been right; it seemed Rericha had hand-picked the people in his group, people who were vulnerable in one way or another—people he could control. And with Rericha gone, it had only taken a year for it to fall apart. Probably because Piotr was keeping all that cash to himself; Hudson had likely been right about that too. Actually... maybe that was why Lewis was pissed.

"Piotr cut you off, didn't he?"

Lewis's eyes blazed, but he nodded. *Figures.* Piotr stops shelling out the cash, Lewis loses his wife, goes on a bender, kills a couple of people, and blames Piotr, the man who started his downward spiral. As if it was anyone's fault but his own.

"It wasn't right, what Piotr did; that asshole ruined everything. We used to have a community with Joe, and all of a sudden, no one got together anymore, people stopped returning my calls, and one day there was no one left. Just Roman, Lucius, and Piotr, doing whatever they did with Joe's money, and I didn't get shit—I wasn't blood. If my wife had hung around just a few more years until Joe got out..." He sighed. "When I couldn't pay the mortgage, I guess she decided there were better places she could be."

"Talk to me about the women," Petrosky said. "It sounds like your wife understood there was a better life out there. A place where she wouldn't be abused." He wasn't positive on that last part, but with what Hudson had overheard, his mention of rape accusations against Rericha, combined with Piotr's actions, with Lucius's and Roman's actions...the group didn't think too highly of the fairer sex.

Lewis had stilled, his eyes tight and shining—defensive. "It's not about abuse. It's about obedience."

"And the women were supposed to be subservient? Your wife was supposed to be—"

"They all know what's expected of a righteous woman." He shrugged, the patchy salt-and-pepper stubble on one cheek catching the light in a way that made it appear as if he were glittering with agitation.

"And their place was where exactly? At home? Having babies?"

"They took care of other stuff too." But he did not elaborate. And Petrosky didn't really give a shit what this asshole thought women were supposed to do; he cared what the men did when they disobeyed. Because Rebecca...she'd obviously disobeyed when she'd filed that domestic violence report. And she'd suffered immensely. So had Louisa. Guilt stabbed at his chest, but he inhaled deeply and said: "What happened when wives stepped out of line?"

Lewis shook his head. "They didn't."

Maybe not when Rericha was in charge, but Hudson believed things were more violent under Piotr. He wasn't positive how that had translated into members' home lives, but a woman who feared for her safety was more likely to seek outside help, and Piotr hadn't even been offering financial security. "Devil's advocate, okay? You were still out for a few years after Rericha got locked up. When Piotr was in charge, what would he have done if one of the women disobeyed, say if she called the police on her husband?"

Lewis's nostrils were flaring like a sea cucumber's asshole. "Piotr...he'd have taken them to confession."

Petrosky frowned, his hands still clasped neatly on the table—his knuckles ached. "And what does 'confession' mean to you people?" While Petrosky would rather gargle bleach than enter a confessional booth, having to confess your sins wasn't likely to make a rape victim recant.

Lewis's nostrils expanded, contracted, expanded, contracted. "Not sure. You'll have to ask someone else."

"I think you know exactly what happens in *confession*." He spat the last word as if he were hocking up a bug.

"I don't!" Lewis slammed his hands on the table, the words ringing sharply against the bars, but he recovered quickly and settled back in the chair. Petrosky watched, numb; he should have at least leaned away, right? *It's the booze —too much or not enough.* When Lewis spoke again, his tone had softened. "My wife…she was a good woman. That's why I didn't tell them that she left me, and I don't think they cared much after I got tossed in here. So no, I don't know anything, because my wife never had to go."

Had to go. And he obviously thought it was bad if he'd lied to keep his wife from it; he'd protected her, maybe the only way he knew how. He'd tried. Petrosky's shoulders relaxed, and he finally released his fingers and drew his hands into his lap. "You don't know what happened, but how about where?" he said softly. "Where did Piotr take these confessions?" *Maybe he taped them. Maybe that's what Rebecca was after at Piotr's house.* Even with this new information on the group, he couldn't figure out what she'd been looking for. Just cash, a bank account number? It couldn't be that simple.

"I don't know, no one ever said. And the women definitely didn't say much of anything after." And when Lewis met Petrosky's gaze, the look in his eyes said *that's how you knew it worked.*

Any sympathy he'd had for the guy evaporated. *Goat-fucking piece of shit.* Petrosky cleared his throat, pressing his shoulders against the back of his metal chair. "Should I ask Joe?"

Lewis froze; even his nostrils stilled. "Ask that asshole, Piotr."

"He's not around right now, Mr. Lewis."

Lewis's brow furrowed as if trying to make sense of what Petrosky was saying, then the hint of a smile touched his lips and vanished so quickly Petrosky was half-certain he'd imagined it. "Gone, huh?"

"Ran off like he had something to hide. If only someone knew what it was." But from the steely look in Lewis's eyes, he didn't know; he only wished he had a way to put Piotr behind bars so he could shank Piotr's ass himself.

13

"No hits on Rebecca's photo from the press release?"

"Nope," Jackson said, taking a hard left into the parking lot; her eyes had tightened. Trouble in reporter-detective paradise? She gestured to her console. "You're not bringing your phone with you? It hasn't rung in a while, and you're due for one of your trademarked scowls while not looking at the screen."

He glanced at the cupholder where his cell now sat—he'd tossed the empty stainless coffee mug onto Jackson's floorboard to make room. "I don't need it." Shannon seemed to have given up. He hated himself for pushing her away, but she'd be able to tell from his voice that he was drinking or thinking about drinking, thoughts which had intensified since meeting Lewis, and would intensify further still if he had to listen to Evie's high, squeaky voice saying that she missed him. Or if he had to bring up Morrison. His boy, her late husband, had been involved somehow with Rebecca's case, even if it was just sitting vigil outside Lucius's house during Rebecca's kidnapping, but with that missing file... Everything smelled wrong. At least Carroll wasn't calling;

she was probably relieved as hell not to be his sponsor anymore.

He didn't need anyone—he could get this under control. He'd done it before.

Is that why you were sneaking vodka out of the neighbors' cabinets at seven a.m.?

He silenced that voice with a cough.

The parking lot for Joe's Hardware was almost as small as Piotr's postage-stamp garden: room for a dozen cars on the outside, and right now, it was empty. No way this place made enough to necessitate a full-time bookkeeper, family or no. But that bookkeeper was now missing; hopefully, Rericha knew where Piotr was and why he'd run off. They'd started with a bloody home invasion, and had now added kidnapping, domestic abuse, rape, cults, switched dental records, stolen corpses, arson, double homicide, and a missing undead one-handed burglar, so chasing that dickhead wasn't on his priority list. But everything on that list led back here —to Joseph Rericha.

Jackson slid her Escalade into the spot nearest the door. The cold bit at Petrosky's bare Adam's apple like a tiny, but very hungry, vampire. The asphalt crumbled beneath his shoes like the lot was trying to protect the store owner by swallowing them whole.

And what a store. It belonged in some podunk town in Nowhere, USA and was just as Petrosky remembered it from his investigation into the Louisa Parson case. The high windows were too dusty to allow much natural light, and the deer-antler candelabras cast harsh shadows over long shelves of hammers and pliers and assorted fasteners, the aisles too narrow for the CrossFit folks. It was at the far end of one of those where he'd interviewed Piotr five years ago, a spot he'd chosen because of its proximity to the register; the store had been just as empty then, which made sense if it was a front for something else.

Joseph Rericha had stood behind the counter the whole time, eyes cast down on some hunting and fishing magazine, bored by the idea that his employee—his grandson—might be a rapist.

And in the end, it had amounted to nothing. Louisa had dropped the charges, and Piotr had kept his job and gone right on being a douchebag.

And now he had vanished.

Petrosky headed up the narrow aisle, Jackson at his back, thankful, for once, that his bulk was all in the front and not at his sides. Joseph Rericha was perched behind the counter, as usual, his craggy face a mess of thick wrinkles even deeper than Petrosky's own. His watery blue eyes lit on them as they flashed their badges.

"What can I help you find?" He blinked and glanced back down at the magazine in his lap—*Hunter's Quarterly*—as if he couldn't wait to get back to it.

"I think you know why we're here, Mr. Rericha."

He closed the magazine and set it on the counter beside him, resting a bandaged left hand on the cover, his clubbed fingertips peeking from beneath the swath of white. Petrosky frowned at the gauze. *Interesting.* Did they have it wrong? Had he been the one fighting with his grandchild at Piotr's house? But there had definitely been a female's blood at the scene, not Rericha's, and someone had seen Rebecca leaving. Injured. *Maybe it was two on one. Maybe Piotr beat her, and after she turned that corner onto the next street, Joey snatched her up along with a bag of cement and dumped her in a lake.*

"I can't say I know what you're doing here, but I'm sure you'll tell me," Rericha said, his voice a monotonous drone. His eyes looked sleepy, the lids heavy and sagging.

"We'd like to talk to you about Piotr and his connection to Rebecca Kowalski," Jackson said. "I'm sure Piotr told you someone broke into his home early yesterday morning?" Non-confrontational. Trying to make him comfortable.

Rericha kept his eyes on Petrosky. "I have a lot to do, so if you don't mind hurrying this up..." Refusing to even address Jackson. Refusing to even look at her. Petrosky had known Rericha was a dick—they'd learned as much from Hudson and Lewis, plus the family's history of rape and misogyny—but this... The asshole wasn't even trying to hide it.

Jackson stiffened. Petrosky waited, fully expecting her to go off on Rericha's old, pasty ass, but she turned on her heel and headed for the aisles, giving Petrosky space to interrogate the man. But Petrosky didn't want to ask questions; he wanted to punch Rericha in his stupid face. Maybe Rericha's jowls would flap the way his Great Dane's did when the dog was snoring. That'd be fun to watch, and goddammit, he deserved a little fun, didn't he?

His fist clenched, but he kept it locked at his side. "When was the last time you talked to your grandson, Piotr?"

If Rericha was surprised that they knew exactly how he and Piotr were related, he didn't show it. He blinked those sleepy bulldog eyes and said, "Oh, I saw him...yesterday. Came in, worked, left, like usual. But I suppose it might have been the day before—the days run together. Getting old, you know." He raised one age-spotted hand and tapped his temple; he left the bandaged hand on the counter.

But though the man was pushing eighty, though the bags under his eyes could hold four dollars' worth of quarters, the way his nostrils flared, the way his eyes twinkled was anything but confused—antagonistic. Rericha knew they didn't have anything on him. He hadn't had a single arrest since he'd gotten paroled ten years back, and there was no evidence of other wrongdoing, but at the very least, he knew what Piotr had done to Louisa—Petrosky had made sure of that. And Hudson said Rericha paid to cover up rape allegations for Roman, got that girl in Bloomfield to recant. Guys like this didn't change—they couldn't.

"We stopped by Piotr's place," Petrosky said. "Looks like he left in a hurry."

"Well, I'm not that boy's keeper." Rericha shrugged. "I do know he got his laptop stolen. It belongs to the hardware store, and I'd like to have it back."

"Is there anything of particular interest on it?"

"Nah. But it was expensive."

He leveled his gaze at Rericha, but the man's face seemed made of wax—expressionless. *Do you know what Rebecca wanted with that computer?* "What happened to your hand?" Petrosky asked instead, nodding to the arm still resting on the countertop.

Rericha shrugged and glanced down as if he'd never seen the bandage before. "I was straightening up, broke a lantern."

Petrosky scanned the front counter, then the far wall, the shelves sparser than they'd been a few years before. And uncluttered, unlike the aisles of dusty nails, the rows of claw hammers and measuring tapes. "You used to have lots of lanterns here, didn't you?" Petrosky edged toward the endcap—empty. But there were clean circles on the otherwise dusty shelves. The floor was clean here, too, despite the film of dust an aisle farther up, as if someone had swept a perfect rectangle at the end of this aisle. "You knock the whole endcap over?"

The man shrugged. *Huh.* Either this asshole had bumped into a shelf that had been collecting dust for a good five years, or someone else had. He imagined the shattered glass at Piotr's place, the upended coffee table. Maybe Rebecca had broken in here too. "Looks like someone smashed up the place, Joey. Maybe a victim of your cult."

Rericha blinked slowly. "Never had a cult, just family. And I stumbled against the shelf. Old men sometimes do things like that, which I suspect you know."

From somewhere down one of the back aisles, Jackson chuckled.

Petrosky approached Rericha once more and leaned an elbow against the counter. "Are you calling me old, Rericha?"

"I call it like I see it." He narrowed his eyes. The silence stretched.

He's fucking me around. Maybe a few bait-and-switch questions would trip him up. "You still have a Glock under that counter?"

"It ain't illegal to be near one."

"But you shot someone with it, didn't you?"

Rericha stared, eyes blank. Cold. But could he maintain that once they were talking about a person instead of an object? Probably—his congregation saw women as objects anyway.

"Do you remember Rebecca Kowalski?" Petrosky asked.

Rericha shook his head as if intending to deny it, but then he said, "Poor girl." His sorrowful tone was betrayed by the dull, unremorseful gleam in his eyes.

"What do you remember about the fire that killed Rebecca, your son Lucius, and your grandson Roman?" He watched carefully, trying to discern whether this topic distressed him, whether the man knew Rebecca hadn't actually perished in that fire, whether he was bothered by the fact that they had DNA linking him to both Roman and Lucius, but the man's eyes revealed nothing. His jaw remained slack, lips loose—bored.

Finally, Rericha blinked. "Terrible thing. Good help is hard to find."

Seriously? *Good help is hard to find*, and not *it's hard to lose your children*, or even *funerals are a pain in the ass*? As if realizing that he'd made an error, Rericha leaned back in his chair and crossed his arms, tucking his injured hand beneath his bicep. "You know what I mean. Family isn't always easy to deal with."

Which still didn't answer his question. "Do you know why they were all in that warehouse?"

He nodded, just once. "They were buying it."

"The warehouse?" No wonder their presence at the

building hadn't been suspicious. Maybe he'd been wrong about Gargano's "lacking" report.

"Lucius thought they might open a...well, it sounded like a farmer's market," he scoffed. "Arts and crafts, cheese, vegetables." The man was practically rolling his eyes, and it was by far the most emotion Petrosky had seen out of him.

"Sounds like a ridiculous idea to me," Petrosky said slowly.

"That it was." He sniffed. "All this hippie stuff people think they need. But they don't."

"Rather make your money on hammers and nails, right?" But the fact that he agreed with Rericha about hippie stuff—about anything at all—turned his stomach. "Buying it or not, it seems like a weird place to hang out in the middle of the night."

"I'm sure they were sharing a bottle of wine. It's good luck."

"Good luck? That doesn't appear to be true, Mr. Rericha." The man's face still did not change. Petrosky tried again: "So you think they got drunk and passed out? Seems a little strange to celebrate a sale when the ink isn't even dry."

Rericha cleared his throat—phlegmy. He swallowed. "It's a sign of confidence—the decision was made because they'd made it, and nothing was going to stop them. Why not celebrate?" But his voice did not go up with this question—no inflection at all. Like a robot.

"You're used to getting what you want, aren't you?"

Down the aisle, something crashed, and Rericha's jaw tightened, but his eyes remained locked on Petrosky.

"Do you hate women, Mr. Rericha?"

His gaze drifted beyond Petrosky, then back again, though he appeared to be looking through Petrosky's forehead—no footsteps, so Jackson was still hidden somewhere up the far aisle. "I don't think much about women at all, not since my wife died."

"What about your daughter, Miranda?" *Your dead daughter, who surely deserved better than you.*

Now Rericha met Petrosky's eyes, his gaze flickering like a dull flame on the verge of blazing to life. "Suicide." He blinked heavily. "We done?"

"How many children do you have, Rericha?"

"Enough."

"Lots of them have died though. Lucius was your son. Roman, your grandkid. And then there's Piotr, your grandson, the only one you raised as a son, and he ran off somewhere. And I've got a few more of your boys in the system." He leaned closer over the counter. "Any other daughters besides Miranda?"

Rericha glanced at his magazine—was he smirking? "I'm sure."

"An unfaithful man, are you? Was your wife cool with that?" Petrosky forced his voice to remain even, but his blood was boiling. This man didn't care about his own kids, didn't care what became of them. He didn't care about anything except spreading his seed as far as he could.

"That isn't illegal, Detective."

Enough. "We found your daughter's body," Petrosky spat out.

Now the man raised an eyebrow. "I could'a told you where she was."

"So you knew she burned in that warehouse fire? The one that killed Roman and Lucius?"

Rericha blinked, but the dullness in his eyes did not clear —he looked as bored as ever. Petrosky's shoulders knotted, and the space around his heart tightened as if those muscles had been formed in clay that had suddenly dried to stone. If he had heard that Julie's body had been stolen and used as a pawn in another crime, that someone had taken her and burned what little he had left of her, he'd have lost his shit. How much longer until he was off duty? A shot, maybe two, and this ache in his chest should loosen up, right? He didn't want to have another heart attack. "That doesn't bother you, Rericha? That someone used Miranda—"

"She's just as dead now as she was before." He sniffed again.

That might have been true, but the words made the room feel smaller, the air thinner than it had been just moments ago. Rericha shouldn't be numb to it; no father should. The man was a sociopath, and one who didn't believe he should bother to fake being shocked—he thought he was above the law. And like Hudson before him, there wasn't a damn thing Petrosky could do about it.

STEPPING outside the hardware store was like walking into another world; the air felt more oxygenated, and smelled sweeter, too, as if being in the presence of that evil bastard had made everything else nicer by comparison. "Guy's an asshole," he snapped as he climbed into Jackson's SUV.

"And yet, you're not threatening to punch him in the dick for my honor. What kind of partner are you?"

"I figured you'd want to do that yourself." He shrugged, but the knot between his shoulder blades already felt looser. Lean on friends, not liquor. That was good advice, right? But just the word *liquor* made his mouth water.

"Eh, my ego's not that fucked that I need to go around punching geriatrics." She pulled out of the lot and squinted as a blade of sun hit her square in the face. "You notice all the missing merchandise on the endcap?"

He nodded. "Yeah. I think Rebecca was there, maybe looking for the same thing she was at Piotr's, but there's not a single camera to help us prove it. And whatever she's after, none of them want to cop to it—she could be sitting in Rericha's back room, and he'd deny knowing her just to cover up whatever they did." Abused by her husband. Kidnapped, maybe. Then the loss of her hand in that car wreck—

"But you remember who this woman is, right? She planned and executed a scheme to steal a corpse, fake her death, and murder two people. We have to find her, and we have to arrest her. Let the court sort it out."

He leaned back against the seat and closed his eyes. "She had her reasons."

"She doesn't need your sympathy or that thing you do where you think you can save her. She's clearly desperate—dangerous. Stop trying to be her hero."

Hero. The idea that he'd be anyone's hero was a joke. He opened his eyes and straightened. "There's an electronics store up the way. Let's see if anyone came in trying to break into a laptop." Piotr said Rebecca couldn't get in without a passcode, so if she wasn't a hacker herself, the easiest way to get in was to go to an electronics store with techs on site. And unlike the smaller tech stores in the area, the big-box one near here had thirty-foot ceilings and cameras mounted too high to see faces dead-on. If she'd cased it, she'd know all she had to do to hide her identity was wear a hat.

Jackson hit her blinker. The water had evaporated from the roads, leaving behind the opaque sheen of dried salt. "I just can't believe he didn't bat an eye about his daughter," she said. "He didn't even ask for her body back."

Daughter, his dead daughter. Petrosky's gut clenched, his heart ached, but he swallowed it down and forced out: "All white women look the same anyway. And everyone looks the same once you burn their skin off."

Jackson's jaw dropped, but the tightness at the corners of her eyes had vanished.

"Why are you looking at me like that?" he said. "If it wasn't true, someone would have noticed Rebecca Kowalski and Miranda Rericha were two different people." But though his tone was light, his chest hurt like the dickens. *Just one drink, just one.* He couldn't, not now, but after the sun went down, he'd hit the bar—one and done, that was his new motto. Okay, two today, maybe three, but who was counting?

Jackson raised an eyebrow. "Do we need to play 'Is it Racist?' again?"

"What? I'm white, why can't I say white women look alike? Unless..." He squinted. "Is this about the other day when you said I can't say 'bougie' because it's hip-hop slang? I like hip-hop too, Jackson."

"No, you do not."

"I hate country, but no one cares if I say 'hee-haw!'" His heart was loosening up, just a little—*no heart attack today, old man.*

"Shut up, would you?" She wheeled them into the electronics store lot and cut the engine. Uniform white lines marked the parking spots, and square floods stood vigil along the store's roofline. They entered the store beneath a blinking neon-green sign that would have put any strip club to shame, the chill air biting at his nostrils.

Inside, a wall of flat-screen televisions chattered from the far end of the room, and to their right, row upon row of cell phones lay along low shelves, half of them lit up in promotional mode. A hundred phones, all on the verge of ringing. His own personal hell.

Jackson was already headed for the computer section, where half a dozen customers browsed the laptops along three waist-high shelves. At a fourth counter, a man carrying a small child on his shoulders squinted at chargers. And behind all that stood a circular cubicle of Formica manned by five people in button-down shirts the same garish green as the sign outside.

"They call these people professional dorks? They don't even have suspenders."

"What?" Jackson stopped and looked at him. "Why would they have suspenders?"

"Scott says that's how you can tell a real dork."

"He's messing with you." But she wasn't looking at him anymore. "You think that's her?"

Like we'd get that lucky. He followed Jackson's gaze. A woman stood at the Dork Patrol's counter, her back to them, hand hidden—small but strong, blonde hair with just enough wave to make it interesting, cut severely just below the shoulder. Familiar somehow, though she seemed a little taller than their suspect, and—

She turned. The world stopped spinning.

The woman staring back at them was Shannon.

"Only enemies speak the truth; friends and lovers lie endlessly, caught in the web of duty."
~Stephen King

14

OF ALL THE scenarios Shannon had run over in her head on the flight up, none could have prepared her for the look of utter shock on Petrosky's face. But it wasn't just surprise. Disappointment? Was he upset she was there? *Well, fuck him then.* But the rage was muted, made uneven and slippery by the aching throb just beneath her lower ribs, her emotions changing with each heartbeat—fury, grief, anger, worry. And beneath it all, a rising panic that this, of all things, she would not be able to fix.

She climbed into Jackson's back seat and tossed her duffel to the floorboards; the bag was inconvenient, but she'd taken an Uber from the airport straight to the electronics store after talking to Decantor. She'd told Decantor she was just trying to find Petrosky—not a stretch, she'd been talking about coming up since Petrosky's voicemail had gotten full—but what she really needed to ask him was what Rebecca had stolen from Piotr's house. The news had said it was a home invasion, but Rebecca wouldn't have gone there without a damn good reason, a goal, and Petrosky surely knew that too. But what else did he know?

Her lungs tightened, but she drew her shoulders up

straight. She wasn't about to let him see her squirm, not only because of her pride; if he worried, he drank. And for the moment, he appeared sober. That eased the pressure in her chest a bit, but not enough to get a full breath.

"You have a lot of explaining to do," Petrosky said, sharply enough to cut into her thoughts.

She yanked the seat belt into position. "I tried to explain. I've been calling you for a goddamn week. You couldn't answer the phone once?" *Who am I, right? I'm only the mother to a little girl who calls you Papa Ed.* And still, her heart went on: grief, anger, worry, rage. Petrosky vanishing like that was never a good sign. She leaned back against the buttery leather and forced her lungs to expand.

Jackson was staring at Petrosky with an I-told-you-so look, her fingers tapping on the steering wheel in time with Shannon's heart, and something in the set of Petrosky's jaw, even from her seat behind his... Not upset—he was worried. But as much as she wanted to keep him out of it, wanted to keep his stress to a minimum, she'd need his help. And they couldn't do this by the book, or she'd lose her job, get disbarred, maybe even arrested. And how would she support her kids then?

"Are you in trouble?" he asked finally, reading her mind the way he always seemed to, and the fact that he still could, when she had no idea what was happening in his head, made her want to kick the back of his seat until the springs broke.

"Does it matter?" she fired back. But it was her nerves talking—she'd made a huge mistake, one that might upend her life, one that might destroy her late husband's reputation, and she was here to fix it. She glanced at Jackson, at the tight set of her shoulders—Petrosky would keep everything close, protect her even if she was wrong, but Jackson? Maybe she should level with Petrosky later.

"Sorry. No, I'm not in trouble." But Morrison's voice whispered: *liar.* She touched her wedding band, still circling her ring finger; in the last few years, touching the ring had become second nature when she considered him—when she was wondering what he might think of her. She'd been fussing with the ring a lot lately.

Petrosky grunted, and to her ear, it sounded like *bullshit*. "Where's the case file on Rebecca Kowalski's kidnapping?" he asked, his voice low, almost like he was apologizing to the windshield. But even the back of his head looked irritated.

Heat burned through her chest. Apparently, he was intent on keeping his partner in the loop—she had no choice. She sighed. "Morrison stole it. I didn't know until afterward."

It was technically true, but he'd done it for her, to help stop the nightmares, to ease the pressing feeling that someone would find out what she'd done. She'd gotten dragged in so quickly, and after it was all over, there was no going back. She'd been manipulated—her, of all the people. Manipulated by a killer.

"Well, do you still have it?" Jackson asked, her words sharp as blades.

"He burned it in the fireplace a few months before he…" She swallowed hard, and Petrosky twisted around in the chair, his jaw tight. A lump rose in her throat, but she forced herself to finish: "There was nothing more I could do, and the thought of the case being reopened when I'd already been snatched away from Evie once…" The scars around her lips throbbed.

"I can't be hearing this." Jackson's fingers stopped tapping, and the silence felt far more oppressive, the air wound tight like a spring, loaded with pent-up energy. Ready to explode.

"You're fine," Petrosky told his partner. "Just pretend we're talking about Acharya and his crazy journalist ass—you sure did enough for him during our last case."

Jackson's face jerked in his direction so fast Shannon thought she heard a snap come from somewhere in the area of her neck. "I swear to god, Petrosky…"

But Petrosky didn't seem to hear his partner; he kept his steely blue gaze on Shannon, more father than friend. Like he wanted to ream her out for smoking dope but was far more worried about whether she was high right now—whether she was okay. "You can trust Jackson. I trust Jackson."

Jackson harrumphed as if she'd never heard him say that before in her life, but if he was saying it, it was true. And he didn't trust anyone, especially when he was sober...and despite her initial fears, he really did appear to be now. Clear eyes, steady gaze—irritated as hell, sure, but his face usually looked like that. He did look older than the last time she'd seen him though. More frail somehow. Tired. She swallowed hard over the thick burning in her throat.

"So, what are you doing here, Shannon?" His voice was soft, pressured. "How are you mixed up in this?"

I'll never work as an attorney again. They're going to throw me in jail. The silence in the car was electric with anticipation—she could almost see Jackson's ears straining in her direction.

She took a deep breath to calm her heart. "I'm here because Rebecca called me."

Petrosky raised his eyebrows, the look almost comical peeking around the SUV's headrest. "And what exactly did she say?"

"I'll let you listen." Shannon pulled out her phone.

"Wait, you mean *you* didn't answer your phone?" Petrosky balked. "Looks like we're living the same life, Shanny."

Was that a smirk at the corner of his mouth? But her chest brightened with a new ache—*Shanny*. When was the last time someone called her that? Petrosky never called her that. And hearing it from his mouth, the inflection so similar to the way her brother used to say it...

I don't have time to break down now. She pulled up her voicemail and put it on speakerphone, willing her hands to stay steady. Her kids were counting on her to fix this, and goddammit, she was going to. She wasn't going to let a killer fuck up her life twice.

Rebecca's voice was tight with panic but still somehow melodic, her vowels long and round—almost a British accent. "Shannon, it's Becca. They found me." The recording deteriorated into unintelligible garble, then: "I need you to watch your kids. Watch them to make sure—" More static. The line went dead.

"Where are Evie and Henry?" Petrosky barked—he suddenly sounded terrified.

"At home. In Atlanta." *I didn't want them to see me like this.* And she hadn't known what she was walking into—still didn't, not really, nor did she know what the consequences might be. But she was tired of running from it. She was so damn tired. "They're staying with friends in law enforcement. People who know what the stakes are; who carry big guns and know how to use them."

"Someone else who knows what you're doing here?"

"They think I got a threatening letter related to an old case I worked, and that I came back to look into it. That's all they need to know."

Petrosky shook his head. "You're tangled in a web of lies."

This time, both she and Jackson stared at him.

"What the hell was that?" Jackson asked.

He shrugged. "Don't hate, that's my poetic side." He turned back to Shannon. "So…why'd she call you? You still haven't explained how you're involved. Back up, spill it, and don't leave anything out."

Shannon did. She'd started her career representing the bad guys, which Petrosky knew. What he didn't know is that she had represented and successfully defended, the man accused of attacking Miranda Rericha in the months before she killed herself: Miranda's boyfriend, Roman Wójcik. Petrosky's nostrils flared harder with each word she said, maybe disapproval, but she couldn't find it in herself to care

—her body had gone numb, and even the painful throbbing in her ribs had vanished. "It was one of the last cases I tried before I moved over to prosecution. Roman hit Miranda so hard she had a goddamn miscarriage, and I was still expected to defend him. I couldn't get out of there fast enough." The silence was so thick it felt like it might choke her.

"How does this relate to Rebecca's kidnapping or to the case we're on now?" Jackson asked, pumping the brakes at a red light. When the car had stopped, she turned in her seat, craning her neck to meet Shannon's eyes. "If Rebecca and Miranda were friends, maybe it's a motive for Rebecca to kill Roman, especially if she'd been abused by the family too. But how does that make you complicit in those crimes? Because you're sure acting complicit—hiding shit. Stealing files." She raised an eyebrow pointedly, then turned back to the road.

Petrosky glared daggers at Jackson, but he kept his mouth shut. Because she was right.

"It's how I met Rebecca," Shannon said, watching an old Monte Carlo zing by through the tinted glass. "I interviewed Miranda at my office during Roman's case, and Rebecca came with her for moral support. But pretty soon, Miranda stopped cooperating, and I had no choice but to push for a dismissal—the charges against Roman were dropped. But Rebecca knew I was sympathetic, that I didn't want to help Miranda's boyfriend. I never did have a great poker face."

She shifted and rubbed her neck, her shoulders aching from sitting so rigidly. "Rebecca called me six or seven months later, the month after Miranda died—four months before the fire. I met her at the lake. She was paranoid, convinced her husband knew she had talked to me during Miranda's case. I felt like Miranda's suicide was partly my fault, but Rebecca believed someone else had killed her; she had no evidence, though, just a hunch." And there was nothing they could do now—Miranda's body was as crispy as a bug left in the sun. "Then Rebecca told me her husband was beating her, raping her, and after Miranda's death, she seemed panicked enough to act—to get out. After some convincing and providing her a list of domestic violence shelters, I called over to the station and had them take a report. But before that went any further...someone took her."

"The kidnapping," Petrosky turned back to the windshield, shoulders slumped, the gray in his hair sparkling in the sun, but he turned back just as quickly. "So Miranda... you're saying she was banging Roman?" His nose wrinkled—disgust.

Why did he look so shocked? But Jackson's jaw had dropped too. "What is it?" Shannon asked.

"Roman was Rericha's grandson," he said, "and Miranda his daughter. So Miranda was fucking her...um...nephew?"

Jackson shrugged. "Rericha didn't really claim any of his kids—not like his name was on their birth certificates, and Piotr was the only one he raised besides Miranda. Maybe they didn't even know they were related."

Petrosky looked like he might puke. He grimaced. "Cults are so gross."

Shannon stared. Cults? What the hell were they talking about? And...Miranda and Roman were related? But Jackson brought her back.

"I still don't get it. What exactly *did you do*?" Jackson's voice was hard, her syllables punctuated by the pads of her fingers on the leather wheel.

Shannon took a deep breath, considering. She didn't want to tell them—didn't want to tell anyone. But it was going to come out. *You came here to clear this shit up, get out from under it, Jesus Christ, let them help you put these demons to rest.* If anyone would, it was Petrosky—he'd put himself on the line if it meant she got to go home unscathed. "I got her a car and a fake ID," she blurted before she could change her mind. "Just before the fire. It wasn't a great fake; she wouldn't be able to use it for anything critical once she got where she was going, and me knowing her new name was a loose end she didn't need. But if she did the speed limit, managed to get to another state without getting pulled over..." She shrugged.

"What about a credit card?" Jackson asked. "Did you get her that too?"

"No, I didn't get her money." But here's where things got sticky. "She said she was going to use Miranda's body to fake her death and that she planned to slip her husband something to make sure she had time to get away—sleeping pills or whatever. She was going to take what cash she needed from the house when he fell asleep."

"But she didn't just take his money," Jackson said. "She killed him and his nephew, a man you defended, however reluctantly. And because you knew the victim, knew about the drugs, knew about the fire, knew about Miranda's body, procured the getaway car and helped her plan her escape, a jury might see that as complicit—might see you as an accomplice to at least some of those crimes. At the least, the bar association might take a hard look at your professional status." Jackson's fingers were still tapping on the wheel, but the sounds outside the car seemed suddenly louder—the buzz of the tires on the road, the whoosh of displaced air, the whining engines as other cars passed them, the occasional bleat of a horn. It was oddly soothing, though it did nothing to ease the frantic pace of her heart. "Did anyone else know you were involved?" Jackson asked. "That you knew Rebecca was alive?"

"Just Morrison." *And he's...* Even in her head, she hated the word: *D-E-A-D.* Reduced to four letters. Her husband had been so much more than that. The flesh beneath her ring vibrated, and heat rose in her guts and burned her chest. "Listen, I know how this all sounds. But after the kidnapping, I really believed he would kill her, and I couldn't be responsible for that. Miranda died because I couldn't help her, and with Rebecca…I was just trying to help her escape an abusive husband. I had no idea she was going to hurt anyone. She convinced me her life was at stake, maybe tricked me, and I was stupid enough to believe there was no other way." She turned to Petrosky; she'd almost forgotten he was there during Jackson's interrogation, but now she leveled a steely gaze in his direction. "In my place, you would have gotten her out of there yourself."

Petrosky's eyes widened. What did he see in her face? Maybe guilt. Because while what she'd said was true, she had made a grievous error: she had accidentally helped a killer disappear.

Finally, Petrosky blinked. His mouth softened. He turned back to the windshield. "So why would she come back, Shannon? Yeah, maybe someone found her like she said in that voicemail, but why wouldn't she just run again, find another place where no one knows her? Do you have any idea why she'd come back here?"

Shannon's muscles relaxed. She did know—or she thought she did. She forced her voice to remain steady. "She's here to find her baby. Joseph Rericha took him."

15

SHANNON. *She's here. And how could you call her Shanny? What is wrong with you?*

Petrosky still felt like he was living in some surreal fantasy world, the sky outside his Caprice strange and nearly violet in the early morning light. If exhaustion were a contest, he was winning. He watched the tobacco smoke creep toward his windshield on the superheated air from the vents.

Last night had been awkward at best. Jackson, Shannon, and himself had spent hours at his dining table, writing down every last thing Shannon could recall about Roman's case, the Rericha family, and her meetings with Miranda and Rebecca. Where she'd bought the car, and how Rebecca had given her five hundred dollars cash for that piece-of-shit Nissan. How Shannon had met Rebecca twice on the shore of Lake Saint Clair: once the month after Miranda's suicide, when she'd told Shannon her husband was abusing her, then again just before the fire, when Rebecca had told Shannon about the kidnapping and the baby who'd supposedly been taken just after Miranda died. He could see it, Rebecca sobbing beside that lake, telling Shannon that a man had locked her in a little room until she'd agreed to drop her claim against Lucius; that once he was satisfied, he'd tossed her into her Jeep with a pair of keys. Shannon claimed that Rebecca hadn't known anything else, that she'd never seen her kidnapper, couldn't even remember what had happened to her hand. Trauma was funny like that, but it was more likely she was too scared to name names in case her escape plan failed. And Shannon, already feeling guilty about Miranda's suicide, had agreed not to say anything about the missing kid until Rebecca was gone. And days later, the fire. The bodies. Then Shannon couldn't say anything without looking complicit. She'd called in an anonymous tip on the baby, but it had already been four months, and there was no evidence that a child had ever existed—without Rebecca, the police had nothing to go on. They'd filed it away. Like Rebecca's death.

He lit another cigarette and glowered at the sunrise, listening to the *pip-pip-pip* of the turn signal—weird how it sounded like a ticking clock. He hadn't had a drink last night, not even one; Shannon might have been breathing deeply in the spare bedroom, but he hadn't been positive she was sleeping. She'd probably been waiting to catch him in the act, listening for the clank of the bottle against a glass or the plasticky rattle of the cap. Maybe not though; she hadn't tried to come with him this morning, just waved and pulled her laptop onto the table. Maybe he was waiting to catch *her* in the act. The act of what, he wasn't sure, but she was the one who'd done something wrong. It wasn't *that* wrong, but the justice system and the bar association wouldn't likely see it that way.

He ground his teeth and crushed the cigarette out in the car ashtray, the nicotine not nearly potent enough to calm his nerves. The pieces were starting to fall into place, but there was still far too much he didn't know. Miranda's suicide, coupled with the abduction of Rebecca's child only weeks later, had apparently prompted Rebecca to seek Shannon's help. But instead of help, Rebecca had gotten kidnapped—vanished for weeks, just like Piotr's victim, Louisa. And three months after her return, Rebecca faked her death and murdered both Miranda's husband and her own. Revenge was definitely a motive. But this baby thing...

He tightened his fingers on the wheel, a headache taking root behind his eyes. Was Shannon correct that Joseph Rericha had stolen Rebecca's child at birth, that Rebecca had come back for the kid—that she'd had a child at all? There was no birth certificate, and Shannon hadn't seen a belly, but Rebecca would have been in her first trimester when she'd gone with Miranda to Shannon's office, and nearly a month postpartum when she'd first met Shannon at the lake. And while there were cults known for sending children to be raised elsewhere, that didn't appear to be the case with whatever bullshit Rericha had been leading—the relatives that had popped in the system all lived in the immediate area, and the detective who'd put Rericha away said there'd been children running around calling him "Father." Hell, Rericha had let his daughter hook up with his grandson, a fact that still skeeved Petrosky out.

So why would Rericha take Rebecca's child, his grandchild, the first kid born into that family in fifteen years? Why would her husband allow it? Maybe Rebecca had wanted out of the group—that was probably a motive to take the baby, either to force her to stay or as punishment. But if Rericha had taken the kid, why had Rebecca gone after Piotr instead of Rericha himself? Did she think Piotr knew where the child was? Maybe Rebecca was just a whack job, but then why had Piotr run off when Rebecca had returned? Where was Piotr now? Where was Rebecca? He had more questions than answers, and it made him want to scream. Or drink.

Mostly drink.

Rita's Diner approached, the interior lights spilling out

onto the front walk. Inside, the place was like a summer ghost town: bright and eerily empty, save the waitress behind the long counter, the same woman who'd waited on him last time—red lipstick, auburn hair, and a tiny baby belly beneath her apron.

"Morning shift, eh?" He stepped up to the register, aiming for nonchalant, but his brain was on fire with unanswered questions; the words came out strangled.

"No rest for the wicked." She smiled, revealing that chipped front tooth, her hand on her barely pregnant belly, and he could almost imagine freckles across the bridge of her nose, that her hand was missing beneath the counter—he was suddenly terrified for the woman in front of him and for her child. Bile burned low in his esophagus, threatening to choke him.

"You want a table?"

He swallowed hard. "Not today. Just two coffees to go." He raised a hand to massage his aching temple.

"Cream or sugar?"

"Just black and…" He dropped his arm—was his hand shaking? His head was definitely throbbing. But of course he had a headache; Shannon had colluded with a fugitive and helped hide a killer. His abdomen suddenly felt feverish and heavy, like molten lead. "Can you toss a shot of Baileys into one of them? Got a friend going through a rough patch."

She tapped the screen to ring him up. "The coffees I can do, but we don't have Baileys, and we don't actually serve alcohol."

His chest constricted. "Yeah, I know, but you have rum cake and stuff, right? Whatever liquor you have in back will be fine. I won't tell anyone."

She frowned. Bit her ruby-red lip with that sharp chipped tooth. Uncomfortable. Because of him.

Yeah, the world was definitely spinning the wrong way.

JACKSON WAS ALREADY at her desk in the bullpen when he arrived with their coffees—well, her coffee. He'd finished his in the car and chased it with mouthwash and another cigarette for good measure. She looked up as he set the cup on her desk beside a photo of her two boys, one of whom was still alive. He glanced at his own desktop, free of pictures or any other signs of life outside of yesterday's coffee and a dirty napkin.

"Where's Shannon?" she asked.

"Working from home."

She raised an eyebrow. "I don't like it, Petrosky."

"I know. But I also know that you'll look the other way."

"The other way? All she did was try to help a woman she believed was being abused—gave her the keys to a car. If I thought she knew what Rebecca was up to, that she was complicit in a double homicide, I'd drag her in without a second thought. I just meant I'd rather have Shannon here where she can help us." She grabbed her coffee. The booze roiled in Petrosky's gut—amaretto. He could still feel the sweetness cloying in the back of his throat, but his chest felt looser, and his headache was all but gone.

Jackson replaced the cup, stretched her arms over her head, then planted her elbows on the desktop. "Now that we have some idea why Rebecca returned, hopefully, we can figure out where she's going next—who else is involved with this baby thing or who she might go to for help."

If Piotr, the family's bookkeeper, had something to do with her missing child, had even a single record of it, coming back for him made sense—waiting seven years to come back didn't, but he'd cross that bridge later. Right now, he just wanted to know if the kid existed.

"Shannon said Miranda miscarried, right?" Jackson asked. "After the domestic violence incident?"

He nodded. "Yeah, but we can skip the OBs; Miranda used a midwife, and Shannon said last night that no one in the family used hospitals—even after the miscarriage, Miranda was treated at home. When I interviewed him in prison, Lewis said his wife had their daughter at home too." Which was a bonus for them if they wanted to verify that Rebecca's pregnancy had been real. There were fewer midwives than OBGYNs, only twenty-five listed within a thirty-mile radius of Rebecca's old house. If Petrosky wouldn't drive more than twenty minutes for cardiac care, he couldn't imagine a pregnant woman would drive much farther. Not that he ever made cardiac appointments these days. "I'll print the list of midwives, and you can take the bottom half. Hopefully, now that Rebecca's dead, they won't pull that patient confidentiality shit."

"She's not dea..." Jackson smirked, picked up her half-full coffee cup, and brought it to her lips. "Yeah. Fingers crossed they didn't see her face on the news, or they'll know she's out there."

He frowned, eyes already burning. *I should have bought more coffee.*

IT TOOK TWO HOURS, but they were able to locate the midwife who'd worked with Rebecca—Tanya Jervis had tawny skin, amber eyes, and black hair adorned by tasteful streaks of red. Not yet thirty-six, she was young for a woman with a swanky office in downtown Farmington, a building shared by plastic surgeons and endodontists, all high-income earners that should far surpass what she'd pull in as a midwife. She met them at the door wearing turquoise beads the size of mothballs, a yellow suit, and an infectious grin. A yellow diamond, or some other glittering rock, sparkled from her ring finger—no wedding band beside it. Her hand would be heavy as hell once she got married.

She walked them into a cozy office with bookcases on one wall, posters of the uterus in various stages of labor on the opposite, a painting of wildflowers on the third. No desk. The only other furniture was a straight-backed wooden chair and a little end table topped with a half-empty bottle of water, Jervis's coral lipstick on the rim. That was probably where fathers-to-be sat while Jervis checked out their wives. Jervis leaned against the exam table near the stirrups, white paper crinkling.

"That whole thing was so sad," Jervis said, shaking her head. "I remember Rebecca well."

Sounded like she hadn't seen the news, didn't know Rebecca was still alive. *Score.*

"Anything might be helpful," Jackson said, taking the reins. Petrosky wasn't squeamish—you've looked into one eviscerated abdominal cavity, you've seen them all—but this seemed more her lane. Or so she'd told him in the car. Seemed fair; he hadn't been there for most of Linda's prenatal appointments, and he'd barely made it to Julie's birth.

He leaned his shoulder against the doorframe as Jervis said: "Rebecca came to me in her third trimester."

"Did she have care before you?" Jackson asked. "At a doctor?" Jackson was really asking why Rebecca hadn't had prenatal care until her last few months of pregnancy—hopefully, Jervis would read between the lines.

Jervis showed no sign of offense; she shrugged. "Rebecca never mentioned another healthcare provider, but most of my clients don't have one." The white paper rasped as Jervis shifted position. "And everything was fine with the pregnancy. She planned to have a water birth." He wrinkled his nose, but who was he to judge? Pouring Jack Daniel's down his throat and sucking tobacco into his lungs weren't exactly health-conscious. Or neat.

Jervis crossed her arms. "She did miss quite a few appointments, though, skipped most of her ultrasounds, but she made it to the one where we checked for the sex." A wan smile. "Her baby boy was growing as expected."

"Did you follow up to see why she wasn't coming in?" Jackson asked. *Trouble at home?*

"I called, but that's all I can do. Sometimes you get a mom who just isn't...reliable." Jervis shook her head again. And Jervis...that name. So familiar.

"And as she approached her due date?"

Jervis's eyes narrowed—remembering or agitated, he couldn't tell. *Shit, how much amaretto was in that coffee?* "She missed her last four weekly appointments," Jervis said finally. "Her due date came and went. When I called, she said the baby came fast, and she delivered in bed before she even knew she was in labor. Not common, to be sure, but possible."

Jackson nodded. "And did you have contact with her after the birth?" *Had Jervis ever seen the boy?*

"Well, I did call. The service I provide includes two in-home meetings postpartum. I make sure the new mom is okay, I help if there are any questions or concerns, that kind of thing. But Rebecca refused, said everything was fine, that she had help there with her. She sent me a check that included the normal delivery fees, but I didn't cash it."

"Why not?"

"I wasn't there for the birth—that wouldn't have been right. I would never take advantage of the family." She looked down, and something in the set of her shoulders made the hairs on Petrosky's neck stand on end. *The* family. Not *her* family.

"Is the baby okay?" Jervis asked, raising her head. "I really thought he just came fast, but..."

"We have no idea." Jackson's voice remained level, almost comforting if you weren't being interrogated. "Do you know where the boy is now?"

"No, but after Rebecca died, I'm sure someone would have taken him in." Jervis's gaze did not falter—she appeared to be telling the truth. But her lip trembled. The flower picture over her shoulder shuddered in the breeze, but that was certainly just his eyes.

Petrosky pushed himself off the doorframe and stepped closer. "It seems you suspected something wasn't right, Ms. Jervis."

"I didn't suspect anything." Her gaze hardened. "The way you're talking…it's like you think I did something wrong. But I had no reason to doubt that she had support even though her husband didn't come to her appointments; even she missed them half the time."

"Lucius just opted out?" Jackson said. "Any other indications that there was trouble between them?"

Her jaw dropped. "I didn't say there was—"

"Is it possible the child wasn't her husband's?" Not likely, not with a man that controlling, but uncertain paternity might be a reason for a narcissistic cult leader to steal a baby.

"No, the baby was his; obviously, it was her husband's, it wasn't like she could just…" She stiffened, her eyes widening as if she'd said something out of turn. But of course it'd be outlandish to think that any woman in Rericha's cult—or Piotr's newfangled version—would go outside her marriage. No one wanted to go to… What had Lewis called it? *Confession*. And it seemed Jervis knew that all too well.

"What do you know about Joseph Rericha?" he asked.

She froze—she didn't even appear to be breathing. "Nothing, I don't know a single—"

"What about the group he was in charge of?" Jackson cut in. "The one his grandson took over when he went to jail?"

Jervis's nostrils flared. She cleared her throat. "No group, just family. They were all very close."

Just family—the same thing Rericha had said. "Not close enough to come to prenatal appointments, though," Jackson fired back.

"Lucius was just busy!" she said quickly, her voice high—anxious. "And support…that's what family is for. Rebecca even brought Piotr with her a few times."

That smarmy bastard had been here with Rebecca? Was he the baby's father? But that wasn't the part making gooseflesh prickle on his arms; how had Jervis remembered his name so quickly? Most would have said "Peter" or some variation, and… *Oh shit.* Now he knew why her name sounded so familiar. Tanya *Jervis.* Clark Jervis. Hudson had mentioned his name, one of the murdered men pulled from the waters of Lake Huron. One of the men who'd been involved in Rericha's cult once upon a time. If Tanya was Clark Jervis's child, she was involved in Rericha's cult, too—born into it.

"How well did you know Piotr, ma'am?" *Did he kill your daddy?* Hudson sure thought Piotr had done it.

Jervis dropped her gaze to the floor again. The white paper crinkled in one clenched fist. Yeah, something was definitely wrong. And Piotr hadn't come here to support Rebecca, no way—not him. If he was here in the midwife's office, he had a vested interest in the kid. Or his boss did.

"I take it Piotr's not one of your favorite people," Jackson said, edging closer.

Jervis sniffed and released the paper, righting herself once more, her coral lips pressed together. She shrugged.

What are you hiding? But from the steely look in her eyes, she wasn't going to tell them regardless of her feelings about Piotr, and the reason wasn't hard to figure out. Dr. Purcman had his dental office paid for by Rericha; Piotr got Rolexes and god knew what else. And this office, right up the hall from a plastic surgery suite, was proof enough that Jervis had something to gain by keeping her mouth shut…and lots to lose. The group might not meet anymore, didn't even appear to be in close contact, but Rericha was still taking care of those he considered family. His eyes lit once more on the single visitor's chair—the water bottle on the wooden table beside it. The coral lipstick on the rim.

"Thank you for your time, ma'am," he said, nodding. Jervis nodded back with tight lips, and turned to the exam table, settling a fresh sheet of paper over the top. He grabbed the water bottle on his way out, thankful he'd decided to wear a suit jacket—it made him look like less of a drunk, and it was easier to steal things with a jacket than with a sweatshirt pouch.

The air in the parking lot felt colder than it had on the way in.

"The family is strange, way too secretive," Jackson said. "Like you'd expect from a cult, I guess. Everyone they deal with has a reason to keep quiet."

He pulled the bottle out and squinted at it in the sun—the lipstick was definitely Jervis's shade. "We need to talk to someone who's been on the inside." No one outside the group would know where Rericha would hide a baby, how Piotr might be involved, or what motivation Rericha had to steal a kid in the first place.

But they wouldn't get anywhere with Rericha or Jervis. Piotr had conveniently vanished, and Rebecca was in hiding. Lewis had told them all he intended to from behind bars. And all the other members of the group that Hudson had identified were long gone—dead or far, far away—and they needed someone involved more recently, anyway. Someone who knew the group after Rericha's fall from grace, when Piotr was in charge. From the time Rebecca was there.

There was only one person he could think to ask, but she might tell him to fuck off too.

16

Louisa Parson had an apartment in Ann Arbor, only an hour from Ash Park, but apparently far enough to get Piotr to leave her alone. But from the look in her hazel eyes, it wasn't nearly far enough to knock out the fear. She sat at her dining table and wrapped an oversized navy cardigan around her thin frame, trembling hands clamped under her armpits as if she was worried Petrosky and Jackson might attack her too. *Damn, honey, what did he do to you?*

"Did you ever meet Rebecca Kowalski?" Jackson asked. It was a good place to start. *Do you know if someone stole her kid and kidnapped her, leading her to murder her husband and later return to Ash Park for revenge?* did not have the same ring.

Louisa shook her head, releasing a tendril of dark hair from behind her ear. She squinted at it and blew it out of her eye instead of touching it. "No. By the time he and I started dating, she was gone already." *Gone—dead.* Her gaze darted from him to Jackson and back. "Is that all you needed?"

Jackson and Petrosky exchanged a glance, and Jackson continued: "Did Piotr ever mention Roman or Lucius? Other family members?" *Other people who might be complicit in whatever happened to Rebecca? Who might know where her son is?*

Another head shake. She shifted in the dining chair, leaning one wool-clad elbow against the table. "No, he didn't talk about his family, and I only met Joe. They're super private people. Not just introverted the way I am, but like... really private." More confirmation that there was nothing left of Rericha's group besides Piotr—if Jervis or anyone else was getting funding from Rericha, he was doing it on the sly, even if they'd found no evidence of it yet. But Louisa had met Piotr right after the fire. No mention of his dead brother, Roman? His dead uncle Lucius or Lucius's wife, Rebecca?

She swallowed hard and shook her head again, fast, fast, fast, more of a vibration in her neck. "I don't know anything, and I have some stuff to do, so..."

His hackles rose—why was she so jumpy? Drugs? But her pupils looked normal.

"Did you ever wonder if Piotr and Joe were up to no good?" Jackson said, her voice low and careful, obviously trying not to scare her off. "Maybe they had something to hide, and that's why they were so secreti—I mean, private?"

Louisa sighed shakily. She leaned away from the table and moved her hands to her lap.

"Let's start simple," he said gently. "Tell us about Piotr. Before things got messy." He stared at her until she met his gaze. "I'm sure you were happy together once."

This appeared to relax Louisa somewhat—her shoulders slumped. "Well, I liked that we could just be alone. That he wanted to take care of me, didn't want me to work." But despite her more relaxed posture, the words spilled from her lips rapid-fire. And keeping her at home, isolated...abusers commonly cut their partners off from the rest of the world, leaving them with no one to tell when things went wrong.

"Can you just go? I have to go." She shot to her feet, narrowly missing smashing her hip into the table.

No, this was not right, not right at all. Petrosky stood as

well, his knees creaking as he stepped around the table toward her.

Jackson stayed seated. "Louisa, we know something is off with Piotr's family—that they hurt people. Maybe you're afraid of Joe? Of your ex?"

Her shoulders...god, she was trembling, and it made his own shoulders ache in response. "We can help you." He reached for her elbow. "Let us help you."

The moment his fingers brushed her arm, she leapt back as if she'd been stung by a wasp. "No, you can't help."

His chest spasmed—hot, painful. He dropped his hand. He should have stalked Piotr after Louisa recanted, watched until he did something else. Or just taken him into a back alley somewhere. But this level of terror so far after the fact... Whatever Piotr had threatened her with, she believed he'd follow through. What was he hanging over her head now? And why was she so sure that just talking to them would get her into trouble?

He lowered himself back into the chair, as far from her as he could get while still being at the table, and waited until she'd eased once more into the seat across from him. When he spoke again, his voice was hushed, but at least it wasn't shaking. "When you came to the station, I sat with you—hours we sat there before you told me about the rape. And I told *you* I'd do everything in my power to help you if you would just talk to me." He inched forward in his chair, palms up. "That's still true. We can't help you if we don't know what's going on. Just tell me what you need," he said. "What do you need to feel safe?"

"I need him dead," she blurted, and immediately raised one sleeve-clad hand to cover her mouth.

"I wish," he said, and Jackson shot an elbow into his ribs. He rubbed his smarting side. "Hey, I'm just saying what we're all thinking." He turned back to Louisa. "But my partner's elbow is right: I can't kill him. All I can do is set you up somewhere else. If you tell us what we need to know, so help me, I will pay for your move myself." He'd just have Shannon get her a car—what were the odds of two frightened women in a row being murderers?

Her jaw dropped. "You're…allowed to do that? I don't have any money; it's the only reason I'm still here."

The chief would have his head, but whatever. "I don't care whether it's allowed, do you?" He could feel Jackson's eyes burning into his forehead—she definitely cared what was allowed.

Louisa sniffed and straightened her shoulders, but she was still trembling.

"Please, Louisa. There's another woman out there, a woman who was abused by her husband, then kidnapped after filing a police report. Whatever they did to you, they probably did to her too." Maybe worse.

"Oh…oh god." Her eyes dropped to her lap.

"You said you didn't know Rebecca—did you ever hear about her child?"

Louisa closed her eyes so long, Petrosky thought she'd forgotten the question, maybe fallen asleep sitting up. But when she opened her eyes again, her voice had steadied. "If this woman had a kid, she'd have agreed to raise it…their way. The way her husband wanted. In the family, you know?"

"And if she didn't agree?"

"They'd punish her." Her voice was a hissed whisper. Almost exactly what Lewis had said—*send her to confession*.

"What about the baby?" Jackson asked. "Would they take the child if she wanted out? Make sure it was raised up right?" Raised right. What a laugh.

She frowned. "No, I don't think they…knew anyone who would raise a baby. It was just Joe and Piotr when I was around, and I don't think Joe liked kids—he'd be more likely to sell it or something."

For a guy who didn't like kids, he sure had a ton of them.

But sell it? Hudson's voice echoed in his head: *Joe did whatever he could, to make as much cash as he could, and didn't give a shit beyond that.* "Do you have any reason to think he sold a chil—"

"No one had a baby when I was around, so..." She was staring at him, maybe trying to decide if she believed him—if this was safe. "They were more worried about money than people, that's all. About...power. Everyone owes Joe a favor. Everyone. Every doctor we saw, every dentist, the people we bought groceries from, everyone knew him."

"Or were related to him," Petrosky said. "A regular gigolo, that guy."

Her nostrils flared, and Jackson frowned at him, but then Louisa nodded. "Yeah. They never came out and said it, but a few of the guys called him 'Father.'" She hissed an inhale and let it out slowly.

"Sounds like it was more of a group than just you and Piotr and Joe." Jackson cocked her head.

"It wasn't, though, not really. I don't think I could name a single other person—they weren't involved with us, they were just people who wanted to keep Joe happy. And I did too." She let out a long shuddering sigh. "I know it sounds insane, but you have to understand, they were all I had. By the time Piotr raped me, I didn't have any friends. He was my only family. Hell, I was one step from thinking the rape was...*normal*, that it was okay because I wasn't listening to him. They were big on listening." She snorted. It was a bitter sound.

"Can you tell us more about that?" Jackson asked. "What your life with Piotr looked like?"

Louisa blinked, her eyes on some faraway point over Petrosky's left shoulder. "It was...quiet, honestly. I was in college when I met Piotr, but pretty soon, I was taking online courses. And when we talked about what I would do after I finished... Like, I would talk about working at a graphic design firm, and he'd say it would be better for me to work from home, that he could help me start my own graphic design business, or that I could work for the store the way he did. Back then, I was still allowed to talk to my friends online."

Allowed. It wasn't a religious cult, but it was a cult all the same; a group of control-freak domestic abusers, experts in gaslighting. "So Piotr trusted you? Must have if you were still talking to your friends."

She nodded. "For a while, yeah. I mean, until I filed that report. And then...Piotr fixed me." Her voice shook, and her chest was rising and falling much too quickly—panting. Or hyperventilating. "That's what Joe always called Piotr. *The fixer.*"

The fixer. Very 1940s gangster, but maybe there was something to it. When Rebecca had become a problem, someone had to fix it—someone had made that report against Lucius go away.

Louisa was shaking her head. "I should have taken the money to leave. I should have—"

"Ma'am?" Jackson said, and Petrosky jumped. He'd nearly forgotten she was there, but now his partner leaned closer to Louisa, her brow creased with concern. "What money?"

"From Joe."

"Why would he pay you to leave?" It seemed Rericha's goal should be to expand his network, his power, not reduce it, especially once she was already indoctrinated. It took time to brainwash someone—energy.

"I don't know, but it was back before Piotr...hurt me. I just thought Joe didn't like me." She wrapped her arms tighter around her body as if she were trying to comfort herself. "He came to me, told me to leave Piotr alone, but I didn't have anywhere else to go—no job, no family, nothing. When I was still there the next month, he offered to pay me. I refused. And then...my student loans were rejected—something had been filled out wrong on the application, but I know I did it right. I went to see Piotr at work, sobbing, and Joe...he was just staring at me, you know? And then...he smiled." She shuddered involuntarily. "I had never seen him smile before, and for him to do it then, when I was crying about having to drop out of school... Joe did it, I know he did."

"Did he know anyone at the university?" Jackson asked.

"No, I don't think so."

But if he'd sabotaged her application, he wouldn't need to have an inside man. They'd have to make another visit to their friend, the hardware-store-owning sociopath. "Why didn't you tell me this before?"

"I couldn't prove it, and it sounds insane—it isn't like a smile is an admission of guilt. But after that, I couldn't look at Piotr the same way. Couldn't be in the same room with him or Joe without my skin crawling. I know Piotr felt it, too. And when I tried to leave, he beat me—raped me."

And then you vanished. And when you reappeared, you recanted. Just like Rebecca.

Louisa was trembling so hard she looked like she was having difficulty staying upright. Her knuckles were white, the edges of her cardigan sleeves balled in her fists.

"Louisa?"

"I want you to leave. I don't think I can...do this." She released her arms and rested her hands in her lap, the cardigan clenched tightly around her fists, only a slip of index finger visible. Clenched so, so tightly.

Jackson's eyes were fixed on Louisa's hands too. And Rebecca's missing limb, the stump of her arm... "Can I see your hands?" Jackson asked gently.

She shook her head. "No. I can't. He'll kill me."

"Piotr's gone," Petrosky said.

She stilled. Louisa's eyes widened.

"His clothes are gone. His car. He knows we're onto

him. And if he did something to you, if he knows you have information on him, your only way out of this is to help us." The words were bitter in his mouth. When all else fails, threaten the victim? *There's a special place in hell for you, old man.*

She leveled her gaze at him. "I won't testify."

"Then you'll walk away from this like you did before and hope he doesn't find a reason to show up again. But walking away last time, recanting, knowing he's still out there...it didn't help, did it?"

She bit her lip, tears glistening in her eyes.

"Please," Jackson said. "He's right—we can help. But only if we know what we're dealing with. Show us what we need to protect you from."

Louisa blinked at Jackson, then drew her eyes once more to Petrosky. She took a deep breath. Dropped her gaze to the table. And released her sleeves.

Petrosky winced. The deep scar was a gorge in her flesh, bisecting the back of her hand from just below the little finger to the hollow beneath the fatty pad of her thumb. Several other serious but shallower wounds cross-hatched their way from mid-hand to wrist bone. Louisa's scarred hand; Rebecca's hand missing—Piotr had done this to both of them. And Rebecca hadn't given Shannon Piotr's name because she'd been just as terrified as Louisa.

Her eyes remained locked on the tabletop as she said: "When I came back from making that report, he was waiting for me—I thought he'd be at work. He...dragged me downstairs. And he made me call you the next day, told me he'd kill me if I didn't." Her words were half sob.

Heat rose in Petrosky's chest. He remembered that call—she'd left a message saying she was taking a trip, needed time to decompress. And two weeks later, she'd come back and recanted. He was so pissed she'd decided to let the asshole go. *I should have known better.*

"Piotr kept me handcuffed in that basement for weeks." She choked, recovered. "With the...the tools."

The silence stretched. Finally, Jackson prodded: "Ma'am?"

"There was a table. It had knives, an ax. Rubbing alcohol." She shuddered.

Rubbing alcohol. To sterilize the wounds he inflicted, so she didn't succumb to infection before he was done with her.

Louisa's eyes had gone glassy. "Piotr liked to...watch." Her voice was hollow, low, as if she were whispering to someone they couldn't see. "I don't want to do this." She burst from her chair again so suddenly that Petrosky jolted back, but she stepped away from him, wringing her scarred hand in her good one, tears streaming down her face, her eyes darting from him to Jackson and back like a wild animal caught in a trap. "I didn't want to, I didn't want to do it."

Didn't want to do the interview? But why was she talking in the past tense? Unless... His eyes lit on her scarred hand. *Oh shit.* "Piotr made you do it yourself, didn't he?"

Fresh tears poured down her cheeks. "I just needed to get out, and I tried, but I couldn't...I couldn't... And I saw what had happened to the others. He showed me pictures. Of what he'd done." Her breath hitched. "They were already dead, their skin kinda falling off, but you could see the marks from the knives. He said, 'if I could do this to my own father, imagine what I can do to you.'"

His father? Piotr had killed his...dad? How many crimes did they have to solve?

"Do you know who Piotr's father is?" Petrosky said. They hadn't had any luck on that front.

"He didn't say his name or anything." Her voice shook. "And the picture...his skin was...he didn't really have a face."

No face. No name. Were the photos even real or just part of Piotr's ruse to make her comply? And...he'd let her live. Unusual if he'd killed before, if he'd shown her photos of his victims. Why give her ammunition to use against him?

"Why'd he let you go?" The wound, as awful as it was, didn't look like it would allow her to escape—not enough damage, not enough flayed off to get out of the cuffs.

"Joe made him. Joe made him let me out."

Joe knew. He was an accessory. They'd finish up here and go arrest his ass.

"Did Joe go down into the basement?" Jackson asked. "Did he actually see you?"

Say yes, say yes. Maybe they'd charge him with kidnapping, get him on attempted murder.

She shook her head. "No, but I heard them upstairs, yelling…" She cast her eyes to the floor once again. "And then Piotr came down and uncuffed me. Stitched up my hand. And gave me my keys." She yanked the sweater back over her fists. "Sometimes, I wish he hadn't."

17

THE TIRES BUZZED. His heart throbbed. His head ached. Petrosky stared out the windshield at the field of somber gray, which too perfectly matched his mood. Louisa didn't seem to know anything about the child or Rebecca, but she had been kidnapped like Rebecca—too frightened even now to come forward. But what did this mean for their case?

Had Rebecca been kept at Piotr's house all those years ago, as Louisa had? Probably. Had Piotr forced her to cut off her own hand to escape? Most likely, even if the car wreck was accidental—hard to drive with blood slicking the steering wheel. But though Rebecca had called Shannon and said "they" had found her, she hadn't been abducted this time; the basement had been clean the morning she'd jimmied Piotr's front door, too clean for someone to have been held hostage there recently. But Piotr was missing; maybe he was holding Rebecca hostage now…somewhere.

And then there was the child, Rebecca's supposed motivation for returning. The pregnancy was real, but had her baby been taken by Joseph Rericha? That one was a maybe. Sure, her kid had to go somewhere, but she might have been desperate enough to lie if it meant Shannon would be more likely to help her—she could have hidden the kid away herself. And…Roman. Lucius. Whatever those men had done, Rebecca had murdered two people, and while Petrosky agreed they'd deserved to die, it was a good bet that the justice system wouldn't feel the same. All the pieces were like ping pong balls in a swimming pool, bobbing uselessly against each other. "We should haul Rericha's ass in," he said finally, and in the next lane, a car horn bleated like an exclamation point.

Jackson grunted, less emphatically. They had put out an APB on Piotr and his car—a classic Camaro with paint like iridescent piss—but Rericha was another matter. They had nothing on him except Louisa's statement that he'd argued with Piotr before he let her go, and she wasn't about to go on record—she'd pull her statement back the second they asked her to sign it. They needed other evidence to convict these assholes, and they simply didn't have it. The warehouse where Rericha had lectured his congregation had been remodeled into a series of loft-style apartments complete with a gym. No evidence there. And outside of Dr. Pureman, Tanya Jervis the midwife, and Mr. "Twitchy Convict" Lewis, they hadn't been able to locate other members of Rericha's cult who might help them. Lewis's wife and daughter lived in Toronto and had refused to speak to them as they refused to speak to Lewis himself. Of the six partial DNA matches Scott had found, only two men were alive besides Piotr, but neither had filed taxes in the past five years, and it was unlikely that either would have known Rebecca. They were probably six feet under. Or floating—at least two cult members had been murdered, found in that damn lake, connected only by their relationship to Rericha. So many people, so many connections, and as far as he could tell, all worthless for their case.

Jackson's jaw muscles were working overtime, her eyes on the road—on the approaching intersection. She hit the turn signal. "I don't want that racist bastard to know we're onto him, not yet."

"Maybe he's not racist," Petrosky said. "Maybe he just doesn't like you."

"Oh, fuck off." Jackson wheeled them into the precinct parking lot, kicking up a spray of gravel—dry now. The sky above burned white but cold, like the inside of a freezer. "What about Shannon? You think she knows anything she hasn't told us?"

He turned to her. "Like what?"

"No idea. But she should be here with us, Petrosky." The slam of Jackson's car door echoed against the building like buckshot.

His footsteps were just as agitated. "She's not a cop, and I'm not about to tell everyone that she was involved with Rebecca." But what if Rericha already knew about Shannon's part in Rebecca's disappearance? What if Piotr had vanished so he could go stealth, kill anyone who might have evidence against them? They'd already moved Louisa to a hotel for a few days, just in case, but was Shannon in danger? "Maybe we should put Shannon in protective custody," he said, a ball of heat growing in his guts—*where the liquor should be.* "At least get Decantor over there." Petrosky glanced over in time to see Jackson shake her head—*You're such an asshat*—but she had the decency not to say it out loud.

"Shannon's already in a safe house—your harem, or whatever." Jackson flashed her badge at the door reader and let them into the stairwell.

"She's not with the neighbors, she's—"

"Of course she's at the neighbors'." Their footfalls echoed on the stairs, Jackson's boots clack-clack-clacking, his sneakers sneezing out far more muted squeaks. "That's where I'd be, digging around for dirt on you…and by dirt, I mean hints about how you are since you're so fucking forthcoming."

He frowned. Was Jackson right? Was Shannon with Billie and Candace and Jane? But that was good—safety in numbers. And...*my place has a bottle of Jack.* If she found that, she'd kick his ass, and then she'd leave, making her even more vulnerable. Of all the things she wouldn't tolerate from him, the bottle was top of her list; she'd known better, even when Morrison had looked the other way. The heated ball of lead in his guts radiated into his chest, forcing bile into his throat.

Jackson was frowning at him over her shoulder. She stopped mid-step, and he squeaked to a halt. "Don't look so worried. Your neighbors' place has your giant beast of a dog pacing the front room, and it's full of other people. And I've seen the cameras out there."

He sniffed, but she was right; the neighbors' house had external cameras, glass break alarms, and window sensors—nothing like that on his own home. Shannon would probably be okay so long as he didn't do something to chase her off.

"Shannon is fine," Jackson said again when he didn't respond. "And she's never been hidden. If someone knew what Rebecca did, that she lit up that warehouse, they probably would have known about Shannon too—they'd have gotten to her before she moved to Atlanta." Jackson turned and headed up the stairs once more. "I know you're upset that she's here—that she did this, or that she hid it, whatever. But stop acting like you're going to make her stay home while you work this case without her."

"I'm not doing anything, she was the one who—"

Jackson yanked the door handle. "Shannon is a daughter to you, she knows it, I know it, hell, even Duke knows it. And she's determined enough to keep on this case, no matter what you think about it. Maybe she'll find Piotr before we do."

18

"I STILL CAN'T BELIEVE you didn't call when you got in. What kind of garbage is that?" Decantor's brilliant smile was like a light at the end of a very long tunnel. But Shannon had no right to think she was out of the dark, not yet. Decantor might have been her husband's friend, her friend, but he wasn't like Petrosky—he wasn't going to protect her when she was the one who'd fucked up. Decantor was a lot of things, but an enabler wasn't one of them, which was why he and Petrosky had never really gotten along.

Shannon reached across the table and laid her palm against his knuckles—his big hands were warm. "I'm sorry. It's hard being here, and diving back into this place, all the people we hung out with together…"

He didn't have to ask who "we" was—he missed Morrison too.

Decantor grabbed his lemonade from the table, and Shannon leaned back against the seat, the clatter of silverware on plates clank clanking from the booths behind her. "Seeing Petrosky used to bother me for the same reason," Decantor said. "Because it made me think about Morrison.

Now seeing Petrosky just bothers me because it's Petrosky." He grinned, but it looked forced. Tight.

"I hear you." She smiled back and hoped hers looked genuine, but her chest was on fire. "It's just so weird. All the roads we used to drive down, parks where we went jogging, restaurants we used to go to…" She'd picked this little Mexican place because it hadn't even existed when Morrison was alive—no memories. And he'd still managed to sneak in; she could practically see him sitting beside her, and that somehow made the place feel more like home than Atlanta. "I feel like I'm seeing things," she blurted.

Decantor set the lemonade aside. "Like…hallucinating?"

"God no, just…I'm so paranoid being here. I keep seeing cars on Petrosky's street, thinking they're there for me. That they're following me. I'll look again and *poof*, they're gone. It's ridiculous." *Was it though? Maybe someone* is *after you. Maybe it's Piotr.* She shook the thoughts off. No one knew she was involved except Rebecca, and though Rebecca was a killer, she'd had a reason to hurt those men—Rebecca had no reason to hurt her.

Decantor was frowning. "Maybe I should go back to Petrosky's with you. Hang out in front of the house. You can watch him hurl baseless pop-culture-themed insults at me."

"Nah, I have that giant slobbery dog at Petrosky's. No one's getting near me." She forked a bite of enchilada into her mouth, but it was dry, tasteless.

"You've got a gun, too, right?"

She could almost feel the weight of it in her purse. "What do you think?"

Decantor smiled. "Good." He pulled his own plate closer —ceviche? "So, why are you in panicked paranoia mode? I know it's not just being here." He paused with a bite halfway to his lips, one eyebrow raised—suspicious. Yeah, Decantor was no enabler. And no dummy.

"I've been worried about Petrosky." That, at least, was absolutely true.

"You probably have good reason. How does he seem?"

Not great. All night he'd paced the house, maybe waiting for her to sleep so he could crack a bottle, but she didn't think so. She used to be able to tell when he was drinking, but he'd seemed pretty goddamn sober at the electronics store, and she couldn't imagine Jackson putting up with his shit the way Morrison had. Morrison had an addiction history too—he'd put up with a lot more than he should have.

But so had Shannon.

"He seems stressed," she said now. "But I guess he's like that about every case. Intense. You know how he gets." She watched Decantor's face carefully as his eyes narrowed. He sighed and leaned back against the booth, food abandoned, arms crossed. Her heart launched into her throat.

"You don't have to bullshit me," he said. "I already know."

Her heart stopped. "Know what?" *He knows about the fire, knows about Rebecca and me.* Maybe he'd pull out his cuffs and arrest her right now. No, that was ridiculous.

"About Morrison. Jackson told me he worked on Rebecca Kowalski's kidnapping case back in the day—that woman we're looking for now." He leveled his gaze in her direction. "It's okay if that's why you came back, Shannon. I know he was just involved on the outside, wasn't even a detective yet, but I get how it could feel like a missing piece. Something you can fix for him. He'd be upset if he missed something."

Jackson had thrown Morrison under the bus to explain why she was here. To cover for her. Guilt swelled in her chest. *This is wrong, Shannon. You should come clean, tell Decantor everything.* It's not like a jury would convict her, even if she did look complicit in that fire—in Roman's and Lucius's deaths. Well, probably not. But surely the legal board would look down on her for helping Rebecca escape after a double homicide. A stupid mistake—a bad week—and she might have screwed up her entire life. But if they could solve this…maybe it went away. At the very least, she wanted to be in control of how the story came out. And Morrison would want her here, too—he'd want her to find that kid, make it right. More than once, he'd questioned her on it, pushed her to do more, but he'd let it go…for her sake. Now he was dead. And she'd spent enough years pretending that boy didn't exist, acting like it was someone else's problem. The skin beneath her ring burned.

"So what do you know about the case?" she asked Decantor.

He set his fork aside. "Did you really come here to pry information out of me?"

Yeah, kind of. "Morrison worked on it; I'm just interested. And Petrosky isn't being very open, you know how he is." Would he buy that? She leaned closer over the table. "Let me do this for Morrison. Like you said, it would drive him insane if he thought he missed something. If he thought someone got hurt because of him."

Decantor's eyes narrowed, but he nodded. "Let me tell you a little bit about Joseph Rericha."

19

PETROSKY GLANCED at the fresh coffee Jackson had set on his desk, wishing it was a cigarette and a single malt, then squinted at the pages his partner was sliding onto the wood.

"Piotr was born at home," Jackson said, plopping into the seat beside him. "The home address listed is the warehouse where Rericha used to hold his little meetings, but it doesn't look like anyone else ever lived there." He nodded. Even at the height of Rericha's cult-y reign, members had lived and worked separately; to outsiders, they'd probably just looked like introverts. Jackson went on: "Mother, Kazia Grogan, was admitted to the hospital three days after Piotr's birth and died soon after: preeclampsia. It took a few high-priced lawyers with his history of illegal activities, but Rericha eventually got custody and raised Piotr as his own."

"And no luck on Piotr's real father," Petrosky said. "Nothing in the records. He's not listed on Piotr's or Roman's birth certificate." They knew from the DNA that this mystery man had fathered both Roman and Piotr—the two were full brothers—and that Piotr's father was Rericha's biological son. But the man was a ghost. Knowing his last name, Wójcik, hadn't helped—no one with that name was ever associated with Rericha's cult, not that they could find. They'd even called Pureman to see if he knew the guy since he'd been involved in the group when Piotr was born—nada. All they really knew was that Piotr was the only child aside from Miranda that Rericha had groomed from birth. And what a bang-up job he'd done.

"What about Roman?" Jackson crossed her ankle over the opposite knee, stretching her arms over her head. "He's Piotr's full brother. Why didn't he end up living with Rericha?"

"He was older when Piotr's mother died—almost seventeen—so he went off on his own. And..." He passed her a page, the one Scott had come up to deliver personally. "Remember our midwife, Tanya Jervis? According to her water bottle, she's Rericha's daughter, even though Clark Jervis is listed as the father on her birth certificate." It appeared impregnating as many women as he wanted came with the cult-leader territory. "And Jervis got that clinic of hers fully funded ten years ago by a mystery donor. Can't trace it to Rericha yet, some out-of-country bank account, but..."

Jackson set the page aside and frowned. "I guess we know why Jervis wasn't talking. If she was indoctrinated from the time she was small, got paid off because of her relationship to Rericha... Hell, maybe that's why Rebecca kept skipping appointments, didn't want the family involved with her child, whether or not Jervis was doing anything wrong." They hadn't found evidence of wrongdoing by Tanya Jervis, hadn't found evidence that there was any cohesion or even communication among the group now—no leadership, just Piotr trying to keep their women in line with brute force. Roman, Lucius, and Piotr had been nothing but domestic abusers. Manipulators. Narcissists. Strip away the guise of religion, and that's all any cult really was.

She sighed. "Well, we can't prove Piotr killed his father,"

she said. "We don't even know who his father was. Of the things he told Louisa, we don't know which are accurate and which were lies he used to keep her in line."

"Maybe that doesn't even matter now," Petrosky muttered. No one would miss one more potentially abusive dickhead. "I mean, we had to look into Piotr's father-killing confession, but our more pressing issue at the moment is our two missing suspects: Rebecca, who is guilty of at least a double homicide, and Piotr, who kidnaps women and forces them to hack off their limbs for fun. And of course, we've got this baby thing. For Rebecca to come back here...it's like finding that kid suddenly became more important to her than self-preservation." After seven goddamn years.

Jackson seemed to be thinking the same. "But why now? Because they found her, and she figured it didn't matter anymore? That's what she said on Shannon's voicemail: 'they found me.'"

"But she could have escaped again, gone anywhere." He shook his head. "I think Shannon's right: a missing kid would make returning to Ash Park worth it. And she has to believe he's alive, otherwise what's the point?" His gaze drifted across the bullpen to the window, the afternoon sky gray and dull like the skin of a corpse tossed into a lake by an evil bookkeeper.

"But her being back puts that child in more danger," Jackson said. "One blood test to prove they're related, and we can take Rericha in. The child is as much of a threat to that family as Rebecca herself."

Maybe that's where Piotr's going, to make sure no one ever finds her kid. "So we have to find the child, the same way Rebecca is trying to. Head her off at the pass." But that's what they'd been doing, wasn't it? Getting insight into the group, talking to cult members, looking for links to anyone who might have taken the boy and raised him—Rericha and Piotr sure hadn't.

But Louisa's first thought had been that Rericha would have sold the child. And Hudson had said the same, that Rericha just wanted to make as much cash as he could—that he didn't care how he did it. And after years without a clear source of income…would he have sold Rebecca's baby?

Petrosky glowered at the pile of useless papers on the desktop—birth certificates, DNA reports, Kazia Grogan's rap sheet and death certificate. Nothing that answered their questions. "I'm going to visit Tyrone," he said. "See if he has an in on Rebecca's missing son."

Tyrone was new to the Ash Park force, but he'd worked trafficking in Phoenix for five years before he transferred up to Detroit. Seemed like a demotion, really, but he had taken the job so he could look after his aging mother—or so Decantor said, that gossip. Either way, his track record spoke for itself. Tyrone had located more missing kids than any other officer in the state. If smoking like a warehouse fire and bitching out suspects were Petrosky's superpowers, Tyrone's was finding children.

But Tyrone was not alone.

Shannon was sitting in the chair across the desk from Tyrone, her blonde hair in a bun, her face scrubbed clean. When she glanced over at Petrosky, his breath caught—god, she looked young. Maybe not teenage young, but young enough to make that "daddy" place in his heart ache.

But instead of telling her that, he snapped: "What are you doing here?"

She sniffed, one side of her mouth turning up, a little spot at the corner puckering. It looked like a freckle, but Petrosky had been there when it held a stitch—when a kidnapper, a killer, still had her locked in a deadly metal collar. "I'm trying to find a child. How about you?" She turned away before he could protest and said to Tyrone: "So how do we track a missing kid?"

"Going broad out of the gate, huh?" Tyrone chuckled, his thick eyebrows dancing over the top of his PC, a computer every bit as decrepit as the one on Petrosky's desk. The overheads caught the shine on his bald head. "When did the kid go missing?"

"About seven and a half years ago," Petrosky grunted. Just after Miranda's suicide. Before Rebecca's kidnapping. "Newborn, male," he finished.

Tyrone pulled his gaze from the screen as Petrosky wedged himself into the seat beside Shannon. The walls here were too close, the chair backs pressed against the plaster—no windows. Had this room once been a closet? But at least the guy got his own office.

"Any idea who might have taken him?" Tyrone asked. "Or where they were headed? City, state, family name?" The PC buzzed, internal circuitry whirring and screeching as if begging them to put it out of its misery.

"If we knew the name of the family who took him in, we wouldn't need you." Petrosky leaned back in the plastic chair, trying to keep the desk from digging into his gut, his shoulder hitting the wall. Shannon smelled like his shampoo.

Tyrone chuckled again, clearly unbothered. Decantor had probably warned the guy that Big Bad Petrosky was an asshole. Or maybe Shannon had.

Maybe they didn't need broad anyway—Rericha wasn't an idiot. "Where would someone stand to make the most money selling a kid?" Sure, Rericha might have simply abandoned the boy, but he was inclined to at least research Louisa's and Hudson's guess that Rericha would follow the cash.

"Babies can be sold for as little as a hundred bucks—sometimes they're re-homed to abusers without a fee. If your suspect found the buyer himself, if there's no other paper trail, you're peeing into the wind." And Rebecca had never filed a missing child report; she didn't have a birth certificate. There was no paperwork whatsoever to link her to a kid outside of the one ultrasound Tanya Jervis had on file. The only thing that would make it more perfect for a baby snatcher was a dead mother, and until this week, Rericha and Piotr thought they had that too.

"But if we're peeing into the wind, at least we're getting something back, right?"

Tyrone blinked. He did not smile. "If you want to get back piss, sure." The silence stretched.

"Maybe we can narrow the search," Shannon said.

Petrosky squinted, imagining Rebecca's face, her brown eyes, then the driver's license picture of her husband—dark hair, dark eyes, square jaw. "The baby was white. Probably has brown eyes, since both parents had brown." He'd briefly entertained the idea that the kid was Piotr's, but it was more likely that Piotr went with her to Jervis's to check out the merchandise. Or to make sure Rebecca showed up for her appointment—make sure she was *listening*. Louisa had said they were big on that.

"Having dark eyes just isn't enough information. Heck, sometimes women pretend to be pregnant if they know the kid's coming; it'd take a blood test to know for sure, and if there's no one to suspect the kid doesn't belong with the new family..." He shrugged.

"So, our best bet is birth certificates?" Shannon asked. "I can't imagine he'd have one unless someone else pretended to be his mother—pretended to give birth to him. So we can look at women who had a baby boy around that time, a home birth so she could sneak the new kid into her household. If the baby's still alive—"

"It's thin as hell," Tyrone said. "You have no clue what country the kid was sold into, or even if he was sold at all. Shit, if they wanted to get rid of the kid, all they'd have to do is drop him off at a fire station, or one of the safe haven baby box things at the hospital. And this is one kid, right? A singular incident? Your suspect isn't likely to have outside connections—he's not hooked up with a trafficking ring. Those are the cases I usually get in here." He said it nonchalantly. His eyes looked haunted.

And he was right. They could look into abandoned and surrendered infants, they could look at birth certificates, focus on home births, but in the end, it was an exercise in futility that wouldn't necessarily help them find Rebecca—wouldn't help them find the child. They'd have better luck beating it out of Piotr. Or Rericha. Were thumb screws still illegal?

Petrosky's phone buzzed, and he pulled it from his pocket —Decantor. Shannon raised an eyebrow—*oh, look at you, answering your cell*—then turned back to Tyrone. But he paused, the cell buzzing again, the air suddenly too thick to breathe. This past week, she'd called him often, and he had avoided her, told himself he didn't want her to know about the liquor, about Morrison…but he'd ignored her when she was in trouble. He really was an asshole. He slapped the cell to his ear hard enough to sting. "You get tired of surfing the web for pictures of J-Lo, or what?" Shannon rolled her eyes at him, but Tyrone chuckled once more.

"Hey, man. Sloan needs you out in Grosse Pointe."

"What the hell is your partner doing way out there? Isn't he with Louisa?"

"Louisa's here; I'm taking her home now. But you know the APB we put out on Piotr Wójcik?"

"Yeah. Did they get him?"

"Not exactly." Decantor paused. "They just found his body."

20

The waves of Lake Saint Clair slapped at Piotr Wójcik's graying cheek, far softer than he deserved, but at least someone had hit him harder before they'd arrived; the man's temple was a gaping crater. Much of the blood had been washed away, but fragments of shattered bone poked through the flesh around his eyebrow and above the eye socket, his lid distorted and angry. The other eye stared blankly at the sky.

"Couple of kids came out to walk the beach, found him near the shore." Jackson crouched, careful to avoid the driftwood scattered amidst the rocky sand. Definitely evidence of a struggle—splintered branches, sharp stones, deep gouges in the earth from someone digging in their heels. "They're giving their statement to the locals, but whoever did this was long gone by the time the kids got here; he's been dead a while."

"Looks like he didn't make it far after he ran off." Petrosky squinted, examining the crown of bone along Piotr's brow ridge—no sign of splinters or muck, not what you'd expect if he'd been bludgeoned with a piece of driftwood, and none of the branches here appeared stained. Pipe?

Maybe a metal bat. Tire iron. Something substantial, but more critically, not something you'd find lying around the shore. The killer had probably brought it with them—premeditated.

"Hopefully, Scott will be able to find some DNA," Jackson muttered to the dead man. "Water probably compromised a lot of it, though. It was smart, doing it here, I'll give her that."

Petrosky nodded, mute, and stared into Piotr's glassy eye. *Did you do this, Rebecca?* But he already knew the answer, and while she might be cleaning up a mess the justice system had failed to, he couldn't let her run around murdering people.

Jackson looked up. "What?"

Had he spoken out loud? "Nothing." He cleared his throat and straightened, squinting past the body where footprints dented the sand: smaller, two pairs of shoes, probably the kids who'd found Piotr's corpse. Behind him, his sneakers and Jackson's boots marred the shoreline along with several other sets of prints—work boots from the tread, maybe the first responders. Nothing that looked like Piotr's or their killer's; too big to be Rebecca's. They might find some prints closer to the lot, though; in the summer, the low metal benches were surely surrounded by bluegrass and wildflowers, but now, the ground was heavy with thick black mud, the kind that sucked at your shoes. All he could see of the lot itself were the tall spires of sodium lights ready to bathe this place like a football stadium once the sun went down—Jackson's Escalade wasn't visible from here, and the entrance to the nature trails was hidden behind the hill. But he didn't see signs of a struggle anywhere between the dump site and the lot. When Piotr had fought back, he'd already been by the water where the tide could wash the remnants of the scuffle away. "Looks like Piotr walked down on his own."

Jackson straightened. "He probably thought he could get the upper hand with her. He was a decent-sized guy, two hundred pounds of muscle."

Petrosky raised an eyebrow. "You sweet on him? Does Acharya know?"

"Shut up, Petro—"

"I'm just saying, he can be as big as he wants, it doesn't take a bodybuilder to kill someone with a lead pipe." And if Rebecca had been down here waiting for him, maybe he hadn't seen the weapon until it was too late.

He headed away from the body, up the hill, and dragged his gaze from the vehicles parked on the asphalt to the green trash cans to the tree line beyond. "You see the car?"

"Eyes failing you, old man?"

"If Piotr drove here to meet her, we should have another car—his car." He gestured to the lot: police cruisers, Jackson's ride, but no Camaro. Had the killer moved it? Why bother? She hadn't even tried to hide the body. *She stole it so she could run off again—she's probably halfway through Indiana by now.*

Jackson was staring at the lot as if Piotr's car might suddenly materialize. Maybe they'd been wrong about the motivation—the kid. Maybe the only thing Rebecca had wanted out of Piotr's house was Piotr himself.

Piotr was *The Fixer.*

And Rebecca had fixed him.

21

THE VULTURES SHOWED up as dusk was falling, their makeup cartoonish after staring at Piotr's gray corpse, their flashing cameras brighter than the sodium lights that illuminated the shoreline, brighter even than the floods Scott was using to collect evidence. Piotr's body was already on the medical examiner's gurney, but that didn't stop one particularly testy reporter, a man wearing more makeup than the most ostentatious prostitute, from stepping past the crime scene tape and onto the muddy shoreline. They'd already swept it, but damn if it wasn't a dick move.

"Idiot," Jackson said as they passed. The sound of the flatfoots running their way to pull the reporter back was music to his ears, but Petrosky paused as they stepped beside the journalist, his fancy reporter suit shiny even in the dim. The man smiled. Petrosky smiled back. Then Petrosky jumped, mud splattering his jeans, but more critically, covering the man's fancy khaki-colored slacks.

The reporter leapt back, leg tangling in the crime tape, his eyes blue marbles surrounded by concealer. "Hey, what the hell?"

"Oh man, sorry about that." Petrosky stooped and wiped a

hand across his jeans, gritty, wet, then reached over and touched the man's white shirt and watched the streaks of brown materialize—twin smears of mud on the douchebag with the microphone. "You're standing in the wrong spot, fuck-o."

The man's face twisted grotesquely, a vengeful, angry clown. The muddied reporter lunged, but the officers who'd rushed up behind Petrosky grabbed the journalist's arms, and as Petrosky stepped over the crime tape after Jackson, the man was already being escorted to his news van.

"Real mature," Jackson muttered, but she was smirking. "Wipe your shoes off before you get into my car, I don't want mud all over the floor mat."

"I wouldn't dream of messing up your precious floor mat." He shuffled across the lot, dragging his feet, a harsh grinding sound cutting through the din of the reporters—fresh salt, little grains of white glimmering in the dusky light. But the salted ice gave way to water as they headed toward the pines where Jackson had parked, and soon he was dragging his sneakers through puddles, and his feet were already cold and wet from splashing the journalist. He couldn't feel his toes. *Still worth it.*

"Piotr wasn't tortured like you'd expect if she was trying to get information," Jackson said, unlocking the car with a *blip*. "Whatever she was after when she broke into Piotr's house, she's moved on to revenge now. We might need to get Rericha into protective custody."

"I'm not protecting that shithead." Misogynistic cult leaders didn't deserve protection.

"We can't just let her kill him."

"Why not?" The wind hissed against his forehead as if trying to drive Jackson's point through his thick skull. "Rericha's not going to agree to protective custody anyway." Not any more than Petrosky was going to get a sweet security system for his house when he was the only one living there—Shannon would be gone again soon. He tried to ignore the way that made his heart squeeze and went on: "And admitting that he needs protective custody means admitting guilt." His cell buzzed.

"No, it doesn't," she scoffed, heading for the driver's side. "Being a whack job's target doesn't mean you've done anything wrong. He's smart enough to know that."

"*Fine*." His phone rang again, and he pulled it from his pocket and glanced at the screen: a local number, but he didn't recognize it.

"You gonna get that?"

He climbed into Jackson's SUV. "Nope."

Jackson slammed the door behind her. The cell buzzed again. "For god's sake." Jackson snapped the phone from his hand and put it to her ear. "Edward Petrosky's answering service, state your business."

Petrosky snorted and buckled his seat belt. "Better you than me," he muttered, but Jackson had gone stock still, her eyes wide. He frowned. "You okay? Is it a telemarketer?"

She pulled the cell from her ear and put it on speaker.

"He got what he deserved, but I didn't do it, you have to believe me." A woman's voice, but Petrosky had never heard it before. Believe her about what?

"I believe you," Jackson said. "Why don't you tell me where you are? We can come to you, talk about it."

"There's nothing to talk about."

"But—"

"I did not kill Piotr."

Realization dawned. Rebecca? He opened his mouth as if to speak, but his tongue had gone dry, a useless lump against his teeth.

Luckily, Jackson had no such issue. "We know there's a lot more going on here—we know about your husband, Lucius, about the kidnapping. We know you've been hurt. But running makes things worse, you have to understand that. And whatever you did to your husband, to Roman—"

"They weren't supposed to die." Was her voice shaking? *Faking, she has to be.* But that thought didn't ease the pressure in his chest.

"We know you worked for Dr. Pureman, Rebecca," Jackson said. "We know about the switched dental records, the—"

"I want to talk to him."

Him. Who? But Jackson was staring his way. *Oh, me?*

Petrosky cleared his throat, and for a moment, he could think of nothing to ask her. Jackson had asked her location already. "Are you injured?" he finally managed.

She paused so long Petrosky thought she'd hung up. "Yes."

"Did Piotr hurt you?"

Another pause. "I just wanted to know where he was."

"Your son?"

A sound that might have been a sob.

Petrosky lowered his voice. "Is he in danger, Rebecca? Do you know who has him?" *Where do we start?* They already knew eye color wasn't going to help.

"Shannon once said I could talk to you. That I could trust you. Can I?"

No, I let people down all the time, Shannon especially, and I can't even make it through the day without a drink. "You can."

"I'll call you back." The line went dead.

22

Jackson was already on her cell, asking Decantor to trace the call. What would they find? The old story about the killer's call coming from inside the house floated into his brain and then dissipated. He looked in the back seat anyway, just to make sure.

Jackson tossed her phone into the cupholder and narrowed her eyes at him. "Looking awfully pensive there, partner."

"We have to at least consider that she's telling the truth. Why would she call otherwise?"

She sighed. "Not the kind of pensive I was hoping for."

Why not, though? It was clear Rebecca was desperate. Until now, she hadn't tried to involve herself in any case, certainly hadn't stuck around long enough to get noticed. There might be other reasons to call—to throw them off, to manipulate them as she had Shannon—but they didn't seem to fit.

He drew his eyes to the passenger window where the charcoal sky had already swallowed the earth at the horizon. "At least we know she's following the investigation. Watching the news closely since she knew Piotr was dead the moment it went live."

"She probably knew before us if she was the one who killed him," Jackson snapped, taking a hard right that made his seat belt lock. "We need to focus on this homicide so we can unravel the rest; it's all connected. This is linked to her kidnapping, linked to her child if she told Shannon the truth about them taking her son. And we know Rebecca is guilty of killing Lucius and Roman—why would she *not* kill Piotr, too? Why stop short of killing the man who made her cut off her hand?"

He frowned, but he couldn't disagree; baby or no baby, Rebecca's kidnapping was a motive in and of itself. The streetlights outside peered down at the car like the eyes of a winged nocturnal predator.

"Let's work Piotr's homicide, and go from there," she said again. "At least this case is here-and-now, which should be easier to solve than some seven-year-old cold case." Her words were tight, louder with every syllable. Either she was frustrated, or she wanted to punch him in the face for suggesting they consider Rebecca was innocent. Probably both. "Rebecca's face is already out there with the press, but if we can track how she got to the lake, figure out what she's driving, if she has Piotr's car...we'll find her. They've got cameras along that stretch of shore, and the security tech is already on his way down to pull the tapes for us."

Petrosky leaned against the door—his body felt heavy. *A drink would help, ask her to stop somewhere, buy her a round.* "At least we can search that asshole's place now," he said instead. "It's even on the way."

Jackson paused. "I don't think—"

"He's dead—he doesn't have privacy protections now, and we need to look for clues about his killer, right? Plus, those tools, the photos of the dead man Louisa mentioned, the dead guy Piotr claimed was his murdered father... With Piotr gone, Rericha could be on his way over there to destroy anything incriminating. Hell, Piotr could even have another victim in there." Better to ask forgiveness than permission, and it wasn't like he could prosecute Piotr now. If he was honest, he wanted to verify whether Rebecca or Louisa had ever been down in that basement, and though he wasn't sure why, he suddenly needed to *see it*, the room that had destroyed so many lives.

"Rericha's not going anywhere; Michaelson's watching him."

"Michaelson. He'll probably see a squirrel and forget what he's doing there."

She rolled her eyes, but she turned on her blinker and eased them off the main drag toward Piotr's place.

The neighborhood was just as he remembered it, right down to the empty carport. Maybe the security cam footage would show Rebecca behind the wheel of his Camaro, a tire iron on the passenger seat, her fingers red with blood.

Petrosky used his Swiss Army knife to jimmy the front door, but the damage from Rebecca's B&E stint made the lock pop with barely a wiggle. The air inside was thick with iron, sweet and cloying in his throat. Had it smelled like this before? He coughed, but the heavy sweetness stuck.

Jackson hit the lights.

Huh. When they'd peeked in the window, the coffee table had been on its back; now, it stood on all four legs in the center of the room. The glass had been swept from the hallway floor, too, but the picture frames had not been rehung—the photos were carefully laid on the hall table, seven pairs of eyes all staring at the ceiling as unmoving and glassy as Piotr's eyes had been. "Looks like we're too late."

"Maybe Piotr came back here before he met up with Rebecca." Her eyes locked on the kitchen. Did that dickwad leave another Rolex out before he bit it? He followed her gaze. No, not the kitchen—the door to the basement was wide open, the blackness beyond a cavernous void. The night of the break-in, there had been no evidence of disturbance, and no reason to sweep the cellar for forensics, not with all the mess upstairs—that had clearly been where a crime had taken place. But now…

The stairway to the basement made his lungs tighten. Not the first time he'd edged his way into a torture chamber, and probably not the last, but the hairs between his shoulders were already prickling with the aggressive energy only a sadist left behind—the air felt wicked.

But the concrete floor was clean. Normal. He gazed at the metal pole in the center of the room, then at the card table against the far wall, the tools on top glinting dully in the meager light. His stomach soured. *That's it—those are the tools Louisa stared at for weeks before she sliced through her own hand.*

"Looks the same as it did before," Jackson said. "Whoever straightened the upstairs didn't bother with this room."

Petrosky could barely hear her; he crossed to the pillar and knelt, the concrete cold beneath his knee as he fingered the metal along the lower third of the pole—deep scratches gouged the finish. Bile rose in his throat. He could almost see Louisa Parson tethered here, her face twisted in agony, her fingers slick with her own blood, and the table…

From down here, it appeared far larger than it had when he'd entered. It was cheap, with folding metal legs, but the items on top confirmed Louisa's story. A small-handled ax. A pair of shears. A set of hunting-camping knives. A hammer. Tools you'd expect for home maintenance, but he'd be willing to bet that Piotr hadn't done a goddamn thing to his yard at any point in the recent past, at least not with these tools. And he had been arrogant enough to just leave them here. Out in the open.

Petrosky squinted at the blade nearest him: some type of hunting knife, once sharp, but the edge was mottled with rust. It'd take a lot of work to get through your own flesh with that, but maybe that was part of the draw—part of the fun. They'd know for sure if they found traces of Louisa's or Rebecca's DNA on the weapons. Or blood from other women they had yet to identify. "I'll call Scott." He pushed himself to standing, his knees creaking in true old-man style. "See what the kid can find with his magical swabs."

THE NUMBER on Petrosky's caller ID, the number Rebecca had called him from, was from the same pay phone Rebecca had used to call the police before her kidnapping—her "help me" call. Shannon's voicemail had come from the same number. No witnesses, but at least they could be sure it was really her; no one else would have known that detail. He was shocked the pay phone was still there, let alone worked—it was an antique, a holdout. Like him.

He squinted at his computer, the bullpen silent save for his irritated sighs. The road that led to the park where Piotr's wet corpse had been found was monitored by surveillance cameras meant to dissuade vandals in the summer months; it had seemed like a lucky break until he'd actually started watching them. He rubbed his aching temples—it was too late for this. Only eight thirty, but it felt like midnight. Maybe he should pop out for a few. Grab a cup of coffee. A shot of Jack. Then he could go all night.

Stop, old man. He ground his teeth, wiped sweat from the back of his neck, and narrowed his eyes at the screen. Early in the day, a couple had driven through with a German shepherd hanging his furry head out the back window. An hour later, they drove out. Around lunchtime, a blond man in a white truck appeared: open back, nowhere to hide Piotr's body, not that he'd thought Piotr had been killed elsewhere and carried to the beach, not with the struggle at the shoreline. Petrosky fast-forwarded. The white truck left, the blond man hanging his arm out the window like a fool—it might be March, but it was still cold. The computer hummed. On the screen, two hours passed, then three. A black man in a green truck zipped up the street, a dozen white bags in the back. And out again. Petrosky paused on the adolescent pair that had found the body, the unfortunate ginger in the driver's seat looking like Carrot Top.

No Camaro. No Piotr. And no Rebecca.

He leaned back in his chair, frustrated. How the hell had Piotr and his killer gotten to the beach? They could have come by boat, but he knew Piotr had been killed on the shore —forensics had confirmed. If they'd come via the water, it would have been far easier to kill Piotr out on the lake and dump his body overboard—less evidence, too. Plus, it was the middle of winter, so a boat would be harder to come by; most boats were winterized and stored during the colder months. That left the hiking paths, but there were at least twenty miles of trails out that way, leading around the lake and through a series of other neighborhoods. No sign of Piotr's car in any of the closer ones, and how far could they really have hiked? How far would Piotr have followed his killer?

Decantor's giant fist knocked on his desk. Petrosky looked up. "What are you still doing here? There a Kardashian reunion special I need to know about?"

"They've never been apart to be reunited, but that's beside the point. Got an Emanuel Latewood in interrogation for you."

Petrosky frowned. "Who?"

"Maintenance guy over on Lake Saint Clair. He watched the reports on the six o'clock news. He might have seen your killer."

23

Interrogation was on the first floor of the Ash Park precinct, a little room with a stainless table that stayed cold no matter how high they cranked the heat.

Petrosky lowered himself into the seat opposite Emanuel Latewood, Jackson at his side, a fresh cup of coffee in his hand. He set the cup in front of Latewood—*Do I know him?*—who glanced at the steaming Styrofoam mug, probably wishing it was whiskey at this hour. Petrosky could relate. Latewood pulled it closer, cupping his hands around it as if they were cold, and... *Ah*, now Petrosky recognized him: the man from the green truck, the one with the white bags in the back. "Thank you for coming down, sir. I hear you have some information for us."

The man's wiry eyebrows kissed in the middle of his forehead. "I think I do, yes. At least, I hope so." He screwed up his thick lips, pucker, relax, pucker, relax. Nervous? But most normal people would be—tattling on a killer wasn't something most took lightly. And they shouldn't.

Jackson nodded to him. "Let's start at the beginning."

Latewood did. He'd been there to apply salt over the lot and to scrape the ice from the front of the trash cans near the nature trail—if they froze up, people tossed things, including bags of dog shit, to the ground, lazy bastards. Latewood had been at the far end of the lot, near the bank of trees Jackson had parked beside, when he heard noises down at the water.

"I didn't think much of it; there are always folks down there. It's a beautiful place to take your dog out. Good thinking spot, too."

Or a good spot to bludgeon someone to death, which is probably why the killer had chosen it. And this man had left in his truck before the teenagers had driven in—the ones who'd found Piotr's corpse. If he'd heard noises down at the water, it was likely he had been present for Piotr's murder. "Did you see anyone at the shore? Or in the park?"

Latewood shook his head. "I feel awful about that. Maybe I should have seen him lying there, gotten help, but I was up at the far side of the parking lot with the salt; it's supposed to ice up again tomorrow, so I was trying to get it done before day's end. But you can't see the shoreline over that ridge there, just the water."

Petrosky thought back to the scene—the sodium lights, the long stretch of beach, the hill. Latewood was right; Petrosky hadn't been able to see the body from Jackson's car or the lot from the shore. It wasn't until they'd stepped off the asphalt and onto that muddy hill that he'd been able to see Piotr's corpse.

"So you were working on the lot, and you heard what exactly?" Jackson said. "Talking? Shouting?" *The wet thunk of metal on brain?*

The man sipped at the coffee and winced. It was hot, but the grimace was probably because precinct coffee tasted like shit—bitter shit. "No, nothing like that. Just a motor out on the water."

On the water. *Goddammit*. Piotr had been killed on the beach, but Petrosky had bumped a boat down his suspect-vehicle list because...it was stupid to kill someone on the beach if you didn't have to. If you were on the water away from all potential witnesses, why not just kill Piotr on board and dump him?

"What kind of boat was it?" Jackson asked.

Latewood took a deep swallow from the Styrofoam cup and then set it on the table. "I'm not sure. A smaller one. White, but it might have been cream or gray, it was hard to tell."

They'd check the boat registrations for people living around the lake, but he doubted it'd be that easy; anyone could have used the boat launch a few miles up the way, and no cameras there, he was almost sure.

"Were there any lights on the boat?" Jackson asked.

Latewood's eyes narrowed. "If there were, he didn't have them on."

He? Petrosky and Jackson exchanged a look. "I thought you didn't see anyone," Petrosky said.

"I didn't see anyone on the shore or in the park, but I saw the guy driving the boat once he got out on the lake."

"You saw a *man* driving the boat?" *Not Rebecca?*

Latewood raised an eyebrow. "Well, yeah. He didn't look especially big, but I'm sure it was a man. Wider shoulders, you know." He raised his hands to demonstrate.

"Hair color?" Jackson said.

"He was wearing a hat and gloves—real cold out there this time of year. All I saw was his back, but I'm sure it wasn't a woman."

Jackson's shoulders had tensed; she didn't feel any better about this development than he did. Either Rebecca had a partner, or they had more than one killer on their hands.

And they had no clue who he was.

24

DAWN. Again. The Jack in his bloodstream made the early morning more bearable, but as lunchtime crept nearer, that warm edge of calm began to dissipate along with his patience.

Piotr had last been seen leaving the hardware store after work on the day he ran off. No one had seen him or his car since—the APB had turned up nothing. Obviously, whatever he'd decided to run away from had caught up with him, and that something wasn't Rebecca; she'd been telling the truth that she didn't kill him. Maybe Rebecca and Piotr had both been scared of the same person. Did that make sense? He couldn't tell anymore.

Petrosky ground his teeth together so hard they squeaked. He'd ran registrations on every boat on the lake— due diligence, but tedious shit, and probably pointless since the killer could have used someone else's. But no one had reported a boat stolen, and there were no names near the lake that rang any bells, no associations with Rericha's group, and though a few boat owners had criminal records—DUIs, marijuana possession, petty theft—none raised his hackles.

A mystery man—perfect. And not even a murder weapon to help them. The ME's guess on the weapon had matched Petrosky's—something long, hard, metal—but it wasn't at the scene. Probably at the bottom of Lake Saint Clair.

He sighed, a headache taking root in his brain. Was it really possible that Rebecca had nothing to do with Piotr's death after she'd broken into his house three days ago? And if that were the case...how were she and Piotr connected to this mysterious boat-driving killer?

He leaned back in his chair and ran a hand over his prickly face as Jackson slid into the seat beside him. "I called Scott about the boats—told him to work his cross-referencing muscles. The kid loves an excuse to research."

He lowered his hand. "You're the best."

"You don't know the half of it." She smirked. "Also, Shannon should be up here soon with coffee."

His heart stalled. "Shannon? She can't just be running around out th—"

"Sloan's with her, relax."

His heart started pumping again, still too fast. Shannon had been pecking away at her keyboard when he'd arrived home last night; no indication that she'd found his booze stash, though she'd barely looked up from the screen. She was obsessed with finding this kid, Rebecca's child, but if Tyrone couldn't do it, he didn't think she'd be able to pull a name and address out of her ass. But it was keeping her occupied. Keeping her *safe*—that was the most important thing.

Jackson was still looking at him.

"Did you send her to Rita's?" he asked. If Shannon was at the coffeehouse, he'd drink the acrid tar in the break room. Bitter as hell, but it kept you honest.

"Of course, I sent her to Rita's. If you're lucky, she'll bring back fries."

He paused. "Did you tell her to bring back fries?"

She ignored him, her eyes darkening—serious. "I've been thinking about that phone call, Petrosky. Rebecca…she has a strategy." He blinked, his brain trying to catch up with the abrupt shift in subject. "Anyone could have gotten Rebecca a car the way Shannon did, and they would have been easier to convince—Shannon's an attorney, less likely to buy into the idea of circumventing the law. Shannon doesn't make sense unless Rebecca was purposely choosing people who were above suspicion."

Or who had something to lose—who wouldn't come forward after she bait-and-switched them. He frowned, thinking. What was she getting at? "I mean, okay, fine, but—"

"She knows how to pick her marks," Jackson continued. "That's my main point. She could be scared someone is setting her up, or she might just want to distract you, but you and I both know Piotr's killer could be involved with her. *That's* the reason she called you directly—to put that doubt in your head."

Ah, there it is. "So, you think *I'm* a mark?"

"I think you have a tendency to believe things other people wouldn't, especially when it comes from a young woman you think you can help. And didn't Shannon deny mentioning you to Rebecca?" Yeah, she had—that *Shannon said I could trust you* comment was apparently a lie. "She has a sixth sense for identifying vulnerability and using it to her advantage."

His shoulders tensed; his stomach burned with acid. The fries couldn't get here soon enough. "This isn't about me, Jackson. She hasn't asked me for anything."

"Not anything action-oriented—yet. But she did ask you to believe that she was innocent, and you sure did that."

"Maybe I considered it"—*am still considering it*—"but we're right to. A man was driving that boat, not Rebecca."

"A guy she probably put up to it; that's what she does, Petrosky. She exploits people's weaknesses and gets them to do things they wouldn't ordinarily do. Even Gargano—he's a decorated arson investigator and FBI consultant, too good at his job not to know something was wrong with that fire. And he was vulnerable then, suffering through a divorce." But that didn't make him complicit, and they had no evidence that he'd done anything illegal. Jackson's gaze drifted to the bullpen beyond him, to Decantor's empty desk. Sloan's empty seat. "At least we know Gargano didn't kill Piotr," she said. "I called Oaklawn. Franklin Gargano was passed out in the hospital when Piotr was murdered, and I don't think he has the strength to hurt anyone even if he had miraculously walked out." And Pureman, a man who had seemed sweet on Rebecca, who had seemed anxious to protect her, had been performing a root canal when Piotr was killed—he'd checked that one out himself, even before this little speech. Maybe they were on the same page, after all.

Petrosky nodded. "Fine, so Rebecca's a manipulative genius of the highest order, an accomplice-finding extraordinaire. Who'd she tap to kill Piotr? And how did Rebecca even know where to find him?" They'd looked for him, used every Ash Park resource at their disposal, but they didn't even know where his car was, and that yellow Camaro was anything but inconspicuous.

Jackson shrugged. "Maybe she, or her partner, were watching Piotr's house—followed him when he left. Or maybe she already knew where he might go; it's possible the family has a hideout somewhere. I'm more concerned with how she got Piotr to Lake Saint Clair. If Piotr had something to do with Rebecca's missing son, if he ran away because she came back, he wouldn't have gone out there to meet her."

How did you get him into that boat, Rebecca? No ligature marks on him, so the killer hadn't tied him up, and the ME hadn't found drugs in Piotr's system. Had to be someone

Piotr knew, right? But if that person was also connected to Rebecca... He cleared his throat, but the mucus there felt thick—heavy with nicotine. "What you said about her knowing who to target, who will help her...what if this man who killed Piotr was someone she knew before she faked her death? Someone from her past, before her marriage even?"

Jackson shook her head, her gaze on the desktop. "We looked into her though, as did Apmada during the kidnapping—no family, and she didn't have any friends by the time she married Lucius, which made her a perfect target for the cult-y shit they were into." Her brow furrowed. "You're thinking before that? A childhood friend?"

"If she's involved, I can't see her hiring it out; if she hired a hitman to stay clear of Piotr's death, she'd have paid someone to break into Piotr's house for her, too. And I think her taking advantage of someone she knows well is more likely than exploiting a new relationship—she'd have to drag a new guy back with her from wherever she's been hiding." Right? He couldn't tell if he was making sense anymore—he needed something to take the edge off, something more significant than fries and coffee and nicotine. He raised his fingers to his temples, where a headache was steadily spreading across the front of his skull. "Maybe it isn't even someone she's involved with," he said. "Maybe it's just someone who cares about her, knows what Piotr did to her, someone who—"

"Are you kidding?"

He massaged his temples harder—the pain stuck. "She said she didn't do it. We can't just ignore—"

Jackson threw her hands in the air hard enough to make him startle; he released his head. "That's what I'm talking about, Petrosky! She's screwing with you. Every single time it's a younger woman, someone who seems like they need your protection, you want to give them the benefit of the doubt. But sometimes, the young, pretty woman is a goddamn murderer."

He watched her stalk back to her own desk, his brain throbbing, throbbing, throbbing.

Yeah, maybe Jackson was right. Rebecca was a killer.

But something had turned her into one.

25

"Alright, you go first," Jackson said, setting her manila folder on the desk.

Petrosky shoved a cold french fry into his mouth. Shannon had brought burgers, too, Detective Sloan in tow, the stocky Irishman looking a little too gleeful that he got to play chauffeur—was he married? *Better be.* Petrosky washed the fry down with coffee and turned Jackson's way. "Rebecca was a foster kid, spent her entire life being bounced from house to house until she married Lucius just weeks after she turned eighteen." Sounded like she'd been desperate for love; McCallum would have called it "attachment issues" or some such shrink-y melodrama. Rebecca probably hadn't realized how messed up their family was until it was too late.

He slid a few printed pages across the desk toward her. "These are the guys who crossed paths with Rebecca during her foster-home years." If she'd known her accomplice before she left, these were the people she was associated with, and lots had criminal records—it was a stretch, a big one, but one of them might have met Piotr, accidentally or intentionally, and been able to lure him to that boat. No friends more recent that he could find; once she met her husband, she stuck to Lucius's immediate family, and none of them were alive now except Rericha.

Jackson took the sheets from him. "I'll pull these guys up, see if there's anything glaring—maybe one has a history with a lead pipe." She squinted at the names of the foster kids, or maybe at his scribble-scrabble notes about the crimes they'd been convicted of, but when she raised her face, she had a glimmer in her eye.

"While you were looking at her old friends, I found something more interesting." She set the pages aside and snatched up his last fry, then said around the potato: "We know she set that fire and ran off without much cash, right?"

He nodded. Despite what she'd told Shannon, Rebecca hadn't taken any money from the house, and Lucius's bank accounts had remained untouched. Which meant no one had a reason to suspect her of foul play—or faking her death.

"Broke and living under an assumed, she'd have had to think on her feet—maybe seek help," Jackson continued. "There are a few domestic violence programs across the country that hook women up with under-the-table jobs, but I didn't get any hits on the fake-ID name Shannon gave us; she must have dropped that the moment she crossed state lines. But she had worked for Pureman, so I thought she might have gotten into something similar after the fire: dental receptionist, office worker, candy striper in a small-town health clinic that might pay an employee cash. And I found one clinic where the doctor herself is a survivor—someone who might make a good mark if I were trying to hide. And with that missing hand, who'd say no?"

"Cold." Manipulative. *Desperate.*

She leaned back in the chair, pulled a printed photo from her manila folder, and slapped it onto the desk in front of him. "Meet Deanna Nowak."

He narrowed his eyes at the image. "Is this from social media?"

"Yup. It's the only picture of her on the web, from the doctor's Christmas party. A tiny town in Briddiss, Pennsylvania. I doubt Rebecca even knew this photo was taken; she doesn't have a profile that I could find, and the doctor hasn't called back yet—hopefully, she can fill in some blanks for us."

Petrosky studied the grainy shot. Her hair was lighter, but "Deanna Nowak" had the same heart-shaped face as Rebecca, the same freckles, and one hand short of a pair. Face in a perpetual frown, as if she'd forgotten what happiness looked like. Her good hand rested on the shoulder of a little boy: slight, five or six years old, dark hair, lots of freckles. But where Rebecca had brown eyes, this little boy had bright blue eyes, the color of a sapphire.

"Who's the kid with her?"

"Her son, Christopher Nowak. At first, I thought this was the kid she accused Rericha of stealing, but he was born in the hospital seven months after the fire. This boy isn't the same child."

What a ride this case is. So, Rebecca had been pregnant with her first child, as confirmed by the midwife. That baby had been taken by Rericha. Soon after, she'd been kidnapped and had returned without her hand, maybe in retaliation for filing a police report. And right after the kidnapping... *Shit.* She'd found out she was pregnant again. "Well, there's our trigger for faking her death—she knew she had to get out of here, or they'd take the second kid the way they did the first."

Jackson nodded. "Right. And here's where the plot thickens." She pulled another page from the folder. Petrosky blinked, trying to force his eyes to focus on the tiny print—a death certificate, dated three weeks ago. For...Christopher Nowak. *Damn.* He ran a hand down his face, the stubble long enough now not to catch on his fingers. When was the last time he'd shaved?

"The reports say hit and run," she said, but her tone whispered *bullshit*. "No witnesses. There was blue automotive paint at the scene, but it's too common to trace. They also found part of a muffler from an old Chevelle, so Briddiss PD looked at every Chevelle within city limits, and checked registrations within three hours of the crime scene—nada. And no body shops in the state reported a car coming in with that piece missing, and none ordered that part for a customer in the weeks following Christopher's death."

So the driver was laying low. But they didn't need to solve the hit-and-run case to solve their case, did they? Something about it was nagging at him, a needle deep in his gray matter. What was he missing? Yeah, the timeline was too perfect for Rebecca's return to be unconnected, but the connection could simply be that she no longer cared what happened to her.

Jackson seemed to be thinking the same because she said: "She probably always wanted her first child back, but she had to consider that they'd take Christopher, or hurt both her and her son if they found out she was alive. Rebecca protected Christopher by staying away."

And now that was over. Now she was back here, looking for her stolen child because she'd lost her…. *Oh.* The needle in his brain wiggled, a persistent stinging itch. *They found me*—that's what she'd said on Shannon's voicemail…and then she'd told Shannon to protect her kids. At the time, it had struck him as odd—Shannon's kids weren't involved in this—but had Rebecca seen firsthand what this family was capable of? Had she watched them kill her son?

Petrosky tapped the page. "This hit-and-run thing… I'm not buying it was an accident."

Jackson nodded. "You check if anyone in Rericha's family has access to a Chevelle. I'll call Woolverton."

26

Dr. Woolverton was a smarmy little twerp with the attitude of a much larger man. They met him in the morgue, his thick glasses halfway down his nose, his eyes on the stainless table as he tugged a blue sheet up over a dark-skinned man with an ice-pick sized hole in his cheek.

"Thanks for seeing us," Jackson said.

Woolverton nodded and peeled his gloves from his thin fingers, then took the file from Jackson's outstretched hand. "It's easier to make an accurate assessment if I can examine the body, but I'll give you what I can." He frowned as he read. And flipped. And read.

Cold air crept down Petrosky's shirt. He shuddered, though it might have been more from the images within that file—the pictures of that poor boy's body, first on the curb, then on the slab. Had Rebecca come outside to find his shattered corpse unmoving on the concrete, sidewalk chalk clutched in his still-warm hand? Had a neighbor held her back? Had she cradled his head and screamed at the sky, all the while trying desperately to find the words to say goodbye for the last time?

But he had done none of those things with Julie's body. Maybe Rebecca had just stood on the porch and stared, feeling her last shred of hope evaporate.

"Well, it looks like a hit and run on the surface," Woolverton said, bringing Petrosky back. "There are a few inconsistencies, though." He pointed, thin finger sliding over one of the glossy images, over pale flesh and bloody bone. "Here, you've got a compound fracture, which almost always occurs on the side opposite the impact—this one is as I'd expect. But there's a second compound fracture on the other side, which likely means the vehicle ran over the body again."

The car had backed up just to make sure he was dead? The cool air on Petrosky's back heated—his chest burned.

"So, this *was* a homicide," Jackson said.

"Not necessarily. If the vehicle ran up on the curb and then had to reverse to the street, it's possible this was the result of them backing up for that reason. It could also have happened if the boy was thrown from the initial impact; if he was struck and landed on the concrete in front of the car, then the driver panicked and pressed the gas, hitting him a second time..." He shrugged, but his face was stricken; his nostrils flared. *He's as angry as I am.* "I can't testify that it was purposeful. But from the photos of the scene, the position of the body near the curb... They'd have been able to avoid him if they wanted to. My gut says they didn't want to."

Petrosky frowned. "You're not really a gut guy, Doc."

"No, I'm not." Woolverton closed the folder and leveled a steely gaze at Jackson, then Petrosky. "Whoever did this, accident or not...I hope you find him. And I hope you throw the book at him."

"I'll throw more than that at him, Doctor." He took the folder and tucked it beneath his arm, the photos of young Christopher Nowak's broken body hiding within it. Dead. Because someone had wanted it that way.

This wasn't about a stolen baby years ago—this was about

a dead boy weeks ago. She'd lost her child, and as soon as his body had been taken away, Rebecca had packed her things and headed for a place she'd killed to escape from.

She'd come here to punish the man who killed her child. And Petrosky was inclined to let her.

27

Shannon watched Petrosky's face as he shook his head and leaned back in his dining chair. "I don't know, Shannon. I don't see anything we can use." Duke grumbled his agreement, his giant head pressed firmly into Petrosky's lap, the flecks of graying fur around his muzzle vibrating with his flapping lips.

"I'll keep on Christopher, see where that leads," he said. "It's bullshit that Rebecca has you running around looking for her stolen baby when she doesn't even have the decency to give us an interview." But Petrosky's eyes looked more defeated than irritated for once, the hair on his cheeks soft with the beginnings of a beard. Evie had always liked it when he grew it out—maybe that was why he was growing it out, actually, waiting for a snippet of video chat. You never could tell whether the beard was because he was depressed or because he was doing that father-grandfather thing, but Shannon hoped it was the latter.

She shoved the laptop aside. Decantor had said the same as Petrosky, that Rebecca was jerking them around, and she knew it was true, but fucking hell. Every day here felt more pointless than the last, and what Petrosky had just told her about this second child, this dead child...it was not just the pointlessness. Every new piece of information felt like a punch to the gut—they were due for some good news, but she wasn't sure it would ever arrive.

She had hoped to locate a kid related to Rebecca in one of the genealogy databases or among other missing and exploited kids. Decantor had sent off a sample of Rebecca's blood from Piotr's living room, but there was nothing in any database, official or non-official, that they could find. And there were far too many birth certificates to sift through, especially since they couldn't even be sure the kid had stayed in state. She'd even looked up the couple who'd lived next door to Rebecca at the time of the missing baby's birth, chatted them up for an hour. No one even appeared to recall that Rebecca had been pregnant, and they had no reason to lie—no connection to Rericha. She'd found no one he might have passed the kid off to. After Rericha had been arrested, the congregation just vanished along with the lease on the warehouse.

Tyrone had been right; this kid could be anywhere. "I hate fucking everything," she snapped, planting her elbows on the table and resting her head in her palms. Her hair fell like a curtain over her eyes.

"I'd imagine anyone would," Petrosky said, his voice low, serious. "You'd chafe after a while. Maybe better to only fuck *some* things, see if you hate that as much."

She straightened in time to see Petrosky shrug, his eyes still on Duke—rubbing the dog's silky ears without even a hint of a smile. "You're impossible, you know that?"

"No more impossible than you, kid." He met her gaze. "And that's okay. Impossible people get things done, even when we have to put ourselves in places we don't want to be."

Was that a dig at himself? But no, he probably meant that she was away from her children.

She sighed. If she'd gotten Miranda away from Roman,

managed to get him convicted, even protected Rebecca sooner, maybe Rebecca's kid would be with his mother right now instead of god knew where. But that wasn't the only reason she was pushing this: her husband wouldn't have let it go. How many times had Morrison tried to get her to look at this case again—at the kid? She glanced down; her fingers were already twisting her wedding band, around, around, around. "It's hard being away from Evie and Henry, but I have to do this. If Rericha stole her child, we'll make him pay for that and make sure Rebecca's son gets the life he deserves."

"I understand." His voice was so low she barely heard him over the throbbing of her heart—when had it started racing?

"I'm not sure you do, Petrosky."

"I understand." His eyes were steady, patient, but edged with heat.

Why did this feel like an argument? "I mean, I know you want to find the kid so you can get the killer, but—"

"Morrison wouldn't have stopped until he found that kid." His eyes suddenly dropped to the table as if the woodgrain held a mystery he had to solve. He raised his hand from Duke's face and rubbed at the center of his chest. "He would have been pissed at himself for just sitting in that car outside her house, eating granola bars; he'd be sorry for burning the file, even if it was for a good reason; he'd be feeling like he missed something important. We can't read that surfer boy's mind, but we both know he would have wanted you to find Rebecca's boy." He released his chest and put his hand on her arm, gaze still on the wood as if he couldn't bear to look at her. "I. Under. Stand."

The heat of his palm radiated into her chest, calming her heart, making all the muscles in her body suddenly heavy—weak. "Then why aren't you looking for this kid just as hard as I am?"

This appeared to pain him; his jaw went tight, and he

released her arm, leaned back in his chair, and finally looked her way. Duke stared as if waiting for his master to scratch his ears again, and when Petrosky didn't, the dog grumbled and stalked from the room. "I wish I could do more," Petrosky said, "but I've got nothing. Our best bet to find the boy is to jam up Rericha—if he knows where the kid is, and I get him on something else, maybe he'll cough up a location to ease his sentence."

Yeah, right. "That means he has to confess to taking the baby in the first place."

Petrosky crossed his arms over his gut—bigger than the last time she'd seen him. She'd gotten some groceries yesterday, but when she'd arrived, the man hadn't had a single vegetable in his house. "I can be very persuasive," he said.

But they had nothing on Rericha, no official statements, no witnesses to any wrongdoing. *You need to get a warrant, toss that asshole's house.* Rericha had owned that place for fifty years, had lived there when Rebecca's child had been taken—there should be something there. *Anything.*

He sniffed, and his eyes drifted over her shoulder toward the kitchen. "Once we have more evidence that links Rericha to the child, to Piotr's disappearance, to Rebecca's kidnapping, to *fucking anything*, I'll work on a warrant."

Dammit. How did he read her mind like that?

He pushed himself to standing, a low sound rumbling in his throat, almost like a groan.

Her heart seized. *Just take care of yourself, you jerk!* But her agitation was muted by worry. "You okay?"

"Yeah." He opened the fridge. "Want a beer?"

Her jaw dropped. *No, no, no, no, no.* She whirled in her seat, fists clenched. "What the…? You can't—"

He peeked over the top of the refrigerator door. Smiling. And…there was no beer in there, she'd filled that fridge herself. She slumped back in the seat. "Jesus. You're killing me, Petrosky."

"Yeah, I'm killing us both." He slammed the fridge empty-handed and swiped a wide rectangular donut box from the counter; he'd had it when he arrived home, but she'd ignored it and waved him over to her computer. Now, he tossed it onto the table in front of her. So much for that healthy grocery thing. And yet, her mouth watered—one more night of junk food wouldn't hurt.

She flipped the top and peeked inside. All Boston cream; her favorite. She raised her eyes as he slid back into the seat across from her. "You remembered?" And there it was: that inexplicable kindness that often showed up at the least opportune times...like when she wanted to be pissed. He might be a dick sometimes, might vanish because he had no way to cope with his demons—a skill she'd had to learn, being a single mom—but he was her friend, and the closest thing she'd ever had to a real father. And in her desperation to distance herself from her grief, she'd just left him here. Alone.

He reached across the table and grabbed a donut from the box. "Remembered what? I love these."

She raised an eyebrow. "Evie told me you said they taste like snot."

He took a bite, chocolate clinging to his lips. "See? So good." But he winced as he swallowed.

She laughed and snatched up her own. "There are so many, though. We should share with the neighbors."

He set his donut on the table and wiped sugar from his lips with the back of his hand. "They have their own box, I dropped them off on the way in—bear claws. Jane doesn't like these. She says they taste like snot."

"Well, aren't you generous," Shannon said, shoving a bite into her mouth. Creamy, sweet, and perfect. "We should eat this every day while I'm here."

He nodded, but his gaze dropped to the table again. Strange how it looked like shame.

28

The heated seats in Jackson's Escalade were making his ass sweat, an affront matched by the little smear of dirt that glared at him from his door, probably from the day he'd kicked mud at the journalist. He stretched down to wipe it away, though Jackson had probably already seen it, but kept his eyes focused on the window in case she hadn't.

With Piotr gone, Louisa seemed safe, though Petrosky had paid for her hotel for the rest of the week anyway—she had cried when he told her Piotr was dead. And laughed. Good riddance to that asshole. But regardless of his thoughts on the family or Rebecca's motivations, they still had to find the man who'd had killed Piotr and left him on that beach. Surely someone working with Rebecca—she'd had help with past crimes, why not now?

Their hunch had been confirmed this morning. They'd finally spoken to the doctor Rebecca had worked for in Pennsylvania and the landlord of the house she'd rented for the last five years along with every Pennsylvania neighbor of hers they could find. They all said the same thing: Rebecca had been living with a man in Briddiss, though none were certain of his name—he'd told one neighbor it was Chuck, and another it was Tom, so he clearly wasn't using his own. And according to her employer, this man was not a new love interest; Rebecca had told her they'd been friends since high school. It was possible Rebecca had lied to the woman, but he didn't think so, which meant his long-shot idea about Rebecca's early associates had been *right*—he'd never let Jackson live that down. And if this man and Rebecca were involved during the warehouse fire, if he'd been her accomplice then as well as now, that would explain how she'd managed to get Roman and Lucius into the building. If she'd drugged them in the warehouse, they wouldn't have just stood there while the drugs took effect—one or the other would have tried to stumble out. It was more likely they were already unconscious, maybe kissing death, when Rebecca and her partner had dragged them inside and lit the building aflame.

But despite knowing that this partner existed, he had no name. The man living with Rebecca in Briddiss had no driver's license. No job that they could find.

"I wish we could prove Piotr was the one who hit Christopher," Jackson said, her eyes fixed on the hazy afternoon beyond the dashboard. "He's an abusive psycho; I can see him killing a kid, and he was the one Rebecca seemed to be after. Plus, that douchebag sure does love his muscle cars." But they hadn't found a Chevelle registered to anyone in the family, and Piotr had no credit card receipts going toward Pennsylvania in the last month. That didn't mean he hadn't, though—the family was careful, and they knew how to hide their money. But still...why kill Christopher? If Piotr had found Rebecca, why not kill her instead? To make her suffer the way Piotr himself had suffered the loss of his brother and his uncle?

Jackson frowned at the road as she eased them up the freeway off-ramp.

"We can confirm it was Piotr if we talk to her," he said. "Whether she came here to find the kid Rericha took, or for revenge for Christopher's death, she went right for Piotr's house." And she'd made the decision quick—she vanished almost immediately after the hit and run, didn't even talk to the police; she was still a person of interest there. But so far, Briddiss PD hadn't connected their hit and run to Rebecca's current case in Ash Park, probably because of the different names—Nowak and Kowalski weren't similar enough to raise any red flags. But it was only a matter of time; Rebecca's photo was all over the place.

"Yeah, like she'd start helping us." Jackson shook her head. "And this partner has to be as screwed up as she is. Shacking up with her, playing daddy to her kid, becoming an accessory to multiple murders? That's a lot for anyone to swallow." Jackson squinted out the windshield, hit the blinker, and pulled into the drive of a modest beige-brick colonial; three windows on the upper floor, each flanked by bookends of red aluminum. Red door the color of fresh blood. Hopefully, the last house of the day—they'd already been to five other foster homes. Lots of good people in these places, but a lot of sorrow too. The slamming of the car doors echoed through the air as they strode over the front lawn.

The hairs pricked on the back of his neck, and he adjusted the collar of his sports coat—Shannon had frowned when she'd seen his sweatshirt this morning—but no breeze was brushing the skin there. Maybe he was just irritated in general. It was weird to have other people in his house, but nice, so long as he didn't think about the liquor beckoning him from under the kitchen cupboard. Shannon was better than Jack, of course, but a piece of him didn't believe that. And that made him hate himself all the more.

He rubbed harder at his neck, the skin still prickling with a familiar kind of unease; it wasn't the jacket—someone was watching him. He looked up to see a young moon-faced child staring down from the middle window, his nose flattened against the glass. The boy waved.

Petrosky smiled.

"You coming?"

He lowered his gaze. Jackson stood at the front door, her fist raised like she might punch someone, but she was probably just getting ready to knock. Less interesting, but more professional.

The woman who answered the door had hair the color of the muddy front lawn, cut as severely as the sharp line of her mouth. She looked like the type of person who never smiled. Maybe she didn't know how.

She raised an eyebrow when they introduced themselves, then both eyebrows when they mentioned Rebecca's name, but stepped back so they could enter. They followed her into the living room, the foyer strangely pristine despite the six children who supposedly lived there—shiny wood floors, no scrapes from toy trucks, no errant sneaker marks. No shoes kicked off by kids running in and out. This was the house where teenaged Rebecca had stayed the longest—she'd been here with Patty and Carlo Moletti nearly six months near the end of her high school career. Moletti gestured to the sofa and sank onto a high-backed wooden seat across from them.

"Moletti, like the mathematician?" Petrosky said when he and Jackson were settled on her couch. The plastic cover squealed under his ass.

Jackson gaped at him—*dammit, Jackson, I know lots of shit*—but Moletti just frowned. "My daddy was a plumber."

Tough crowd. And this place... Silent as a tomb. "Where are all the children, Mrs. Moletti?"

"It's studying time. They'll be down for dinner."

Dinner? It wasn't even two o'clock, and the little boy in the upper window hadn't looked like he was studying. He didn't look like he was even old enough to study on his own. At five, you shouldn't be studying anything more than how to shove twelve cookies into your maw while someone else read Dr. Seuss on repeat. "You must run a pretty tight ship here."

"No other way to do it." She sniffed. "Not that it ever mattered for *that* girl."

"Sounds like you remember Rebecca pretty well," Jackson said. Her tone was low, careful, but Petrosky could hear the tense undertones beneath it, the accusation no one but him would be able to discern. She probably didn't like the tomb-like atmosphere in this place any more than he did.

"*She* was trouble. I'm not surprised you're here asking about *her*." Moletti crossed her legs, her knobby knees spiderwebbed with thick blue veins that looked like bulging coils of yarn. "She came to live with us halfway through her junior year. They told me she might be trouble. Sounded like she'd accused her last foster family of"—her eyes darted behind them—"rape." The last word she whispered. "Accused her foster brother, if you can believe that."

He could believe it. He could also believe that the family had conveniently forgotten to mention it when he and Jackson had visited them this morning. They'd have to research that one a little further, even if the statute of limitations was up by now. "Were charges filed?"

She shook her head. "No, it didn't stick; she was known for making up stories."

Making up stories about rape? Perhaps this was where Rebecca had learned that the police and her "family" weren't to be trusted—where she realized that taking justice into your own hands was the only option. He forced his face to remain neutral. And bit his tongue.

If Moletti sensed his disdain, she didn't show it; she laced her fingers primly on one veiny baseball of a kneecap. "Anyway, she came to live here, and things went wrong *right* away." She looked at them pointedly, as if they were supposed to read her mind.

"Meaning…" Jackson prompted.

"If you had kids, you'd understand." Practically patting herself on the back.

His hackles rose. "Explain it to me like I'm an idiot. Or some dumb kid." Petrosky flashed her a smile that he hoped didn't look too malicious, but his toes were itching to kick her brittle shin. "Was she giving you attitude? Kids these days…no respect, right?"

"Right, *exactly*." One corner of Moletti's tight little mouth turned up. "No respect at all. She didn't want to come down to family dinners. Didn't want to study."

Withdrawn, after a rape? Crazy. "Sounds like she was depressed, Mrs. Moletti." There were so many sympathetic, loving, downright fantastic foster parents out there—how'd Rebecca get the shit luck to end up here?

Moletti leveled a hard glare his way, a look that was probably effective with ten-year-olds, but it only made him want to kick her more. "Depressed or no, we tried to make it better for her. But she never did like us. *Me* especially."

"I can't imagine why, Mrs. Moletti. I mean, it's not like you ever hit her or anything, right?" He watched her face, looking for signs of guilt or regret. The woman's nostrils flared.

"No, I didn't hit her. She was too old to spank."

If that was the only reason, maybe they should be worried about the other kids under this roof, even if spanking wasn't technically illegal. But they weren't just here to discuss Rebecca's history—they needed to know who her friends were. They needed to find the man she'd run off with, most likely, the man in the boat. The man who had lived with her in Briddiss—someone she'd known since high school.

"Was there anyone, friends, other kids in the house, that she seemed to have a special connection with?" They'd asked the same of the other foster parents they'd met, but none had remembered any significant relationships or conflicts—not even the couple from the home where she'd been raped.

"Ah, yes, she and Stewart had…something." Moletti leaned back in the chair as far as the straight back would allow, but she only ended up looking more rigid. "From the day she moved in, those two were inseparable."

"Romantic?" Jackson asked.

Moletti scowled. "I don't allow *that* under my roof. But with that girl…" Her nostrils flared again, and she peeled pale slivers of lip back from her teeth. "*She* was trouble. *He* was a dear. Stewart was here for over a year before her, and we never had a single issue. The month after she arrived, the two of them got suspended for smoking in the school parking lot. Rebecca practically *ruined* his high school career."

A single episode of—*gasp*—smoking wouldn't ruin someone's high school career. "Was he a good student?"

"Absolutely."

"Charming?" *Narcissistic? Sociopathic?*

She crossed her arms. "What are you getting at?"

"Where is he now, Mrs. Moletti?"

"I have no idea. We didn't speak often after graduation, but he came to Thanksgiving until…six or seven years ago, I suppose."

Right around the time Rebecca left town. "And her previous foster brother, the one she accused of"—he paused dramatically and said in a whisper—"rape. Any idea where that kid is now?"

"Oh…" She shifted in the chair. "I think he's in jail now, actually."

"For what?" Jackson asked.

"Well…" Moletti swallowed hard.

Petrosky stared daggers at her. He waited until she met his eyes before he said: "Did he rape someone else, Mrs. Moletti?"

Her nostrils flared. But she nodded.

No wonder Rebecca had lost her shit.

29

Jackson texted Stewart's photo to the Pennsylvania doctor Rebecca had worked for from Moletti's front porch. The reply came immediately: Stewart Baird was definitely the man who'd lived with Rebecca in Briddiss, the guy who'd brought her lunch and picked her up from work. And a few more phone calls told them that none of the neighbors or the landlord had seen Stewart since Rebecca left Pennsylvania. He had to be their guy in the boat—Piotr's killer.

"Sounds like she had a good reason to distrust the police," Petrosky said. "She learned pretty early that we aren't worth a damn." He climbed down from Jackson's SUV, sneakers splashing in the precinct parking lot; he might be wearing a suit jacket today—he'd gotten tired of Shannon frowning at his sweatshirts—but he'd be damned if he gave up his sneakers. "Hopefully, McCallum can give us a little insight."

The walk to the brown brick building felt extra far, his body heavy and slow like he was moving underwater. Shaky too. He hadn't had a drink since yesterday—a single shot when Shannon was in the shower, then straight to bed before she got wise—but would McCallum notice? Would he see right through Petrosky's bullshit? Nah, the doc was good, but he wasn't psychic. The outer door squealed. Petrosky's chest throbbed.

The psychiatrist met them in his interior office, his head bent over a chart, little Benjamin Franklin glasses Petrosky hadn't seen before sitting primly on the bridge of his nose. He didn't get to his feet as they walked in and sat across from him.

"How's it hanging, Doc?"

"A little to the left."

Petrosky raised an eyebrow. The psychiatrist grinned, the round balls of his cheeks pushing his eyeglasses up to his eyebrows. "Jackson says you two are dealing with a battered-wife-turned-killer situation?"

Petrosky glanced at Jackson. He hadn't liked the description when she'd given it on the phone, but it was probably the most concise. "Well…maybe." He filled the doctor in on their suspicions regarding Rebecca Kowalski. The weird-family-home-birth-cult vibe, the hardware-hoking cult leader, Miranda Rericha's suicide, Rebecca's allegedly stolen child. That she'd reported her husband for abuse, and ended up being kidnapped and discovered under her car, less one hand. How Rebecca had faked her death; even if she'd done it in desperation, the murder of Lucius and Roman showed she had a tendency toward revenge as well as self-preservation—she could have lit the warehouse with only Miranda's corpse inside and still gotten away. Then the running, living in Briddiss, the hit and run and Christopher's death. Soon thereafter, the break-in at Piotr's place and his subsequent murder. The man in the boat who might be her missing foster brother turned roommate. They'd look more closely at Stewart after they got out of here; McCallum only had this one appointment available until next month. Sounded like the horrors of the Ash Park police force were pretty time-consuming.

McCallum leaned back in his chair and folded his thick

fingers over the curve of his belly. "We all know the signs and consequences of domestic violence, so I won't waste time describing battered woman syndrome. Yes, I know it's not an official diagnosis, but we all know it exists as a subcategory of post-traumatic stress disorder."

Petrosky nodded. Battered woman syndrome came with a plethora of awfulness—flashbacks, dissociative states, nightmares, depression, anxiety, even psychotic breaks. Bullshit way to live.

"From her history with foster care, the suspected rape, the near-constant assaults on her psyche, we have to assume some form of attachment disorder, which made her more prone to accept her husband's abuse. Most cults attract people with similar issues."

Which they already knew.

"One of the bigger issues for this case," McCallum went on, "is the grief. This is the fuel that's driving her. This earlier child, the first baby Rebecca lost, that Rericha took from her —do we know if there's any truth to that?"

"We spoke to her midwife," Jackson said. "The pregnancy was legitimate. We suspect that Rericha took him at birth or soon after." They'd conveniently left out Shannon's involvement—hopefully, the doc wouldn't ask too many questions.

McCallum nodded, the corners of his eyes tight with sympathy: the ultimate "shrink face." "And the pain of that loss compounded by the recent death of her second child… it's quite possible, her safety is no longer a priority. She's going to do whatever she can to take control. To feel less helpless, to feel that life is worth living again."

"I can't imagine she'll ever feel that," Petrosky muttered. McCallum leveled his gaze at Petrosky, and for a moment, those eyes bored straight into his soul—*he knows, he knows about the drinking.* His tongue felt heavy on the floor of his mouth, his lips dry, the muscles along his spine tightening, because he *did* need a drink—he could suddenly taste it in the back of his throat. But the moment passed just as quickly as it had come. "What I mean is, she's graduated from stealing Piotr's laptop, maybe looking for her missing child, to murdering one of the men she holds responsible for the shit hand she's been dealt." Or having him killed—Rebecca hadn't been the one in the boat, but that didn't mean she was innocent, no matter what she'd told him. Right? *Don't do that, Petrosky, you know how you are, stop it now, you sucker.*

McCallum had not moved; it felt as if his gaze was scooping Petrosky's soul out through a soft spot in the middle of his forehead. He took a deep breath and let it out slowly. *Check me out, I'm caaaaalm, and totally not wasted. Yet.* He forced his voice to stay even. "So, what does she want, Doc?"

"Closure."

Jackson cocked her head. "Not revenge?"

"Revenge makes sense as a bonus, but I believe that missing baby remains her core motivation. If she only wanted revenge, she could have killed Piotr that first night, shot Rericha at any point over the last week. But she didn't. And if she thinks her child is alive, killing Piotr doesn't further her main goal." The doctor laced his fingers on the tabletop and leaned over them, his bulk pressing into the wood. "You said you had a man at the scene, not Rebecca. It's possible this man was supposed to scare Piotr, get information on the child, and things got out of hand. But I can't imagine that her goal will have changed. She'll still be trying to figure out who else knows where this child might be." And Rericha had no reason to tell them a damn thing—even admitting there *was* a child was incriminating. Better Rericha didn't know they were onto him until they could back his ass into a corner.

"You also have to consider the psychology of your patriarch," McCallum said. "Your cult leader, as you seem so fond of calling him. If he is a sociopath, as you believe, he's not going to take the murder of his grandson, his right-hand man, lying down. You aren't just racing against this woman and her partner."

Shit. He was right. People like Joseph Rericha didn't enlist the police when they needed help. If Rericha figured out who had killed his grandson before they did, that person was as good as dead.

30

SHANNON'S LUNGS felt tight and flimsy like they'd been drained of tissue and rebuilt in plastic—a pair of sandwich bags between her and death. She forced air through her nose and into her chest, listening to the sounds of the house. Silent, save for the ticking of Rericha's grandfather clock, which had scared the shit out of her a moment ago. The whole place reeked of old dust tinged with the vinegar tang of fear—probably to be expected for a house owned by a psychopathic cult leader for nearly fifty years.

She shuddered, but she was tired of messing around. Tired of waiting for search warrants, of waiting for something else to happen. She had wasted enough of her life on this family, enough time spent worrying about the boy, stolen from his mother, and passed off to god knew who. Not that she thought Rebecca was a better parental option, but Shannon needed to know the child wasn't in the care of a sex trafficker, an abuser, or some other horrible human who shouldn't be allowed to procreate. Morrison wouldn't have been okay with that either. The skin beneath her ring prickled.

She tapped the flashlight icon on her phone, and the desktop in front of her lit up; photos of Rericha as a younger man, a pretty dark-haired woman sitting beside him, a little girl on her lap. She pulled out the drawer on the right, wincing as the wood squealed, but the only things inside were a stapler and a box of ballpoint pens. The left drawer held sticky notes. She stepped back, scanning the scarred leather desk chair and the braided rug. No other furniture in this room, not even a bookcase, but more framed shots of that toddler through the years adorned the walls: here, a ten-year-old atop a brown pony, there a twentysomething woman with a dark braid over one shoulder, grinning with a rabbit-like overbite that somehow managed to be cute—Miranda. No matter how many children Rericha had, it was clear that this girl had been the only one to steal his heart, but that wasn't relevant right now. That wouldn't help her find a stolen child.

Shannon sighed and edged back toward the hallway. Nothing of interest yet, not a damn thing in the living room or the office or the master bedroom. She didn't know exactly what she expected to find—it wasn't like Rericha would have the contact information of whoever he'd given the kid to under "BABY SNATCHER" in his Rolodex.

She headed for the guest bedroom. Dust coated the little end table, the motes whirling into the air and attacking her nose as she passed. The bedspread, too, appeared dirty, like dust might plume up in a cloud if she patted the comforter—once white, the edges of the cloth had gone yellow. She stifled a sneeze and crept closer, trailing the cell-phone light over the end tables, the—

She leapt back, heart in her throat, smashing her elbow against the wall.

Above the bed, a giant golden tiger's head loomed, sneering at the room, far larger than life-sized with teeth like railroad spikes. *Super relaxing, Rericha.* Who would ever be able to sleep with that snarling down at them?

She kept her gaze off the thing's monstrous jaws and edged forward again to paw through the drawers in the end tables, but it was more of the same: a pencil and a single handkerchief in one, a paperback novel with tattered edges in another—well-loved. But... *Huh.* She hadn't seen even one other book in the rest of the house.

She pulled the book from the drawer, careful not to tear the cover, though one corner was already missing. Not a paperback novel, as she'd originally thought—the pages looked lined beneath the missing edge. A ledger? *Bingo.* She rested the cell phone on the table, balanced against the wall, and gingerly flipped through the pages. At least twenty...no, thirty names in the first two pages alone, all listed on the far left in neat columns, dates beside them. Birthdays? Were these all members of his crazy cult?

After the birthday column was another set of numbers, ranging from 35 to 52. Ages—each corresponded to the birthday listed, some of the paper, thin beneath the penciled digits, rubbed nearly through as if he sat here every year and changed them. The following column was yet more numbers, but these had dollar signs. What the... Was it a debit sheet? What he'd paid out to each of them? But the dentist wasn't on the list, and she knew from Petrosky that Dr. Pureman's business had been funded by Rericha.

Tanya Jervis, though—*475k*. She was Rericha's daughter, right? But even if he'd gotten her set up, would she really owe him that much? Midwifery schooling didn't have the same costs as a medical degree, and she'd been working for a decade. If she owed him this much money, that meant he'd paid for her office all these years, maybe bought her a house too. Shannon shook her head. That didn't make sense. The woman was engaged, and Shannon had checked out her fiancé, an investment banker, a man who seemed like he'd pay off his wife's debts if she had them. Maybe…wait, was this list of numbers net worth? That didn't make sense either; it wasn't like Rericha could tap into Tanya and her husband's finances unless Tanya gave them to him freely. Maybe he was just a crazy narcissist who liked to see his riches—considered anything his offspring produced a direct reflection of him, an extension of his own wealth.

She flipped again. Damn. More pages. More names. More numbers. So many, there were so, so many. Could this be what Rebecca had been looking for when she broke into Piotr's? But why would this help her?

Shannon drew her finger down over the list of names. Roman was there, Piotr too. Lucius. It appeared that Rericha looked at his grandchildren the same as he did his sons and daughters—no differentiation between them in the book. Only one name looked different: Stewart Baird, scrawled in red ink. No birthday, no numbers at all. Who was he?

She frowned and resumed her flipping. No child so far with Lucius's last name—Kowalski—as if Rebecca's missing infant had never existed. She might believe that Rebecca had made it up, used the story as a manipulation tactic, if not for Tanya Jervis's records. The midwife would be more likely to claim the kid wasn't real to protect her father.

Shannon turned another sheet. As the pages went on, the ages were decreasing, the birthdays more recent, though, thus far, no one in the book was younger than seventeen—all born before Rericha's incarceration.

She shifted the book, leaned closer to the light, and turned to the last page. She froze. Christopher Nowak's name stared back at her—Rebecca's younger son, the one who'd died just three weeks ago in a hit and run. A birthdate that matched what they knew of him.

The dollar amount by his name was zero.

Creak.

Shannon jumped, fumbling the book against her chest, where it vibrated with the angry energy of a trapped rattlesnake. What was that? The wind against a door? Maybe the house settling. She held her breath, listening.

Thud, thud, thud. Footsteps. Coming up the hall.

She was no longer alone.

"These children that come at you with knives, they are your children. You taught them. I didn't teach them. I just tried to help them stand up."
~Charles Manson, testimony from the Tate-LaBianca murder trial

31

McCallum's outer office door banged open, and Petrosky didn't think it was from the wind.

"I can't believe that's what you got out of what he said," Jackson huffed.

He listened to their footsteps on the asphalt, the pointed squalling of a nightbird, but the sound of Jackson's heels was sharper, louder still. "McCallum said she's looking for her kid, not revenge, and we can't be sure she told her boyfriend to kill Piotr—Stewart Baird might have done that without her blessing." The precinct loomed. Shadows crept away from the streetlamps, threading themselves like black vines beneath the cars. "If her motivation is to find her child, she wouldn't kill a guy who might know where the boy is."

The door to the precinct slammed into the wall with a hollow metallic *clonk*—definitely not the wind. "Rericha knows," Jackson snapped.

"But she'd have more luck getting it out of Piotr—Rericha's a goddamn vault." Their feet on the stairs thrummed in time to his heart. "Let's, just for a moment, assume it wasn't her who wanted to kill Piotr—maybe even that she's telling the truth and didn't kill her husband in that fire."

Jackson's shoes ground to a halt on the stair treads, her knuckles pale on the railing. She turned. "Are you out of your—"

"Just listen, okay? Stewart…he's a player here, a new suspect. We shouldn't rule out his involvement in any of these crimes. And he's been with her since high school. He left with her, moved to Briddiss with her, which means they were associated when the fire happened."

Jackson shook her head and turned away once more, but she sighed. "Fine. Okay? I'll humor you for a minute, just until we can find Baird, but Rebecca was the one who was desperate—the one who had a reason to fake her death. She was the one with a motive to kill her abusive husband and any of his family that she blamed for kidnapping her or stealing her baby. She's the common denominator, not this Baird asshole." She flung open the door to the bullpen, and the acrid stink of old coffee and copier ink assaulted his nostrils.

He waited until they'd plopped down at his desk before he said: "That fire thing…it's still bothering me."

"It was a double homicide. It should bother you."

"I just want to know exactly how she pulled it off. Accomplice or no, those men were big, heavy—maybe Baird was strong enough to get them into the warehouse once they were unconscious, but he couldn't have fought them both, not the way he did Piotr. So how did Rebecca knock them out without one or the other noticing?" If she'd slipped them something, and one of them had shown symptoms before the other, the remaining fellow wouldn't keep drinking the Kool-Aid.

Jackson was shaking her head. "You don't want to believe she did it at all, that's the problem. But we suspected from the beginning that she had a partner, and now we know who her accomplice was." She put her elbows on the desk and slumped over them, looking his way from the corner of her eye—bloodshot. Exhausted. "But I need you to get this through your head: she didn't *need* help, not really. With a little imagination, she could have committed those murders by herself."

He opened his mouth to protest, but Jackson sat back and put up her hand. "If Rericha was telling the truth, that they were at the warehouse to drink and celebrate the upcoming purchase, then all she had to do was spike the wine, wait until they were unconscious, then set the place on fire. Plus, she was *married* to one of them—misogynist abuser or no, she could have leveraged his trust. Convinced him to go in and have a drink, even told them she was going to get help once the drugs started to kick in. She wouldn't have had to carry anyone, Stewart or no Stewart. Mystery solved."

"They'd have noticed a moldering corpse on the floor," he muttered, though she clearly would have dragged that in later, after they were unconscious. "That's not even what's bothering me, though. It's more...the taste."

Her nose wrinkled. "The taste? All this she-might-be-innocent shit over the flavor quality of their wine?"

You just want a drink, old man—you just want a taste of Jack. But he pressed on: "To drink a bottle of wine laced with GHB... Hell, any commonly used knock-out drug gets nasty in a dose high enough to render two grown men completely unconscious. That wine would have been slimy." He'd notice if someone spiked his wine with that, probably even his whiskey, strong as it was. He glanced around the bullpen—empty save the two of them—then at the window, the sky outside black and heavy. Another hour, maybe two—he'd get a drink on the way home today...and another bottle of mouthwash.

"Fine, so she'd need something *not* commonly used, something that would make them pass out quickly and stay unconscious long enough for the place to burn. That doesn't mean she's innocent, just that she knew what she was doing." If only someone had run a tox screen at the time; then they could put this argument aside. Why did everything about this case have to be so complicated?

Jackson rolled her eyes and pushed herself to standing. "I'm going to poke around on Stewart Baird, the man doing her wet work. We'll nail him and Rebecca at the same time. Does that make you feel better?"

His desk phone rang. He stared at it. It rang again.

"For god's sake, Petrosky."

"I know, I know." He grabbed the receiver.

"Guess who has a boat on the lake where Piotr was killed?" Scott's voice was high with excitement.

"Who?"

"Kazia Gorgan."

Petrosky frowned. "Who's Kazia Gorgan?" It sounded familiar, but…

Jackson slid back into her seat as Scott said: "Piotr's mother, but her name's misspelled on the boat license, G*o*rgan, not G*ro*gan, which might be why it got missed before…I mean, if you looked under her already."

What the hell? "Isn't she dead?"

"Kazia is definitely dead. But I dug around on her because she was one of the cult members who didn't have a clear-cut history; an addict-prostitute turned cult-warehouse caretaker, but she never filed a single W-2, never graduated high school, had no debt, and the father of her kids is totally MIA. With zero connections to anything, she seemed like a good… I dunno…scapegoat? Not like anyone would come looking for her property."

Good thinking, kid. Piotr's mother had died well before Rebecca's time, but Rebecca could have known about the boat if she'd ever gone out with Lucius. "Where's the boat now, Scott?"

Jackson shifted in the chair, watching him intently, her eyes wide but still tired.

"That's the other thing that made the boat hard to find. It's stored at a landing strip about forty-five minutes out under her *father's* name: Janek Grogan. He was a friend of Rericha's back in the day, or must have been; Rericha paid to have him buried beside Kazia."

"You're an evil genius, Scott."

Scott chuckled, but there wasn't much humor in it. "I wish I had more for you, like a picture of whoever actually took the boat, but they don't have cameras—it's an unmanned slip. No witnesses unless someone else was cruising the lake in the middle of the winter." Which was highly unlikely. "I'm heading down now to take swabs and dust for prints."

"Thanks, kid. I owe you." But the pit in his belly felt heavier as he hung up the phone.

"So?" Jackson asked.

Petrosky ran a hand over his face, imagining Lucius and Rebecca on that boat, out for a cruise around the lake, then Miranda and Roman, then Piotr and Louisa with their hair flying. Had those women watched at least one good sunset before the men in their lives had beat the hell out of them? When had it all gone bad, from holding hands to flying fists? And... Petrosky blinked, but this time it was Joseph Rericha's hands that he saw behind his eyelids. That thick white bandage. And clubbing on his fingers, right? That happened with long-term heart and lung issues, and that chesty way he breathed... *Shit.* Rebecca hadn't used GHB to put Lucius and Roman out the night she burned them to death. She had access to something far better, and it was easier to steal pills from a medicine cabinet than to buy drugs off the street. "Nitroglycerin."

Jackson cocked her head. "That's what Scott said? What the hell does that have to do with a boat?"

"No, he said… Scott found the boat."

Jackson nodded, her face brightening—waking up. "Great, then we should—"

"We will, but just wait a second, okay? Nitroglycerin has a sweet taste that can burn a little, but if Roman and Lucius were drinking it in wine, they might not have noticed."

"Back to this, huh?" She frowned. "I thought you had to put nitroglycerin under your tongue."

"If you want it to work fast to stop a heart attack, yeah, but she had a few minutes. Doesn't have to be nitroglycerin, either. Any heart med will mess up someone without heart issues—she could have even given them a pill, told them it was aspirin. And adding alcohol to the mix is far more dangerous. Lucius and Roman might have been almost dead before the fire started." He'd gotten a hell of a lecture from his doctor about drinking while taking heart medications. Not that he was on those anymore.

"Did you just spontaneously talk yourself into the idea that Rebecca did it herself?"

He frowned. "I don't want to talk about it, Jackson."

"That sounds like a yes."

It was. But he'd be damned if he would admit that to his partner, and with Piotr's death, the boat, the missing kid, there were still too many unanswered questions.

Screw tipping Rericha off. Maybe they wanted that asshole a little nervous.

Maybe then he'd finally screw up.

32

THE NEXT MORNING was a brilliant shitshow of sunshine and ice smooth as glass, a mirror effect that blinded you the moment you stepped outside; it was like being stabbed in the eyes by Mother Nature. Shannon appeared to share the sentiment. She had met him in the kitchen for morning coffee, her face drawn, her jaw tight. Pale. She'd been edgy since the night before, had even refused the Mexican takeout he'd brought home, and that wasn't like her at all. Had something happened? Not at his house; flatfoots had been driving by his place all week, and they hadn't noted anything strange. He still wasn't sure what Jackson had told them, but none seemed to suspect Shannon of any wrongdoing. But Shannon... Was the case getting to her? Maybe she'd found his booze after all—maybe, despite his trusty mouthwash, she'd smelled it on him last night...or this morning. But she'd still waved goodbye. Told him not to smoke too much.

As if.

"We need to pull Rericha in officially," Jackson was saying, her voice raised to be heard over the heat belching from the Escalade's vents. "Chatting him up in public is a backward way to go about it."

But they had nothing on the man, nothing to encourage him to cooperate—unlike Piotr, Rericha was still alive and maintained all rights to privacy afforded under the law since they didn't have enough for a warrant. Piotr was the one who appeared guilty of domestic abuse, kidnapping, and torture, not Rericha. The boat wasn't in Rericha's name, and they had nothing to connect him to it; though he wasn't a suspect in Piotr's death, being connected to the getaway vehicle would have at least given them some legal leeway. The only thing Rericha was accused of doing directly was taking Rebecca's child, but Rebecca, their only witness, wasn't around, and using Shannon's secondhand account meant she'd have to explain her involvement to the authorities beyond him—and to what end? No one would believe a husband-murderer, and even Shannon would lose any credibility once they realized what she'd done to help Rebecca.

Petrosky would have to settle for trying to trip Rericha up; could he get Rericha to hint at where the kid was? They were looking for Stewart Baird, too, had already put his nondescript face on TV along with Rebecca's—a brown-haired, brown-eyed poster boy for boring white men—but if Rebecca was still looking for her missing child, they'd be closer to locating Baird and Rebecca if they found the boy. Plus, finding a missing kid felt more important than arresting a man who liked to kill assholes.

Joseph Rericha wasn't at the hardware store, nor was he at his house four blocks from the place Rebecca had shared with her dickbag husband before his untimely barbecuing. But it didn't take them long to figure out where Rericha had gone; the funeral home he'd used to bury Miranda was six miles from his store, and it hadn't changed hands since he'd buried her the first time.

They flashed their badges at the door and strode past a showroom filled to bursting with silk-lined coffins, all open to show their cotton-stuffed innards, as if any putrefying body would give a shit what shade of cream they were rotting on.

Jackson headed off to find the funeral home director. Scott had said Rericha paid for Janek Grogan's burial, so the director might know something about Grogan's relationship to Rericha, and this was even more true if the director himself had ever been involved with Rericha's group. They had no evidence of that, but with the way Rericha tried to keep things in the family, it was worth a shot.

Petrosky found Rericha in the back room poring over a death catalog on a faux leather sofa that had already begun to wear, the arms and edges pale as if it, too, were in the beginning stages of decay. His nostrils burned from too-strong potpourri and something that could only be rubbing alcohol. Or vodka.

Stop it. Later.

"Looks like you're the last of your sadistic little family," Petrosky said, sliding into the wooden chair across the coffee table from Rericha.

The man did not look up. "What's it to you?"

"Well, I still have to figure out who killed your grandson. Probably Roman and Lucius, too, I guess."

Now Rericha raised his head. "You said that girl did it."

"Yeah, but I say a lot of things." He glared. Rericha stared back at him, his gaze not nearly as irritated as Petrosky wanted it to be. He'd have to try harder.

"Did she use your drugs to knock Roman and Lucius out?" He wasn't sure this theory was accurate, but sometimes the easiest way to get to the truth was to monitor a reaction.

Rericha laid the catalog on the coffee table—headstones—beside a stack of photos he must have brought with him: pictures of Piotr, maybe for the service, though who he'd invite would be more interesting than whatever was in those shots. "I don't know what you mean," Rericha said.

"What medications are you on?"

Rericha appraised him with a cool, dull gaze. "I'm getting up there; it's easier to list what I'm not taking."

"Diabetes meds? Something for hypertension?"

Rericha blinked.

Come on, fuck-o. "What about nitroglycerin? Captopril?" Any of a dozen heart medications, especially combined with downers, could have made Lucius and Roman hypotensive—hard to stay conscious when you don't have enough blood going to your brain.

But Rericha just sniffed. "You don't have the faintest idea what you're talking about."

Fine, he didn't want to talk about his meds; if Rebecca hadn't stolen too much, Rericha might not have noticed them missing anyway. "What do you know about the boat witnesses saw speeding away from Piotr's dead body?" *Bait and switch, dickhead.*

"Boat?" He scratched at his cheek with one clubbed finger. His hand was still bandaged as it had been the other day, a strip of gauze wound tight over his papery flesh.

"Come on, Rericha, you know exactly what I'm talking about—Piotr sure knew it existed. And you don't seem like the kind of guy people keep secrets from." Would that work? Playing on his need for control? He couldn't tell—Rericha's face did not change. Petrosky leaned closer over the table, his elbows on his knees, and said, "Who else knows about that boat?"

Rericha appraised him coolly, then raised one shoulder. "I'm not sure. It's not a secret."

"It sure seems like a secret. The slip is in a dead man's name—Piotr's maternal grandfather, a man you knew well back in the day. Janek Grogan's daughter birthed Piotr and Roman while your son was off god knows where."

Rericha shrugged. "It was his boat."

That's it? It was his boat? *Give me something, prick.* "Does Rebecca have keys?"

"I doubt it."

"If it wasn't her, maybe it was you." Petrosky fingered the photo of Piotr nearest him—the man smiling, that damn silver cross glinting on his chest—and narrowed his eyes at Rericha. "Maybe you got sick of Piotr fucking up, didn't want to worry about what he did to Rebecca or to anyone else. Didn't want anything traced back to you." Rericha had no reason to kill the boy he'd raised as his own, especially while the police were watching, but Jesus Christ, he needed this guy to *react*. That was half the reason he'd ambushed Rericha at the funeral home.

Rericha shook his head, but his eyes stayed steady. "Guessing just to see if I'll crack isn't going to do much for you." He glanced nonchalantly at the catalog of headstones, then back up at Petrosky the same way he'd glanced at the hunting magazine at the hardware store.

"You really are a cold bastard, aren't you?"

Rericha sniffed again. "Think what you want. You have nothing to charge me with."

"You're right on that, but all this does beg some questions, doesn't it?" Petrosky straightened, his back popping with a sound like that of angry bubble wrap. "I don't think Rebecca's targeting your family on accident, Rericha. I think she's got it in for you."

"Why do you care what a murderer thinks?"

"What makes you think she's a murderer?" Petrosky fired back.

Rericha chuckled, though his lips did not cooperate. "You told me she was alive—that she killed Roman and Lucius, burned my daughter's body in that warehouse. You think someone else stole my Miranda's body? That someone else set that fire with the sole purpose of helping Becky disappear?"

The world spun a little slower. Petrosky watched the man for signs of distress, for a signal that he realized he'd fucked up, but Rericha just stared. "Now, that's interesting, Mr. Rericha."

The man raised an eyebrow. "You knew she was a murderer, that's not new."

"Calling her Becky," Petrosky said slowly. "I've never heard you use a nickname for anyone else." Becky was personal. "If I didn't know better, I'd think you care about her."

Rericha blinked sleepily, bored…but he wasn't. Oh, he wasn't. *What's it gonna take, jackoff?* Cold bastard though he was, this guy wasn't immune to rage.

Petrosky lowered his voice. "If you care about her, Joey, why would you take her kid?"

"I did no such thing."

"But you knew Rebecca was pregnant; Piotr even went with her to see the midwife. Where did you think the baby went?"

He raised one shoulder as if the question wasn't worth a full shrug. "That isn't my business."

"Bullshit it isn't." The congregation might have dissipated, but men like Rericha didn't give up control without a fight. "Did Lucius ever ask you about his son? It seems he'd have to agree to make the boy disappear; maybe he thought the baby wasn't his."

"I don't know anything about that kid." Rericha's gaze stayed level, but his nostrils flared—*I'm getting to him.* "You came here, interrupted me planning my grandson's funeral, to berate me about someone else's baby? Accuse me of stealing a child?"

"Maybe two of them." Did he know about Christopher?

Rericha's eyes twitched, widening, then tensing once more, tiny movements that might not mean much on any normal person, but Rericha wasn't a normal man. Shocked? But he kept his voice steady as he said: "You better start making sense, and soon."

Petrosky crossed his arms, letting the silence of the funeral home wash over them, the pregnant hush of old and new sorrow, the collective grief of a multitude of anguished families. When Rericha just stared, he cleared his throat. "Rebecca had another son while she was away. Christopher was only six when he died." Petrosky locked his gaze on Rericha's face, on the lookout for the tiniest of twitches that might indicate knowledge, or conversely, surprise, but this time, Rericha kept himself composed. The quiet hummed.

"Did you kill Christopher? Maybe send Piotr to make Rebecca's second child disappear the way you did the first?"

Rericha leaned back against the sofa, as far from Petrosky as he could get without walking out—criminals did the same thing in the interrogation room when they wanted to run. "Kill him? I haven't been anywhere but my house and my store in months, and I didn't even know about the boy; Christopher was it?" Rericha crossed his arms, his bandaged hand tucked into the hollow of his armpit. They hadn't found evidence that he'd left the state, but this bastard was sneaky.

"For a leader, the head of the household, a man who should know everything that's going on in your family, you're not great at keeping track of information."

Rericha's dull gaze sharpened, a pair of icicles aimed Petrosky's way, and when Petrosky didn't blink, he dropped his eyes to the table—the photos of Piotr. *What's on your mind, Rericha?* Petrosky snatched up the picture on the top, a close-up shot of Piotr's face: strong jaw, dark hair, silver cross, as always, at his clavicle. The only one who showed any sign of religiosity now that he thought about it.

"He looks like you." Petrosky brought the photo closer to his face, studying the angular plane of Piotr's nose, his eyes bluish gray like the water where he'd met his maker—blue like Joe's eyes. "You fought awful hard to adopt him; you didn't want him being raised by someone else, right?"

"Family belongs together," Rericha snapped, and Petrosky

lowered the picture, his shoulder muscles knotted. The way Rericha said it, severe, decisive…he believed it.

Rericha picked up the catalog again, his gaze cast down at the pages. "Charge me or leave me in peace," Rericha growled.

Yeah, this douchebag wasn't going to tell them shit, but they'd get him anyway. Somehow. "You won't have peace for a long time, old man," Petrosky said, getting to his feet.

None of them would.

33

"I don't know what to tell you." Scott's voice echoed from the desk phone's receiver, or maybe it was echoing in his brain. "The DNA doesn't match. I had Briddiss pull a sample for me since Christopher is still in their morgue, and I compared that to the blood I took from Piotr's house. Piotr is not the father of Rebecca's son. None of the guys in that family are related to Christopher: not her husband, not Rericha, not anyone."

Damn recessive genes. Rebecca had brown eyes, as did Lucius and Stewart Baird, but Christopher's were a brilliant blue—Piotr and Rericha had been worth a look. But Baird had gone with her to Briddiss to raise her kid; it would make sense if Christopher was Baird's child. Petrosky ran a hand over his face, feeling the soft hair against the pads of his fingers. He wasn't sure why it mattered; yeah, she'd gotten pregnant before she left, and cheating on her husband might be a motive to hurt her or the boy, but no matter who Christopher's father was, no one had the right to kill him. The phone was a weight in his hand, the bullpen buzzing around him, the drone of Jackson's irritated voice from her desk a subtle but persistent reminder that they had nothing to go on.

He dropped the receiver into the cradle with a *clunk* and shook his head, trying to clear it, but there was only one thing that would really help, and he had to wait until quitting time for that. *So what next?* They'd already released Rebecca's and Stewart's photos to the press, but so far, no hits. The APB on Piotr's Camaro had gone nowhere—perhaps that car was at the bottom of the lake, along with the weapon used to murder him. They were still looking into the Chevelle that had killed Christopher, hoping to link it to Piotr or Rericha, but if the car was in the area, no one had it registered—every single Chevelle they'd found had an owner with an alibi if the car was even drivable. That was the thing with those old muscle cars, especially in the Motor City: collectors didn't always need them to work. Sometimes they were just fun to tinker with...or so he'd heard.

He rubbed his temples. Over the last hour, a headache had taken root and sent branches of pain twisting over the surface of his skull. Petrosky looked up as Jackson plopped into the seat beside him.

"Bullshit," she muttered.

"What now? Did someone shoot Rericha in the face? Because I think you're overestimating how upset I'd be about that."

"No, this is about Stewart Baird. If he and Rebecca were involved while she was with Lucius, they were better than 99% of the population at hiding it—not a single phone call or credit card receipt to connect them. And he wasn't involved in the warehouse fire, so your girl did that herself. He was an inpatient out of state, a week from completing a 90-day rehab program when Rebecca killed her husband and vanished. Looks like he's been in and out of rehab centers since his teenage years, and he also has a string of arrests for burglary, so Moletti was full of shit about him being the poster child for good behavior."

Addiction and burglary—fun.

"I think we can rule Baird out as Christopher's father too. Based on the boy's birthdate, she would have had to get pregnant between the kidnapping and the fire. If Baird was in rehab…" Jackson paused. "They get conjugal visits in there?"

"Nope." At least not with the people from their using days.

"Worse than jail, eh?"

"You don't get to have sex in jail either unless you're sweet on the guy in the top bunk." He frowned at the desk phone. So, they were wrong about Baird helping Rebecca with the fire, but that didn't mean he hadn't helped her kill Piotr. He had obviously gone with her to Briddiss, and he could have come back to Ash Park with her. It was even possible that her son's hit and run really had been an accident; maybe she'd just wanted an excuse to kill the man who'd assaulted her, who'd been responsible for the loss of her hand.

They needed to talk to her. And they couldn't do that if they couldn't find her.

His desk phone rang, sending bolts of pain through his temples. He glowered at it—he'd rather sweep the thing off the desk than answer it—but he lifted the receiver to his ear.

"You're never going to believe this one."

Shannon? He fumbled the phone and brought it back to his head. Jackson narrowed her eyes at him like she was watching a duck try to walk a tightrope.

"You there?" Shannon asked.

"Yeah, sorry."

"You don't even know what to say when you actually answer, do you?"

"I know what to say. So…you miss me or what?"

"Oh, fuck off, Petrosky." She sighed. "I've been trying to

track down Stewart, that guy Rebecca knew from high school."

"Wait, how did you know about—"

"Doesn't matter, just listen, would you? He's in a hospital in Ohio where he's been for the last three weeks. Since the day someone tried to kill him."

34

"How the hell did he get all the way over here?" East Valley Hospital wasn't anywhere near Pennsylvania; an hour and a half from Detroit, the hospital where Stewart Baird was currently admitted sat between Briddiss, where Rebecca had spent the last seven years, and Ash Park, her last known destination. Petrosky let his eyes rest on the gray sky, a sea of boring nothing through the Escalade's windshield—dammit, he could use a little boring. But his brain would not relax. "What'd she do, just drop him here on her way?" he muttered to the passenger window.

Jackson's fingers tightened on the wheel. "Maybe he got injured in Ohio, near the hospital." But from Jackson's tone, she didn't believe that for a second.

Try as she might, Shannon hadn't been able to get details about Baird's condition from the hospital employees: confidential. They did know he'd been in a car wreck and had been admitted the day after Christopher Nowak's death. Which meant he wasn't Piotr's killer—that fact alone was a brainfuck of the highest order. Every time they took one step forward, someone kicked their asses down the stairs.

So, who had killed Piotr? Had Baird been in a separate

but unrelated accident? That was much too coincidental for Petrosky's taste, but there was no mention of Baird at the crash that had killed Rebecca's son. Hopefully, the guy would have something for them; Baird was probably the only person who knew Rebecca well enough to tell them where she might be.

The orderly at the front desk eyed them suspiciously but directed them to the third floor, the top level at this tiny institution—more a glorified clinic than a hospital. Though it was bright and had the requisite stink of disinfectant, this place had something else wafting through the air, too... lavender?

The elevator opened on the third floor to four people clustered around a circular desk that appeared to function as the nurse's station. A woman with a curly red ponytail turned as they approached...nope, not a woman—a slight man in green scrubs. Latewood's voice, the witness who'd seen the boat, echoed in his brain: *I'm sure it was a man. Wider shoulders, you know.* The redheaded worker nodded solemnly and headed off, frowning. At them?

"Does he know why we're here, or does he just hate showing his teeth?" Petrosky muttered under his breath, but he knew the answer—all three of the other scrub-clad people at the desk were turned their way now, looking at them with that mix of contrition and sympathy common to cops and emergency room doctors. *We all get to see people on the worst day of their lives.* "I should have been a clown," Petrosky said.

Jackson turned to him, "What the hell are you talkin—"

"Detectives?" A brunette in pink scrubs had pulled away from the rest of the pack, her face drawn. But she had a clipboard in her hands, thank god. Usually, hospitals gave them shit—wouldn't even tell them if a patient was there. Actually...was it weird that they'd sent them upstairs in the first place? "I'm Gina."

Jackson was already nodding. "I'm Detective Jackson, and

this is Detective Petrosky." Just their names, not where they were from; they didn't have jurisdiction here. "We're looking for Stewart Baird."

"Did you find out who did it?" Her eyes were tight, sad. Looked like Stewart had made an impression on the nursing staff. The two other nurses—one man, one woman—standing near the circular desk weren't even trying to pretend not to listen; they watched with unabashed focus.

"Not yet, ma'am, but we're working on it," Jackson said. "It would help if we could speak to him."

Her eyes widened. "They didn't tell you?"

Uh-oh. That was never good. "Tell us what?"

"He's braindead. Has been since the day he arrived."

Great. "Sure glad we wasted our time coming out here," he grumbled. Looked like it was back to that boring sky for another hour.

Gina glanced his way, but Jackson pressed on: "Did he come via ambulance?"

A young man with an earring in his nose stepped away from the counter to stand beside his *Pretty in Pink* counterpart. "No, I was here when he was admitted," he said. "His wife just burst into the ER out of nowhere."

His wife? "Can you describe her?"

"Um... I think she had blonde hair. At the chin." He made a swiping motion just below his jawline, like someone threatening to slit your throat by way of the lymph nodes. "Pale, but I mean, she was freaking out. Screaming that her husband had gotten hit by a car."

Hit by a car—the same car that had hit her boy? But why drive Stewart all the way here? They had to be six hours from Briddiss.

"Was he alert?" Petrosky asked.

"Oh, no, he was unconscious in the lot, kinda sprawled on the curb. He was breathing on his own, though—well, he was then." The man nodded, the ring in his nose catching the light like a shiny rogue booger. "We went out with the gurney while she started to fill out the paperwork, and by the time we got back to her...well, she wasn't here anymore. She didn't get beyond writing his name."

Gina nodded, met Jackson's gaze, and passed the clipboard over.

Jackson took it, squinting. "She used his real name. That's strange for someone trying to travel incognito."

"Maybe she knew he was too far gone already," Petrosky said. "Figured it didn't matter." But she had to know they'd connect it to her if they came here—why not just throw John Doe on the paperwork? Not like he had family to notify.

Gina was staring at them, brow furrowed.

"Did she give her name?" Petrosky asked.

Gina cleared her throat, and her nose-ringed comrade crossed his arms, oddly confrontational; the tips of Gina's ears had gone pink. Whatever the nurses had expected after Shannon's call, this was not it. "No, she just said that she was his wife, that he was hurt, and that she didn't want him taken off life support. That's why he's still here, though there's really nothing left. Like I said, he's braindead."

And yet Rebecca had asked them to keep him on life support. *Maybe she killed him and didn't want to add another homicide charge to her list.* "Do people in his condition ever wake up?"

"I guess there have been a few isolated cases," Nose-ring said, "but it's rare enough to be basically impossible."

Jackson was frowning. "When people come in with a loved one, is that a usual thing to say? That they want them on life support?"

Gina and Nose-ring exchanged a glance. "Now that you mention it...no," Gina said. "I mean, they beg us to save them, tell us they'll do anything if we'll just help, etcetera, etcetera, but asking us not to remove life support...they aren't usually thinking that far ahead."

"But you still listened," Petrosky said.

"She said she was his wife, and that's how we listed it in the file." She crossed her arms and glared. "We're a small hospital; we can't afford a lawsuit."

"What do you think happens if the person who brought him in was the one who injured him?" He suddenly wanted to wipe that haughty look off Gina's face.

It worked—Gina raised a hand to cover her gaping mouth. "Oh god…she was the one who… She did that to him?"

"What room is he in?" Jackson asked.

Gina swallowed hard, and Nose-ring laid a hand on her shoulder. "Three-eleven," he said.

Petrosky nodded. "I'd like to sit with him for a bit, if that's okay."

Gina dropped her hand from her mouth, revealing tight lips—her eyes had tightened too. Small hospital or no, people probably did weird shit to coma patients. The world was full of sickos.

"Did you…know him?" Gina asked.

Petrosky shifted, the edge of his jacket falling away to reveal the badge on his belt, and leveled his gaze at her. "He was a good man. Someone should care."

Her face softened as she studied him. Finally, she sighed. "I can't see any harm in it. I'll show you in."

The "hall" was short, all of fifty feet long, and they were in Stewart Baird's room before Petrosky could say "you call this a hospital?" Baird was a stocky bulge beneath gray sheets that matched the sky outside and further muted the color in Baird's already pale face, making the man appear as if he were already dead. Which, for all intents and purposes, he was.

Petrosky watched Gina walk out. The moment the door clicked behind her, Jackson said, "He was a good man? Someone should care?"

Petrosky approached the bed and pulled a vial from his jacket: a little test tube with an attached cotton swab. He leaned toward Baird, the air sweet and tangy, thick with impending decay and alcohol so strong it made Petrosky's mouth water. *Disgusting, you're disgusting.*

"What the hell are you doing?"

"He's got a little wax in his ears, Jackson, what?"

"You won't be able to use that DNA for anything in court." But she turned her back on him and stepped between him and the door, blocking the view for anyone who might enter unexpectedly. "Why does it matter anyway? You're just curious if he was Christopher's father?"

"Maybe," he said quietly, sliding the tip of the swab between Baird's slack lips. "It just matters." He felt the truth of that in his bones.

His task complete, he replaced the swab in his jacket pocket and straightened, preparing for another hour of car horns and gray sky, but he stopped short when his eyes lit on the table beside the bed. A glass vase adorned the top—tulips, half of them still blooming.

Huh. Was this hospital a thousand times nicer than any other, providing fresh flowers for all the rooms? Doubtful. He glanced back at Jackson, but her gaze remained locked on the door.

He scanned the flowers, the buds, the greenery, but saw no tag, no writing at all save a little etched logo on the side of the vase: a line drawing of an old-fashioned pair of undies. Either Baird had a friend who knew he was here, or their "please keep him alive no matter what" murderess had sent them herself.

35

"You can go ahead home," Petrosky said. "I won't be long."

Jackson raised an eyebrow. "You sure?"

"Yup. I'll get some of this paperwork done, then see if Shannon wants to play poker if I can stay awake. Today kicked my ass." Petrosky's head hurt, maybe from the stale hospital air, maybe from lying to his partner.

Jackson frowned, but she nodded. "Okay. See you in the morning?" Her eyes were like daggers in his forehead as they had been all the way back to Ash Park. She knew something was up, and even he wasn't sure why he didn't want to include her—maybe because Jackson deserved a few hours off. It was bad enough she was saddled with him when she could do a hell of a lot better in the partner department.

He pulled the files closer and kept his eyes on the paper and pen as he listened to her boots *tap-tap-tap* toward the stairwell. The door squealed open and thunked closed again. Surely it had seemed plausible that he was tired, though it was barely dinnertime, but hell if his adrenaline wasn't pumping electricity through his veins.

Because he had a lead. Maybe.

He abandoned the files and grabbed his keyboard.

It only took him fifteen minutes to figure out where the flowers had come from—the old-fashioned underwear logo led him to "Bloomers," the most hilarious flower shop name he'd ever heard. And while the chain did have locations across the country, only one was local.

His knees creaked, the stairs groaned, the breeze outside biting and frigid, but his Caprice had never smelled more glorious, the stink of salt and grease and old cigarettes invading his nostrils as he pulled onto the main drag—his headache was all but gone. Maybe it was because he was finally alone for the first time in days. Maybe it was the shot of Jack he'd taken from the airline bottle under his seat.

That bottle...that's the real reason you didn't tell Jackson.

He sniffed and lit a cigarette, squinting through the smoke at the street signs.

Bloomers was located in a strip mall, sandwiched between a frozen yogurt place and a "Virtual Reality Lounge" —whatever that was. The nice woman inside—"Call me Tammy"—was all smiles despite him banging on the door after hours. She knew nothing about virtual reality lounges, but she knew plenty that should help him; his heart beat faster with every word she said. The woman who'd ordered the flowers a week prior had done so in person; definitely Rebecca, but she'd paid cash, so no paper trail. *Bummer.* Rebecca wasn't driving Piotr's Camaro; the flower-shop windows offered a wide view of the parking lot, and Tammy had a general description of Rebecca's station wagon. *Better.* And Tammy had noticed a motel key on Rebecca's ring. *Bingo.* There was only one Lodge Motel in the vicinity of the flower shop—three blocks over. It all seemed a little too easy, but nothing in this case had been easy yet, so he was surely due for a break.

His Caprice smelled even better when he slipped back behind the wheel.

The glowing sign for the Lodge Motel approached on his

right, and he hit the brakes, easing the car into the lot, the warmth in his guts a heavy, peaceful pressure that steadied his breathing. She probably wouldn't be here. Maybe she had already left town since Piotr was dead. Or maybe she was at Joe's Hardware right now, setting up some explosive device for Rericha to walk into in the morning. There were worse ideas.

He crushed out his smoke and kicked the car door closed; the gravel crunched under his sneakers. Calmer than he'd felt all day despite the excess adrenaline, and the breeze was almost friendly, a slightly chilly kiss against the back of his neck.

Petrosky scanned the lot, bathed in yellow floods.

The motel was set up in a large, angular U-shape, a square missing one side—not much privacy. A single parking space for each unit sat directly in front of the corresponding motel room, all marked by lines of yellow paint, and a room number near the curb. The woman at the flower shop hadn't seen the number on the key, but she had seen the beige station wagon Rebecca had gotten into. Of all the inconspicuous cars...

But inconspicuous or not, there was only one vehicle that met that description here. It sat, unassuming, in front of the very last door on the right, just beyond the edge of the streetlamp's glow. Tricky. There was probably a window on the back side of the room for easier escape, provided whoever you were escaping from showed up alone. Maybe he should have considered backup.

Too late now. He drew his shoulders up and marched across the lot toward the door—green, like the other doors. So normal-looking. The *thunk, thunk, thunk* of his fist on the wood echoed across the lot in time to the steady throb in his temples.

For a moment, there was no other noise. Then he heard it: the subtle *shht* of someone moving on the opposite side of the door, leaning their weight against it. Was she checking him out? *Probably aiming a weapon.*

But no crack of gunfire cut the air—the knob turned. The door creaked open.

Her shiny hair was pulled into a bun, brilliantly blonde—not the same shade as in the pictures they'd seen, but there was no mistaking that heart-shaped face, the slapdash of freckles across the bridge of her nose, the deep intelligence in her brown eyes.

Rebecca blinked at him. "Hello, Detective." She opened the door wider and smiled. "Come on in. You look like you could use a drink."

36

The first shot she gave him went down easy. So did the second. The mattress groaned beneath his weight.

Rebecca had yet to say a word. Her white-blonde hair was in a tight bun at the nape of her neck, her freckles barely visible in the dim lamplight, but the gauze around her arm, tightly wrapping the stump above her wrist, practically glowed. What was she waiting for? She stared at him from her perch on the corner of the little motel desk, her eyes deep pools of amber—nearly the same color as the whiskey. She even had his brand. Had she researched him? Did she know all his vices? Was she manipulating him the same way she'd manipulated everyone else? It appeared so; she extended the bottle of Jack his way, and he let her fill his plastic cup. He didn't even consider refusing.

The third shot burned a little, maybe more than the others, and his eyes dropped to his empty glass. Was it poisoned? Maybe that's why she let him in. She figured she'd confess, unburden her soul, and he wouldn't be around to tell anyone else. But she didn't look ready to spill—her chest was barely moving at all, barely breathing, her lips pressed together in a tight line. Angry. Not at him, probably, but the tension in the air was palpable. From his years of interrogating suspects, he sensed she was trying to decide what to do, teetering on the edge of cooperation, oscillating between running and spilling her guts. Gooseflesh prickled on his forearms.

If he said the wrong thing, she'd shut down. He listened to the screeching mattress springs and the weak hiss of his own breath, then said, "Quite the mess you're in, Rebecca."

She squinted at him…no. At the cup? *That's what she's waiting for; she wants me to be incapacitated.* Useless. Unable to chase her, unable to arrest her—like he was going to run anywhere. And between the alcohol he'd had in the car and what she was feeding him now, his insides were already pleasantly warm, his eyes a little bleary. But his mouth was still working.

He loosened his tongue, trying to make his words slur in case she was using that as a measure of his incapacitation. "Who killed Piotr?"

Her eyes narrowed. She shrugged.

"Who killed your husband?" Surely she knew they'd already figured that one out.

Rebecca just stared.

Fucking hell, woman. "Why am I here, Rebecca?" *Why're I ere, R-becca?* Nice. And…he *was* faking, right? He blinked. The bleariness stayed.

She paused, maybe deciding whether she believed him, then her gaze softened. He wasn't sure why it took so much calculation; drunk or not, he wasn't about to win a foot race. "They took my baby," she said. "Joe took my baby, and everyone knew, my husband knew, and none of them did a thing about it. I want my child back."

"And here I thought you were after revenge." *Don't piss her off, Petrosky.* But he didn't seem to have the ability to hold back his thoughts—the ideas came tumbling from his lips, uncensored. *Uh-oh.*

Rebecca shook her head. "I named him Carl—it means 'free man' in German. I want that for him even now, and if Joe sent him off somewhere, if he has someone raising Carl the way he raised Piotr... I don't want my son to be a...a monster." Her voice cracked on the last word, but she recovered quickly, clearing her throat and drawing her shoulders up. Defensive.

"Understood, those guys are assholes of the highest order. But why come looking for Carl now?" *Bu-why.* "You didn't look for him for seven year—"

"I couldn't come back for Carl!" Her fingers tightened on the neck of the bottle as if she might hit him with it, but he didn't have it in him to care. "They would have taken Christopher, and even if I hid him, they might have killed me and left Chris without his mother. Chris deserved...better." Her eyes filled—grief and guilt and a bright and vibrant rage. She dropped her gaze to the bottle. "Christopher had a chance. I gave him a chance." She pushed herself to her feet and turned her back on him, resting the base of the bottle against the desk. Her thin shoulders shook.

Stand up, Petrosky, get her. He still felt steady enough—he could grab her now, cuff her, perp walk her back to his car. This would be over.

But it wouldn't be, would it? Not until the real criminals were behind bars. Who could blame Rebecca for killing the men who'd abused her and Miranda and Louisa? Who'd forced her to cut off her own hand? The group who had taken her first child, maybe killed her second? Rericha was still out there, and he should be in jail before Rebecca. But Petrosky said none of that. Instead, he asked the question that had become lodged in his chest, a burning ache behind his breastbone: "Were you there when Christopher died? Did you see who did it?"

She released a long shuddering sigh, and said to the wall: "You know what it's like, don't you?"

He blinked, trying to focus on her face as she turned to him once more, but his eyes were fuzzy, and a hazy warmth had settled over his limbs. "Know what what's like?"

"You lost a child too." She eased herself back onto the edge of the desk, her big brown eyes steeped in sorrow. "Did you watch your daughter die?"

Julie's burned flesh wafted into his nostrils—melted fat and char. Had she screamed for him in the final moments of her life? *Help me, Daddy, please!* His chest burned hotter, as if he were on fire too. The way his baby girl had been.

Petrosky cleared his throat; the stink in his nostrils remained. "No. I didn't watch her die."

Rebecca nodded, but her shoulders were trembling again. "Christopher was already gone when I got to the curb, half on, half off like he had been sitting there watching the sun set. He did that sometimes." Her voice shook. Rebecca looked away, her sorrowful gaze drifting to the ceiling, but when she lowered her head once more, her irises were bright with fury. Pink had risen on her cheekbones. "I saw a blue muscle car speeding away down the street, and Piotr's the only one I know who's into those. He found me, and instead of kidnapping me again, he decided to hurt me in a way that would never heal—he killed my son. And I'm not letting those bastards keep the other one."

"That's why you went to Piotr's house?"

She nodded. "Piotr was in charge of the records—in charge of everything, really, all the bad stuff. Joe didn't usually get his hands dirty. I thought Piotr might…have something on Carl."

Because Piotr was the family bookkeeper. The fixer. The one that did the dirty work. But…

"Why not ask Rericha himself?" That would have been safer, and if the current situation was any indication, Rebecca didn't have a problem dealing with old men.

She snorted. "He'd never tell me—that psycho never tells

anyone anything. But Piotr…he was a braggart. The whole time I was in that basement, he talked about other people he'd hurt, men he'd killed, other women he'd…" She shuddered.

"Maybe we should talk to Rericha again. Together." He tried to cross his ankle over his knee, missed, and settled for leaning over his lap with his elbows on his thighs. "If you file a report, let me get it all down on paper—"

"You know I can't do that."

No, she couldn't. She'd find her child just in time to go to prison.

"Tell me what we're missing," *Mssssssng*. "Tell me how to find your boy."

Rebecca blinked those giant doe eyes. She extended the bottle toward his cup.

The fourth shot went down easier still.

37

SHANNON LEANED back on the couch and rubbed at her aching neck, the blue of the computer screen making her eyes burn. Duke snorted from the cushion beside her.

"What am I missing, boy?" She tried to smile but failed. He wagged his tail anyway, which was far better than barking out the front window; the growling had been going on for hours, making the hairs rise on her neck every damn time, though she hadn't seen anything suspicious on the street, and no one had a reason to be after her. *So stupid, Shannon.* But maybe paranoia was okay. She clearly hadn't been cautious enough when she'd broken into Rericha's; someone, probably Rericha himself, had shown up while she was there, and she'd had to sneak out the bedroom window —scratched the shit out of her lower back on a patch of thorny bushes in the process.

She stretched her arms toward the ceiling, her leg warm with the weight of Duke's furry head. So many pieces of this case were driving her crazy. One of them was the death of Christopher Nowak, and not just because someone had killed a child; it was that Rericha knew he existed—he had Christopher's name listed in that book she'd found in his house. And Christopher had been born in Briddiss, so the only way Rericha could know about him was if he'd known where Rebecca was this whole time.

Fuck. She hadn't told Petrosky about Rericha's little book yet; she should have called him right away. Yeah, it'd probably give him a goddamn heart attack to know what she'd done to obtain that information, and no, they couldn't use it in court, but really she'd kept it to herself because she wasn't sure what it meant. Was Rericha the one who had found Rebecca? Had he sent Piotr after her? Had they killed the boy on purpose? Had anyone else known where Rebecca was? And beneath it all, a little voice in her head whispered: *It's all your fault this kid is dead, you'd better make it right.* She never should have helped Rebecca, never should have allowed her to run away, never should have allowed that missing baby to vanish into the cold-case abyss. Just thinking about that kid made Evie's and Henry's faces pop into her mind, their brilliant blue eyes—Morrison's eyes—their little bodies, healthy, happy, safe. To lose them would be... No, she couldn't even think about it. Her wedding band vibrated, hot and sharp against her flesh.

Your fault, your fault, your fault.

So now what? She dragged her gaze over the coffee table, the couch, where pages of research and reports lay scattered like enormous errant snowflakes—the hit-and-run photos, the Briddiss PD's report that Christopher's death had been an accident, young Christopher's death certificate. Not a single witness had seen the boy go down, despite the fact the accident had happened in the middle of the day. She wasn't even sure what she was looking for. Something to connect Christopher's death to Baird's injuries? But everything in the hit-and-run report had been checked and double-checked—Rebecca hadn't convinced anyone to delete Baird from the paperwork, so how had he gotten injured? Hopefully,

Petrosky and Jackson were having more luck with the hospital than she'd had.

Thunk, thunk, thunk.

Shannon jumped, her heart in her throat, but she was not as fast as Duke who leapt from the sofa and ran for the door like he had fire at his heels; his deep growl rumbled through the living room like thunder. Shannon pushed herself to standing. Petrosky had told her at least forty times not to answer the door, but her gun was in her purse by the jamb, and she wasn't going to sit here and hide in this little room. She squinted through the peephole and paused, her hand on the knob. Then pulled.

Petrosky's partner walked in like she owned the place, Duke nuzzling his face against her hip. Jackson reached down to scratch the big dog's head, but her eyes scanned the living room then the tile by the front door where Petrosky's sneakers usually sat. "He's not here, is he?"

Petrosky? But she didn't have to ask. "Is he supposed to be?"

Jackson frowned at the mess on the coffee table. "Yeah. He is." She made her way to the couch and slumped onto it, her face drawn—tired. "We saw Stewart Baird; the guy's braindead. Looks like he was hit by a car on the same day Rebecca's son was killed."

Shannon eased back against the opposite arm of the sofa, her skin smarting from the scrapes she'd gotten in the bushes outside Rericha's house. She let the stinging steady her, trying not to worry—it wasn't that late, Petrosky was probably scrounging up an after-dinner snack. "So, same accident, both hit at the same time? Stewart's not in the reports on Christopher's hit and run; did Rebecca just toss him in the car and speed off before the police arrived?"

"Looks like it. She vanished that day, probably right from the scene—she's still a person of interest there because she was gone before officers could question her. I think she didn't want the police to connect her to her past. If they realized who she was, they'd have figured out she faked her death, killed her husband, and Baird had a record; his prints would have popped in the system. So she shoved Baird in the back seat, drove until she cleared the state, then dumped him at the first hospital she passed."

Cold. And Stewart was someone Rebecca cared about, a man she'd spent her life with. Heat rose in Shannon's abdomen, her chest prickling with concern—*where is Petrosky?* Maybe… Was he at a bar? Was that why Jackson was here checking up on him?

"How is Petrosky?" Shannon asked, though she suddenly wasn't sure she wanted to know the answer.

Duke climbed onto the sofa between them and put his giant head in Jackson's lap. "How does he seem to you?" Jackson said. But her eyes… *She's worried about him too.*

"He's not sleeping," Shannon said finally, though the confession felt like a betrayal. Every night, she listened to him shuffling around, pacing the living room, the kitchen, the hall. She didn't want to admit that she was listening for the sound of a glass on the countertop, but he'd been so distant… She didn't know what to think. But she did know that he retreated into himself when the pain got bad—like she did.

"He'll sleep when this is over, I suppose." Jackson raised a hand and gestured at the coffee table, and Duke nudged her palm like they were doing some synchronized dog-human dance. "Find anything else worth mentioning?"

Shannon shook her head. "No. I was just…reading." *Looking for a nonexistent clue.* Something was still bothering her about the accident, but she couldn't put her finger on it. "I appreciate you including me even though the situation is… well, it's weird at best." Illegal at worst, especially since she'd broken into Rericha's.

"I know you're motivated to catch her." Jackson shrugged.

"Everyone screws up sometimes, and your adopted daddy is case in point."

Yeah, I did screw up. Rebecca's poor kids. Shannon sat straighter, guilt writhing in her abdomen. Her ring itched. She was opening her mouth to reply when Duke leapt from the couch, one long leg catching her just above the knee, and raced for the entrance. Shannon startled, the scratches on her back brightening with pain against the arm of the sofa. She and Jackson both turned to the door.

Petrosky's face was ruddy with cold. He dropped a paper sack on the coffee table on top of her research and nodded to each of them in turn. "You can stop talking about me now."

"We're not talking about you, you narcissistic bastard." Jackson's eyes narrowed. "You said you were heading home hours ago."

He collapsed onto the Lay-Z-Boy across from them; Duke sat at his feet. "You said the same, Jackson, and yet…" He gestured to her, then to Shannon, and his eyes…bloodshot. Stressed? He did tend to get overzealous if a case was eating at him. "You find any other useful tidbits, Taylor?"

It took her a moment to realize he was talking to her, using her last name—her maiden name. He hadn't called her that for years, not since… She frowned.

"We were just talking about that," Jackson said, but she was squinting, studying Petrosky the same way Shannon was.

"And what was the answer?" he growled. But then he grinned and opened the paper sack and pulled out…a cheeseburger. "This hit-and-run thing with Stewart, I don't like it." Crumbs hit his jacket—he hadn't even bothered to wait for their response. A sesame seed clung to his lips. "I think we're looking at this all wrong." Petrosky lowered the burger, and Duke licked his lips, his long, thin tail whipping the leg of the coffee table. "Maybe Christopher's death wasn't about the kid at all. Maybe it was about Baird."

Shannon blinked at him. All the rape and amputations and kidnapping and murder, and this was about...what? "Because the killer thought Stewart helped Rebecca with the fire? Revenge for Lucius and Roman?"

"We know Baird didn't kill Lucius and Roman—he was in rehab." Petrosky took a giant bite of his burger.

"It's still more likely that someone just wanted to hurt Rebecca," Jackson said.

Shannon nodded agreement. Once Rericha found out Rebecca was alive, it wouldn't have taken him long to realize she'd killed two of his children—maybe he had returned the favor. And he knew about Baird, too, that name was in his little book...in red. Yeah, maybe Rericha hadn't left the state that day, and he didn't own a Chevelle, but he didn't seem opposed to hiring out.

Petrosky kept his eyes on Shannon. "I don't think Rebecca killed anyone at all. I don't think she even knows about the boat used in Piotr's murder." He blinked, and her breath caught. His eyes weren't just bloodshot—glassy.

Her fists clenched, and it took every ounce of strength she possessed not to punch him; she'd wait until he sobered up for that—when he'd feel it. "Rebecca knew about the boat, Petrosky," she said, forcing her voice to stay level. "When I met her the first time, she was with Miranda and me in the office, but after Miranda's suicide, I met her twice on the same beach where you just found Piotr's body. That's not a coincidence."

Petrosky frowned. *Does he think I'm lying?*

"Shannon's right," Jackson said, her eyes on Petrosky. "Rebecca's obviously comfortable with the area."

"It doesn't feel right," Petrosky said. "Maybe this killer, the one from the boat...maybe he's not working with her at all. Maybe he just hated Piotr."

So some mystery person had killed Piotr for reasons unconnected to Rebecca, just days after she was seen breaking into his house? *He's drunk, he's just drunk.* But still, she blurted: "Stop talking." *Until you sober up and quit saying dumb shit.* "Desperate or not, she's manipulative. And I fell for it—*me.* Why are you falling for it? Of all the suspicious bastards in the world—"

"I don't think you're right about her. We need to get back to what we know for sure." Petrosky shoved another bite into his maw, then said around a mouthful of burger: "She admits to drugging Lucius and Roman with heart meds so she could get out of the house—maybe gave them a little too much, but not enough to kill them. We also know that she stole Miranda's corpse and put the body in the warehouse about an hour before the explosion. Roman and Lucius weren't drinking at that warehouse—they were at home, unconscious, when she left to start the fire."

What in the…? *Where'd he get all that?*

"And then she blew up the building with Lucius and Roman inside," Jackson said. "Which seems to be the part you're forgetting." Her voice had gone soft, the deadly kind of silence before a gunshot—like she was taking aim. "What do you know?"

"Lots of stuff, Jackson, I tell you that all the time." He smiled again; he had ketchup on his chin. Duke gave up on the food and collapsed onto the floor, shooting reproachful glances at his master, but Jackson's eyes were lasers directed at Petrosky's face. Shannon wouldn't have been surprised if his flesh started smoking.

"Where did you go tonight, Petrosky?" Jackson said.

"I don't have to tell you everything I do. You're not my mother, even if you are old enough." He frowned at his burger as if it had disappointed him.

"I know you weren't doing paperwork."

He raised his eyes once more. "Yeah, I never should have said that. Dead giveaway." He winked.

Enough of this. "You smell like booze," Shannon said. "We

should have this conversation once you sober up." She wasn't close enough to smell him—the fried oil was permeating the room, sticky in her nostrils, covering all other scents—but the point hit home.

He stilled. "That's your concern? The liquor? People are dying, a kid is missing, and you two are worried about—"

"Of course, we're fucking worried about it!" Shannon yelled, throwing her arms into the air; she probably looked like a petulant child, but she didn't give a shit. "And you're not even trying to hide it—do you just not care anymore?"

He shrugged. "Sorry I'm not better at stealth."

"This isn't about stealth," Jackson said. "You're always careful, and you had to know we'd realize you were trashed the second you walked in. But you didn't even consider it, didn't think...at all. Which tells me that you're more worried about whatever else you were doing." She leaned closer to Petrosky, her eyes narrowed. "You talked to her."

He blinked. But he did not deny it.

Shannon's jaw dropped. "How?"

He sniffed. "She called me."

"The hell she did," Jackson snapped. "I've had Scott monitoring your cell since she called the first time."

Shannon glanced at Jackson, then back in time to see the muscles in Petrosky's jaw tighten. "Fine," he said. "I found her. She said she'd tell me what we needed to know to catch the person who killed her husband if I had a drink with her."

Rebecca, that bitch. She was the reason Petrosky had fallen off the wagon? *I'll beat her ass myself.* "She's a liar, Petrosky. She knew alcohol was your weak spot, and she knew about me, too, telling you that *I* said she could trust you... She's messing with your head. How do you not see that?" The words were hot on her tongue—acidic.

His voice stayed low, far too calm. "I just wanted to know the truth, and I didn't think she'd tell me otherwise. She wanted me...vulnerable." He averted his gaze, not quite ashamed—not of the drinking anyhow. "I let her have her way."

"We need to go pick her up," Jackson said, rising. "We need to—"

"She's gone. She promised she'd be out of her room at the Lodge within the hour, which would be right about..." He raised his wrist as if checking the time—his arm was bare. "An hour ago."

"An hour..." Jackson was trying like hell to control herself, her words pressured like the steam escaping a teapot. She lowered herself back onto the sofa, and Duke followed her with his eyes from the spot he'd chosen near Petrosky's feet—near the food. "You were there with her, you knew she was getting ready to run again, and you just *let her?*"

"I didn't say that." He took the last bite of the burger and tossed the crumpled wrapper back into the sack. "I'm just saying that she's faster than I am."

"You chased her? You're telling me that you—"

"If you need plausible deniability, Jackson, yes, I chased her. And I'm a fat, drunk old man, and she got away."

"Now you sound like Rericha."

"And you're not that old," Shannon said.

"Don't stroke his ego." Jackson leveled her gaze at Petrosky. "Everything you know. Right now."

He ran a hand over his face. His cheeks were still pink—from the booze, not the cold. "When she started the fire, Rebecca believed that only Miranda's bones were in the warehouse; she says she didn't know about Lucius and Roman until she saw it on the news."

"How did she not notice two grown men on the floor?" Jackson asked. "They weren't invisible."

"Right, but she didn't go inside again once she put Miranda in there. And she left for about an hour to go pick up the detonator from our good friend, the arson investigator. It sounds like Gargano rigged the place for her sometime during the day, and they met at his house after he got off the late shift so he could pass her the device."

"The...what?" Jackson said. "How did we not know about this sooner?"

"Because the only way simple detectives like us would have known about a detonator is if we'd read about it in the arson investigator's report. And everything in that report is a fucking lie."

The room felt smaller, the air tight against Shannon's skin. Duke grumbled, his eyes on the take-out bag, his bull head on the floor. If they believed Rebecca, then there was an hour between her dropping Miranda at the warehouse and her returning to trigger the blaze. An hour where someone else could have moved Lucius and Roman. And Gargano had known she was going to blow the building. It was bullshit, had to be, but Petrosky seemed to believe it. "So you think... that Franklin Gargano killed Roman and Lucius?" Shannon said finally.

Petrosky shrugged. But his eyes said *yes*.

Jackson crossed her arms. "That doesn't make any sense. Gargano has no motive. And if she drugged them at home, then got the detonator from Gargano and went straight over to start the fire, then Gargano *couldn't* have done it. She was *with him*. Even if he watched her leave then drove fast, there's no way he could get from his place, over to Rebecca's to collect Lucius and Roman, then back to the warehouse to dump the men inside in the same amount of time it took Rebecca to drive directly to the warehouse—her trip would take half that time, easy. She has to be lying. I mean, shit, if Rebecca wasn't planning to kill them in that fire, why drug them at all?"

"Maybe Frankie's just crafty, or maybe he drives really, really fast," Petrosky said, his tone low—breathy. When he was drunk, he didn't show it the way other people did, but that weird way he exhaled made the skin along her spine crawl. It was the only time he sounded like her father. "I don't know how he did it. But Rebecca didn't kill Lucius or Roman or Piotr."

"You seem awfully sure," Jackson said slowly, her mouth pinched. "There's more, isn't there?"

"Not about this, but she told me about her baby—the first one. She remembers pushing, remembers Rericha at the bedside, remembers passing out. But she saw Rericha take the baby out of the room before she lost consciousness; she was absolutely certain. He told her he gave the kid away; that someone was going to adopt him."

What? Rebecca had never told her that part.

"So she told you a story," Jackson snapped. "Completely unsubstantiated."

"That doesn't mean it's a lie." He grimaced at the paper sack as if the thought of food suddenly made him ill. "I want to talk to Gargano about Lucius and Roman, maybe Piotr too —he was in the hospital, but he could know a guy. And I want to check out the adoption circuit. Carl is all she has left."

Carl? Gargano? He was grasping at straws, and Shannon was tired of them being the wrong ones, drunk or not. "Rericha knew she was alive," Shannon blurted. Both Petrosky and Jackson turned to her, eyes wide, and Shannon pressed on before she could change her mind: "I broke into his house. He has a book with the names of all his kids and grandkids, their ages, and then dollar amounts—maybe net worth. Christopher's in there. And Stewart. He has their worths both listed as zero." The words were coming faster and faster, tumbling from her lips. "And he's obsessive. Rericha wouldn't give that baby to someone outside the family to raise. He probably killed her first child the way he did Christopher." That made the most sense, didn't it? Even if it meant she'd failed. Her ring burned as if the metal was in this moment being forged against her flesh.

245

"What the shit, Taylor? Are you kidding right now?" Petrosky's words slurred. Maybe he was only able to hold it together when he was…less furious. Her hackles rose, but when he met her gaze, he looked more hurt than angry—disappointed. In her. "Why do you make it so hard to protect you?" he practically whispered.

Her heart twisted—*that's why I didn't tell him. That right there.* He didn't mean to do it, but damn. "The guilt trip isn't going to solve anything, Petrosky. I'm not trying to make it hard; I'm trying to help, trying to help *you*."

"But we can't use the book," Jackson said. "Can't even ask Rericha about it; no charge will hold up if he—or the DA—finds out what you did. Which you know." Jackson pushed herself to standing and headed around the coffee table, stepping carefully over the dog, who was now snoring like nothing at all had happened. "I'll head to the Lodge, in case you're wrong about Rebecca leaving. Tomorrow morning, we'll go back to the hospital and ask Franklin Gargano about the detonator. Shannon, we'll need a statement from you, so think about whether there's anything else you might have left out." Jackson paused at the door and looked over her shoulder, her gaze on Petrosky. "And if I find out that you've taken another drink after tonight, I will call Carroll. And she'll have your badge."

Petrosky's eyes narrowed. But from the agitated gleam there, Shannon thought he believed her.

38

JACKSON'S FINGERS were already doing their manic dance on the steering wheel, the brilliant morning sun sharp as pokers in Petrosky's eyeballs. Rebecca had been gone by the time Jackson had gotten to the Lodge Motel last night—his partner was surely still pissed at him, but he didn't have it in him to care, not when they were trying to chase down so many crimes at once. He'd wait to worry whether she liked him until they were dealing with just one weirdo cult member. One kidnapping. One dead body. Just one of *anything*. But right now... Jackson was talking. Instead of passing out last night as he had, she'd actually done some work.

"So, Franklin Gargano was the first responder after Rebecca's kidnapping-turned-auto-wreck—the accident they thought took her hand. We didn't see a connection to Gargano before, because we didn't look far enough into his employment; arson investigators aren't usually a part of crashes, especially when the vehicle doesn't burst into flames. But—surprise!—he briefly moonlighted as an EMT after his divorce. EMTs work in pairs, so his name wasn't on the paperwork, but it only took one phone call once, and…" She shrugged.

So much do-gooding, so little time. He squinted at Jackson, then at the blinding road ahead—no ice now. Almost spring. Funny how fast things could change. "So he was going through a divorce, emotionally vulnerable, and with all those damn medals, we know he has a tendency toward heroics. Sounds like her kind of mark." The skin along his spine prickled, and Petrosky looked over to see Jackson watching him, probably trying to tell if he was drunk. Which he wasn't. Shannon hadn't left his side since yesterday—he'd had to step over her pillow to get out of bed—and Jackson had picked him up at his front door.

He studied his partner right back. "Problem?"

She shook her head and maneuvered the SUV into the hospital parking lot. "Nope. Well, unless you count Gargano giving Rebecca a detonator a problem." Her tone said she wasn't sure she believed it, but they had to check it out.

"At least it explains why Gargano failed to mention that he knew Rebecca." He snatched his coffee from the cupholder—Shannon's stainless steel mug, like the ones the girls next door used. It made the coffee taste less like Styrofoam, but he'd have liked it more if he'd been able to sneak in a shot on his way out. He slugged back a brutally hot sip, then said: "I think you were right on the timeline, though—Gargano wasn't the one who brought Lucius and Roman to the warehouse." Sometimes liquor cleared his head, but sometimes it made him dumb, and last night, it had left him incapable of calculating things like mileage and minutes. From Gargano's house to get the bodies at Rebecca's was twenty minutes. From there to the warehouse, another forty. Gargano needed an hour to move the bodies. But Rebecca told him that she'd gone straight from Gargano's to the warehouse after picking up the device—thirty minutes tops. She had no reason to lie about that part, not when her story left less of a window for someone else to move those men.

He set his coffee cup back in the console. "Plus, someone like Gargano wouldn't kill Rebecca's husband without telling her; he'd want her adoration, her thanks, an emotional medal to go with the ones he has on that damn night table." Not a single picture of his kid, but he had his ribbons. He'd want to see Rebecca's face when he told her she never had to worry about her husband again. That he'd saved her.

Jackson eased the Escalade into a parking spot made tight by a dumb-shit Camry, its back tires edging over the line. "Yeah, I think Gargano got roped in the way Shannon did. He probably thought he was helping Rebecca escape, that she was just faking her death, and didn't know about the men inside that building. And after it was over, he was on the hook for rigging the place—he couldn't say shit. But that leaves Rebecca as our killer."

"Or whoever killed Piotr." They knew that wasn't Gargano; he'd been sleeping at the hospital while their suspect was leaving Piotr's body on the shore.

"I can't believe you're falling for this. She did it, and you know she did it—she's involved in every one of those deaths." Jackson was shaking her head as she cut the engine. "But clearly Gargano knows more than he told us; maybe he's aware of another friend at least. Or a hideout where she's lying low with her boat-driving accomplice. Let's focus on that, shall we?"

"Fine." He followed her toward the building, the mild air dewy against the tops of his ears. *Boat-driving accomplice indeed.* They knew Stewart Baird wasn't involved in either the warehouse fire—*rehab*—or killing Piotr—*braindead*—and they couldn't find anyone else that she'd spoken to now or in the past. They hadn't even found evidence that she'd been talking to Gargano before she vanished, yet she clearly had if he'd given her a detonator. The woman was careful.

Franklin Gargano was exactly where they'd left him, sitting up in bed, face drawn in pain, hands limp at his sides. He offered them a wan smile. "Back for seconds?"

"Something like that. Just had a few more questions for you." Petrosky pulled a chair to Gargano's bedside, careful not to catch wires from the bank of monitors that flanked the headboard.

Jackson stood at the foot of the bed as if afraid what Gargano had was catching, but Petrosky knew better—she wanted a different perspective, and it was always more intimidating to tower over the suspect. Or maybe she was trying to avoid karate chopping him in the dick for having wasted their time. "Tell us about the night you and Rebecca met," she said.

Gargano closed his eyes for a beat longer than a blink and sighed. "You know, right? That I was there for her car accident?"

Petrosky nodded. "We want to hear it from you."

Gargano hissed a long, wet breath through his nostrils—phlegmy. "I found her on the west side of Chattel Road, the car inverted. I managed to pry the door open and pulled her free." He swallowed hard. "But she was terrified."

"Most people would be scared after a wreck like that, her hand torn off and all." Petrosky watched Gargano's face, the tremble in one eyebrow. *Take the bait, asshole. Take it.*

"You don't understand; I had to help her." Gargano's voice was strained, not the gravelly rumble from before: a defensive panic. *Here we go.* "She wasn't scared about the wreck," he said. "She was afraid of her husband, of his relatives. She said someone in the family had kidnapped her, and that she'd escaped." Yeah, by cutting off her own hand the way Louisa had begun to...until Rericha had stepped in.

"Why not call the police?" Jackson said.

"She said she had called the police, and her husband found out—Lucius had her kidnapped, tortured because of it." Just like Louisa. Just like Miranda. Weird that Miranda had gotten to keep her hand—maybe because she was Rericha's daughter—but it hadn't helped her in the end.

Jackson snorted. "You're a smart guy, Gargano. You're trained in domestic abuse."

"Does that sound like a run-of-the-mill domestic abuse case to you? Lucius didn't punch her; he had his relatives cut off her *hand*—she had the stump to prove it." Gargano hissed in a quick breath, his face tightening; he winced. "I made her a promise while my partner drove us to the hospital: to keep it to myself until she had an escape plan. But I honestly thought she'd change her mind and tell the police what really happened once she wasn't in crisis mode, in pain—that she'd tell the docs it wasn't just a car wreck. But…she didn't. And after the hospital, she went back home. To *him*. And by then…" He shook his head. Another grimace. "I didn't want to be responsible for something worse. I honestly don't know what I was thinking; it was so…stupid." He sighed, but his eyes were pleading—almost desperate—and his voice came out a whisper. "Would you believe I just got sucked in?"

Sucked in during the ride to the hospital—he'd fallen for her story fast. But Shannon had too. *Maybe even you, old man.* Yet Gargano's situation felt different; he'd rigged a building to explode, a major legal infraction on its own, and the detonator idea hadn't been hatched and handled in the back of that ambulance.

Jackson nodded as if she understood, commiserating, but Petrosky recognized the glitter in her eye. *Bring it home, partner.* "You must have had some strong feelings about her family," Jackson said. "About her husband."

Gargano's face hardened, and this time it wasn't one of his trademarked pain spasms—he was furious. "Her husband deserved to die," he spat. "Roman too."

"Sounds like a yes to me," Jackson said.

"Yeah, I have strong feelings; I wish I'd killed them all." He sniffed. "But unfortunately, I didn't."

"Well, you kind of did." Petrosky leaned one elbow on the bed, and half smiled when Gargano shifted his leg farther away, wincing. "She blew up a warehouse with two men inside it using a detonator she got from you." But any evidence of the detonator had vanished long ago, probably cleaned up by the very person sitting in front of him. All they had was Rebecca's word.

Gargano's lips tightened against his teeth like a cornered animal, and maybe that's exactly what he was. "Yeah."

Wait…yeah? *That was easy.* "So, you admit you gave her the detonator?" Jackson said.

"Yes, okay? Yes." He leveled steely blue eyes at Petrosky. "She said that was the only way she could escape—if they thought she was dead."

"What about Lucius and Roman?" Jackson asked. "They were in the building, too, and you just said you thought they deserved to die."

"I had no idea anyone else was in there." *Like Shannon.* "I thought she was using a dead body, some girl she knew, to fake her death; it felt like a victimless crime. Even the building was already falling down." His shoulders slumped. "I rigged it up and made her a little remote control so she could set it off without going inside where she might get hurt—she just had to be within 100 feet of the warehouse. She would have figured it out even if I hadn't helped, but this way…she was safer. And the burn was more controlled—none of the nearby buildings were damaged." He grimaced and shifted his weight as if his hips were aching.

"Let's back up," Jackson cut in. "You made the detonator—easy enough for a guy in your field. How did you give it to her?"

"She came by the house that night—my house."

"What time?" she snapped. Rapid-fire, trying to catch him in a lie.

"I was getting off a medic shift, pulled up right after her; I was still moonlighting then. So it must have been...maybe midnight? Eleven thirty?" That meshed with what Rebecca had said and the time of the fire in the reports.

"And after you handed the device off?" Jackson asked. "Did you follow her to the warehouse to make sure it worked?"

"No, I knew it would work. I just...watched TV. I couldn't sleep." He raised his arm and scratched at one pale cheek; the flesh looked paper-thin, sagging from the bone. "How'd you know about the detonator anyway? Not that it matters now, I guess."

Petrosky leaned back in the chair and waited to see if Gargano would shift his legs now that Petrosky's elbow was gone. He didn't. "She told me last night," Petrosky said.

Gargano's eyes widened. He sat straighter, though it must have hurt like a bitch. "Wait, she...she's here?" His voice was high, cracking like that of a fourteen-year-old. Excited? Or scared?

Petrosky ignored his question. "If I pull you in as an accessory to a double homicide, even just the two deaths secondary to arson, you'll die in jail before trial instead of in this cushy bed." He gestured to the IV. "And I hear they like to forget pain medications on the inside."

The man did not appear to have heard him—his eyes stayed wide, mouth gaping in shock. "No, wait, just...did you say she's *here*?"

Did this asshole not watch the news? Then again, it wasn't like Rebecca's photo was getting prime billing—the person-of-interest story they'd put out wasn't juicy enough. They should have led with the cult.

"Do you trust her?" Jackson asked, making Gargano turn to her. "Trust that she didn't set it up this way to frame you?

Maybe that's the real reason you covered it up—because you knew you'd look complicit in Roman's and Lucius's deaths. They'd arrest you. As soon as you got her the detonator, fudged that paperwork, you had to choose between keeping her secret—your secret—and never seeing your daughter again. It isn't much of a choice, that's for sure." She raised one shoulder. "Maybe I'd have done the same."

Gargano grimaced and lowered himself to the raised bed, the dented pillows—he stared at the wall. The silence stretched.

"What about Stewart Baird?" Petrosky asked. "How does he fit into all this?"

He turned back, frowning. Confused. "Who?" Did he really have no idea who Stewart was? Maybe Rebecca didn't like to overlap her marks.

"As close as you two were, Rebecca never mentioned her best childhood friend?" He needed Gargano to get upset with her—to stop protecting her—but it looked like he was clueless. Rebecca had been careful; she hadn't told Gargano anything she didn't want him to know.

"He's dying because someone mowed him down three weeks ago," Petrosky went on. "Hit him with a car along with Rebecca's son, Christopher. That child is dead now too."

Gargano's nostrils flared—angry at the unfairness of it all, or did he need more morphine? But then he said: "She's been through so much." His lip trembled. "More than anyone should have to go through."

"You seem pretty emotional there, Frankie."

The man's eyes cleared, a pair of sapphires in his otherwise sallow face. "What do you want me to say? That I made a mistake? That I fucked up? Okay, guilty, you got me. I should have known, right? I mean, I called her that night, and she was freaking out, but I didn't know it was because she'd hurt anyone, that those men were inside. I thought she was panicking because she had to light up the building—because she had to run away. And I told her to take deep breaths and hit the button when I should have been telling her not to do it." His voice had risen on the last sentence; at least his cheeks finally had some color. "How was I supposed to know?"

Petrosky crossed his arms and stared. "It's just hard for me to believe that you didn't get anything out of it except a smile and a pat on the shoulder."

Gargano's gaze steadied. His face relaxed—resigned. "I slept with her. You needed to hear that too? Fine. Drag it all out of me before I kick off."

Some hero you are. Rage burned in Petrosky's gut. "You took advantage of an abused woman, a woman trying like hell to get out of her situation, and—"

"I slept with her, but it wasn't like that!"

Petrosky met the man's eyes—that bright sapphire blue. Like Christopher's. "Are you the father of her child?"

Gargano was shaking. "No. She was pregnant when I met her."

Was she? Christopher had been six pounds at his birth in Briddiss, seven months after the fire; the kidnapping, when Gargano had met Rebecca, was three months before the fire. If she'd conceived before the kidnapping, or even during the kidnapping, Christopher had taken his sweet time coming into the world.

"Weird thing, though…her son Christopher didn't belong to her husband or to Piotr Wójcik, the man we think kidnapped her. Or to her friend Stewart Baird, who's been living with her for the last seven years."

Gargano's nostrils flared again, but he shook his head once more, harder this time—clueless and frustrated as hell about it. "There might have been someone else at the kidnapping. She didn't talk about that. Ever. It was very… traumatic."

"Or maybe the kid was yours, and she didn't want to tell you."

He snorted. "Yeah, right."

Had the thought really never occurred to him?

"Maybe she didn't think you'd want to be involved." Jackson edged her way around the bed until she was standing on Gargano's other side, directly across from Petrosky. "Or maybe she knew she couldn't take you away from your family here—your daughter. Maybe she believed it was cruel to let you walk around with the knowledge that you had another child you couldn't be with." *Or she used you and didn't want anything more to do with you.*

Gargano's face had gone still, pink spots blooming high on his cheekbones like a pair of welts from highly coordinated bees. "No, she loved me; she would have told me."

"Did she tell you where she was going?" Petrosky asked.

The man turned his way. "She couldn't. It would have been too dangerous."

"So, how were you supposed to contact her?" Jackson said. "How were you supposed to continue this alleged love affair?" Now Gargano looked at her—back and forth, back and forth. Poor guy was going to get whiplash. Which was exactly the point.

"She…she said…" He stopped talking, and in that silence rose another sound; the heart-rate monitor, until now mere background noise, punched through Petrosky's consciousness. *Beep. Beep. Beep. Beep.* How had he not noticed the monitor before? Had Gargano's heart rate changed? He should have been paying attention—the monitor was like a built-in lie detector.

"She was supposed to come back for you, wasn't she?" Jackson said.

"Not come back, she was never supposed to come back."

"But she was supposed to contact you." Petrosky drew his eyes to the monitor at the head of the bed, the fine lines of red and green, the little blipping dot in the corner—faster, definitely faster. At the foot of the bank of monitors, a silver trash can gleamed, the top lip reflecting the blinking lights like a mirror—inside, a bloody bandage lay amidst tissue and gauze, the spots of gore like a broken heart.

Gargano's breath hitched. His eyes filled. "She was supposed to call—I had a burner and everything. She wasn't supposed to vanish. In the end, I understood; she was terrified, and she did what she had to do, did what was best for her. Like my wife did."

"Two in a row must have hurt, though," Jackson said, leaning over the bed, her face inches from Gargano's. "But I still can't believe you didn't know what she was up to. Maybe you were okay with it; figured once her husband was dead, she wouldn't have to leave—the guy was an asshole anyway."

"That family...it would have gone on without Lucius and Roman. They were sociopaths, but not near as bad as Piotr."

"Is that why you killed him too?" Petrosky knew the answer to this one, Gargano had been here in the hospital when Piotr was killed, but he was more interested in what it might do to Gargano's heart. He leaned closer to the monitor, to the trash can, reaching into his pocket for...a gum wrapper? *That'll do.* He reached down toward the can, squinting at the blinking dot on the screen.

Gargano shook his head. "I didn't kill Piotr." *Beep-beep-beep.* Fast, but steady. If the guy knew anything about Piotr's death, even secondhand, his heart rate should have changed.

Petrosky straightened once more as Jackson said: "No, but you put your career on the line for her, your freedom. And she left you in the cold."

The monitors accelerated. *Beep-beep-beep.*

"Were you mad, Frankie?" Petrosky said, his voice low. "Mad that she used you and left you alone?"

Gargano scowled, but his lip trembled. Hopefully, he was

upset enough to throw her or her new accomplice under the bus; or the boat, as it were.

"Who else did she know here?" Petrosky asked. "Another man? Someone you thought was a friend?"

"No one that I know of. You think she would have told me if she was stringing me along?" The monitors droned on: *beepbeepbeep.* "There's a lot I don't know, obviously."

"It's time to stop this." Petrosky met Gargano's eyes—bright with pain. "It's not like you have anything to lose now. Just tell us where she might be."

"I have no idea! I guess I never really knew her at all." His words were a hissed whisper. "I tried to save her, and then I watched her walk away. Apparently, with someone else." The monitors shrieked. *Beepbeepbeepbeepbeep.*

"You need to leave."

Petrosky turned. A young ponytailed doctor in a white coat stood in the doorway, her face tight with agitation.

"May we talk to you instead?" Jackson asked.

She looked to her patient with caring brown eyes—worried.

"Tell them. Tell them whatever they ask." A tear slipped down Gargano's cheek, but he kept his gaze focused on the doctor. "That's why you're looking at me, right? To see if it's okay?" He choked, recovered. "I don't have anything left. I don't have anything left to hide—don't have anything left at all."

And from the anguished set of his mouth, maybe that was actually true.

They followed the doctor into the hallway. "You should be ashamed of yourselves, interrogating a dying man like that," she said the moment the door latched. "Even on his best days, the drugs barely touch the pain, and anxiety makes it that much worse." She crossed her arms and stared them down like a schoolmarm waiting for a good reason to whip out her ruler.

"I hear loneliness is bad for pain, too." Petrosky had been there himself after his heart attack. "We were just keeping him company."

She frowned and brushed a dark curl from her cheek. "I'm sure he's lonely, and I don't want to refuse him the only visitors he gets, but keep it kind. Stop jacking up his heart rate."

"We can't be the only ones visiting," Jackson said. "Doesn't his ex-wife ever come by? His daughter?"

The doc shook her head. "Not in the two months he's been here. I don't think he's had any visitors outside his coworkers from the fire department. Which is unusual, especially so close to the end."

Huh. Gargano must have done something nasty if his family hadn't even come to say goodbye.

"Maybe he doesn't want his family to see him like this," Jackson said.

"Maybe," the doctor agreed. "Most people opt for more drugs, sleep their way to the end, but he wants to be alert, at least awake—he's in agony. I think he's hoping his family will show. But the thought of his child watching him grimace in pain… That can be scary for kids."

"Sounds like an awful existence," Petrosky said.

"You aren't wrong." She sighed and shoved her hair back once more like she was mad at it for existing. Maybe she was mad at Petrosky for existing. "Look, he's in enough pain to want to die already. It's my job to keep him as comfortable as possible, for as long as possible, and what you're doing…" She met Petrosky's eyes. "He seems like a nice man. Don't make him suffer more than he has to."

39

"Sorry-ass motherfucker. He's getting what he deserves." Petrosky tore off his jacket as they hustled toward the parking structure, though it wasn't all that warm—it was his guts that were hot. He hadn't felt it while they were interviewing Gargano, but the anger had built as they'd made their way back outside. Yeah, Gargano had been used, as Shannon had, but it sounded like he'd used Rebecca right back. And she'd been used enough.

"What he deserves? Because he fell in love with her? Slept with her?" Jackson's words echoed across the quiet lot. "If anyone got screwed, it was him—he was the one who got manipulated."

"He never said he was in love with her." And they'd moved so *fast*. It had only been three months from the time she showed up with a severed arm to the day she'd burned her husband in that warehouse. Petrosky's sneakers squeaked on the damp pavement, the sound combining with the tap of Jackson's boots to create a horrid cacophony of percussion and errant squealing. "He fucked her; he didn't save her. Some goddamn hero."

She slammed the car door so hard the whole vehicle shook. "What is wrong with you?"

I need a drink. "Nothing." Maybe his moderated drinking wasn't working out so well, especially since he'd expanded to include airline bottles in his car and shots with killers in their motel rooms.

"Let's back up, okay?" Jackson cranked the key, releasing a blast of superheated air from the vents. "Gargano admitted to helping with the fire. Admitted to sleeping with her, to having a relationship with her that started the day of her car wreck. Maybe that's motive to kill her husband, but he wouldn't have had time to move those bodies between Rebecca picking up the detonator and lighting the building up. We have no evidence that he knew where she was these last seven years. No evidence that they maintained a relationship. It sounds like Rebecca just…vanished. As she'd planned. Which means he's not involved with her now—he's not the guy with information on where she might be or who she might be with."

"Maybe that's the problem," he said. "Her tendency to vanish after making people care about her. Partners are always suspects, and she seems to have a lot of them." His chest felt lighter, his rage softening to a steady ache; Gargano was an accessory to arson, but maybe beyond that, he was just a lovesick shmuck.

She eased them onto the freeway and sighed. "We know Gargano didn't kill Piotr since he was passed out in the hospital, but I guess we can entertain the possibility of a jilted lover going after Stewart Baird and hurting Christopher by accident. But I think Rericha-by-proxy is far more likely, especially since he knew Rebecca was alive—knew about Christopher. He has to have contacts out there who owe him a favor." She hit the turn signal. "The thing that gets me is how fast Rebecca packed and headed here. Can you imagine not sticking around to bury your child?"

No. Then again, he couldn't have imagined being *there* to bury his child...until it had happened. Petrosky rubbed at his aching chest and watched the sky—blue like Gargano's eyes. According to Rebecca, she hadn't even packed, just drove with her critically injured, but still conscious, boyfriend toward Ash Park as if she'd had that plan in the back of her mind all along. But she hadn't planned on Baird passing out; on dumping him at East Valley. If she'd gotten him admitted sooner, he might have made it through with his brain intact. "I wish we could find that Chevelle, get the asshole who killed Christopher," he muttered. Rebecca thought it was Piotr's car, but he wanted to be sure.

"And Piotr's killer. Whatever big, bad, boating man Rebecca enlisted after she lost that fight at Piotr's house."

"And Rebecca's kid." Petrosky squinted at the fast-approaching sign for their exit, the sunshine glinting off the steel, everything too goddamn bright. Was the world so different from yesterday, or was it him? He'd lost track of how many shots he'd had last night, but...he'd slept in his car for an hour before he'd driven home. His belly rolled, sour and sick. "Let's get lunch before we head back—at least more coffee. I want to look into that adoption thing, and I don't want to do it on an empty stomach."

"I thought you were drunk when you mentioned the adoption circuit." Jackson eased them onto the main drag, her fingers tap-tap-tapping on the wheel. "I think Shannon already looked into adoptions anyway."

Shannon—he'd lose her once this was over, he'd lose her and the kids for good. His chest spasmed and released; he cleared his throat. "Rericha would make sure the boy was cared for—every member of the group was set up financially on Rericha's dime even if we can't prove it." That bastard kept family close to home. "I just want to see if any of the adoption agencies have connections to Rericha's little cult—just one person he might trust to place the boy."

Jackson paused, the hiss of air from the vents the only sound in the car besides the buzzing drone of the tires. "So how do you propose we go about it? Drag in everyone who worked in adoptions seven years ago? Maybe you can call and pretend to be Rericha, act extra haughty. Shouldn't be too hard for you." She muttered something that might have been *with your bitch ass*.

He almost smiled. "I've got Shannon pulling files on those who worked at the nearest five adoption agencies at the time Rebecca's son was born. If one of them was suspiciously lucky finance-wise or has any connection to Rericha or the other cult members we've already identified—"

"It's a waste of time." Her cell buzzed in her pocket. "I know what we said about trying to do it this way, going around Rericha and not involving Shannon, but we can't just let Rebecca run around killing folks because you don't want Shannon to get into trouble. Shannon needs to give a statement—officially. Rebecca has dragged us all into the mire, and I'm not going out like that, not for her, and not for this case." Her fingers stopped tapping as she reached for her phone. "Not even for you."

Petrosky drew his gaze up to the smattering of clouds above the telephone wires, wispy and white—innocent. He had known this was coming, but he'd hoped he could buy a few more days before he had to drag Shannon into the station. "If we find the kid, figure out who has him, Rebecca will come to us." And Shannon could go home without signing a thing. "Trust me."

Jackson's cell rang again. She snapped it to her ear, still shaking her head, and he turned back to the window—to those innocent clouds. "Jackson." She listened. And took her foot off the gas.

He glanced her way, expecting to see her rummaging for a pen or adjusting the vents, maybe just eking toward a stop sign, but her mouth was open, her brow furrowed, her knuckles pale around the cell. *Shit, what now?* But he didn't have time to ask; Petrosky's shoulder slammed against the door as she hooked a U-turn. "What's going on, woman?"

She ignored him. "Rericha should have listened to us." She tossed the cell into the cupholder and clutched the wheel. "You did call him about protective custody, right? You said you were on it."

Nope. Michaelson had been watching the guy's house, albeit mostly to see if Rebecca or Piotr showed up. But after Piotr's death, Petrosky had ratcheted the monitoring down, told the flatfoots to stick to hourly drive-bys. He raised an eyebrow. "Why, what happened?"

"Goddammit, Petrosky." She sighed. "Shots fired at the hardware store. Looks like Rebecca decided to go after Rericha herself."

40

THE STREET in front of Rericha's hardware store was crawling with black-and-white cars, their red lights flashing in a way that would incapacitate an epileptic.

"What've we got?" Jackson snapped at a broad-shouldered patrolwoman—shit, his partner was *furious*. Likely at him.

"Two inside; appears to be the store owner and a female, mid thirties," the patrolwoman said. "She's armed. Screaming about a baby, but we've seen no evidence of a child—could be hallucinating. Probably cranked out of her mind."

Petrosky headed over the lot, his footsteps vanishing into the din of sirens and murmuring cops.

"Hey! You can't go in there!" the patrolwoman called after them.

"She knows us," Jackson barked back, but Petrosky ignored the woman altogether and addressed his partner. "You should stay out here, Jackson. Rebecca trusts me; I can get her out safely."

Jackson's eyes stayed locked on the building, scanning the high windows, then the wooden door. "Yeah, she trusts you so much she decided to take matters into her own hands less than twelve hours after talking to you." They stepped onto the walkway.

"That stings, Jackson."

"You just want to take her back to your harem."

"I don't have a—"

"House full of dog walkers, whatever." She drew her weapon.

The front door squealed as it had the first time they'd come—the final terrified scream of a dying bird.

And inside…more screaming. Of the human variety. It filtered down the aisles and out the door like a strong smell —like smoke.

"I don't have him, Becky." Rericha's voice was just as calm as it'd been in days past, not an ounce of anxiety-induced inflection. Either he didn't believe she'd shoot him or he wasn't afraid to die.

"You do, I know you do!" Rebecca shouted.

Jackson headed left, down the far aisle where she'd spent their last visit, and Petrosky took the middle; the front desk would be waiting up this row at the far side of the store, the place where Rericha always sat with his hunting magazines.

Petrosky sidled up the aisle, his weapon heavy against his hip. "Rebecca Kowalski!"

Silence. His sneakers made a dull *thip, thip, thip* against the dusty wooden floor.

"That's not my name anymore," she said, her voice muted by distance and angle—she was still facing Rericha, had to be. She was too smart to take her eyes off him.

Petrosky stepped toward the endcap, his shoulder against the shelving, and peeked around the edge. His heart spasmed —god, she was so *small*, innocent-looking if you ignored the gun in her hand. Rebecca's back was to him as he'd suspected, her white-blonde ponytail askew as if she'd been in a fight. Maybe she had; she had a smudge of something on the back of one sleeved elbow, maybe dirt, maybe blood. The sleeve on that arm had been cut and tied just above the swath of heavy gauze that covered her stump; red stains seeped outward from a spot near the middle of her forearm. And Rericha…his hair was mussed too. Petrosky took another step, and something crunched beneath his sneaker—glass. Maybe from whatever she'd shot, but he couldn't tell what it used to be.

Rericha kept his gaze on Rebecca, or perhaps on the weapon—he didn't appear to see Petrosky at all, didn't acknowledge the *click* that sounded from the left of the store. Jackson's boots? Probably her gun.

"I know why you're here, Rebecca," Petrosky said. "You want him to pay for what he did, but this isn't the way."

"I don't care if he pays," she snapped. "I. Want. My. Child."

Rericha blinked slowly, his shoulders hunched as if he were bored of the accusation—as if he didn't have a gun pointed at his face. "There is no child, I told you—"

"There *is* a child. I was pregnant. I didn't make that up." She took a step closer to Rericha, the gun steady and sure in her hand, her finger on the trigger. "You were there when he was born, when Lucius was out of town. I remember how fast he came like he couldn't wait to make his way into the world; I pushed a few times, and he was in your arms." Her voice cracked. "And you…took him. You gave him to someone; I know you did."

Rericha stared blankly. *Cold, cold bastard.*

"If you tell us who you gave him to, we can cut you a deal," Petrosky said, stepping away from the endcap. "She just wants her kid, so if you help us with that, Rebecca will walk out of here with us, and you get to keep your head. That sounds good, eh, Rebecca?"

Rebecca did not look back—she kept the weapon trained on Rericha. Her hand was shaking now, maybe with nerves, more likely with rage from the set of her jaw. He was shocked that he couldn't hear her teeth grinding together, but he couldn't really hear anything save their words above the frantic throbbing of his heart.

"I didn't take him." Rericha blinked, but this was not the usual sleepy blinking he was known for—rapid-fire, as if he had something in his eye. But...*huh*. He'd interviewed Rericha twice this week; when he lied, the man didn't have any tells. Was this how he looked when he was telling the truth?

"You did this to me," Rebecca said in a voice that was half sob. "I passed out, or maybe you gave me something, and when I woke up—"

"I'm sorry," Rericha said. "I'm sorry those boys took it out on you. That Lucius came home and hurt you, that he...did what he did."

Had Rericha just admitted that he'd known his son had attacked her? Was he referring to the kidnapping? Petrosky couldn't be sure—and nor could any jury.

"You think I'm here about that?" Rebecca spat the words. "About Lucius? Piotr's dead, and so is my husband. But my baby...he's all I have left."

"Put the gun down, Rebecca," Petrosky said. "Just lower the weapon and—"

"I wish I had him, Becky, I do." Rericha's words had started low and crescendoed into a passionate appeal, as if he were begging her not to kill him, but Petrosky didn't think that's what he was asking for—a plea for forgiveness? "I wish I could take it all back and start over. Because I was wrong, it was wrong what I did. You should have been able to say goodbye."

Say goodbye? Was he admitting to something worse than they'd expected? Had he killed the boy? Petrosky's fist tightened on the weapon, but Rebecca had frozen. Her hand had stilled. Even her jaw had gone slack. She wanted to know, needed to know, but she couldn't ask. And that, Petrosky understood. He hadn't even been able to open the case file from Julie's murder, hadn't solved it for ten years, and Rebecca'd only had ten seconds to process that she might never see her child again. Outside, voices rose then fell: shouting. Backup would come in soon.

Rebecca didn't have ten years. If she wanted an answer, she needed to get it now.

"What'd you do, Rericha?" Petrosky asked for her. He should be telling Rebecca to drop the gun, not giving her a reason to shoot this man in the face, but Rericha would never be as motivated to spill his guts as he was right now.

Rericha's eyes flicked to Petrosky and back to Rebecca. "He was so little, Becky. More than a month early. There was nothing I could do."

Wait, the baby was a month early? They hadn't known that, had they? *Maybe the liquor's messing with your brain.*

"What are you saying?"

Rericha did not respond; he stared.

Rebecca advanced on him unsteadily as if her legs had stopped working right, her soles on the wood hissing like the first sharp breath of new grief. A pinprick of pain stabbed at his chest and swelled to a throbbing ache. He recognized that sound—he'd made that sound.

Her shoulders trembled. "What are you telling me?" Her words screamed down the aisles, ringing in his ears, though she'd barely spoken above a whisper.

"Rebecca," Petrosky said. "Put the gun down. We'll get him; we'll figure this out."

Neither Rericha nor Rebecca appeared to hear him; their gazes stayed locked on each other, a tenuous dance that felt too much like a death march. Rericha blinked, his eyes no longer cold: resigned, and just as sorrowful as Rebecca's likely were—Petrosky couldn't see her face from his position at her back.

A beat passed, then two. Finally, Rericha spoke in a voice so soft Petrosky had to strain his ears. "I'd just lost Miranda,"

Rericha said. "I watched that bastard break her; she died well before I put her in the ground. Roman killed her soul when he made her lose that baby." Rericha's eyes twitched, and his nose was trembling, too—his whole face was spasming. "I thought it'd be better if you believed your boy was alive. At least if he was walking around somewhere...that's a little piece of hope still living." He blinked heavily. "Maybe that would have saved Miranda too."

Doubtful, Miranda had been abused, depressed—she had other reasons to choose suicide—but Petrosky recognized the desperation in the man's eyes and in his words. His daughter was the only soft spot he'd had, and his sons had poked that spot until it bled.

"How could you?" Rebecca whispered. "All these years, all this time and—"

"I built a house full of monsters." His eye twitched again. *Ah...guilt, that's what* guilt *looks like for him.* "I knew what they were, and I let them go—let them feed on each other. The fire...that was the first step toward cleansing." He looked Petrosky's way as if challenging him to deny it.

Oh shit. *Rericha* had killed his son? His grandson?

Rebecca had gone stock-still, every ounce of her attention on Rericha, and as the man drew his gaze back to her, his face calmed entirely—no more twitching. Accepting of his fate. "I knew what you were up to after the cemetery, the mausoleum; only so many reasons to steal a body, only so many reasons to steal my meds." He shook his head. "That fire was a means to an end."

Rebecca had been telling the truth. She'd had no idea anyone else was in that building when she lit it up. "Was Piotr a monster too?" Petrosky asked, the air electric with anticipation.

Rericha drew himself up and squared his shoulders. "He was the worst of them. And I gave him what he deserved."

I'm going to kill Michaelson—that asshole had still been

watching Rericha at the time of Piotr's death; he'd let ol' Joe wander right by him.

Rericha appraised Rebecca with a look more anguished than any Petrosky had seen from him. "Someone should walk away from this." He raised one shaky finger in Rebecca's direction and nodded at Petrosky. "She should walk away from this."

Maybe true, but it'd be tricky to get her out of a hostage situation scot-free. And there was still one more set of crimes that hadn't been solved. "Did you know where Rebecca was all this time?"

Rericha's face hardened. "I didn't want to know where she was. I was glad she got out."

Liar. He'd known—he'd known about Christopher, had the boy's name printed in his little book.

"Did you kill Christopher, Rericha? Or did Piotr kill him?"

Rericha shrugged one shoulder, but it seemed to take far more effort than was normal. "I think we're done here. I'm tired." Rericha pushed himself to standing, his face twisted in pain, and Rebecca stepped to her right, mirroring Rericha's movements—out of Petrosky's reach, too far away to grab her. "I'll get the key," Rericha said. "To the crypt."

Rebecca's thin shoulders convulsed. "Oh god." She cocked the gun. Tightened her finger on the trigger. Petrosky kept his gaze locked on her hand, on the weapon—if he launched himself in her direction, it'd surely go off.

"Rebecca—" Petrosky said.

Another click hit his ear, then a footstep from somewhere off to his right. Behind Rericha. Jackson? Petrosky drew his gaze from Rebecca and... No, not Jackson, but there were eyes in the shadows beyond Rericha's counter, beyond the arch that led to the back room. And out of that shadowed arch came the barrel of a weapon. Aimed at Rebecca. *Fuck.*

Three things happened at once: Joe shifted right, bending

low enough to be out of the line of fire, hidden behind his register. Rebecca stepped forward, gun trained on the spot where Rericha had disappeared like she might shoot him straight through the counter. And the officer in the shadows stepped into the room—the burly woman from out front. Rebecca saw her too late; she startled, swinging her weapon away from the counter, aiming the gun at the officer.

The cop fired.

The first shot caught Rebecca in the chest, just under the right shoulder, the one with the mangled stump, the hand Piotr had taken from her. The impact spun her around, her eyes wide with fear, with pain. A second shot rang out, and Rebecca lurched forward, taking the round in the back, the force propelling her body toward the shelving. Rebecca stumbled, gasping, and he rushed toward her in time to catch her around the armpits. She groaned. His hand was wet—blood.

There was so much blood.

He eased her to the floor, his knees creaking, screaming, but she was already limp, panting against his arm, her breath much too fast. Around him, people were shouting, Jackson was saying something, Rericha was yelling, but it was all muted in his ears, the hushed din of funeral-goers.

"Don't leave me," Rebecca said, and her voice, too, was quiet—much too quiet. "Please don't leave me."

"I'm here," he said. "I'm here."

She raised her hand to his face. Her lips were moving, but he could no longer hear her over the shouting, the beeping of walkies, the thud of boots.

Petrosky bent his head lower and listened.

41

The next three hours were a blur of cops and first responders. He watched Rebecca's body being wrapped in black by the EMTs; the material zippered over her face, hiding that smattering of freckles and covering her white-blonde hair. He felt numb as he scrubbed the red from his hands. Outside, people with cell-phone cameras skittered around the hardware parking lot like insects looking for cookie crumbs. Petrosky flipped them off, an act that would surely make it to the internet before the fast-approaching sunset, which meant he'd be getting an earful from the chief.

Maybe he should "accidentally" leave his phone here.

He squinted at the hazy dusk that had already settled over the lot until Jackson pulled onto the main drag, tucking her cell away. "Scott didn't find prints on the boat," she said, "so Rericha wasn't ready to get caught."

Nothing like having a gun shoved in your face to spawn a confession. "But if he was that angry, why'd he wait so long to kill Piotr? Why not kill the jerk seven years ago when he was cleaning house?" Or literally any time between then and now?

She shrugged. "Maybe he needed Piotr to help with the

business. He was all alone trying to run that place, and no way he'd bring in an outsider." Rericha, the whole family, was secretive as fuck, and with good reason.

"How long until Woolverton gets to the baby?" They'd sent Decantor to the cemetery with a transport while they finished up at the hardware store. Decantor had found the body in the crypt exactly where Rericha said it would be—in the spot meant for Rericha himself—wrapped tightly in a baby blanket and dressed in a onesie, tiny hands laid over his chest; usually a sign of remorse. He wouldn't have thought Rericha had it in him until today, but even the coldest bastards could surprise you. He himself was a case in point.

"We'll find out in a second," Jackson said, pulling onto the street that led toward the medical examiner's office. "Decantor was at least an hour ahead of us, so hopefully, Woolverton's already doing his thing."

"Good." If Rericha killed that baby, Petrosky would nail the bastard to the wall—not that it would help Rebecca now. And they still had to interrogate Rericha about Christopher's death. Had Piotr killed the kid, and Rericha took him out for it? Or had Rericha killed Christopher? But if Rericha had done it, why not confess when he'd already admitted to murdering three people?

The air had chilled, making gooseflesh tingle on his arms as they marched across the lot. The muted film of twilight outside made the white lights in Woolverton's office even more blinding—they glared down on the stainless table like the burning eyes of some deity who was super pissed that she had to preside over an infant's corpse. Bad guys killing each other was one thing, but two children had died in this—at least one on purpose.

The bulge under the blue sheet was far too small.

The doctor stood behind the body, clipboard in hand. "The crypt kept him remarkably well-preserved—too well-preserved. There's some damage to the skin, so I'm guessing he was kept in a freezer until recently." Woolverton turned his gaze on Jackson, one eyebrow raised.

Jackson nodded. Rericha had admitted to keeping the boy in the freezer while he decided what to do with him, but he hadn't said for how long, and they hadn't bothered asking.

Woolverton shifted, and Petrosky braced himself, but the doctor did not reach toward the sheet. Instead, he pushed his glasses up his nose and squinted at Petrosky and Jackson in turn. "I know what you're expecting me to say: that someone killed this child. But no one needed to. The boy had a significant atrioventricular septal defect. Maybe the defect would have closed a bit if she'd made it to term, but as it was, the kid couldn't have lived more than a few minutes."

Shit. Rericha had been telling the truth. The baby had died, and he'd hidden the body so Rebecca wouldn't see. And he had no reason to lie about anything else. He'd admitted to killing Piotr. To killing Roman and Lucius in that fire.

But he hadn't said anything about Christopher.

"I ran the DNA tests you asked about too."

Oh yeah. He'd almost forgotten about that. *Definitely time to stop drinking.* Or time to start drinking more. His mouth watered, and he swallowed hard, and damn if it didn't taste a little like whiskey. "So, what's the verdict, Doc?"

Woolverton pushed his glasses up his nose again. "Lucius Kowalski was this baby's father."

Petrosky frowned. He'd been hoping it wouldn't match, that he could run the baby's DNA through the system and find some other man with a claim on Rebecca's kids, someone who might have a reason to go after Christopher, or Baird if he was the jealous type. Because something about these killings was still bothering him: bludgeoning a man to death (Piotr), arson (Roman and Lucius), and hit-and-run (Christopher) were wildly different MOs. It felt like they were down a suspect…maybe two.

"I also ran your DNA comparison on Christopher, out of curiosity."

"You must have been really damn curious to take that job from Scott. He loves that shit."

Woolverton half smiled. "He let me have it. Said he had enough to do."

The silence stretched. "Come on, Doc, the suspense is killing me."

"As if we would be that lucky."

Jackson snorted, her lips twitching like she was trying not to laugh. *Little dorky twit.* Woolverton sniffed, looked at his clipboard, and said, "According to his hospital trash, Christopher's father is Franklin Gargano."

Petrosky froze, the lights from above suddenly hotter, like a spotlight aimed directly at his brain. "Well of course he fucking is."

Both of Woolverton's eyebrows hit his hairline, rising fully above the upper rim of his glasses. He stared at Petrosky disapprovingly.

"Gargano didn't know he was the kid's father, though," Jackson said. "He seemed genuine about that."

Petrosky nodded. It was true—Gargano had balked at the idea that he was Christopher's dad. But after they'd gone to the hospital and told Gargano that the boy didn't belong to the usual suspects…he'd surely thought about it. Had he figured it out? Had he realized that she'd had his baby, that Rebecca had taken his kid and vanished? Would he even care? It didn't sound like he had a strong relationship with his other child—his ex-wife and his daughter hadn't gone to visit him in the hospital since he'd been admitted two months ago.

Maybe it was time they asked why that was.

Just in case.

42

Franklin Gargano's ex-wife, Juno, answered the door with sweat on her brow and a rag in her hand, her curly black hair piled on top of her head. Despite the hour, despite her bleach-speckled sweatpants and oversized tank top, Juno somehow managed to appear pulled together, like she was shooting an ad for Clorox. Damn. Eight thirty, but it sure felt like bedtime to him—Petrosky's eyelids were sandpapery and hot. His throat was even worse, but he knew that was a thirst water wouldn't quench. She raised an eyebrow, curious, but her face went hard when they told her why they were there.

Juno let them into a foyer that smelled of lemon furniture polish, but didn't invite them beyond—her kid was probably sleeping. She set the rag on the already shiny hall table and crossed her arms. "So what do you want to know about Franklin? I haven't talked to him in over a year." She squinted. "Is he in some kind of trouble?"

Jackson cocked her head. "Does he seem like the kind of man who might be?"

She smiled, but her tone was sarcastic. "Him? Nah, he's an All-American hero, right? Firefighter, EMT, always in the paper for saving someone else's kid."

"But not yours, huh?" Petrosky said.

"She doesn't need saving. She has me."

The implication was clear: Gargano was a deadbeat dad. These assholes never knew how good they had it—didn't appreciate the fact that their children were even alive. *Did I?* Rage, or maybe guilt, heated his chest, and he cleared his throat. "We're investigating a false report made by your husband when he was working as an arson investigator."

She chuckled. "I knew he wasn't perfect, but I'm not sure what I can tell you; I'm an electrical engineer, I don't know anything about Franklin's job."

"We're mostly looking at personality stuff," he said. "Changes in behavior, motivations, that kind of thing."

"Motivations?" Her eyes narrowed. "Ask your questions, detectives. I don't have anything to do with whatever he's into."

"When was the last time your daughter saw her father?" Jackson said. Starting broad—good call. The woman seemed willing to help them, but you never could tell; some people clammed up the second you asked about things like arson and faked deaths.

"It's been close to six months; he had lunch with her at school one day. I didn't even know he was going to be there." Her nostrils flared.

Jackson nodded. "Was he more involved before the divorce?"

"I...sometimes. It's hard to explain." Her face fell.

"Ma'am?"

She sighed. "Sometimes he was wonderful—attentive, caring...it's like he threw himself into loving you. And I fell in love with him for that."

"But?" Jackson pressed on.

She pursed her lips as if considering what to say...or how to say it. Somewhere in the house, a clock chimed—eight forty-five—and this seemed to snap her out of it. Juno raised her gaze to Jackson's. "He always ran obsessive," she said. "Especially when he was stressed; he'd reorganize silverware, straighten already made beds—I caught him cutting the grass with scissors once. What woman wouldn't love that?" She laughed again, but it was a bitter sound.

"All that anal retentiveness get to you, or what?" Petrosky asked. "Was that why you divorced him?" Petrosky's level of clean-freakiness was on par with Duke's; someone else bitching at him about how he creased the bedspread would drive him insane, and he was already close enough.

"Well, kinda." Her eyes drifted to the floor. "It changed... *he* changed. I married him as a firefighter, but then he wanted to be an arson investigator, and, of course, I supported him. Hell, I figured that might give him a place to channel all that extra energy—it's tedious stuff, right up his alley, and...it seemed okay at first. He worked long hours, way more than anyone in his department. They gave him awards. But at home, he was pulling away. He was very single-minded when he got something in his head, but Clara and I just didn't stick there like whatever pet project he had going. We were stable—not as exciting, I guess." She raised her head. "That's why we split."

Gargano was after excitement? No wonder he'd gotten sucked into Rebecca's world.

"And after you divorced?" Jackson asked.

"He hated me, acted like it was my fault; the moment the papers were filed, he shut down. Even took a side job as an EMT to get away from us. It was like his own daughter didn't exist, despite the fact we still lived together for a year afterward—he had some money issues, but he had no problem affording his projects." She met Petrosky's eyes and grimaced as if to say *what an asshole*. "I don't give a shit if it's depression, obsessive-compulsive disorder, whatever, I just don't care. I don't have any sympathy for him."

Depression? Maybe. Or guilt over helping set that fire.

Though Rericha had admitted to dragging the bodies inside, finding out you'd helped kill two people, however unwittingly, might change a man. But Gargano seemed to believe that Roman and Lucius had deserved it—he couldn't be that sorry. Had he been depressed over Rebecca leaving him? Maybe she'd become his new pet project, and he'd lost his shit when she vanished. "Is that why you haven't gone to see him?"

Juno shook her head. "I'm not about to go where I'm not wanted."

Huh. The contentious divorce might be on Gargano, but…not wanted? No matter how pissed she was, she had to know he'd want to say goodbye to his daughter—that her daughter might want to say goodbye, too. Unless…

She doesn't know he's sick.

Jackson beat him to it, saying, "Do you know your ex-husband has bone cancer?"

"No, I…" Juno backed up a step as if she could walk away from that little tidbit of information. She crossed her arms again. "Are you sure?"

No, we just wanted to see what you'd do. "Unless he's faking the IVs and the death rattle, yeah."

Her eyes locked on Petrosky's face as if trying to read him, maybe hoping it wasn't true—or hoping it was. When she finally spoke again, her voice had gone quiet. "He didn't tell me, but it's not like we're a support system for him any more than he was for us. Clara used to cry because he spent all his spare time in that damn garage, tinkering instead of playing with her." The silence stretched. Lemon furniture polish tickled his lungs. But his brain was sizzling, itchy and hot. *That damn garage.*

"What was he tinkering with?" Petrosky asked.

She sniffed. "His car—well, my car since he keeps it here. I'll sell it eventually. He doesn't want to be a father, but he can at least contribute to Clara's college fund."

But Gargano didn't have a vehicle registered; he'd sold his truck right before his hospital admission. They'd checked that back when they were looking for the Chevelle.

"When was the last time he drove it?" Jackson said.

"Maybe…three or four weeks ago?"

Gooseflesh prickled between his shoulder blades. "I thought you hadn't seen him in a year."

"I haven't; I wasn't here, Clara has basketball practice Saturday mornings. I didn't even know he'd been here until I went to get meat from the Deepfreeze, and the car was gone." She frowned. "He brought the car back the next day, not like he can drive it far without a plate, but I was pretty pissed. Thought he was trying to take it back or something."

Returned it. Three weeks ago. Saturday. And it wasn't hard to slap a plate on it for an afternoon—Gargano was too obsessive to forget that detail. But he had been in the hospital three weeks ago, hadn't he? Maybe it wasn't even the right car. "Can we see it, ma'am?"

She raised an eyebrow, but she nodded. "You can go around the front. I'll open the garage."

He and Jackson retreated down the porch steps and headed for the driveway, blinking as the porch lights then the garage lights clicked on.

"You think he tracked her down?" she said.

Yes. "Rebecca stayed hidden all this time because no one else knew to look for her, but you found her in a few days. Gargano's obsessive ass had seven years."

A low rumble came from the garage. The door started up. They stood, shoulder to shoulder in the drive. Staring.

Wheels.

Bumper.

Blue hood, still shiny despite being nearly as old as Petrosky.

Shit. Gargano had been there. At the hit and run.

And he hadn't just killed Rebecca's child.

He'd killed his own.

"To me, death is not a fearful thing. It's living that's cursed."
~*Jim Jones*

43

SHANNON TAPPED the button on the computer to exit the site: another video of the shootout at the hardware store, another reporter, another headline—*Hardware Store Invasion, Female Intruder Dead*. Just wait until the news got wind of the full story.

Decantor had texted her an update hours ago, but her head was still spinning. Rericha had killed Lucius, Roman, and Piotr, his own family. Damn. Surely, Rericha or Piotr had run over Christopher and Baird, too, though Rericha had yet to admit it. And Rebecca's first son was dead. Case closed, right? She hadn't talked to Petrosky yet—after a shooting like that, cops stayed busy for a while—but she hoped he was holding up okay. It'd be a hard few weeks for him, though; watching a woman bleed out on the floor wasn't easy, especially when Rebecca had been innocent, at least of murder.

Shannon glanced over at Duke, his giant head planted on the cushion beside her, eyes closed, peaceful—too peaceful. She was relieved, god knew, her shoulders looser, the tension in her back finally melting like ice during the spring thaw, but that just made the guilt worse, hot and sharp in her belly. It wasn't justice, not even close, yet Rebecca's death meant she'd be able to sleep at night because no one had reason to dig too deeply into the warehouse fire—no one would link anything to her. When had she become so selfish?

But at least it was over. Now she could go home to Evie and Henry. They were alive, happy, healthy—they had a chance Rebecca's kids never would.

Tears smarted in her eyes, and she swiped them away angrily. *You're better than this, Shannon, stop crying.* But she couldn't. She'd come all this way and solved nothing, helped no one—she'd never even had a chance to save that kid. Her fingers grazed her wedding band, the metal warm from the heat of her body. "I miss you," she whispered. Duke nuzzled her elbow, and she let go of the ring and scratched his head. "Not you, boy. I know you'll be here as long as I rub your ears."

The dog snuffled in agreement, and she leaned back against the arm of the couch, her gaze on the now-empty coffee table. She could almost see Evie here, sitting on the floor with Petrosky, chattering nonstop. And Henry, cautiously scooting closer, first playing with Legos by the door, then near the couch, until he wound up in Petrosky's lap. She knew what Petrosky was capable of—the affection he kept close, the kindnesses he meted out when you least expected it, the grandfatherly smiles he always had ready for the kids no matter how awful he felt. But would he stay sober? Could he? Her eyes burned. She sighed and wiped her face again.

Bzzzzzt-bzzzzzt-bzzzzzt. She reached into her back pocket and squinted at the cell. She didn't recognize the number; it wasn't Petrosky or Decantor, and it wasn't Marlene or Jake, the couple who was watching her kids.

Bzzzzzt-bzzzzzt-bzzzzzt.

Shannon pulled the phone to her ear.

"Shannon?" The voice was a gravelly rasp—unfamiliar. "This is Franklin. Franklin Gargano." Was he crying? She couldn't blame him. Her own face was still wet with tears, but he was surely crying for different reasons—less selfish ones. And...why was he calling her? "Is it true?" he said. "Is she... Did they shoot her?"

Her heart spasmed; the ring burned. "Yeah, it's true."

"Oh god. I didn't think it would end like this."

She sniffed, her throat aching with guilt at the pain in his voice. Franklin had obviously cared about Rebecca a great deal, which was not a shock. He'd done more than Shannon had—he'd overtly broken the law for Rebecca, rigged that warehouse to explode so she could get away from her abusive husband. And for seven years, Rebecca and her son had known peace. Because of him. "I know, Franklin. I'm sorry for your loss."

"You helped her, too, right? Rebecca... She said..."

The muscles in her shoulders tightened, and Duke raised his head, his ears pricked. Rebecca had told him about her? *Shit.* That's why he'd called—he thought they were in the same boat. The smart thing to do was to say nothing, but this man... He was dying, and he'd spent years covering for a woman he'd known only a few months. How likely was it that he'd tell Shannon's secrets? Franklin might be talking about her legal help anyway—Shannon had tried to help Rebecca go the legal route first, even if it had failed spectacularly. "We all did what we could, Franklin," she said carefully. "And now it's over."

"I... We shouldn't talk about this on the phone. I don't want to say anything...you know."

Her shoulders loosened; Franklin was still trying to protect everyone else despite his own pain. Kinda like Petrosky.

"Would you be willing to talk in person?" His voice cracked. "I just feel so lost all of a sudden, and I feel so stupid, and...no one else will understand." He hiccupped and sniffled. Her ring was hot enough to blister her flesh. *Dammit.*

She had been worrying about herself again when this guy just wanted to talk to someone who understood. Maybe the one good thing she could do here was give this man some peace before he died. Like the peace he'd afforded Rebecca.

"Of course." She scratched Duke's ears one more time and pushed herself to standing. "I'll come to you."

44

"That's why we couldn't find a registration." Petrosky watched the thick black of night encroach on the SUV—a cloud of nothingness. He could almost imagine the precinct wouldn't be there when they arrived. "He'd been buying parts, building it himself."

"But it's been finished for years. Maybe he didn't register it because he planned to go out there and kill her boyfriend."

"That makes more sense than him going after the kid, but I'm not entirely sure he planned anything ahead of time," Petrosky said. "We don't even know when he figured out where she was." Juno said he hadn't taken the car before now, but he could have been sneaking it out without her knowledge; she admitted she hadn't changed the locks because he never came around.

Petrosky squinted in the glare from an upcoming streetlight, then relaxed as it passed. "Maybe he figured it out just last month, went up there to confront her, or to say goodbye before he died, then saw Baird and lost it. Either way, that rage built for a long time. She left him despite what he saw as this ultimate heroic act; he put his neck on the line, his career, and she just walked away, the same way his wife did."

Jackson was nodding. "What his ex said about him being an All-American hero…the mentality fits. I could see him being pissed enough to take out Rebecca's new beau—maybe he didn't see the boy until it was too late."

But something still wasn't right, Petrosky could feel it in his bones. It was like a little jigsaw piece that wanted to fit, the space and size were right, but the colors didn't quite line up. "Doesn't this seem too easy?"

"There's nothing easy about this, Petrosky."

He frowned at the window. It wasn't just Christopher's death that was eating at him. Rericha's confession had been too…neat. *Convenient*. And nothing in this case had been convenient. "How'd Rericha do it, Jackson? How'd he carry Lucius and Roman into that warehouse?"

She raised an eyebrow. "You're still on Rericha?"

"Even with the boat thing, Piotr's death… Michaelson was supposed to be watching the guy."

"You said yourself that Michaelson is a tool, and you were right, okay? You were. Michaelson admitted that he left for an hour to get lunch; Rericha's car was still in the drive when he returned, so he just assumed Rericha was there. Rericha probably took Piotr's car or had Piotr pick him up. Not like anyone thought Rericha was going to murder his grandkid, Piotr included."

"Then where is it? Where's Piotr's car?"

"We'll ask him in interrogation; I'm sure there's an explanation. But you need to stop second-guessing a confession."

He glowered into the night. "Rericha's confession doesn't fit."

"Rericha doesn't fit? Aside from being a sociopathic cult leader with a criminal history who hid a dead baby in his freezer? What the hell are you talking about?"

"Motives matter, Jackson. If he killed Roman and Lucius for hurting his daughter, for hurting Rebecca, he would have killed Piotr, too. Piotr made Rebecca cut off her hand for god's sake. Why not kill him?"

"He did, Petrosky! He *confessed*." She jerked her face in his direction so suddenly he startled back against the door. "Are you drunk? Did you manage to—"

"I'm stone-cold sober, Jackson." *For now*. And at the moment, his head felt remarkably clear, because he suddenly knew why that little piece didn't fit: it was from a different puzzle. He sat straighter in the seat. "Rericha killing Piotr makes sense if he thought Piotr was going to hurt Rebecca again." Or had. "But Rericha hid a dead baby to protect Rebecca's *feelings*. And today, Rericha basically confesses to framing her for murder? Does that sound like someone who'd hide a child because he thought it would hurt her? Framing Rebecca for killing Lucius and Roman would have fucked her over as badly as Roman fucked over Rericha's daughter." *Shit*. Rericha…he'd been protecting Rebecca this whole time. "Jackson, Rericha didn't take responsibility because he did it. He took responsibility because he thinks *she* did it. He was trying to save her. That's why he confessed."

But Rebecca wasn't guilty. The person who'd burned her husband alive was still out there. And only one man had a murder weapon in his garage—that they knew of. "Gargano killed Roman and Lucius. I don't know how, but he did."

"But the timeline. She picked up the detonator—"

"She and Gargano both said he was just getting home from work, that he pulled up right after her." He frowned. "I think he had the men with him then." In his trunk, maybe. He'd followed her all night, waited for her to drug them, watched her drive off. Then he'd loaded the unconscious men into his car and sped back to his place to meet her.

Jackson's fingers were a frantic metronome on the wheel. "And at the warehouse…he called her, remember? He said she was freaking out, that he happened to call her and talk her down, that it took her a few minutes to get over the panic attack."

Dammit. He'd called her because he was buying himself time; Gargano had followed her to the warehouse with the unconscious men in his truck, but he'd still needed to get Roman and Lucius into the building. And for a guy like him, a firefighter adept at throwing heavy shit over his shoulders, it would only have taken a minute or two.

He'd tricked her into killing them. And he'd walked away free.

"But why would he frame her for that?" Jackson said, the streetlights painting her face in white lines, a brilliant carbon copy of prison bars. "If he loved her—"

"Maybe he realized she was going to leave him for good."

Her fingers stopped tapping, and the resulting silence was deafening—he could hear the *thud-thunk, thud-thunk, thud-thunk* of his own heart. "If that's the case, he sat on this all these years. Left her alone out in Pennsylvania. Why go after her now?"

"He's dying," Petrosky said, his voice hollow. "Now, he has an endgame." *Revenge.*

"At least he's drugged out of his mind." She frowned, surely realizing the same thing he had: Gargano should have been drugged out of his mind three weeks ago, too, shouldn't have been able to drive that car to Briddiss in the first place. But he wasn't a prisoner; just because he'd been hospitalized for two months didn't mean he was locked up 24/7. Maybe leaving meant checking himself out for a day trip, maybe it just meant the bed being empty for eight hours—yeah, rounds might miss him, but would they call the cops? Probably not. The doctor's words echoed in his head: *Most people opt for more drugs, sleep their way to the end, but he wants to be alert, at least awake—he's in agony.* Perhaps that pain had fueled his rage even more.

Jackson grabbed her phone, and he watched her face

grow more grim as she snapped at the nursing staff, or maybe the doctor they'd met with before—*uncool, Jackson*. Finally, she slammed the phone into the cupholder. "Gargano checked himself out against medical advice two hours ago. Probably stopped taking any meds at all after we met with him last time."

Of course he'd stopped taking the drugs after their visit. That was when they'd told him Rebecca's baby didn't belong to her husband; that was when he realized the kid was his, that he'd killed his own son in a fit of jealous rage. Was he even sick? No, he was...he was. But acting frailer, weaker, had helped with his alibi. It was the same thing Rericha did with his "I'm an old man" bullshit. It had all been a ruse.

Gargano hadn't gone to Briddiss to beg Rebecca to come back, to be with him for his last few months. He hadn't gone to pledge his undying devotion. He went to get even with the woman who had cuckolded him, who'd gotten him to risk his job and his freedom in the process—and who had vanished without so much as a text.

And now, Gargano knew Rebecca was dead; it had hit the press two hours ago, almost the same time Gargano had checked himself out. Was he headed home to kill himself? That seemed a little too easy for a guy like Gargano. He'd be dead anyway in a few weeks, maybe sooner; no reason to stop those meds and up the pain unless he had another agenda. So what was it?

Was Gargano after someone else? Was he angry about Rebecca's death? If so, maybe he blamed them—it was a cop who'd shot Rebecca—but Gargano might appreciate that they'd gotten Rebecca killed if he was still furious with her, especially since he probably blamed her for Christopher. After all, if he had known the boy was his...maybe he'd have been more careful.

Petrosky stared at the horizon, the inky blackness that seemed to stretch forever. No, this wasn't about them, wasn't about this case, wasn't even about her death. The only time Gargano had shown real emotion was when he talked about Rebecca leaving him—that was the ultimate slap in the face, the reason he was pissed.

And there was one other person out there who had helped Rebecca vanish.

One other person Gargano might blame for prolonging his misery.

He pulled out his cell and dialed with shaking hands.

45

Bzzzzzt-bzzzzzt-bzzzzzt.

Shannon could feel the vibration in her back pocket, but she didn't dare take her eyes off Franklin. Something was wrong. She wasn't entirely sure what it was, but he'd been twitchy since she got here, the air in the room agitated—the energy of a nest of wasps. Not that she was afraid, not really; the man was clearly sick, and she did CrossFit three days a week—there was no way he could take her. Unless he had a weapon. But she probably had a bigger one in her purse, and she saw no bulges near the pockets of his sweatpants, no gun on the coffee table, and he'd had no trouble turning his back on her as he led her through the kitchen and into the living room where they now sat.

She shifted in her chair. The phone buzzed again. "I love what you've done with the place. Rustic." But overkill. She gestured to the ceiling, the wooden chandelier adorned with mason jars instead of decorative candleholders. More jars littered the end tables, all full of wax. There'd been some in the kitchen too.

He nodded. "All homemade." His face was tight.

"Are you okay, Franklin?"

"No, actually." He grimaced. "I'm in a lot of pain."

No wonder things felt off. "Is there anything I can get for you? Maybe we can sit on the sofa." The little wooden stool he was sitting on couldn't be comfortable. Even her recliner would be better.

He shook his head. "Maybe I should have stayed at the hospital, but the medications… I couldn't just lie there, thinking about her. And the drugs were making things hazy, all my memories. That's really all you have at the end." He sniffed—was he crying? That's what she'd thought on the phone, but his eyes weren't glassy, not even a little; his mouth was a bloodless slash.

The hairs on the back of her neck prickled.

Gargano shifted his weight, wincing as if the act hurt him, and it surely did. "Anyway, I'm glad you came. I didn't want to die without talking to even one person about what really happened. And I couldn't have you come to the hospital, not out in public like that." He sniffed again. "Might not matter so much for me, but for you…"

Right. She didn't want them being connected—the wider world knowing she was involved. That might haunt her later, even if her actions weren't as serious as Franklin's; most DAs found arson more concerning than car buying, even if it was a getaway car. "Thank you for being discreet. I think we both have some…regrets."

His eyes narrowed, but not with understanding. She frowned. Yeah, his eyes were definitely wrong. Despite his words, he didn't look sorry, didn't seem guilty, not the way she felt. Not so much grief as…rage.

"Do you think she ever loved me?"

Did she really know you? It was just a few months, right? She realized that despite knowing that he'd helped Rebecca with the fire, she wasn't exactly sure what their relationship had been. "I'm sure she cared about you, but I think she had her own agenda."

"You let her go, though—you helped her. If it wasn't for you, maybe she'd have stayed."

Wait, what? "She couldn't have stayed, Franklin. Even if all she did was steal a corpse and light up a warehouse, she was still going to jail. Having that baby in prison, having to give it away…no mother would want that."

His eyes glittered darkly. "You knew, didn't you?" he said, his voice low.

She sat straighter, but her blood had run cold. "Knew what?"

"That it was mine. That her child… That she was going to take him from me."

Huh? They'd been…sleeping together? She'd thought Gargano had been duped the way she was, and she'd kept her pants on the whole time. "No," she said, shaking her head. "I didn't know she was pregnant before she left, didn't even know you and her had a thing. I just knew she was scared, that she needed to get away."

"My wife, she left me, took my daughter. Then Becky… she did the same thing." His lips peeled back from his teeth, the scowl of a hungry wolf. "Both of them raised my children without me."

But his wife hadn't wanted that, had she? Not that the truth mattered here, not anymore—not when you were dealing with a crazy man. And looking into his eyes, Shannon was certain that's what Gargano was.

She put her palms on her knees, preparing to stand. "I think I should go. It's been a long day and—"

"Don't even think about it."

She froze, still on the seat, every beat of her heart sending icicles of panic stabbing through her veins. *You've dealt with assholes worse than him, Shannon.* The old scars around her lips throbbed. Her lungs ached. She glanced at the purse near her foot—the gun inside was calling her name, but she kept her voice steady, calm. "I know she hurt you, Franklin." *Stroke his ego. Keep him happy.* "I wish there was something I could do to help." *Like smash a fist into your crotch.*

He gestured to her chair. "Sit back."

She leaned forward. "I'd rather not." If she had to fight him, even shoot him, she would. She forced herself to avoid looking at her bag, but her hands clenched into fists. *Come at me, shithead.*

"There's a detonator under the cushion on my stool. If I stand up, neither of us will make it out alive. Look around." He gestured to the end table, the makeshift candelabra—the jars. *Oh shit.* They weren't homemade candles. Accelerants? And... hell, she couldn't shoot him. If she did, he'd fall off the stool, and then—

"You're the last piece. The last one." He put his elbows on his knees, and leaned over his thighs, staring at her accusingly—his gaze had teeth. "I need you to do something for me. The way you did for her."

Her throat was so tight it was difficult to breathe, let alone force a sentence. "Get you a car? That's all I did for her. I can't make you disappear."

"Oh, I don't need you to do that—I'll be gone soon enough."

He gestured to her chair once more. "Sit back, Shannon. All the way. We need to talk."

But from the look in his eyes, talking was the last thing he wanted to do.

He just didn't want to die alone.

46

The tires were a buzzing drone that needled a soft spot at the base of his spine—painful, but not as painful as the stabbing in his chest. The phone was a weight in Petrosky's hand, a hot brick of plastic. Useless.

He hit redial anyway.

"She's not at your neighbor's. Billie says she left in your Caprice about half an hour ago." Jackson tossed her phone in the cupholder and hit the gas, propelling the Escalade through the darkness.

He should have driven himself to the station today—he shouldn't have left his car at home.

"She has to be with Gargano," Jackson said. "Scott used his superpowers to look at her phone. She got a call from the hospital right before she left."

Fuck. Gargano called her, and she went right to him. So, where would they meet? Gargano's house felt too easy, but what other options existed? They'd already put out an APB, and Decantor was on his way to Juno's, but she would have called if Gargano was there.

The tires squealed as Jackson cranked a hard right onto

Gargano's street. She flicked the headlights off. The Escalade crept up the road, slowly, stealthily, so the occupants of the house wouldn't know they were there. They didn't need an address; his Caprice was parked three houses up, hulking in the driveway floodlights of an unsuspecting one-story stucco, the overgrown bushes a dead giveaway that whoever lived there no longer gave a shit. In the summer, the front yard was probably a mess of clover and creeping thistle.

Jackson eased to a stop one house down.

A thin yellow haze eked from the front window—lamplight. But it was not the glow that concerned him. He stared at the little bundle of red and yellow wires at the top corner of the garage, an electrified rat's nest. "Is that what I think it is?"

Jackson squinted. "You think he's got a detonator up there? Damn, he planned ahead—probably set up his endgame as soon as he got back from Briddiss."

Petrosky nodded, but the tendons in his neck were so tight they felt as if they might snap. The asshole probably had the whole place wired. If they tried to get inside through the garage, probably the windows or the back door, too, the house would go up with Shannon inside. But Gargano had to have left one entrance free if he'd let Shannon in: the front door. Petrosky couldn't breathe; he couldn't fucking *breathe*.

"Had to be a goddamn fire expert," Petrosky muttered; his words came out strangled, and for a moment he wondered if he'd be able to talk, if he could see Shannon with a gun at her head or a bomb on her chest and actually function. And if he had to watch her die—

Get it together, old man. If you do nothing else in this life, you need to do this. Get her out. Don't fail her the way you did Morrison. The way you did Julie. He hissed a breath through clenched teeth, his lungs burning, burning, burning, and stared at the wires. They didn't have time for a bomb squad.

Gargano wasn't going to make it out of this alive, and he knew it.

And Petrosky was not about to lose another daughter to flames.

47

THE JARS above Shannon's head glistened, swaying in their candelabra holsters, their explosive liquid viscous like chicken fat. Would they fall? All it took was one, and the whole place would ignite.

All it took was one, and her children would be orphans.

Her ring vibrated, prickling angrily against her skin. *I'm sorry, Morrison, I'm so sorry, honey, I fucked up.* "Just tell me what you want, Franklin. Anything within my power, I'll make it happen." She wanted to move, wanted to leap from the chair, but what if there was an explosive device beneath her seat as well? Would she accidentally set it off?

"Is it true that Stewart is alive?" he asked.

Yes, but his brain isn't. "I don't know who Stewart is." If she could just buy a little time, Petrosky would be there. Cell phone avoider that he was, he always showed up when she needed him—really needed him. "I can make a call, find out for you."

His nostrils flared, and he shifted in his seat, eyes shining like flecks of blue flame beneath his brows.

The stool squeaked. Shannon gasped. *Please don't light us*

up, please, I don't want to die. But even as she thought it, her rage was building, a primal, visceral thing that encased her lungs and slithered through her soft tissues, turning her muscles to stone. *You will not do this to me.* She'd been here before, survived monsters more savage than this prick. *Fuck you, Franklin, you absolute piece of shit.* She forced her breathing to slow. "If you don't want me to call, I can send an email. That way, you can make sure I don't say anything you don't want me to."

"Do you see a computer around here, Shannon?" He leveled his gaze at her, smug, sadistic—he thought he'd already won.

I will kill you. "I can use my phone." She watched his face, trying to tell whether he'd wired her seat, but he didn't bat an eye when she leaned forward—*just a little*—to see whether it concerned him. And while he might plan on dying today, he'd said he needed something from her. He wouldn't go through all this without even telling her what it was…right?

"I don't need an email." His face contorted as he shifted in the chair once more, and once more, her heart rate exploded into a frantic dance of panic. "I need to know Stewart is dead. If he isn't, I need you to make it happen."

Um…he wanted her to kill Stewart Baird? From here? Did he think she had a drone in her purse? And once he knew Stewart was dead, he'd what? Kill them both? She drew her fingers to her wedding band. *Help me, Morrison, get me out of this.* "How am I supposed to—"

He leaned closer, his chest over his knees, and again she tensed—the muscles in her back were screaming. "You got her that car, got her a fake ID. And you're a lawyer; you've got some lowlife friends, Rebecca told me that, said you knew people way worse than she or I could ever be. So, figure it out."

What the hell had that bitch told him? *I just got her a car; I don't know a goddamn hitman.* But she couldn't say that. "You're right. I can make a phone call. I'll make sure—"

"Hey, Frankie!"

She jumped. Petrosky? His voice echoed through the house, and Franklin's eyes narrowed, his gaze on the hall at her back. She turned her head in time to see Petrosky striding down the hallway toward the living room like he didn't have a care in the world. No gun. How did he look so damn calm? But her heartbeat evened.

I knew you'd come; I knew it. Help me kill this bastard.

"Hey, Shannon. I guess you've met Frankie." Petrosky stepped into the room, the hem of his jacket brushing the glass jars on the hallway shelf.

Fuck, fuck, shit, fuck.

Franklin's eyes darted from her to Petrosky and back again. "You guys know each other?"

"Oh yeah, we go way back, like you two do, I guess. Or like you and Rebecca, but I'm not screwing this one, you know what I mean?" He jerked his thumb in Shannon's direction.

Franklin's eyes twitched, then his lips. "That is not what I did, not what we had." He practically spat out the words.

Oh shit—Petrosky was trying to make Franklin go after him, maybe so she could run. But Petrosky didn't know about the explosives under Franklin's seat, didn't know that the second Franklin lunged at Petrosky, they were all dead.

She opened her mouth, maybe to tell Petrosky to shut up, maybe to tell him about the detonator, but Petrosky had paused dead center in the room, hands out at his sides—surrender.

"Shannon should go."

"She and I have business." Franklin's eyes locked on Petrosky, probably trying to stare him down, and she could almost hear Petrosky's voice in her head: *Good luck with that, fuck-o.*

"You don't need her," Petrosky said. "Anything she can do, I can do better." He took another step closer to Franklin, and the bastard raised an eyebrow. "I think I know what you want, Frankie. The same thing I'd want in your position: revenge." One more step, and now Petrosky was between Shannon and Franklin, beside the coffee table—the table topped with those terrible jars. "I needed to solve this case, put Rericha away, but I don't give a shit about Stewart Baird."

Petrosky must have heard the tail end of their conversation. Shannon watched, but she couldn't see Gargano's face around Petrosky's bulk, and she was too afraid to move. But from the way Franklin's leg shifted...he was leaning back. Less confrontational.

"You know...I actually believe that's true, Detective."

"You should," Petrosky said, shrugging. "He's just another lowlife, a user, living off her dime out there. He didn't deserve her."

"None of them did." Franklin's disembodied voice floated toward her. The world felt strange and wrong, every muscle tense, every molecule of air in her lungs electric.

"Oh, trust me, I get it. You and I, we're the same—I lost my wife, too, my daughter. We always try to do the right thing, and where does it get us?" Petrosky grunted, almost a chuckle, but it was not his usual laugh; to her ear, it sounded like he was choking. "And I know you never meant to hurt that boy, either. Stewart was the one who deserved to die."

Wait... Christopher? *Franklin* had killed Rebecca's son?

"The boy..." Franklin coughed—a wet, heavy sound. "He was sitting behind another car, right at the curb. I didn't see him until it was too late."

Creak. The wooden floor moaned as Petrosky shifted closer to the man once more, only a step from Franklin's chair, his hands still out at his sides. Not a single tremor in his fingers. How did he do that? Her entire body was vibrating, and... *Oh shit, am I shaking the chair?* She inhaled deeply, trying to calm her twitching muscles.

"See, Frankie, I knew it was an accident. And I think, deep down, you loved her, despite everything she did to you. She took your boy, went off with that asshole, Stewart, and you stayed strong; you waited for her, never even got remarried. Most men wouldn't have done that." Petrosky raised a hand, and her breath left her—*Is he going to snatch him off the stool?*—but he pointed a finger gun at Franklin's face. "Trying to do the right thing," he repeated. "Like you always have. The FBI doesn't tap just anyone."

Petrosky shifted to the side, unblocking Shannon's view, but Franklin didn't appear to notice—his eyes had dropped to his lap. "I wish I could take that back; that the kid would have made it. That Rebecca..." He sighed. "Doesn't matter now, I guess."

"Rebecca didn't know you were driving, did she?"

Franklin shook his head, and when he raised his face again, his eyes were clear, though the corners were tight with pain. "Maybe I deserve to die for that—for Christopher. But Stewart...it's *his* fault. That bastard stole them from me. I need to know he's dead before I go." His lips shifted into a tight, anemic smile, but it was less smug, more...desperate?

"That bastard is braindead," Petrosky said. "He'll never wake up." Petrosky gestured to the stool. "Am I going to blow myself up if I tell you a secret?"

Franklin shook his head. "You can say it from there."

"No." Petrosky nodded to Shannon. "This is between you and me, Frankie. Just us."

Shannon straightened. Did he really have something to tell Franklin? If not, Petrosky was going to die here, but maybe that was the plan: to have Franklin take him instead of her. But she sure hoped he had a better idea than that.

Franklin frowned, considering.

"No arms on that chair," Petrosky said. "If I hurt you, and you fall, there's no way I'll get pressure on the device before we all die. You thought of everything. But I've got one last way for you to be a hero. To make up for what happened to Christopher. Trust me."

Franklin glanced at Shannon, his eyes fiery, his mouth tense. But he nodded. Petrosky leaned closer until his face was at the man's ear—blocking her line of sight.

Shannon counted.

One. *What the hell is he telling him?*

Two. *Please get us out of here, Petrosky.*

Three. *I hate you, Franklin, you sorry sack of shit.*

Four. *This has to work, please let me go home to Evie and Henry.*

Petrosky straightened and took a step back, and Franklin's face...something was wrong. His steely eyes had gone glassy, his stiff upper lip trembling.

"I still need—"

"I know," Petrosky said. "Text it to me; I'll take care of it for you."

"Promise?" Franklin's voice was so low it was almost a whisper. Shannon wasn't sure whether he was talking to Petrosky or himself.

Petrosky met the man's eyes and nodded, just once, but that was enough. Franklin smiled, not an ounce of smugness left on his face. Just relief. He pulled out his phone.

Oh god, what does he want? What had Petrosky promised him?

Petrosky turned his back on Franklin and hustled in her direction, again blocking her view with his body. He pulled her shoulders, trying to get her to stand, and when she resisted, he pulled harder, practically lifting her from the seat. She opened her mouth to protest, barely noticing that no bomb had gone off—nothing beneath her chair. But her legs were made of pins and needles. She couldn't feel her toes.

He shoved her gently but quickly up the hall, his fingers a steady pressure against her bicep. "Go, Shannon," he said. "Fucking go!"

She did, stumbling as fast as she could, the living room paneling giving way to the tile of the kitchen, then to the concrete of the front porch. "What's going on, what did you tell—"

Bang!

Percussion ripped through her eardrums, vibrating her marrow, but Petrosky had her arm, and with one hard jerk she was flying, the concrete of the porch gone, just air and panicked weightlessness, and then she was falling, landing hard on her back, the wet mud of the front lawn seeping through her shirt. She couldn't breathe—heavy, something heavy on top of her. *Petrosky.* Oh shit, it was Petrosky on her chest, squeezing the air from her lungs. One of her arms was wrapped around his back. Their legs were a twisted mess.

He wasn't moving.

Oh shit, he shot him, that bastard fucking shot him, Morrison will never forgive me. She tried to force an inhale, tried to call his name, but a thunderous boom, far louder than the first, stole her thoughts and her breath. A wave of heat rolled over her, searing the hair from the arm that was wrapped over Petrosky. She winced.

"Don't move." The words were a harsh whisper against her neck, though he was probably yelling. *He's okay! Oh, thank god.* Petrosky twisted to grab her wrist, then tucked her arm beneath his bulk. Not a gunshot. A bomb. A bright crackling like snapping tinder assaulted her ears.

She shook her head, dazed, but she could barely move, could barely breathe beneath Petrosky's weight. "Sorry about my donut-eating ass, Shannon. Just stay still. Let it burn a second."

The heat—the place was on fire. She blinked, squinting to focus her eyes, but all she could see of the house was concrete; they were wedged beneath the lip of the porch, protected by the foundation. Where he'd thrown her. Above them, orange flames licked the black sky.

Petrosky shifted his weight, rolling onto his back beside her. "Crawl toward the street," he rasped.

She did, pushing herself forward over the sodden grass, her muscles screaming, her lungs aching, the fire hot against her back. The sidewalk inched closer.

Petrosky hauled himself to sitting on the curb and grimaced, rubbing at the back of his neck. "You're a hard girl to keep track of, Shan—"

"I'm moving back home," she blurted.

He dropped his arm. "What?"

Maybe he actually couldn't hear her. The fire was louder than she'd realized, a harsh roaring in her ears, and now there were other sounds too: the bleating of firetrucks, the wail of an ambulance. She raised her voice, forcing the words out over the angry snapping of burning wood. "Evie misses you, and Henry will love you, and I know you love them as much as Morrison did. And I need there to be *one* person on my team who will be there for them if something happens to me."

His eyes were orange, reflecting the flames. "I'm not good at this, Shannon."

"Shut the fuck up." She was screaming, but she could barely hear her own words. "You will get good, or I will slap you. Again."

His eyes drifted beyond her to the fire. Her own eyes felt sunburned.

"You can stay in my spare room," he said finally. "Until you get settled." He kept his gaze locked on the house; red and blue lights flashed against the front lawn. And there was

Jackson, running toward them over the sidewalk, her hand up against the heat of the blaze.

"You let him kill himself," she said. "You let him die quick."

"It's not justice," Petrosky said. "But it is over."

She squinted back at the house. They both watched it burn.

48

The steady thrum of alcohol buzzed in his veins, dulling the angry glare from the sun, but the park bench was still frigid beneath his ass. At least it was dry. No ice now, unlike the day they'd found Piotr's body at the shoreline.

Petrosky took the last drag from his cigarette and crushed the butt under his heel, watching the smoke bloom from his lips like a cloud and dissipate into the air; the lapping waves vanished behind the tobacco and reappeared in a single plane of gray. Soon, the lake would be blue again, welcoming a spring that would never be warm enough to burn off winter's ache.

Rericha was awaiting trial for Piotr's death, though Petrosky wasn't sure how he felt about that one. Sure, the world was better with fewer Joseph Rerichas in it, but Rericha's intentions here had been pure. Psychopathic maybe, fucked-up definitely, but righteous nonetheless.

The biggest surprise had been Franklin Gargano. His charred body had barely been dragged from the rubble before the lawyers showed up with paperwork. The house was ruined, but he had more holdings than he'd let on—he'd even hidden them from Juno. Most of the cash went to his ex-wife and his daughter, as it should have, but someone had transferred a portion of his funds via an online service to one Christopher Nowak. Which had promptly vanished. And despite what the nurse had said about people very occasionally waking up from comas, Petrosky had no doubt that Stewart Baird was still lying immobile in his hospital bed when Christopher's account had been drained.

He shook another cigarette from his pack and listened to the click of the lighter, relishing the acrid burn in his throat. His lungs tensed, then accepted the nicotine.

"How'd you know?"

He glanced up as she slid onto the bench beside him—short black hair and heavy makeup, goth style, her eyeliner painted into those weird thick wings that hide the real shape of your eyes. That was the best she could do with Gargano's cash? "This is where you and Stewart came when you were kids. Where you came to meet Shannon." A place she'd come to escape the confines of her foster home and shed her psychological chains, if only for a moment. Where the water stretched forever.

She leaned back against the bench. "Got another smoke?"

He reached into his pocket and passed her the pack. "These things will kill you."

"Good thing I already died."

He snorted and flicked the lighter, waiting while she lit up. "Twice. You're just lucky that gal didn't shoot you in the face instead of in the vest. Overkill on the blood packets, though. Next time, one or two'll do it." He'd thought Rericha would have pulled his Glock from under the counter as he had once before, that he would have been the one to shoot; if that failed, Petrosky would have "accidentally" done it himself. It wasn't supposed to be another cop taking the kill shot, though. He regretted that.

"What makes you think there'll be a next time?" she said.

He smoked. The silence stretched. The water lapped at

the shore, the steady, peaceful hush of depths unknown—beneath those waves, none of this mattered.

"Can I ask you something?"

Out past the break, a fish leapt into the air and splashed back down into the gray. "Shoot."

"Why did you do it?"

He listened to the hiss of burning tobacco, felt the ache in his throat. "You've paid for your sins, Rebecca." A hundred times over. Plus, it had been the only way to get Rericha to confess. A man like that didn't spill his guts for the sake of it, and definitely not for the cops, but even psychos had a soft spot for family—for people they believed they were supposed to protect. And Rebecca...she was the only one he'd ever called by a nickname.

Not to mention that Petrosky'd had a favor to call in; by the time he needed another favor from an EMT, he'd probably be on his way out. *Pack her up, leave the door unlocked, lose the paperwork.* If someone came looking for Rebecca's body, he'd have some explaining to do, but he could probably pawn the blame off on Gargano. Maybe the consequences didn't matter anyway; maybe it was enough to reduce suffering where he could. But Petrosky wouldn't be able to verify how well that worked. He'd never speak to Rebecca again.

She hit her cigarette one more time and dropped it to the sand in front of the bench; the coal sizzled and vanished. He registered a gentle pressure on his thigh, and then she was gone.

He lit another smoke and watched the gray of the water, rippling, rippling, rippling, hiding god knew what beneath those sparkling waves.

"I HAVE, INDEED, NO ABHORRENCE OF DANGER, EXCEPT IN ITS ABSOLUTE EFFECT - IN TERROR."
~*EDGAR ALLAN POE*

EPILOGUE

THE EVENING WAS FAR MORE interesting than the day, he'd always thought, mostly because of the way the shadows spoke. It wasn't that he was deranged, some lunatic actually hearing voices; no, that was for other people—crazy people. But he'd always believed that if you looked hard enough, listened hard enough, the dark had more to tell you. Not about what was out there—that hardly mattered. The whispers you heard at night were almost always about yourself.

And today, those shadows said it was time. He agreed; he felt it in his marrow, an urgent…itching.

He squinted at the moving truck in the driveway. Just a few blocks over from the detective, a cute little place with the hedges all sharp and neat. The ground cover beneath the bushes rustled quietly in the breeze. He leaned back against the headrest, his vehicle safely hidden in the mires of dusk, and watched Shannon emerge from the house once more, the girl at her heel. So much bigger now than she'd been, and the younger one too! Henry, was it?

Shannon reached the back of the moving truck and slung another box onto her shoulder, nodding to something in the dark interior. Her little girl reached, higher, higher—*got it.*

He smiled as she pulled the tiny box down and eased it onto her own shoulder, then waited while her mother tugged the door closed—smart. She wouldn't want to walk across the lawn alone, and there wasn't another person in sight.

Where was the detective? Surely he was around, but the moving truck had only arrived a few hours back; perhaps Petrosky thought there'd be no unloading until the morning.

He was wrong. As he so often was.

Shannon and the girl vanished into the house, and in the flower beds, green leaves waved as if saying goodbye, shiny in the wan porch light. Quite pretty, really. He'd always liked pachysandra; it grew where it wished, had a mind of its own, like Shannon. She'd always come off as rather tenacious, though he'd never had the pleasure to meet her himself. Her husband had that about him, too, that perseverance, even if the man had been a bit of a coward at the end.

A coward, but he followed the rules. He had been a good cop.

Unlike Edward Petrosky.

He started the engine and put the truck in drive, easing it up the road before flipping on the headlights. He rolled the window down, the warm air a balm in his lungs, the flowers sweet in his nose. Summer. It was almost here, and it might be the best one yet.

Want to find out what happens next? *Get Savage* on https://meghanoflynn.com, then read on for a sneak peek! *Petrosky's back, and so is his most vicious rival: the man who killed his partner.*

SAVAGE
CHAPTER 1

The cobblestones in the alleyway were sharp as tacks beneath the soles of her boots, not that Regina Jackson was particularly bothered by that little bit of discomfort. Everything hurt lately, her eyes aching from the moment she awoke—her bones felt sore like they were straining to burst from their tendon prison but were just too damn exhausted to follow through. That was how Petrosky felt every damn day if you believed his bellyaching, but she didn't have time to feel bad; she'd spent yesterday trying to get her son set up with a new caregiver. He'd head-butted the last one. She loved him, loved him with all her heart and soul, but people didn't like to talk about the hardship that went along with special needs. The pain. The abject terror of what might happen when you were gone. And in her line of work, that possibility was always a little closer than she liked.

A breeze hissed up the alley, bringing with it the subtle tang of rot, sweet and bitter, the fragrance like grass clippings and cut tulips tossed into a pile of long-stagnant water. It was possible that was exactly what the stink was—she couldn't see much past the enormous set of dumpsters that blocked half the alley, and the bricks on either side of the crumbling cobblestone walkway seemed to be grappling with the clouds. But though she couldn't see the police cars, she knew they were there; red and blue lights flashed maniacally against the dumpsters, the reflection turning the metal sides into pulsing strobes—no grass on the breeze now. Just the stench of decaying flowers, like someone had dumped perfume into a sewer. She sidestepped a particularly large puddle of black water, the top shiny, reds and blues dancing on the top like fireworks on a dark lake. She was still squinting at it when her feet splashed into another puddle, sending a spray of gray water over the tops of her boots and the cuffs of her navy suit pants. *Just great.* She stomped a little extra hard past the strobing dumpsters. *Click-thunk. Click-thunk-squish.*

The far end of the alley came into focus first, a line of cruisers and crime tape and barrel-chested officers just itching to get the first glance at whatever mess waited for her on the other side of the trash bins. She paused. A car? The little green Fusion sat tucked behind the dumpsters, unassuming like a wart on a toad. A bumper sticker that said "Life is Better with a Beard" adorned the back window, a sign Petrosky would surely take to mean whatever hipster lay inside had deserved to die slowly. But it didn't look as if this was the case. The victim lay prone beside the back door on a piece of thick plastic sheeting, his shirt soaked in ruby, his blue eyes wide to the clouds. Bloody hands grasped at nothing, crimson nails facing upward as if prepared to accept some offering that would never be enough to repair the gash that bisected his throat—his neck had been slashed open like a gaping secondary smile. Beneath the neat lines of his close-cropped facial hair, both the carotid and the jugular appeared to have been severed; even the pale tube of esophageal tissue was slashed. The hair along his jaw was stained with gore. It wouldn't have taken long to bleed out from a wound like that; unconsciousness would have claimed him within a minute, probably much less. Efficiency was the name of this killer's game.

She sidestepped the body and peered through the open back door into the car's interior—a fast-food bag on the floorboards, a few slips that looked like receipts. But no blood. She drew back and frowned at the body, at the plastic sheeting beneath the man where wide swaths of red marred the opaque material. Smears, but nothing that resembled spray. She scanned the walls of brick, the dumpster, the cobblestones, but she saw no signs of struggle, no splatters of red. The victim hadn't been killed here. Premeditated, probably, a bloody mess, absolutely, but Decantor had sounded strange on the phone, too tense for this to be a standard homicide. What was she missing?

"Thanks for coming."

She looked over. Decantor was approaching from behind

the crime tape at the far end of the alley, breaking from the pack of uniforms for the twenty feet of vacant cobbles between them. No one with him to jostle the cup of coffee he held in one hand, no one to knock the manila folder he carried in the other. But...that was strange too, wasn't it? Why weren't there techs here scrambling for evidence? Maybe he'd been waiting for her—it was always good to get a peek at the scene before the techs started picking things up. Helped you get into the mind of your suspect. She stepped around the body and met Decantor by the car's front bumper.

He passed her the coffee cup. "For your trouble." His voice was tight, lower than usual as if apologizing for giving her coffee.

She nodded her thanks. "Is Petrosky on his way?"

Decantor sniffed, his eyes easing to the brick wall off to their right before coming to rest on her face. "I didn't call him."

No wonder he sounded strange. Was he trying to keep Petrosky from getting in on this case? Did he know how far her partner had fallen? It wasn't exactly a secret. Sure, Petrosky never smelled of liquor, and he still showed up and did his job—some might argue more professionally when he had whiskey running through his veins. He even wore suit jackets these days. But it was in the eyes. In the way he talked. You had to know him well, but the signs were there. If she saw him drinking, she could justify getting him fired, could rationalize taking him away from her son. Petrosky was the only person Lance had never been violent with; her son had punched her more times than she could count, but he'd never so much as raised his voice to Petrosky.

She sipped at the coffee, trying to refocus. Decantor's gaze was tight, hard, his eyes deep pools of onyx that suddenly resembled the muddy water she'd walked through to get here. Unlike her, unlike Shannon, unlike the girls next door to Petrosky—street girls he'd adopted and put up, who seemed to look at him as a father—it appeared Decantor was done with Petrosky's bullshit. Maybe he'd already gone to the chief.

Her phone buzzed, and she dropped her eyes to the screen: her partner. *Speak of the devil.* Maybe he already knew; maybe the chief had already talked to him. But she wanted to know for certain before she called him back. "So, does Petrosky know you're boxing him out, or what?"

"I just wanted to make sure there was something to tell before we brought him in," Decantor said, too slowly. And it wasn't just his eyes or his voice; his face was drawn, his dark skin shiny with sweat. His lips, usually so easy to smile even when greeting her at a crime scene, remained downturned—anxious. There was more on his mind than not wanting to upset Petrosky, more than thinking her partner was unstable.

She frowned. "What the hell is going on, Decantor?"

He was no longer looking at her—his gaze dragged along the brick wall, then the car, and stopped on the body. The silence stretched. "You know the serial I've been working on?"

Yeah, she did. Her boyfriend—well, ex-boyfriend now—had been considering doing a book on him. Everyone loved a good serial-killer story, he'd said, but she thought it was exploitative. That it encouraged more bad guys to go out and act in the hopes that the media would write about them too. Fame was as good a motivator as any. "Didn't he go underground? It's been a year since he killed anyone, right?"

Decantor nodded. "Yeah."

She waited. So what was new? What was the problem all of a sudden? Why was she here? He had Sloan, his own partner—he didn't need her.

He sighed and shook his head. "I just can't believe no one saw it before."

"For fuck's sake, spit it out, Decantor!" She sounded like Petrosky—the old man was rubbing off on her.

Voices floated over them, the murmuring of the flatfoots beyond the crime tape…or maybe the techs were finally here. Decantor extended the manila folder, his eyes grave. "I'll let you take a look. Call it a case consultation."

She leaned closer, narrowing her eyes at the tag—the name. The world around her froze, her lungs useless and icy in her chest. *Oh fuck.*

Her phone buzzed again, the world around her started spinning once more, and she snatched the cell from her pocket. "You're too late, Decantor. I've got my own case." Was her voice shaking?

His eyes widened, the file still held aloft like a little boy with a flower for an indifferent girl. "But—"

"But nothing. You call me when you have something concrete."

No way she was playing messenger on this one.

No way in hell.

CHAPTER 2

The buzzing came again, a persistent brainfuck that would not quit. A bee…was it a bee? A goddamn wasp, surely, here to shoot a stinger into his eye, a needle that would pierce through his gray matter. Would his brain leak onto the bed? Would he care?

Bzzzzt. Bzzzzt. Bzzzzt.

Duke grumbled, thick lips flapping—too close. The dog's breath was warm against his neck. The side of Petrosky's face was wet. "Aw, fuck." He pushed himself to seated, wiping the slime from his grizzled jowls. "What are you doing up here anyway? You're not supposed to be on the bed."

Duke licked Petrosky's elbow, then collapsed back onto

the pillow as if he hadn't heard a word of it. The phone buzzed again.

Fuck, fuck, fuck. Petrosky squinted at the night table, the vibrating phone, the half-full bottle of Jack. The digital clock read eight thirty. Yeah, on the later side, but they'd just solved a case yesterday. Another rapist in jail, getting his three hots and a cot. That bastard would be locked up for far too short a time, counting down the days until he could abuse another unsuspecting victim. Castration...that'd be better.

Bzzzzt. Bzzzzt. Bzzzzt.

Fine, asshole, fine. He reached for the nightstand, paused briefly when his fingers grazed the bottle, and then fumbled the cell to his ear. "Yeah."

"You're not just waking up, are you, you cantankerous bastard?" Jackson's voice was clear and alert. She'd probably woken up at five, worked out, eaten a sensible breakfast, taken care of her kid, and done god knew what else while he and Duke were snoring. Damn overachiever.

Petrosky tucked the cell against his shoulder and grabbed the bottle of Jack. The top made a high-pitched *zzzz* sound as it unscrewed, far more pleasant than the incessant buzzing of the phone. "Are you kidding? I've been up for hours; gotta get my pedometer steps in." The amber liquid sloshed in the bottom of the bottle—lower than he'd thought, though he didn't recall drinking it. Didn't recall much of anything last night after Shannon and the kids had left. At least he'd managed to hold it together until he was alone; fucked up though he was, he still had something worth holding on to, and things had been good, hadn't they? Great, really, having Shannon and the kids around.

The phone had gone silent. Had she hung up? "Fine, I lied about the pedomete—"

"I need you at Rita's."

He heaved himself to standing, clinging to the neck of the bottle for dear life. "I already ate."

Again, the silence stretched. The Jack sloshed. And then... clanking, like silverware against dishes, the low beeping of a walkie, and the uneasy din that could only be described as the drone of a crime scene. *Shit.* He drew the bottle to his lips and let the liquor burn down his gullet and into his belly, the warmth spreading, calming the too-fast throb of his heart. He hadn't even noticed his heart going haywire, but now the thudding broke into his temples. The world around him pulsed. "What happened?"

"Kidnapping."

Not homicide—not yet.

"If you're at Rita's...is the vic someone we know?"

A loud noise blared through the phone, the bright clang of shattering glass. "Just get your ass down here, would you?"

He opened his mouth to reply, but the phone had gone silent—Jackson was gone. He tilted the bottle back and drained it dry.

THE RIDE to Rita's Diner was punctuated by the stink of a breakfast burrito—Shannon had made him stop smoking "for the kids," but it was nicotine or grease, and damn if his waistline wasn't pissed at him. His heart doc would have been pissed, too, if Petrosky'd managed to make it to any of his appointments.

Black-and-whites were already parked in the nearest four spaces, Evan Scott's used Caddy wedged among them. The forensics guy was a genius, and his father, George, was Petrosky's only real friend—at least he used to be. It turned out the man had far less tolerance for bullshit than was necessary to deal with Petrosky's dumb ass. Petrosky still wasn't sure what he'd done to get the guy to finally stop calling. Not that it mattered anymore.

He grabbed his suit jacket off the passenger seat and

shrugged it over his gray T-shirt as he headed across the lot, the buttons too tight to attach. Hot already. The temperate late-summer air that had kept sweat off his brow during yesterday's evening walk with Billie had vanished, replaced by the sticky ball-sweat mugginess of August. Then again, maybe the stickiness was easier to ignore when you were three shots deep as he'd been last night—he'd had only one, maybe two shots this morning. Petrosky cleared his throat, tasting the mint on his breath. Two unmarked cars in the lot besides Scott's ride: an old gray Buick and a burgundy Kia. Did one belong to the victim? Through the glass doors, he could see three, no four, other cops, positioned around the perimeter of the restaurant as if to ward off any incoming diners. One officer sat at the table near the window, a black-haired woman in a pink shirt across from him, her apron clutched absentmindedly in her hand.

He spotted Jackson just inside the glass front doors, her navy pantsuit neatly buttoned, the white of her blouse peeking between the lapels. The fluorescents blared like spotlights against her dark skin, her shorn black hair, the sharp angles of her cheekbones, her narrowed eyes. Her nostrils flared like an angry bull—agitated as hell. *Fuck*. The victim was definitely someone they knew. A cop? One of the waitresses? He tried to prepare himself, tried to guess by examining the tight contours of his partner's lips, but Jackson wasn't looking at him; her attention was focused on a spindly man wearing plastic booties. Not Scott. Must be the new guy. Petrosky had heard that Scott had managed to snag an assistant, but he had yet to meet the man, and he didn't see a reason to change that track record now.

The air smelled of charred caraway laced with the bitterness of burned garlic. Jackson glanced over as he entered, and now he could see that her eyes weren't just narrowed, weren't just agitated; they were sad. His chest constricted, but not near as much as it should have. The booze was good for that—for taking the edge off.

Jackson stepped around the plastic-footsied man to stand beside Petrosky. "Victim's name is Wilona Hyde."

His shoulders relaxed. He knew all the waitresses in this joint, and the names of most of the cops who worked at the precinct, those who might have been regulars at this place—he'd remember a name like Wilona Hyde. *Thank god.* He'd had far too many cases where the vic was someone he knew, and those investigations drove a fucking spike into his heart; it was always harder to work when you couldn't breathe.

"What was the victim doing here? Was she making early deliveries or what?"

Jackson shook her head. "Waitress, working the morning shift."

Petrosky frowned. Must be a new girl. Had she moved to town and started working here because she was running from something else—someone else? Maybe a violent ex had caught up with her. He'd seen that more times than he wanted to admit.

Jackson hooked a thumb at the long front counter, where trays of pastries beckoned from beneath glass cases. On the shelves behind the counter, a coffeepot sat dark and empty—off. "Looks like she came in at five thirty, opened the place up, put in the bagels. When help came in at seven for the breakfast rush, they found the bagels burning in the oven. And no Wilona."

That explained the burned caraway. "Was the front door locked?" Petrosky asked.

Jackson nodded. "Yup. But the other waitress said they usually open the front door for coffee and day-old scones within half an hour of arriving. The place should have been unlocked by six."

Petrosky scanned the register, the gleaming counter, the dark coffeepot. Acrid smoke tingled in his nostrils. The unmade coffee meant the kidnapper had gotten to her after she put the bagels in, but before she had time to scoop the grounds—before they were supposed to open, maybe around five forty-five. If that were true, she'd have had to unlock the door for her kidnapper. Did she know the perp?

"How does she get to work?" Petrosky asked.

"Drives. Her car's still in the lot."

Made sense, most kidnappers had their own rides, but he'd been hoping the guy had made her drive—at least then they'd know what kind of car to look for, put out an APB. He should have figured this asshole was smarter than that—the bastard had abducted her and made her relock the door behind them, thereby ensuring that no customers showed up to report the woman missing before he had a chance to get away. Petrosky glanced at the wall clock behind the counter. The kidnapper was already three hours ahead of them.

"Any sign of a struggle?" He drew his gaze away from the clock in time to see Jackson shake her head.

"Nothing, and no signs of blood or anything else that might indicate he knocked her out. So he was probably armed."

Right. When faced with a gun, most people did as they were asked—no mess. He turned back to the front door and frowned. The tall, slim forensics guy was crouched on the floor near the doorjamb, thin fingers busy with his little bags, his skinny little tweezers. Even his brown hair was thin. *This is some* Nightmare Before Christmas *shit.* "Where's Scott?"

"Out back. That's where Wilona's car is parked." Her gaze darted from the front door to the counter where the register was, and back to Petrosky. "I've got her picture out already. The story goes live next press cycle."

He gaped at her—they didn't yet know if they were dealing with a ransom situation, and some kidnappers went ballistic if the victim's face was splashed all over television.

Jackson raised a hand. "I know what you're thinking,

but we can't risk it; she's nine months pregnant, due any day. And if she goes into labor, we have two victims to worry about. Hell, the kid might even be the reason he took her."

"Lots of sick fucks out there." But his voice rang hollow in his ears. *A pregnant waitress.* His guts tightened as a face leaped into his mind—red hair. Chipped front tooth. Red lipstick. *Fucking hell, not her.* He scanned the restaurant as if the woman would materialize out of nowhere, but all he saw were the flatfoots, the slim forensics guy, and the black-haired pink-shirted woman who had come in expecting to wait tables for tips and not to talk to cops for free. "Her friends call her Ruby," he said.

Jackson met his eyes and nodded, though it wasn't really a question.

Fuck, fuck, fuck. Ruby had been the one spiking his coffee on days he couldn't find a bottle. Ruby had added a little edge to his lemonade, sometimes even when Petrosky was with Jackson—not enough to stink, but enough to help. And he tipped her well for it. Hell, he'd driven her to her last doctor's appointment when her car broke down. Paid the mechanic's bill too.

He'd been trying to help her get back on her feet.

And someone had stolen her away.

GET *SAVAGE*
on https://meghanoflynn.com

What you can't see can kill. A compulsively readable thriller in the vein of Gillian Flynn, *Shadow's Keep* is a mind-bending exploration of obsession, desperation, and how far we'll go to protect those we love.

SHADOW'S KEEP
CHAPTER 1

Witness

For William Shannahan, six-thirty on Tuesday, the third of August, was "the moment." Life was full of those moments, his mother had always told him, experiences that prevented you from going back to who you were before, tiny decisions that changed you forever.

And that morning, the moment came and went, though he didn't recognize it, nor would he ever have wished to recall that morning again for as long as he lived. But he would never, from that day on, be able to forget it.

He left his Mississippi farmhouse a little after six, dressed in running shorts and an old T-shirt that still had sunny yellow paint dashed across the front from decorating the child's room. *The child.* William had named him Brett, but he'd never told anyone that. To everyone else, the baby was just that-thing-you-could-never-mention, particularly since William had also lost his wife at Bartlett General.

His green Nikes beat against the gravel, a blunt metronome as he left the porch and started along the road parallel to the Oval, what the townsfolk called the near hundred square miles of woods that had turned marshy wasteland when freeway construction had dammed the creeks downstream. Before William was born, those fifty or so unlucky folks who owned property inside the Oval had gotten some settlement from the developers when their houses flooded and were deemed uninhabitable. Now those homes were part of a ghost town, tucked well beyond the reach of prying eyes.

William's mother had called it a disgrace. William thought it might be the price of progress, though he'd never dared to tell her that. He'd also never told her that his fondest memory of the Oval was when his best friend Mike had beat the crap out of Kevin Pultzer for punching William in the eye. That was before Mike was the sheriff, back when they were all just "us" or "them" and William had always been a them, except when Mike was around. He might fit in somewhere else, some other place where the rest of the dorky goofballs lived, but here in Graybel he was just a little…odd. Oh well. People in this town gossiped far too much to trust them as friends anyway.

William sniffed at the marshy air, the closely-shorn grass sucking at his sneakers as he increased his pace. Somewhere near him a bird shrieked, sharp and high. He startled as it took flight above him with another aggravated scream.

Straight ahead, the car road leading into town was bathed in filtered dawn, the first rays of sun painting the gravel gold, though the road was slippery with moss and morning damp. To his right, deep shadows pulled at him from the trees; the tall pines crouched close together as if hiding a secret bundle in their underbrush. Dark but calm, quiet—comforting. Legs pumping, William headed off the road toward the pines.

A snap like that of a muted gunshot echoed through the morning air, somewhere deep inside the wooded stillness, and though it was surely just a fox, or maybe a raccoon, he paused, running in place, disquiet spreading through him like the worms of fog that were only now rolling out from under the trees to be burned off as the sun made its debut. Cops never got a moment off, although in this sleepy town the worst he'd see today would be an argument over cattle. He glanced up the road. Squinted. Should he continue up the brighter main street or escape into the shadows beneath the trees?

That was his moment.

William ran toward the woods.

As soon as he set foot inside the tree line, the dark descended on him like a blanket, the cool air brushing his face as another hawk shrieked overhead. William nodded to it, as if the animal had sought his approval, then swiped his arm over his forehead and dodged a limb, pick-jogging his way down the path. A branch caught his ear. He winced. Six foot three was great for some things, but not for running in the woods. Either that or God was pissed at him, which wouldn't be surprising, though he wasn't clear on what he had done wrong. Probably for smirking at his memories of Kevin Pultzer with a torn T-shirt and a bloodied nose.

He smiled again, just a little one this time.

When the path opened up, he raised his gaze above the canopy. He had an hour before he needed to be at the precinct, but the pewter sky beckoned him to run quicker before the heat crept up. It was a good day to turn forty-two, he decided. He might not be the best-looking guy around, but he had his health. And there was a woman whom he adored, even if she wasn't sure about him yet.

William didn't blame her. He probably didn't deserve her, but he'd surely try to convince her that he did, like he had with Marianna...though he didn't think weird card tricks would help this time. But weird was what he had. Without it, he was just background noise, part of the wallpaper of this small town, and at forty-one—*no, forty-two, now*—he was running out of time to start over.

He was pondering this when he rounded the bend and saw the feet. Pale soles barely bigger than his hand, poking from behind a rust-colored boulder that sat a few feet from the edge of the trail. He stopped, his heart throbbing an erratic rhythm in his ears.

Please let it be a doll. But he saw the flies buzzing around the top of the boulder. Buzzing. Buzzing.

William crept forward along the path, reaching for his hip where his gun usually sat, but he touched only cloth. The dried yellow paint scratched his thumb. He thrust his hand into his pocket for his lucky coin. No quarter. Only his phone.

William approached the rock, the edges of his vision dark and unfocused as if he were looking through a telescope, but in the dirt around the stone he could make out deep paw prints. Probably from a dog or a coyote, though these were *enormous*—nearly the size of a salad plate, too big for anything he'd expect to find in these woods. He frantically scanned the underbrush, trying to locate the animal, but saw only a cardinal appraising him from a nearby branch.

Someone's back there, someone needs my help.

He stepped closer to the boulder. *Please don't let it be what I think it is.* Two more steps and he'd be able to see beyond the rock, but he could not drag his gaze from the trees where he was certain canine eyes were watching. Still nothing there save the shaded bark of the surrounding woods. He took another step—cold oozed from the muddy earth into his shoe and around his left ankle, like a hand from the grave. William stumbled, pulling his gaze from the trees just in time to see the boulder rushing at his head and then he was on his side in the slimy filth to the right of the boulder, next to...

Oh god, oh god, oh god.

William had seen death in his twenty years as a deputy, but usually it was the result of a drunken accident, a car wreck, an old man found dead on his couch.

This was not that. The boy was no more than six, probably less. He lay on a carpet of rotting leaves, one arm draped over his chest, legs splayed haphazardly as if he, too, had tripped in the muck. But this wasn't an accident; the boy's throat was torn, jagged ribbons of flesh peeled back, drooping on either side of the muscle meat, the unwanted skin on a Thanksgiving turkey. Deep gouges permeated his chest and abdomen, black slashes against mottled green flesh, the wounds obscured behind his shredded clothing and bits of twigs and leaves.

William scrambled backward, clawing at the ground, his muddy shoe kicking the child's ruined calf, where the boy's shy white bones peeked from under congealing blackish tissue. The legs looked...*chewed on.*

His hand slipped in the muck. The child's face was turned

to his, mouth open, black tongue lolling as if he were about to plead for help. *Not good, oh shit, not good.*

William finally clambered to standing, yanked his cell from his pocket, and tapped a button, barely registering his friend's answering bark. A fly lit on the boy's eyebrow above a single white mushroom that crept upward over the landscape of his cheek, rooted in the empty socket that had once contained an eye.

"Mike, it's William. I need a...tell Dr. Klinger to bring the wagon."

He stepped backward, toward the path, shoe sinking again, the mud trying to root him there, and he yanked his foot free with a squelching sound. Another step backward and he was on the path, and another step off the path again, and another, another, feet moving until his back slammed against a gnarled oak on the opposite side of the trail. He jerked his head up, squinting through the leafy awning, half convinced the boy's assailant would be perched there, ready to leap from the trees and lurch him into oblivion on flensing jaws. But there was no wretched animal. Blue leaked through the filtered haze of dawn.

William lowered his gaze, Mike's voice a distant crackle irritating the edges of his brain but not breaking through—he could not understand what his friend was saying. He stopped trying to decipher it and said, "I'm on the trails behind my house, found a body. Tell them to come in through the path on the Winchester side." He tried to listen to the receiver, but heard only the buzzing of flies across the trail—had they been so loud a moment ago? Their noise grew, amplified to unnatural volumes, filling his head until every other sound fell away—was Mike still talking? He pushed *End*, pocketed the phone, and then leaned back and slid down the tree trunk.

And William Shannahan, not recognizing the event the rest of his life would hinge upon, sat at the base of a gnarled oak tree on Tuesday, the third of August, put his head into his hands, and wept.

GET *SHADOW'S KEEP*
on https://meghanoflynn.com

To save herself, she'll have to face the world's most vicious serial killer. She just calls him Dad. Fast-paced, electric, and barbed with nerve-shredding thrills, the Born Bad series is perfect for fans of Gillian Flynn, Caroline Kepnes, and *Dexter*.

WICKED SHARP
CHAPTER 1

I HAVE a drawing that I keep tucked inside an old doll house —well, a house for fairies. My father always insisted upon the whimsical, albeit in small amounts. It's little quirks like that which make you real to people. Which make you safe. Everyone has some weird thing they cling to in times of stress, whether it's listening to a favorite song or snuggling up in a comfortable blanket or talking to the sky as if it might respond. I had the fairies.

And that little fairy house, now blackened by soot and flame, is as good a place as any to keep the things that should be gone. I haven't looked at the drawing since the day I brought it home, can't even remember stealing it, but I can describe every jagged line by heart.

The crude slashes of black that make up the stick figure's arms, the page torn where the scribbled lines meet— shredded by the pressure of the crayon's point. The sadness of the smallest figure. The horrific, monstrous smile on the father, dead center in the middle of the page.

Looking back, it should have been a warning—I should have known, I should have run. The child who drew it was no longer there to tell me what happened by the time I stumbled into that house. The boy knew too much, that was obvious from the picture.

Children have a way of knowing things that adults don't —a heightened sense of self-preservation that we slowly lose over time as we convince ourselves that the prickling along the backs of our necks is nothing to worry about. Children are too vulnerable not to be ruled by emotion—they're hardwired to identify threats with razor's-edge precision. Unfortunately, they have a limited capacity to describe the perils they uncover. They can't explain why their teacher is scary or what makes them duck into the house if they see the neighbor peeking at them from behind the blinds. They cry. They wet their pants.

They draw pictures of monsters under the bed to process what they can't articulate.

Luckily, most children never find out that the monsters under their bed are real.

I never had that luxury. But even as a child, I was comforted that my father was a bigger, stronger monster than anything outside could ever be. He would protect me. I knew that to be a fact the way other people know the sky is blue or that their racist Uncle Earl is going to fuck up Thanksgiving. Monster or not, he was my world. And I adored him in the way only a daughter can.

I know that's strange to say—to love a man even if you see what terrors lurk beneath. My therapist says it's normal, but she's prone to sugarcoating. Or maybe she's so good at positive thinking that she's grown blind to real evil.

I'm not sure what she'd say about the drawing in the fairy house. I'm not sure what she'd think about me if I told her that I understood why my father did what he did, not because I thought it was justified, but because I understood him. I'm an expert when it comes to the motivation of the creatures underneath the bed.

And I guess that's why I live where I do, hidden in the New Hampshire wilderness as if I can keep every piece of the past beyond the border of the property—as if a fence might keep the lurking dark from creeping in through the cracks. And there are always cracks, no matter how hard you try to plug them. Humanity is a perilous condition rife with self-inflicted torment and psychological vulnerabilities, the what-ifs and maybes contained only by paper-thin flesh, any inch of which is soft enough to puncture if your blade is sharp.

I knew that before I found the picture, of course, but something in those jagged lines of crayon drove it home, or dug it in a little deeper. Something changed that week in the mountains. Something foundational, perhaps the first glimmer of certainty that I'd one day need an escape plan. But though I like to think I was trying to save myself from day one, it's hard to tell through the haze of memory. There are always holes. Cracks.

I don't spend a lot of time reminiscing; I'm not especially nostalgic. I think I lost that little piece of myself first. But I'll never forget the way the sky roiled with electricity, the greenish tinge that threaded through the clouds and seemed to slide down my throat and into my lungs. I can feel the vibration in the air from the birds rising on frantically beating wings. The smell of damp earth and rotting pine will never leave me.

Yes, it was the storm that kept it memorable; it was the mountains.

It was the woman.

It was the blood.

GET *WICKED SHARP*
on https://meghanoflynn.com

PRAISE FOR BESTSELLING AUTHOR MEGHAN O'FLYNN

"Creepy and haunting... fully immersive thrillers. The Ash Park series should be everyone's next binge-read."
~*New York Times Bestselling Author Andra Watkins*

"Full of complex, engaging characters and evocative detail, *Wicked Sharp* is a white-knuckle thrill ride. O'Flynn is a master storyteller." ~*Paul Austin Ardoin, USA Today Bestselling Author*

"Nobody writes with such compelling and entrancing prose as O'Flynn. With perfectly executed twists, Born Bad is chilling, twisted, heart-pounding suspense. This is my new favorite thriller series." ~*Bestselling Author Emerald O'Brien*

"Visceral, fearless, and addictive, this series will keep you on the edge of your seat." ~*Bestselling Author Mandi Castle*

"Intense and suspenseful...captured me from the first chapter and held me enthralled until the final page."
~*Susan Sewell, Reader's Favorite*

"Cunning, delightfully disturbing, and addictive, the Ash Park series is an expertly written labyrinth."~*Award-winning Author Beth Teliho*

"Dark, gritty, and raw, O'Flynn's work will take your mind prisoner and keep you awake far into the morning hours." ~*Bestselling Author Kristen Mae*

"From the feverishly surreal to the downright demented,

O'Flynn takes you on a twisted journey through the deepest and darkest corners of the human mind."
~*Bestselling Author Mary Widdicks*

"With unbearable tension and gripping, thought-provoking storytelling, O'Flynn explores fear in all the best—and creepiest—ways. Masterful psychological thrillers replete with staggering, unpredictable twists." ~*Bestselling Author Wendy Heard*

LEARN MORE ON
https://meghanoflynn.com

WANT MORE FROM MEGHAN?
There are many more books to choose from!

Learn more about Meghan's novels on
https://meghanoflynn.com

ABOUT THE AUTHOR

With books deemed "visceral, haunting, and fully immersive" (*New York Times bestseller, Andra Watkins*), Meghan O'Flynn has made her mark on the thriller genre. Meghan is a clinical therapist who draws her character inspiration from her knowledge of the human psyche. She is the bestselling author of gritty crime novels and serial killer thrillers, all of which take readers on the dark, gripping, and unputdownable journey for which Meghan is notorious. Learn more at https://meghanoflynn.com! While you're there, join Meghan's reader group, and get a **FREE SHORT STORY** just for signing up.

Want to connect with Meghan?
https://meghanoflynn.com

www.ingramcontent.com/pod-product-compliance
Lightning Source LLC
LaVergne TN
LVHW040612250326
834688LV00035B/519